Whirlwind

A NOVEL BY

Robin DeJarnett

OMNIFIC PUBLISHING
DALLAS

Omnific Publishing
P.O. Box 793871, Dallas, TX 75379
www.omnificpublishing.com

First Omnific eBook edition, December 2010
First Omnific trade paperback edition, December 2010

Library of Congress Cataloguing-in-Publication Data

DeJarnett, Robin.
    Whirlwind / Robin DeJarnett – 1st ed.
    ISBN 978-1-936305-50-6
    1. Romantic Suspense—Fiction. 2. Weddings—Fiction.
    3. Contemporary Romance—Fiction. 4. California—Fiction. I. Title

10 9 8 7 6 5 4 3 2 1

Cover Design and Interior Book Design by Coreen Montagna

Printed in the United States of America

One

"The coroner listed the official cause of death as asphyxiation. A memorial trust fund has been set up for Stanton; see our website for details. Stay tuned for traffic and weather."

"Like I need another traffic report." I silenced the radio with a jab. After spending most of the day on California freeways—including a solid hour on a twenty-mile stretch of beach in Malibu—I was intimately familiar with the amount of traffic on the road.

Dial down the attitude, Melissa. You're on vacation! Finals had ended, the weather was perfect, and other than the one spot on the beach, the traffic wasn't really *that* bad. I should have been in a better mood. So what if the summer was starting with my best friend getting married and moving away? I had other friends.

Just none as close as Mitch McAlister.

The first real friend I'd made at college, Mitch had been part of my life for almost three years. After a chance meeting—at, of all places, a rodeo—he'd literally shown me the ropes, cluing me in on everything from how to lasso a steer to where to find the hidden parking spots on the busy Santa Lucia Polytechnic campus. Hell, he'd even taught me to drink, financing my trip down Miracle Mile when I'd turned twenty-one. He was the big brother I never had.

"Turn right on Sepulveda Boulevard." My Dutch-made GPS pronounced it "See-puel-VEED," and I could imagine Mitch's laugh filling my tiny car. I would've snickered too, if only the cold computer voice hadn't been announcing how close I was to seeing my best friend for the last time.

I wanted to blame Ann, his high-class, high-style fiancée, for stealing him away, but I knew better. Our lives had always been headed in different directions. A week ago he graduated from our little school on the central

California coast; that's really what signaled the end. Married or not, next month Mitch was starting work in L.A. at his dream job, designing hybrid cars. I really had no grounds to complain; I was lucky he'd stuck around an extra year to get his master's.

"You can always come down and visit, Mel. It's only a few hours away," he'd said, but I knew it was just a polite invitation. Distance wasn't the issue. Even if Mitch moved in next door, I still wouldn't see much of him. His new job, new friends, and new responsibilities would keep him more than busy enough; he wouldn't have time for any of us still in school. Add in a new wife and I'd be lucky to get a Christmas card.

I ignored my heavily-accented navigator and turned onto Palos Verdes Boulevard with forty-five minutes to spare. Plenty of time to ditch my selfish doldrums, I hoped. I shouldn't rain on Mitch's big day—I wouldn't. Maybe if I pretended this was just another story to cover, my reporter's instincts would kick in.

The Pacific peeked between the apartment buildings lining the street on the right as I scanned for addresses. On the left, a tall A-frame building with a crucifix fit the bill, but it wasn't the church I was looking for. Half a mile farther down I spotted my destination. Or did I?

Is this a church?

The answer was a symphony of horns and a flock of fingers as I rode the brakes in front of the modern stucco-and-glass structure. In sharp contrast to the traditional building I'd just passed, the two-story square pillars and blackened-glass front of Beach Cities Community Church didn't look like any house of worship I'd ever seen. It looked more like a deserted movie theater.

Of course, I wasn't much of an expert on either religion or architecture. God had dispensed with me long ago, and I'd returned the favor without hesitation.

"You have reached your destination," my GPS chanted. I wasn't sure I believed it, but with a belated turn signal I entered the driveway marked CHURCH PARKING.

The one-way alley skirted what I assumed was the sanctuary, taking me down a slope toward a set of dark green hedges. The structure next to me seemed to grow, rising to more than three stories by the time I saw the narrow street curve around the back. My skepticism grew with it, but at least I still had plenty of time to find the right church before Mitch and Ann started their vows.

The road opened up to a boxed-in parking lot, which—as I expected—was empty. Well, almost.

I backed into one of the few shady spots next to a spectacularly clean Lexus and an equally detailed BMW. At least I could get my tired Civic out of the sweltering sun while I decided how lost I was.

With the pale lavender invitation in hand, I verified the address against what I'd programmed into the GPS. The matching numbers didn't reassure me; the GPS had been confused on more than one occasion.

Just as I was about to snag an old-fashioned paper map from the glove box, I noticed a woman in a pink sundress crossing the parking lot. She shaded her face with one hand and waved with the other.

"Melissa! Is that you?" she called.

With a relieved sigh, I stepped out and waved back at Beth Miller, one of my few girlfriends.

"You cut your hair," I said by way of a greeting once she'd reached the cover of the shade.

She twirled, showing off her new chin-length bob. Just three days ago her hair had been as long as mine, trailing down below her shoulders. "Yup, no one will mistake us for sisters anymore."

"You must be so relieved," I said. It'd been weeks since the barista had commented that we must be related; I was surprised she remembered. "So what's going on? I wasn't sure I had the right place at first."

"Oh, shoot! I was supposed to put balloons on the parking sign too." She slumped against my car. "Didn't you see my fabulous decorations?"

I followed her finger, which was aimed at a staircase tucked between the buildings that formed two sides of the enclosed lot. Purple ribbon wound its way up the banister, punctuated by matching balloons floating above every third step.

"You did that? You definitely have a fall-back if psychology doesn't work out for you." I leaned against the car next to her. "I thought you were just a guest. Did Ann conscript you into service?" Ann Linwood was someone who knew what she wanted and would fight tooth and nail to get it. *No* was not a word she recognized.

Beth scowled at me. "Actually, I volunteered. You should cut Ann a break, Mel. She's not the Wicked Witch of the West."

I picked a wayward hair off of my black slacks, this one closer to blond than brown. It was a little late to buddy-up to Ann, but I curbed my tongue. "You're probably right. It's just that she's so different." *Different from me—and from Mitch.* I managed a half-smile, imagining her Jimmy Choo's lined up in the closet next to his dirty cowboy boots.

"That's the thing, though, she's not," said Beth. "She's smart and confident…just like you, now that I think about it. Maybe that's because you both work with so many men." Beth plucked a leaf off the Lexus and traced it with her finger. "Too bad you couldn't come down earlier. She took me and Linda out to lunch yesterday."

To some posh restaurant, I'm sure. "Somehow I doubt you chatted about baseball over pizza and beer."

"No, we went to Panera. Nothing fancy. You would have enjoyed it more than you think." She crumpled the leaf, but it sprang open when she dropped it. "She asked about you. When I told her you had to cover the baseball game—" Beth gave me a disbelieving glance "—she launched into a story about how baseball players had made steroids taboo for any cosmetic use. I guess her company was considering them for some kind of skin therapy."

Steroid-based makeup? Who knew? "You two must've really enjoyed that," I said and was promptly poked in the ribs.

"*You* would have enjoyed it more. Bonds, Sosa, Macintyre—she knew them all."

"McGwire, Beth. It's McGwire." I was impressed Beth remembered any of the names, let alone Ann.

She crossed her arms. "Whatever. The point is she has more in common with you than you think." Glaring at my slacks, she continued, "After lunch, we went over to Del Amo and walked around. We could've helped you find something a little less…practical."

The mall. I should've known. "I like practical. I'm not a girly-girl like you." I couldn't imagine spending two hours every day "putting on my face." The shadow and blush I'd spent way too much time applying this morning now formed an uncomfortable second skin, an itch I couldn't scratch.

"You think you're just one of the guys, but you'd be surprised. With a little effort you'd have them clamoring after you," Beth said.

"I thought we were talking about Ann, not me." My love life, or lack thereof, was not up for debate. "You must've talked about something other than baseball."

With a huff, Beth crossed her arms. "Well, Mitch did come up once or twice." Perking up, she slipped her hand into a well-concealed pocket in her skirt. "Ann loves him to pieces. She'd do anything for him." A folded piece of paper appeared in her hand. "And I mean *anything*."

"What's that?" I reached for the note, but Beth pulled it away.

"Ah-ah-ah, I don't think so. It's a note from Ann to Mitch. I've spent most of the day playing messenger." Beth's lips curled in a wicked grin.

"They're passing notes? Why don't they just text each other?" I followed Beth as she skipped around to the other side of my car.

"Probably because Ann confiscated Mitch's phone. She found out the guys loaded about a thousand pornographic photos on it for...what did they call it? Oh yeah, *inspiration*." She emphasized the last word with her fingers.

I held up my hands in defeat. It was too hot to chase her around the parking lot. "I'm surprised you looked at it, Beth. I always thought you were a good girl." The stereotypical girl next door, Beth didn't even swear.

"I didn't open it when she gave it to me. I'd never do that." She touched the folds of the note with a guilty finger. "But maybe I was looking over her shoulder when she wrote it."

"You devious woman!" I nudged Beth's arm. "It's always the quiet ones."

"Hey, I learned from the best," she said, bumping me back.

"So? What does it say?"

Beth's cheeks turned scarlet. "Um...Do you remember the slogan for Frank's Famous Hot Dogs? Apparently those are Ann's favorite."

"Big Weenies are Better?" I covered my mouth with my hand. "No way! She didn't write that."

"Not in so many words, but that's the gist of it." Beth's hair bounced up and down as she nodded, laughing.

"So that's what Mitch sees in her," I said with a smirk.

Catching her breath, Beth peeked in the passenger window. I cringed, remembering the mess I'd left on the seat. When she looked back at me, confusion wrinkled her brow. "You drove down by yourself? I thought you were bringing that guy from the *Daily*—your replacement."

"Craig? I don't think so." My new freshman charge had followed me around like an eager puppy at the last event I'd been assigned to cover. Like me, his first article for the school paper was about Poly's award-winning rodeo team. *Unlike* me, he got stepped on by a horse, banished to the stands by the team captain, Mitch, and locked in a Porta-John by...well...me.

"But he likes you," Beth argued, batting her eyelashes. "Is there anything you don't know about the rodeo, Ms. Williams? I wish I could be as good as you someday, Ms. Williams. I can call you Melissa? Gee, thanks, Ms. Williams!"

Her imitation of the pimple-faced kid was a little too good.

"Please, stop," I begged, catching myself before I rubbed my eyes and screwed up my makeup. I wrung my hands instead, cracking a knuckle.

Beth picked up another leaf and twirled it between her fingers. "Oh well, I guess you're free to hook up with someone here," she said, a little too casually.

I rolled my eyes. "Don't start. I don't have time for a guy."

Beth grabbed my arm. "But there are so many hot ones here to choose from. Maybe you should come with me. Then you'd have first pick!"

Like *I* was the one who had a choice. "Right. I don't think so, Beth."

I jumped out of the way of Beth's swat. "Give me a break, Mel. You look great, especially in that color. It makes your eyes glow."

I automatically looked away.

"Thanks" was my halfhearted reply. My eyes, like my hair, weren't quite any one color. With flecks of green and blue, they tended to match whatever I happened to be wearing. I could only imagine the nauseating color my teal blouse made them. "Maybe some of your fashion sense is rubbing off on me."

"Ha, you don't need my help. Maybe just more reasons to get dressed up." She smiled and gracefully swept her freshly cut bangs to the side. "When was the last time you went out?"

I sighed. "I go out with the guys all the time, just like you do."

"Let me rephrase the question. When was the last time you went on a date? Specifically, just you and *one* guy—no interview, no story, no business. You know, a *real* date."

"You sound like my mother," I groaned. "Let it go."

Beth put a hand on my arm, but I pushed off the car and walked into the sun. How long had it been since I'd been on a real date? A year? More? I worked with a plethora of eligible, ruggedly attractive men, but none had shown any interest in me. The one time I'd taken the initiative, the polite rejection hurt enough that I didn't try again.

"So up the stairs is where all the action is?" I asked.

With a frown, Beth nodded. "Yeah. I guess I should get back. I'm sure Mitch is freaking out waiting for this." She waved the scrap of paper at me. "He's been a nervous wreck all day. You sure you don't want me to drop any hints to the guys for you?"

"NO!"

"Kidding, Mel. Geez." She took a step toward the church. "Besides, there's always the reception."

"Beth," I warned.

She just laughed. "I'll tell Mitch you're here. That should make him feel a little better," she said.

"And tell him if he doesn't suck it up and act like a man, I'm going to come in there and kick his ass again."

Beth smirked. "Okay, Mel, I will. Should I also tell him you're saving yourself for your biggest fan, Craig?"

Before I could find something to throw at her, Beth took off at a run, slipping in a side door of the huge building. How could she move so fast in heels?

While the freshman reporter held absolutely no interest for me, I did have to give him credit. He took his new job seriously, even if it was one of the worst beats at the *Mission Daily*.

Was I that annoying my first year?

When I'd started college almost three years ago, I'd had visions of becoming the next Murrow—or better yet, a Woodward or Bernstein. When I'd landed a spot on Poly's campus newspaper, Mom had seen it as the perfect job for me to score a husband. She'd sent two books to get me started: *Dating for Dummies* and the latest edition of *A Woman's Guide to Self-Defense*.

"Dad would've wanted you to have this," she'd said of the latter, only half-joking. "It's a man's world you're diving into, and you need to be prepared—for anything."

I didn't get choice assignments that first year. My calendar wasn't filled with the glamour of sweaty football players or muscular bicyclists in skin-tight shorts. No, as the only freshman on the staff, and a city girl to boot, I was sent to cut my teeth on the "real world" of newspaper reporting in the hot, smelly, dirty hell of the rodeo circuit.

I ran into champion steer wrestler Mitch McAlister at my first rodeo—literally—and ended up on my ass in a pile of horse shit. "Road apples" he'd called the green muck, picking me up off the ground like a discarded penny. At six foot two, Mitch was tall, but it wasn't his height that had me withering in my Levi's. Built like a wrestler, the guy was two hundred and ten pounds of muscle, topped with closely cropped dark hair and matching ebony eyes. It was no wonder he'd tied the school record for bulldogging wins. I was pretty sure he could bench press most of the steers he dragged to the ground.

When I introduced myself as a reporter, I thought he was going to push me right back in the crap.

Dubbed the *Mistakes Daily*, the campus newspaper didn't have the love and respect of the rodeo team. I spent most of the day trying to overcome a reputation I had no hand in making. Quoting statistics and obscure rules didn't help. Only when I admitted I really didn't know anything about horses did Mitch finally consent to an interview.

"It's about damn time," he'd said. "Why come all the way out here to ask me about numbers you already know? Isn't the real story what you *don't* already know?"

Almost three years later, those words still adorned the cover of my notebook.

I reached in the car and grabbed my purse, hiding my glum face from the parade of arriving guests. *Get a grip, Melissa!* It wasn't as if Mitch was an ex-boyfriend—he and I were never *that* close. I had no right to expect anything from him. He'd found his soul mate and would have a wonderful life with her. How could I not be happy for my best friend?

A cold ache grew in my chest, a void I hadn't experienced in a long time. Was I jealous? No. Envious, I decided. Mitch, Beth—all my close friends, really—had found someone with whom to share their lives and with hardly any effort. In Mitch's case, it was as simple as offering to drive his roommate, Chase, home for Labor Day. Chase introduced his sister and that was it. Mitch proposed only a month after meeting her.

I couldn't keep a plant alive for a month, let alone a relationship.

In my case, love—or what I'd thought was love—had been unable to withstand the slightest of tests. Perhaps that's why I felt so maudlin. Mitch's wedding highlighted my social ineptitude. Looking down at my dark blouse and black pants, I realized I'd even dressed for a morbid occasion.

No, I'd worn this same outfit to a job interview last week. I could have worn brown slacks, I guess, but what's the difference? As for the blouse, well, pastels did nothing for my complexion.

Yeah, keep up the excuses. Your nose is rivaling Pinocchio's.

Setting my jaw, I locked the car and started toward the church. What I wore or how I felt didn't matter. I didn't need a date to celebrate Mitch and Ann's happiness; I just wished I could share it.

Marching with new purpose toward the ribbons and balloons, I was halfway across the asphalt when two tuxedo-clad men stepped out of the shadows near the foot of the stairs.

One I recognized. At six-and-a-half feet tall with straight blond hair that constantly hung in his eyes, Chase Linwood was hard to miss. He said something I couldn't make out, pointed at his collar, then lifted his chin.

His companion, several inches shorter, turned his back to me and went to work on Chase's tie. His identity was a mystery. Slowing my approach, I tried to paste on the appropriate I'm-so-happy-for-the-bride-and-groom face.

Held up by another passing car, I inspected Chase's friend. Not a strand of his thick, wavy brown hair was out of place, and the tailored fit of his suit coat emphasized his broad shoulders and trim waist. The jacket didn't have tails, but it was long enough to prevent me from checking out his ass. Beth was right: this guy was hot…and *way* out of my league.

I waved another car by. I wasn't in a hurry to make a fool of myself in front of Mr. Sexy-From-the-Back. I had to pace myself.

As if he'd sensed me, the unknown groomsman dropped Chase's tie. He fished something out of his pocket and peered at the small, shiny item in his hand. Giving Chase a chuck on the shoulder, he jogged up the stairs.

"Hey, Chase!" I called after his companion disappeared.

Chase squinted in the bright sun and waved halfheartedly, his hands twisting his bow tie into a floppy mess. "Hey, Mel," he mumbled, continuing to fumble with his tie. Finally he gave up, leaving it hanging limply from his collar.

"Would you like some help with that?"

He brightened a bit. "Could you fix it? Linda tied it this morning, but it came apart."

"No problem." He started to bend his lanky frame toward me, but I dragged him to the edge of the staircase instead. "This'll work better if you stand up straight. Hold still a minute, okay?"

It took me standing on the second step before I could look Chase in the eye, he was so tall. "You've been pulling on this, haven't you?" The ends of the tie were way too long to make a bow at his neck.

"Maybe just a little. Why?" One dimple peeked out of his guilty grin.

"It's too loose. Turn around." Taking hold of his shoulders, I spun him so his back was to me.

As I worked the slide and shortened the tie, Chase craned his head back. "So, did you drive all the way down here this morning from Santa Lucia?"

What's the big deal about my driving today? "Uh-huh." I reached around and checked the length of his tie.

"Oh."

Chase wasn't the most loquacious person I knew, but his reply was uncharacteristically short.

"Why? Is that a problem?" Satisfied with the first phase of bow tie repair, I tugged on his shoulders again. "Turn around."

I ignored the pensive squint Chase gave me and concentrated on his neck.

"No, of course not. I was just wondering why you didn't come earlier."

"I wasn't really invited to anything else," I said without thinking.

"That's not what I heard."

No way. There was no way Mitch told anyone I'd turned down his offer to be part of the wedding. Chase was guessing.

I made the mistake of peeking at his slate-blue eyes. With burning cheeks, I worked on the tie, looping the butterfly-shaped ends around and through each other.

"You heard wrong."

Taking my hands in his, Chase stopped me and waited until I looked up again. "Mitch asked you to be in the wedding, didn't he?"

I didn't bother answering.

"Why'd you say no?"

I started to tell Chase what I'd told Mitch: I was too busy, I knew Ann wouldn't appreciate me there, and I'd much rather see him from the front—not the back—while he made his vows. The disappointment in Chase's face told me he wouldn't believe that story either.

"The truth?"

Chase nodded. "Yeah, the truth."

I tried to swallow, but something…guilt, maybe…clogged my throat. "It's stupid. I didn't want to spoil his big day."

"Spoil it? How? He was more stressed because he didn't think you'd come at all." Anger leaked into his voice.

I hadn't realized Mitch thought I might bail on him. "I didn't mean to worry him," I whispered. "Look, today is about Mitch and Ann starting their new life together. Everyone is supposed to be all happy and excited—"

"And you're not."

"No." Admitting my selfishness out loud hurt more than I'd anticipated.

Chase let my hands go, and I started over on his tie, evening up the ends.

He shoved his hands in his pockets. "I know how you feel. I'm going to miss him too."

My eyes darted to his. "He's marrying your sister. It's not like you're never going to see him."

"Sure, I'll see him. On holidays and at family reunions." He turned away.

"It's better than nothing," I barely breathed. Thankfully Chase didn't hear me.

This was exactly what I wanted to avoid: spreading my selfish melancholy around like a virus. Why couldn't I just be happy like everyone else?

"So, have you found a new roommate yet?" I tightened the knot and straightened the bow.

Chase flinched, and for a second I thought I'd put my foot in my mouth again. "Not quite that tight, Mel. I do need to breathe, ya know." His smile wasn't quite as forced as mine was.

"Sorry. There. I think it's done."

He fingered the tie and nodded. "Thanks. Actually, don't tell Linda, but I have a roommate in mind." His smile widened.

Another perfectly matched couple, Chase and Linda had been together since before I met them. Judging by his grin, whatever he was hiding was going to make Linda one happy woman.

I smoothed the shoulders of his jacket. "When will you break the news to her?" Linda's sources were better than mine; he wouldn't be able to keep her in the dark very long.

"Soon." He winked, but wouldn't explain further. "I should probably help with the seating. May I escort you to the front door, Miss?" he drawled.

With a silent *for Mitch*, I took his arm and we climbed the stairs. Finding it easier to smile, I asked, "How's the groom holding up?"

The answer caught me off guard: Chase laughed. Not a chuckle, but a full, deep belly laugh. "He threw up once this morning—cereal, I think. At least he missed his shoes." We rounded the corner of the building, and he thumbed at the people crowded around the front door. "I wonder if they know what kind of wuss he is!"

His humor lifted my spirits a bit. "Should we tell them about his women's underwear fetish?"

"I'm saving that for the toast," Chase stage-whispered.

Still laughing, he left me in the entryway and headed for the front of the crowd. I waited my turn in the back. Where was Beth?

With a wistful sigh, I checked out the group of ushers at the door. Maybe I should've taken her up on her offer to introduce me—would it be so bad to have someone to talk to?

I'd worried that seeing so many men dressed in black would bring back unpleasant memories of my last trip to church, but instead I found myself drooling over the group like the rest of the women around me.

Chase looked great, but he was only one of an entire herd of *GQ*-worthy, immaculate men—a stunning sight in their matching tuxedos. One of the guys I recognized as Mitch's classmate, and a couple more were from the rodeo team, though I'd never seen them this clean before. The rest were anonymously good looking. They whispered to each other, playing with their ties or cuff links while they waited for their turn to show someone to their seat.

It was my first and only high school dance all over again.

Chase caught my eye and pointed to his neat bowtie before he questioned the guests in line ahead of me. I gave him a thumbs up, happy I could contribute something to Mitch's big day. I stepped forward, expecting the I-got-stuck-with-*her* look from the next piece of eye candy.

A tall, lean stranger approached, stealing my breath.

He didn't look directly at me at first, so he missed my *Exorcist*-like double take. I had two heartbeats to collect myself—and to shut my gaping mouth. The guy I'd seen with Chase earlier moved toward me so smoothly he seemed to skate across the carpet.

I recognized his movie-star hair immediately, the molten-chocolate waves just touching his collar, divided by a soft part just right of center. My previous assumption had been correct; he was exceedingly handsome. I drank in his flawless face, tracing his bold cheekbones and square, strong chin with my eyes, trying to find a suitable description for what I was witnessing. The word that came to mind wasn't *stunning* or *exquisite*, though both were appropriate; it was *familiar*. This animated *David* reminded me of someone. Before I could put a name to his doppelganger, he turned to look at me, and all thought vanished. His eyes were the brightest blue I'd ever seen, and when our gaze met, time stopped.

They say that in the moments before death it's common to experience a lifetime's worth of memories. As I drowned in the sapphirine depths of his eyes, what I saw wasn't the past, but the future. My vision blurred. In my imagination, his vibrant blue eyes appeared inches from mine, and his arms wrapped around me, holding me tightly against his perfect body. I felt every sculpted muscle, every virile heartbeat as he bent down and gently kissed me. As my tongue sought his, the scene shifted and we lay in a darkened room, wrapped in each other's embrace, wearing nothing but the sweat of ecstasy. We panted together in perfect rhythm, and a single strained word left my lips: "Yes."

The scene changed, and he was at my elbow, guiding me into a long black car. Cameras flashed in our faces, and specks of rice crunched under our feet. His azure eyes twinkled as he brushed the white veil away from my cheek and whispered, "My wife." The image darkened again; he nuzzled my ear as his hand slowly stroked the skin of my swollen belly, sending a shiver through me. The pictures flew by faster and faster, flipping like pages in an imaginary scrapbook: we sat on a couch, surrounded by toys, his arm wrapped around my shoulders; we stood in a crowd and watched mortar boards fly into the air; he held my hand as we cut a cake decorated with the words *25 Years and Counting*.

Woven through the fast-forward of my life were kisses, touches, and intense releases of passion—all shared with this unknown, gorgeous man. Decades of life, love, and lust passed before my eyes in just two long seconds. I didn't even know if he liked girls, but I could see myself giving everything I was to him.

He smiled tentatively at me, and as fast as it had appeared, the vision vanished. I blinked, breaking eye contact with him, and inhaled, channeling all my strength to my rubbery legs. He stepped forward, and I realized his lips—his perfect lips—were moving. When I didn't respond, his face fell.

I tried desperately to regain my composure. I'd never experienced a fantasy like that before. *It must be lust at first gawk.*

He tried smiling again, and I was able to respond in kind this time.

"May I show you in?" he asked slowly and extended his arm.

Unable to speak, I imitated a bobblehead doll instead.

"Bride or groom?" The plush baritone of his words washed over me like the incoming tide, and I had to concentrate on voicing my answer.

"Groom," I choked out. I placed my hand in the crook of his arm, easily noting the hard definition of his bicep through his tuxedo jacket.

He laughed lightly, and I actually stumbled, recognizing the inviting chuckle. Why was the sound so familiar?

"Do I know you?" I blurted. The answer had to be no. There was no way I could've met this amazing creature and forgotten.

He looked down at me, carefully inspecting my features. His eyes sparkled when they met mine again, and his mouth turned up in an uneven smile. "No, I'm sure I would remember *you*," he said, echoing my thoughts.

I blushed and looked away. This was foolish. With my luck, this guy was some actor Ann had hired to seat the guests. The thought he could be even remotely interested in me was absurd—and hadn't I decided I didn't need a date?

I carefully controlled my breathing, resolving to enjoy the few moments I had with this living piece of art. He led me gracefully down the aisle, and I couldn't help but notice how we'd become the center of attention.

Feeling the stare of so many people smothered my determination, and I tugged on his arm after only a few steps. "Here is fine," I said. We'd stopped just three rows from the door.

"But I can't see you back here," he said, looking toward the front of the church. His eyes creased together as he seemed to measure the distance to the altar.

"What did you say?"

My escort swallowed quickly. "I said I don't think you can see back here." Before I could comment, he grinned, and I lost myself in his blindingly white teeth. Were they as smooth as they looked?

He led me down the aisle, his smile never wavering, and I startled when he finally stopped. We were only a few rows from the front.

"How about here?" he asked.

I couldn't say no; another guest was being seated right behind me. "If you say so," I said, my voice squeaking.

He chuckled and handed me something.

I turned into the pew, scolding myself for being such an idiot. At least I'd provided him a laugh.

Out of the corner of my eye, I saw Beth waving a few rows behind me. I didn't bother to check what had to be her smug expression and slid down the pew near a couple of other young women. They, too, were entranced with my escort, as were most of the women in the room.

"Who's that?" one whispered, subtly pointing at the unknown groomsman.

"I have no idea. Is he Chase Linwood?" the second asked. At the sound of my friend's name, I glanced over at her. She was peering intently at the program. I looked at the matching page in my own hand. *So that's what he gave me.*

I perused the exotic handmade paper, searching for the list of participants. After skimming the order of service, I flipped the program over. Written on the back, in an elegant curling script, was the information I wanted.

I recognized most of the men listed as groomsmen, but none of the ushers or readers or musicians. How many people did it take to pull off a wedding? Several sported the surnames Linwood or McAlister, including the best man.

The church continued to fill, and I looked around, trying to catch another glimpse of my escort, without any luck. The interior of the building was surprisingly muted. Strips of stained glass broke up the cream-colored walls every ten feet or so, and the pews were the same dusty blue as the carpet. Nothing about this place was what I expected of someone as fashion-forward as Ann.

The music started, and I settled back for the ceremony, grinning when I caught Mitch's nervous eye peeking through the side door. I wagged my finger at him playfully, and he straightened his shoulders and nodded.

"Thanks," he mouthed, and I blew him a kiss. *Damn, I'm going to miss him.*

The organist ducked her head once and the music changed. We all turned to see the mystery groomsman escort the groom's parents to their seats. Suddenly the reason for the familiar feeling became clear.

I'd met Mitch's parents months before at one of the rodeos and recognized his mother immediately. Her escort—*my* escort—resembled her in amazing ways. His hair was exactly the same rich shade of chocolate brown, and he'd inherited her brilliant blue eyes. His smile was reserved, the look of a son who not only loved, but respected, the woman on his arm, his mother. I'd been fantasizing about Mitch's younger brother, Jason.

Unlike me, Mrs. McAlister walked proudly next to Jason. Her ice blue dress had no ornamentation save the sparkling clasp that held the jacket-style top closed. Calm, cool, and collected, she was everything I wasn't.

Mr. McAlister followed behind, his head held high. It was clear Mitch took after him: large, smiling, and bear-like. The elder McAlister put his hand on Jason's shoulder before he sat and shared a quiet laugh with his son. When Jason turned to walk back up the aisle, his eyes flashed to mine, and the corner of his mouth rose, causing my heart to lurch.

The music changed again, and Chase started down the aisle with his mother. Mrs. Linwood was beautiful, like her daughter, but with wavy, auburn hair. Her dress, a pale lilac sheath, emphasized her youthful appearance. She glided down the aisle on Chase's arm, and when he showed her to her seat, he leaned down and kissed her cheek.

Chase retreated to the back of the church, and moments later, the line of delicious groomsmen appeared at the front near the altar. Jason followed Mitch, and their similarities had me shaking my head. Some observer I was; the resemblance was unmistakable. The brothers shared the same strong chin, the same warm smile, and—as I remembered Jason's amusement—the same endearing laugh. He turned toward me again, winking in my direction.

I bit my lip, not taking my eyes off him. One by one the bridesmaids entered. I only noticed because their huge, swishing purple skirts nearly drowned out the music. Jason didn't look away either, equally oblivious to the procession of purple. I felt my expression give way to the dumbfounded look I must've worn when I first laid eyes on him, but his gaze didn't waver.

The vision I'd seen earlier reappeared. Imaginary Jason reached for me…but then the crowd rose, blocking my view. I mentally slapped myself—this fantasy was getting way out of hand. I stood slowly, unable to dispute the fact he was obviously curious about me.

I faced the rear doors, waiting for the bride to enter, the back of my neck tingling. He couldn't be watching me now, could he? The tempo of the music altered, and a quiet murmur rolled through the crowd. I fidgeted, fighting the urge to look over my shoulder just one last time. *Maybe a quick glance…*

Thankfully, I was saved from further embarrassment when the woman next to me whispered, "I'm so happy for them. Aren't you?"

The prickles on my neck disappeared as I forced out my unenthusiastic answer. "Yes, I am."

What a pitiful excuse of a friend I was. Who was I to mourn Mitch's happiness? He'd found the very thing I'd been fantasizing about just moments before: a companion with whom to share his love, his life. Someone tied to him by a bond stronger than anything but death. And he deserved nothing less.

"Yes, I am," I repeated, meaning it this time.

Two

The familiar strains of Pachelbel's Canon filled the sanctuary, and the doors in the back of the church opened wide, revealing Ann and her father. The afternoon sun enrobed her in an unearthly radiance as she waited for her cue. The word *resplendent* came to mind. With a deep breath, she nodded to her father and began her slow walk down the aisle.

Strapless and simple, her gown had an elegance that could only have been conceived by a major designer. A pure, virginal white, the dress emphasized Ann's perfect figure with its wide skirt and tailored waistline. The white satin was completely covered by the thinnest organza, which caught the light, adding to her heavenly aura.

Coronation was another appropriate word, judging by the jeweled tiara holding Ann's immaculate golden bun on the top of her head. The tiara's clear gems glinted in the light that filtered through the stained glass, and I had no doubt it was encrusted with real diamonds. No veil hid Ann's face. Only a few expertly curled tendrils framed her prominent cheekbones and soft blue eyes. On her arm, her father completed the picture: the perfect accessory in his contrasting dark tux.

Ann's expression was fixed in a small, nervous smile as she moved steadily toward the front of the church. Her eyes darted once or twice to the crowd, but she acknowledged no one. The instant she saw Mitch, her face changed. Her lips rounded up the corners, and she blinked furiously. If it were possible, she became even more radiant at that moment. She practically glowed under his gaze.

Surprisingly, Mitch didn't return the smile. With a tangible intensity, he surrounded his bride with wordless adoration, seeming to see nothing but her as she closed the distance between them. He held out a trembling hand and swallowed before looking to her father, almost fearfully. Mitch had once told me he was sure Ann was a dream that would disappear someday, but I'd thought he was joking. Seeing how terrified he was at this moment, I felt bad for having teased him.

Mr. Linwood murmured a few unintelligible words and patted Mitch on the shoulder. Mitch nodded solemnly, then offered Ann his arm. Her aura surrounded them both as she clung to him, and several people in the crowd sighed.

Watching the two of them climb the steps to the minister, I understood exactly why Ann had chosen this subdued venue. Against the soft background of cream and blue, she and Mitch outshone everything and everyone.

Well, almost everyone.

Waiting on the top step, Jason winked at his brother and soon-to-be sister-in-law. The lights meant to frame the bride and groom also illuminated his eyes, adding neon sparkles to his azure irises—especially when they darted to me.

Although I tried to stay focused on Mitch and Ann, my attention kept shifting to the man next to them. Jason's eyes flickered to me a couple of times before he turned to face his brother, and my heart skipped a beat every time they did.

Once stationed next to Mitch, Jason stood motionless, as if locked in a masterpiece, listening intently. Out of the bright sunshine, his hair took on a darker, richer look, and my eye was drawn to a few renegade lengths that curled invitingly toward his ear. Surely some lucky girl would smooth them back into place tonight, and my fingers twitched, wishing they could do the honors.

What was I doing? "No time for a guy," I'd said pompously, as if I was turning them away by the dozen. The truth was I'd never attracted such attention before, especially from someone so devastatingly handsome. Men regarded me in only two lights: tough and equal, or plain and invisible. The only relationships I'd had came about more as afterthoughts than by design—starting with a bored, "So, you don't have a date, huh?" rather than a breathless, "May I join you?" I'd never been pursued, and I had most certainly never done any pursuing.

It's about time, don't you think?

I couldn't believe the words ringing in my head. Me, go after *him?* As crazy as the notion was, I couldn't help but stare at Jason, wondering…wanting…

The minister's words became but a low hum in my ears as I sifted through everything Mitch had ever told me about his younger brother.

Jason had spent most summers in school, I remembered. Mitch had complained about how little he saw him. What was Jason studying…was it pre-med? He went to school in the Midwest somewhere…at Ohio State…no, Michigan. *Crap! Those schools are arch rivals. I can't screw that up—he'll never speak to me again!*

Again? It wasn't like we'd had an actual conversation. Jason had hardly said two words to me.

He and Mitch were close—I knew they corresponded regularly by text and email—but the only photo Mitch had of his brother was a wallet-sized candid from at least ten years ago. The water-soaked boys in the picture looked nothing like the tailored men standing together today.

My tongue slid around my teeth, searching for the wayward piece of hamburger that must be stuck there. Why else would Jason keep looking at me? Maybe my little episode had him thinking I'd be a good subject for his next psych paper.

Laughter erupted, and I looked around quickly, expecting to see everyone staring at me. Thankfully I was not the center of attention this time. Something the minister said must have been funny, not my inability to cope with an overactive fantasy.

Mitch threw a glance over his shoulder at the crowd and grinned tentatively. At least he didn't look like he was about to pass out.

Mitch…what if *he'd* said something to Jason? That couldn't be good. I could only imagine how Mitch would describe me, especially in the acronym-laden world of the internet.

Email…*oh no!* I gasped, and the people nearby shushed me. *The personality profile!*

Last October, I'd received a class assignment to write an extended profile on a real, non-famous person. "A friend, classmate, or coworker—someone local you can find multiple sources on," the instructor had said. Of course, I'd chosen Mitch.

I'd talked to his parents, and they'd given me Jason's email. I'd carefully composed a very dry and business-like message requesting his assistance, but after the basic information had been exchanged, our emails became more of the LMAO variety. The room became exceptionally hot as I remembered those notes…

Jason had cracked a few jokes about me hanging around in the manure with his brother, which led me to send a few of my favorite doctor jokes. He also questioned me about Mitch, seeming innocent at first:

> Mitch mentioned that you met him for coffee
> yesterday. Does he still insist on refusing the
> drink holders and balancing cups on top of each
> other? He takes "green" to the extreme, don't you
> think?

At first glance the question was innocuous enough, but I saw through his weak attempt at fishing out information. If only two coffees had been ordered, Jason would assume we were out alone.

He was a sly one. I smiled as I typed:

> I don't know. I'm into green too, and I brought my
> own cup.

Mitch must not have said much about me, because Jason's email interrogation continued. I purposely kept my answers vague, enjoying stringing him along as long as possible. But when he asked about Mitch's skill as an equestrian, I finally gave in and flat out asked:

> Do you want to know if I'm the one your brother
> is riding?

Normally I'd get a response within the hour—Jason seemed to be online all the time—but in this case I didn't hear back for a full day. I worried I'd offended him; he really didn't know how blunt I could be. Eventually his response arrived, for the first time without any cagey questions.

> To be perfectly honest, yes. Mitch mentions you
> often. He likes you and the way you make him
> laugh. I think he cares about you a lot.
>
> That's all I was trying to do with my
> questions—get a glimpse of what Mitch sees
> in you. I'm sorry. I can see now you are a no-
> nonsense woman.
>
> So, are you my brother's new mount?

I laughed out loud when I read the note—much to the chagrin of the other students on the fourth floor of the library at the time. After apologizing and making a mental note to read my email at home in the future, I carefully composed my response. Jason seemed like someone who could appreciate some friendly innuendo.

That depends. How many brothers do you have?

This time the reply came in seconds.

Just the one. How many men are you sleeping
with?

Apparently I wasn't the only one who was no-nonsense. Quickly I sent him my answer and packed up my books.

Well, sleeping may not be the right term.
Cowboys like to ride a lot…bareback.

Jason's response arrived before I could shut down my laptop, and I left the library snickering.

But that can't be nearly as much fun as playing
doctor.

We continued to joke for another week, but then midterms hit, and I let his last comments go unanswered. It was Christmas before I realized I'd left him hanging. I still felt a little guilty I'd let the teasing end without even a "thank you" for his help with my story. But he must've been busy too, because he'd never restarted the conversation.

How easy it'd been to get completely dirty with a faceless, shameless pen pal and walk away. No regrets, no commitments, and no rejection in the end. Perfect.

But now my pen pal had a face—with a magnificently sculpted chin, inviting lips, and eyes that turned my knees to jelly. All the tasteless, smutty things I'd said to him came back in a rush.

I threw my hand over my eyes, my face redder than Ann's lipstick, I was certain. Thankfully, Jason had his back to me. *Does he know I'm the one who spammed him? Did Mitch rat me out?*

No way. Jason would've said *something* if he'd known who I was—made some comment about my tasteless humor. Or was he waiting for me to figure out who he was—seeing how long he could string *me* along?

No, that didn't make sense, either. He hadn't made any attempts to rekindle our email conversation; it'd died a quick death. It *couldn't* have meant that much to him.

Now that I knew who *he* was, the thought of facing Jason again sent nervous stings up my spine. I considered skipping the reception as I fanned myself with my program.

"It is because of *your* love and *your* support this bond is being sealed today," the minister said, pointing randomly at members of the audience. When his finger stopped on me, I slouched in my seat. "Witness now what you have forged."

Damn it. I'd missed the minister's entire message with my selfish daydreaming. After one more peek at Jason, I swore to give Mitch and Ann the respect they deserved and fixed my eyes on them.

Mitch straightened up, preparing to recite his vows. With a deep breath, he began. "Ann, the first time I saw you, I was reborn. Everything I am, everything I will be became yours. I promise to love you, care for you, and respect you for the rest of my life. No matter what the future brings, good or bad, laughter or tears, we will face it together. I'm yours forever. This I vow."

Mitch's low, steady voice strengthened on the final words, emphasizing his conviction. He'd used the same tone when he told me he proposed to Ann, just weeks after meeting her.

I couldn't imagine falling for anyone so fast. It took time to fall in love and learn about a person before that feeling of *forever* kicked in. I'd never made it long enough to sense that permanence; I doubted there was a forever kind of guy for me.

My eyes drifted to Ann, her lips quivering as a single tear rolled down her cheek. Her forever, Mitch, reached out with one finger and gently wiped it away before she spoke.

Pressing his hand to her cheek, she took a shaky breath. "Mitch, before I met you I didn't know what love was. You swept me off my feet and into your heart, and that's where I found not only love, but my future. Through pain and pleasure, joy and sorrow, good and bad, I promise to be by your side, loving you, respecting you, caring for you, forever. This I vow."

Ann's words were soft but clear, her eyes locked on his. When she finished, she smiled and cradled Mitch's cheek, wiping his face with her thumb. He sniffled loudly, and they both laughed, drawing a quiet response from the audience. I blinked a tear away myself, seeing my big friend so moved.

Lifting a single finger, the minister cued the guitarist standing to the side of the altar. The musical interlude gave us all time to savor the depth of the promises the couple had made. Ann's eyes shined as she whispered to Mitch, and he touched his forehead to hers. Feeling like an intruder into their private moment, my gaze wandered, returning to the dark hair and broad shoulders of the best man. Jason shuffled his feet and tilted his head ever so slightly, as if resisting the urge to turn around. At least that's what I pretended…

The melody faded, and the bride and groom took a more formal stance, their hands intertwined between them. Jason pulled the ring out of his jacket pocket and placed it on the minister's Bible, where it joined one provided by the maid of honor. The minister consecrated the two circles of gold with a simple blessing, the final seals on the bride and groom's holy union.

As Mitch and Ann exchanged rings, my mind drifted back to the strange vision I'd had of Jason. In a flash I saw myself in Ann's place, a thin veil separating me from Jason's smiling lips. Shaking my head, I tried to erase the irrational image, but only succeeded in blurring it. What was wrong with me?

I'd had crushes in the past, even been in love, I thought, but nothing like *this* had ever happened before. It couldn't mean anything; he was just a sexy guy in a tux. A sexy guy in a tux who couldn't keep his eyes off me…

Stop it!

While I appreciated a good-looking man as much as the next girl, it was a guy's wit and personality that had always attracted me. He *is* witty, my hormones argued. Maybe online, but the computer screen clouded a person's true character. I didn't even know who he was when I had the fantasy. Did that make my point or nullify it?

I rubbed my temple, wishing I could shut off my lusty inner voice. Thinking Jason would give me more than the time of day was ridiculous, especially once he connected my face to my electronic banter. Hell, he probably had a girlfriend or fiancée and wouldn't want to explain our little jaunt through the internet gutter to her. If not—and my heart betrayed me with a flutter of hope—my jaw-dropping reaction when we "met" had to have left the impression I was a nut case. He wouldn't want anything more to do with me.

Then why can't he keep his eyes off you? He winked at you, for crying out loud!

I was left shaking my head as the minister concluded the ceremony.

"You may kiss your bride."

With a grin tinged with a hint of mischief, Mitch embraced his wife. Ann melted into her new husband's arms, drawing applause and giggles from the crowd when her lips locked with his.

Clapping enthusiastically, Jason turned his coy smile on me.

Reflexively I smiled back, remembering my earlier fantasy of sharing an equally passionate kiss with him. *If only…*

My cheeks warmed, and his smile grew, as if enjoying the same image. I tore my eyes away, scolding myself for indulging in such an unrealistic daydream. It had to be my childish expression that had him entertained, that's all.

Ann and Mitch led the procession out, and Jason winked at me as he passed. On his arm, the maid of honor and Ann's best friend, Tricia, followed his gaze and sneered. She'd make sure I didn't clutter Jason's time at the reception. Pointing her nose in the air, she tightened her grip on his arm, confirming my supposition. Maybe he didn't have a girlfriend, but he definitely had a companion—whether he wanted one or not.

The parade of black and purple whisked by, and the guests filed out, row by row, behind them. Rather than stand, I turned sideways and let everyone else in my pew pass. I wasn't ready to face Beth—or anyone else—just yet. By the time I'd collected myself enough to scoot down to the end of the pew, the church was nearly empty.

Without warning, the door the groomsmen had used earlier opened and Mitch appeared, escorting his new wife.

"We made a clean getaway," he bellowed before wrapping his arms around Ann and gluing his face to hers.

The rest of the wedding party filed in behind them, and while they whistled and teased the bride and groom, I headed to the back as inconspicuously as I could.

Clapping loudly, the photographer attempted to organize the group. "We only have a few more pictures to take. Pay attention and we'll get done as quickly as possible. Can someone pass the groom a handkerchief? I'm not sure that shade of lipstick suits you, Mr. McAlister."

In the midst of the laughter, a man's voice called, "Melissa, hang on a sec!"

I cringed, but didn't slow. When he called again, I peeked behind me.

"Mel, over here." Todd held up a white cloth and rushed toward me. Behind him, I caught a pair of bright eyes scanning the crowd frantically. I ducked behind a conveniently placed pillar, willing myself to become invisible.

Todd stopped, having lost sight of me. "Over here," I half-whispered, peeking around the pole.

He jogged over, the fabric—a sweater—dangling from one hand. "Can you give this to Beth? She left it in the groom's prep room."

"Uh, sure. No problem." I grabbed the sweater and turned on my heel.

"Thanks a lot. Beth gets cold on the warmest days, so I know she'll need this," he said behind me.

I avoided making eye contact with Jason and raced to the exit, using an older couple as camouflage. Before I could make my escape, I saw him lean in close to his brother's ear and point in my direction. *Great.*

Bursting through the door, I crashed into Beth.

"Whoa, Melissa," she said, half catching me, half steadying herself. "Where's the fire?"

Her use of one of Mitch's favorite phrases snapped me back to reality.

"Sorry! I just…was…" Running from embarrassment? Not when it was standing right in front of me.

While I tripped over my brain, Beth looked down at my hand. "Is that mine?"

Duh. "Um, yeah, here." I thrust the sweater at her, kicking myself for missing the obvious, again. "I was…uh…looking for you, actually."

"Thanks," she said carefully.

After an awkward second of silence while the couple I'd used as a human shield hobbled by, I tugged on my blouse and headed down the path toward the parking lot. "See you at the reception," I said over my shoulder and marched off.

I made it to the stairs before I realized I wasn't alone.

"Who were they?" Beth asked.

Why is she following me? "Who?"

"The couple you just spoke to—the people you're meeting later."

Nice. "No one. I was just being polite." *To you!*

I started down the stairs, taking them two at a time.

"Slow down, Mel. You don't have to rush. They're going to be in there awhile," she said, panting slightly as she trotted next to me.

"I'm not rushing," I lied, stopping abruptly at the bottom. Now that we were out of sight of the front doors, I could finally breathe. "I'm not sure where the reception is and wanted some extra time to look it up."

I expected Beth to call me on the fabrication—she always saw through my lies—but her face lit up like a light bulb. "How about I show you instead?" She caught my arm, suddenly as eager as I was to get to the car.

"What about Todd? I thought you'd ride with him."

"No thanks! The limo ride over with the guys was enough for me. Add the purple people eaters and I'm out." The venom in Beth's voice surprised me.

"Okay," I said slowly. Escaping the wedding alone was clearly not an option. At least having Beth along should mean I wouldn't get lost.

I unlocked the car with the remote, and Beth yanked the door open before I could stop her.

"Hang on. I'll move that stuff," I said. The passenger seat was buried under a load of disheveled newspapers.

"No problem—I've got it," she said, scooping up the stack and plopping down on the seat. She shut the door, preventing me from taking the load off her hands.

By the time I'd gotten my seatbelt buckled, she'd organized and stacked all the papers neatly on her lap.

"I'll take those," I said, reaching for the pile. Beth set the stack in my outstretched arms but didn't let go. She was entranced by what looked like a woman's graduation photo.

"Oh wow, is that her?" she asked.

I tried to figure out what was so special about the woman while she scanned the page. "Who?"

Beth tapped the top of the stack. "Kerry Stanton. Ann knew her." Her eyes bugged out as she read. "She was strangled? How terrible!"

Unable to stand it any longer, I angled the stack so I could see the article.

POLICE SEARCH FOR MOTIVE IN COED'S MURDER

On Thursday the public memorial for Kerry Stanton drew hundreds of mourners to the USC campus. The murder of this popular student and community activist has many questioning why she was targeted.

Stanton's body was found in the park adjoining the Theta Pi sorority house last Saturday morning. An autopsy confirmed she'd been sexually assaulted before she was strangled. The coroner would not confirm whether the scarf found at the scene was the murder weapon.

Police have not ruled out Stanton's acquaintances as possible suspects, but friends of the victim continue to refute this possibility. "Kerry didn't have any enemies. She went out of her way to help everyone she met," said Theta Pi president Janice...

"Ann and Mitch went to her funeral. She was in one of Ann's classes or something. I didn't know she was murdered—how awful." Beth let go of the papers and hugged herself. "Ann said she was really nice. I can't imagine what her folks must be going through."

"That's too bad," I mumbled. I knew exactly what they were feeling, and *bad* didn't come close to covering it. At a loss for words, I slid the papers onto the back seat.

Beth buckled up. "It really is. It would've been nice to meet just one girl down here who wasn't stuck on herself."

I eyed my friend. "I thought you liked Ann."

"Oh, I do," she said quickly. "Other than her. I meant her friends. They are...less than welcoming."

The purple people eaters. I finally got her reference to the lavender-adorned bridesmaids. "Tricia and her groupies?" I guessed.

Beth pointed to the right when we got to the street. "Yeah. You thought Tricia was bad when she came up to the barbecue in Santa Lucia last month? She was Hannah Montana compared to what she's like in her natural environment. Even Ann apologized for her snotty attitude a couple of times. Just this morning I was ready to shove a bouquet down Tricia's throat."

I had to cover my mouth. No one had been surprised Tricia didn't get along with me, but pissing off Beth? That took some seriously bitchy talent.

"Why?"

Beth shook out her sweater and refolded it. "She wanted me to hold an umbrella over her between photos, for Pete's sake. 'The sun's too bright. It's making my eyes water,'" she said with a nasal whine.

"Did you?" I coughed.

"Absolutely not! I'm not a slave girl."

Luckily we'd stopped at an intersection, because I couldn't hold back the laughter any longer.

"It's not funny, Melissa!"

"No, it's—" I choked on another giggle "—not." I couldn't avoid getting smacked on the shoulder. "Ow!"

"She makes me want to spit. To H-E-double hockey sticks with her," Beth muttered, drawing another poorly disguised laugh from me.

Rather than risk another beating, I changed the subject. "So, what did Mitch think of the note?"

Beth blew her bangs out of the way. "He was more interested in your message than Ann's, actually." She sighed, her anger dissipating into a small smile. "Mitch really did look like he was going to be sick for a while. When I told him you were ready to put him on the ground if he didn't pull himself together, he perked up. So did Jason, actually."

The car lurched forward. "*Jason* did?" I hadn't thought about Beth telling him who I was. Did he already know?

"Oh yeah. Before I left, I heard him asking Mitch all about you—what you looked like, did you have a date, where were you staying—but Mitch completely ignored him. Jason got pretty irritated." She shifted so she was facing me. "What was that all about?"

"I have no clue." I hadn't thought about Jason in more than six months—well, until today—but he was asking about me? I consoled myself with the fact that Mitch didn't tell him anything.

The consolation didn't last long. Why *didn't* Mitch say anything?

Wait—do I want Jason to know who I am or not? My stomach filled with something much more violent than butterflies. Jason was mad? What if he only wanted to chew me out for leading him on via email?

"Huh. The way you two were making googly eyes at each other in the church, I figured you must know him. What'd he say to you?"

My stomach did another flip. "Nothing. I didn't know who he was until later." We stopped at a strange five-way intersection. "Which way?"

Beth pointed to the right-hand road ahead of us. "Straight, then around the hill. So you walked all the way to the front of the church with the sexiest guy in the building and didn't say *anything* to him?"

I could hardly breathe next to Jason, and she expected me to have a conversation with him? Beads of sweat formed on the back of my neck just thinking about seeing him again. "I guess."

"Are you blushing?" Beth asked, incredulous. "Goodness, Melissa, you're such a child. You work with guys all the time, but you're afraid of one hot stranger? What's with you?"

What was *wrong with me?* "I don't know. What would I say to him? It's not like I could interview him or something."

Beth straightened her skirt. "You introduce yourself and ask him where he's from, how he knows Mitch, whether he prefers blondes or brunettes. How hard could it be?"

It shouldn't be hard, but my ears burned as I imagined how he'd phrase his answers. *But this isn't email, now is it?*

"He's from Michigan, and he's Mitch's brother." I ignored the third topic, but wondered if having a little bit of both blond and dark hair made me a loser either way.

"But you didn't know that then. I'm surprised he didn't guess who you were. 'Course I guess Mitch didn't know what you were wearing." She opened her window and took a deep breath of the salty air. "Maybe he'll track you down at the reception."

And make me explain my obscene online mouth? *Please, no,* I prayed to no one.

Beth pointed at the rambling ranch homes lining the left side of the boulevard. "Could you imagine living in one of these? Waking up to this view every morning?"

Out her window, the narrow strip of land ended with a sheer drop to the Pacific, distracting me from my internal bickering. In the distance, the sparkling sea was dotted with white sailboats and black cargo ships.

"Nope. I don't think I'll ever see the amount of money it takes to get into one of these houses." As if to punctuate my point, a Bentley pulled up next to me, the driver ignoring my stare. "I have a tough time believing Chase grew up here."

"And Mitch…and Jason," she added with a smirk.

This was news to me. Mitch had always described home as simply "L.A." "Mitch's parents live here too?"

"Yeah, up that way." She pointed at the hill above us. "He and Ann have a condo around the other side. It was their parents' gift to them."

I should've known. Mitch's parents were both successful: his mom was a doctor, and his dad was an executive at a big car company. But I'd neglected to consider the fiscal impact of their chosen professions. The one time I'd met them they'd been in jeans and sneakers and showed none of the snootiness I expected in people of wealth. I'd thought at the time that Mitch was fortunate to have such likeable parents—I just didn't know *how* fortunate.

No wonder Ann had snapped him up. She and the McAlisters ran in the same refined circles, whereas I lived in a completely different social zip code. Attending the same university had given Mitch and me enough common ground to build a strong friendship, but I'd never considered our backgrounds. He liked to play the redneck cowboy part, but on the rare occasion he dressed up, he seemed just as comfortable in a suit and tie. His understanding of the auto industry—from design to production to bottom lines—was endless. To some, his confidence and knowledge came off as arrogance, and I knew firsthand Mitch could be an acquired taste. But no one could ask for a better friend.

What about the younger McAlister? He definitely didn't have confidence issues, that's for sure. And damn, he looked good in a tuxedo. If my imagination was to be believed, he'd look even better out of it.

Ignoring my lapse into lustful daydreaming, Beth let the conversation drop in favor of soaking up the sun, leaving me to continue my mental tail-chasing as we cruised along the cliffs.

Just because Jason turned my world upside down in those first seconds didn't mean he was anything like Mitch. What really lurked behind those brilliant eyes—a snobbish know-it-all, a childish womanizer, or a true gentleman? If he was set on finding the Melissa he knew from the internet, why was he so interested in me, someone he'd barely spent three minutes with? What kept him looking in my direction?

We wound our way around the peninsula, my mind buzzing. The truth silenced the curiosity. None of the questions mattered because I doubted I'd have the chance to answer them. Once Jason realized who I was—and that I'd brushed him off like so much dust months ago—there was no way he'd give me another thought. And after all the rude comments I'd sent him, it wasn't like I'd go looking for him.

This isn't about me. I was here for Mitch. What his brother knew or didn't know was inconsequential. In a few hours they'd both be but a memory.

Three

"*A*re you sure this is the right way?" I asked.

The road turned south and the houses all but disappeared, leaving stretches of dried grass and exposed rock on both sides of us. Even the ocean below was deserted.

Beth's silence didn't help.

"Maybe I should turn around." *And wake up my electronic guide.*

"Well…no, wait!" Her hand shot out toward the windshield. "We're fine. There's the lighthouse. It's just past that."

Beth's hair whipped around in the breeze from the open window. "I love the ocean," she sighed. "Maybe I can move down here when I graduate."

I raised an eyebrow. Beth Miller, psychologist to the stars? Hard to imagine.

"It's not like this every day," I said. "Most days it's foggy, I think."

She frowned. "You're such a buzz kill, Mel. Today is perfect."

"Yeah, perfect."

Beth didn't see my scowl. Sitting up straighter, she turned her attention to the road ahead of us. "Slow down, I think it's just around this bend."

I couldn't see anything but brown. This seemed an odd place to find a four-star hotel, but when we rounded the curve, my mouth fell open.

To the right, the narrow strip of land separating the asphalt from the cliff's edge widened dramatically, forming a huge peninsula that stretched out toward the island in the distance. Sloped away from the street, the property sprawled below us. Gone were the scrub and gravel. The Pacifico Grande Hotel—no, resort—with its pools, palm trees, and putting greens, covered every square inch of real estate in fresh greens, cool blues, and terra cotta reds.

Beth let out a little squeal. "We're here!"

I turned at the fountain-flanked entrance, pausing to inspect a sign with ten arrows pointing to different destinations within the compound. Hotel, golf course, day spa, conference center…where were we supposed to go?

"Where *is* here, exactly?" I asked, feeling behind me for the invitation on the backseat.

"Todd said it was easy to find. We want the Catalina Ballroom. There, third from the bottom," Beth said, peering at the list.

Like tourists we crept along, meticulously reading every sign we passed. Just when I was sure we were about to drive off the cliff, the road ended in a parking lot packed with cars.

Nestled between palm trees at the end of the lot, the ballroom stood apart from the rest of the hotel, isolated from the kid-filled pools and noisy tennis courts. A group of people milled around in front, but by the time I'd found a parking spot, they'd vanished.

"Are you sure this is it?"

Beth hopped out and headed in the direction of the building. "Yes, I'm sure. Come on!"

"Hang on a sec," I called. "I need to grab my gift. Does Todd have yours?"

She giggled. "Of course not. We had it sent directly to their condo. You can do that, you know, Mel."

"Really? I hadn't thought of that," I said sarcastically, but I smiled back at her. I actually had two gifts. The first contained a boring set of towels that I *did* have shipped. I should've had them monogrammed, considering the company Mitch and Ann would be keeping.

The second gift resided in the big silver box covered in metallic red cupids that I hefted out of the trunk. I'd gone in with the guys for the joke gift, hoping to embarrass Mitch's new bride. After hearing of Ann's fondness for frankfurters, however, I had a feeling we'd be getting a thank you instead of a reprimand.

"What did you get them?" Beth asked.

Avoiding her inquisitive gaze, I strode toward the building. "Just some things in case Mitch ever took Ann for a ride," I said, then clamped my mouth shut.

Beth smiled, completely missing the innuendo. "That's nice. She'd look great in a Stetson," she said, eyeing the box. "Did you get Mitch a new hat, too?"

"Chaps," I coughed. *Edible chaps. And a riding crop.*

Thankfully Beth was now occupied with yet another sign.

"I guess we go this way," she said. Turning right, we followed a path that took us past the building and along a low hedge. On the other side, the crowd we'd seen earlier mixed and mingled among exotic flowers and sculpted bushes. We reached a break in the foliage and were greeted by a young blonde dressed immaculately in green. Her gold nametag announced her as Vanessa, Wedding Liaison.

"The Linwood-McAlister wedding?" she asked, and we both nodded. "Welcome. Please enjoy the garden and hors d'oeuvres while we wait for the happy couple. I can take that, if you'd like." She opened her hands for my gift, which I gave her, and she placed it on a nearby cart, hiding it behind several tastefully wrapped presents. "Should you need anything, don't hesitate to ask for me," she added. With a graceful sweep of her hand, she invited us in.

Impressed, I turned to Beth, but she'd already started into the crowd, saying something about starving and missing lunch. She made a beeline for the food, bouncing from one waiter to another like a pink pinball, and I hurried to keep up. In a matter of minutes, she'd sampled every platter of colorful hors d'oeuvres and hand-rolled sushi within reach, charging me with holding two fruity beverages while she ate.

"Don't you want any?" she asked, polishing off what looked like smoked salmon topped with caviar.

Doing my best imitation of my mother, I glared at her. "No, thank you. *I* don't want to spoil my dinner."

With a guilty grimace she wiped her lips. "You're right. I should just enjoy the view." Reclaiming one of the drinks, she stared contentedly across the water at Santa Catalina Island silhouetted against the blue of sea and sky.

Setting my unwanted glass on the empty tray of a passing server, I turned my attention to the guests. Grouped in twos and fours, the crowd naturally divided itself by age. The older generation, in its conservative suits and below-the-knee dresses, congregated on one side of the garden, while the younger set, in miniskirts and tie-less short sleeves, flocked on the other side. Occasionally someone would break ranks, usually chasing down a tray of food or drink.

Whether casual or formal, everyone's attire was runway-ready. I straightened my simple faux-silk blouse, wishing I'd gone with my business suit. Conservative but professional, my suit would've been better than trying to fit my department store fashion sense in with the haute couture around me.

What I wore didn't really matter, since I knew almost no one. The few faces I recognized from Poly weren't friends, just students I'd seen in passing. I entertained myself by sorting the group a different way: *his* and *hers*. Who'd been invited by Mitch and who by Ann?

"Darn, I left my camera at home. Do you have yours, Melissa?" Beth asked suddenly.

"Just my phone. What do you want a shot of?"

"Oh, everything." She opened her arms wide.

"I don't think *everything* will fit. How about one of you and Catalina?"

I dug out my phone while Beth gingerly crossed a small strip of grass and struck a pose in front of the low brick wall separating the garden from the cliff.

"Ready?"

Making sure the island was visible behind her, I snapped the picture. As soon as I lowered the phone, she was at my side.

"Let me see!" she demanded and inspected the display. "Excellent! Let me take one of you." She pushed me in the direction of where she'd been standing and held up the phone.

"Why?"

"For Mitch, silly."

Between the huge resort, Beth's appetizer frenzy, and the stylish crowd, I'd managed to forget this was my last chance to spend any time with Mitch.

Reluctantly I backed toward the wall. With the phone in front of her face, Beth called, "Say cheese!"

I assumed she took the picture, but she shook her head. "That one didn't come out. Take a step back and to the right."

I did as I was told, praying she wasn't sending me over the edge. Her cry of "MY right" coincided with my foot landing on something harder than grass.

Too late I realized I'd stepped on someone's foot. I stumbled forward and managed to stay upright, but my victim wasn't so lucky. The man's ankle folded underneath him, and he went down in the grass, swearing. Shooting another glare at Beth, I spun around and quickly offered him my hand.

"I'm so sorry," I said.

Ignoring my hand and my apology, he grumbled something that sounded like "Watch where you're going," and hurried away, leaving his spilled drink and napkin on the ground.

"It was an accident," I called after him, but he just threw his hand in the air, dismissing me.

Well, I'm *not the worst-dressed person here.* Compared to the immaculate people around us, the man brushing off his knees could only be described as a sore thumb. I should've looked away, but watching him try to straighten his out-of-date, wrinkled suit was as captivating as a slow-motion car wreck. His clothes must've come straight out of mothballs; no matter how he tugged or pressed them, the creases sprang back to their original shape.

"Aw, you stained his best eighties-night outfit," Beth said, snickering. "Maybe he was mad 'cause he didn't know this wasn't a theme wedding. Those wide lapels and thin tie remind me of *Miami Vice.*"

"My mom has an old cowl-neck sweater and some leg warmers I could've worn. Like, gag me with a spoon," I said with a giggle.

"Still, he didn't have to be so rude."

The man glanced back at us with a leer, then grabbed a fresh drink from a passing waiter. A massive cowlick on the back of his head waved at us as he struck up a conversation with the hostess, Vanessa. She gave him an amused once-over before she turned on her professional charm and politely listened.

With one last smirk, Beth returned to the task at hand. "Here, let me try again." She backed away, and I stationed myself against the wall. "*Really* smile this time, Mel. Think of Jason."

Before I could compose an appropriate comeback, I was inundated with the memory of Jason's seductive laugh. I didn't even realize Beth had taken the picture until she touched me on the elbow.

"Much better," she said, handing me the phone.

I inspected the goofy expression on my face, vowing to delete the shot as soon as possible.

"This is fun! Hey, maybe we could get Vanessa to take one of us together." Beth rose to her toes, looking for the hostess, but became distracted by the arrival of yet another waiter and a new tray of phyllo-wrapped delicacies.

I'd started to stow my phone when the unkempt man again caught my eye. Alone now, he lingered near the gift cart and watched the other guests. His expression was hard to read; he didn't appear to be looking for someone in particular, more like he was shopping. Either way, something about him bothered me, and not just the fact he didn't fit in anywhere. *His? Hers? Neither.*

I opened my cell phone and thumbed through the photos, finding Beth's first attempt. In the picture, the man was standing right next to me with his arm raised. I hadn't realized he was so close—he looked like he was about to put his hand on my shoulder…or my hair? I shivered. Maybe knocking him down wasn't such a bad thing after all. My thumb hovered over the delete button.

"Oh no you don't!" Beth said and ripped the phone out of my hands. "If you delete those pictures before sending them to me, I'm going to post the karaoke video."

Karaoke? How does she know about that? "What video? There's no—"

"Promise me you'll send them all to me, or the first person tagged on the post is Craig." Humming what I could barely make out as *Bohemian Rhapsody*, Beth threw one hand in the air, her index and pinky finger extended, and bobbed her head violently. *Shit.* Todd could've told her what I'd done under the influence of tequila, but if there was video… "Fine. I promise. Please stop!"

"I expect to see a message in my inbox when I get home," she said, handing me the phone.

I quickly stuffed it in my purse. The email could wait—there'd be no more picture-taking tonight.

"Now there's a lovely sight," a deep voice said. Beth immediately spun around and captured Todd in her arms.

"Hey, that was fast. I thought you'd be there for hours," she said, her voice warm.

He replied first with a quick but meaningful kiss. "We took a ton of photos before the wedding, so there weren't too many left, thank goodness. How are you, Melissa?" Todd asked, holding out his hand. "Thanks for taking Beth her sweater."

We shared a firm handshake. "I'm doing great, thanks. You look…wow," I said, touching the lapel of his jacket. He smiled shyly.

"Doesn't he, though? I'm going to have to stick to you like glue tonight so no one gets any ideas," Beth purred, keeping an arm around him

"You don't have to worry about me, you know that," he said, kissing her hair.

An obvious third wheel, I decided it was time to find someplace else to mingle.

I scanned the crowd around me but didn't see anyone I could approach. Clustered in small circles, everyone else already had an animated conversation going—and seemed to be paired with someone. Wishing I'd kept my drink, I looked around one last time. I'd even settle for kibitzing with a waiter, but they'd all disappeared.

To my relief, the ballroom's side doors flew open, and the crowd shuffled toward the building. Todd and Beth followed behind me, arm in arm. Before we reached the doors, the mass of people stopped. Strains of classical music filtered out to the garden as we waited.

"I wonder what the holdup is." My toes ached inside my pumps. I shifted impatiently, twisting the thin strap of my purse around my finger.

"It's just the receiving line. Ann wanted to make sure she personally greeted everyone," Beth said.

"And give us all the chance to fawn over her, no doubt," I murmured. Beth admonished me silently with narrowed eyes. "Why aren't you up there, Todd?" I asked, avoiding her searing gaze.

"Luckily, only the family and their escorts have glad-handing duty. I was given a reprieve," he said, wiping imaginary sweat from his brow. "What do you say to hundreds of people you don't know, anyway?"

The line crept forward, the crowd closing in around me with every step. When Todd mentioned *family* I didn't think much of it at first, but then reality slammed me in the gut. Jason and his breathtaking eyes would be in the line, waiting to confront me.

I thought I'd make a quick break and head directly to the tables, but Vanessa was stationed at the door, directing traffic. Wedged between a man resembling George Bush and a short lady with bluish hair, my only option was to go with the flow.

Why was I so nervous? I was nothing to Jason. A quick handshake, a laugh about what an idiot I'd been, and that'd be it. No big deal. Besides, it was Mitch I should be worried about facing, not his brother.

Letting *that* happy thought eat at me, I peeked through the doors at the lavish interior of the ballroom. Enormous gold chandeliers sprinkled with flickering, flame-like bulbs hung from the vaulted ceiling. The wall facing the ocean had to be solid windows, but most were hidden behind thick curtains, blocking out the evening sun. As I made my way inside, the dance floor came into view—an island of open space in a sea of round, white tables. The long head table was staged on risers at the far end of the room. Like royalty, the wedding party would be able to survey the entire crowd as they ate.

First in the receiving line, Mitch's parents greeted me warmly with hugs and a sincere "Thanks for coming." My nerves hadn't subsided, but as I introduced myself and exchanged polite handshakes with Ann's parents, I found myself irritated at the slow pace of the line rather than thankful for it. I caught a glimpse of brown ahead and promptly fingered my hair. *Like it matters what I look like!*

I got a chance to catch my breath when I reached Chase's escort and girlfriend, Linda Yung.

Unaware of my self-imposed drama, she gathered me in a hug and whispered in my ear. "So what do you think of the dress?"

And with a single question, my only other female friend settled my nerves. Slowly releasing her, I answered, "You look *hideous*. Is it inside-out?" My eyes widened in mock horror.

Without missing a beat Linda swayed in the purple taffeta dress, fluffing her skirt and then her hair. "Well, I never!" she said, before an unflattering snort of a laugh snuck out. We hugged again, if only to keep from falling over with hysterics.

"It really is bad, isn't it?" she asked quietly once we'd finished busting up.

The top was fine—sleeveless with a jewel neckline—but the skirt was covered in light purple chiffon ruffles. The color wasn't one Linda should wear; the cool lavender against her warm Asian complexion made her look practically inhuman.

I shook my head no, but mouthed "yes." Luckily her bright black eyes and cascading ebony curls were more than enough to draw anyone's attention away from the dress.

"What are you going to do with it?" I asked, gently lifting a translucent ruffle.

She leaned in to whisper again. "I have a friend in the movie business—I'm going to give it to her to put in a slasher flick." Linda raised an invisible knife and stabbed herself in the chest. I laughed at the thought of some poor girl being hacked to death while wearing the purple monstrosity.

"Will you be around at all this summer?" she asked, but got a glare from her escort.

"Move along there," Chase said, motioning to the long line behind me. His broad smile contradicted his commanding voice.

"Yes, sir," I said to him. "Can we meet up later?" I asked Linda, tipping my head toward the towering table across the room.

Linda squeezed my arm. "Definitely."

Having talked to Chase before the wedding, I obediently followed his orders and gave him quick hug before continuing down the line.

Next to him stood the maid of honor, Beth's favorite mean girl, Tricia. Before I could offer any sort of greeting, I was paralyzed by the same amazing blue eyes I'd seen earlier. Next to Tricia, Jason McAlister grinned, and the burn I expected in my face melted over me, filling me with a comfortable warmth instead. He didn't appear repelled—he still must not have connected the dots.

"Hello, Tricia, you look"—*ridiculous*—"lovely," I said, holding out my hand. She actually looked worse than Linda. The red highlights in her bleached hair totally clashed with the ugly purple dress. She offered her hand, knuckles up, like I should kiss it rather than shake it.

Tempted as I was to demonstrate what a real handshake was, I barely moved her clammy, limp fingers. Why Ann—or anyone—liked her was beyond me.

Tricia smirked when I dropped her hand like it was infected, and she promptly wrapped herself around Jason's arm, clinging to him like a favorite blanket.

"Melissa Williams. I was surprised to see *you* in the crowd," she sneered.

I crushed my lips together, fighting the angry blush I knew was coming. *Well, Jason knows who I am now…*

I cleared my throat. I could feel his eyes on me as I spoke.

"Wouldn't miss this for the world, Tricia." I bared my teeth in something that probably only barely resembled a smile. I slid one foot over and shifted my weight forward. Facing what had to be an amused Jason was better than spending any more time with this shrew.

She wasn't quite done with me, though. "So where's your boyfriend, Melissa? Is he outside munching on hay or are you dateless again?" She looked down her long beak of a nose, feeding the rancor growing in me.

Be nice for Mitch.

I'd intended to make Mitch proud and silently walk away, but something inside me snapped.

"Not dateless, Tricia, *available*," I said. Before I could stop myself, I looked directly into Jason's eyes and gave him a sugar-coated smile.

A sneaky grin crept around his lips, turning into a radiant beam as his eyes locked with mine.

What was I doing?

Tricia snorted, and Jason bit his lower lip, suppressing a laugh. I couldn't speak, happily trapped in a completely unreasonable vision involving *my* teeth holding his lip hostage. When he leaned away from Tricia and winked at me, my heart gave an extra squeeze.

Tricia, frozen in an equally unladylike ogle, recovered first and fired the next shot. "Jason is with me tonight," she said and pulled his arm closer, snuggling it against her unnaturally large breasts. "Right, honey?"

Jason recoiled, covering his mouth with his fist and coughing a little too violently. "What was that, Tee?" he asked innocently.

"Obviously," I murmured, enjoying the distaste on Jason's face as he looked at her. I held out my hand, surprised at how steady it was. Where was this confidence coming from?

"Nice to finally meet you, *Jason*," I said, not so much to irritate Tricia as to…*am I flirting?* Not recognizing myself, I continued to smile up at him, my chest filling with satisfaction when he disengaged his arm from a disgusted Tricia.

He took my hand, but didn't shake it. A fountain of imaginary sparks danced up my arm when our skin touched. I took an awkward step forward—*is he pulling me closer?*

"Very nice, *Melissa*," he purred, and I stopped breathing. Jason continued to draw me to him, then bent down and kissed my cheek.

His lips were soft and warm. *And only an inch or two from mine.* As they left my skin, he exhaled gently on the spot he'd kissed, sending a flurry of tingles down my spine. Thankfully he backed away slowly, giving me a precious second to try to compose myself. His earthy cologne filled my nose—when I finally remembered to inhale.

My imagination instantly spun off into fantasyland. *Surely a kiss is more than a friendly greeting.*

No, no, no. It was only a peck on the cheek, I scolded myself. He was just needling Tricia, or worse, teasing me.

"Jason," Tricia whined, slapping his arm.

He didn't flinch at her warning, and I was too shaken to enjoy her chagrin. A Cheshire Cat smile lit his face; clearly he knew his little stunt had sent me reeling.

Tricia pinched him, making him jump this time.

Jason frowned apologetically at me and turned to the next guest.

Her face as red as a tomato, I expected steam to start whistling out of Tricia's ears at any second. Annoying her was worth any humiliation on my part. As for that kiss…all I could think was if I'd turned my head just slightly, one part of my crazy fantasy would've come true.

My momentary burst of hubris popped like a soap bubble when faced with the man next to Jason.

"Melissa!" Mitch bellowed. I'd never heard my name said with such joy. He scooped me up in a huge hug, lifting me off the floor. "You made it."

I looped my arms around his neck and squeezed as hard as I could. "You did good, Mitch," I said, surprised when my voice cracked.

"Thanks, Mel," he whispered.

My eyes stinging, I loosened my grip. Getting all mushy before I'd even said anything was pathetic.

With a loud exhale, Mitch lowered me to the ground. I recognized his I-have-something-important-to-say look.

No, not yet! "I'm impressed. You clean up pretty well," I said, tweaking his tie. I wasn't ready for this to be the end. Couldn't we have one more minute before he laid the we'll-find-some-way-to-get-together fairy tale on me?

I must not have hidden my uneasiness very well. With a tiny nod to himself, Mitch filed his speech away and grinned. "Gee, thanks, Mel. You don't look so bad yourself."

"Just for you, big guy." The tension lifted, and I snuck a glance back toward Jason. He took the blue-haired lady's hand and shook it. No kiss for her.

Like that matters—she has to be sixty if she's a day.

Mitch's eyes followed mine. "My brother was polite, I hope. He can be an—"

"He was a perfect gentleman, don't worry." *I'm the one acting like a lunatic.* "Hey, I just wanted to tell you how happy I am for you and Ann. You two are so right for each other," I said.

His eyes lit up. "Thank you. You don't know how much that means to me."

As he smiled, I couldn't help but pick out each little detail in his face that matched Jason's. The dimple in the center of his chin, the shape of his jaw…

I mentally slapped myself—gawking at the groom wasn't on anyone's wedding etiquette list.

"I'll find you later, okay?" I said and squeezed his huge hand.

"You bet!" he promised.

Ann didn't hesitate when she held her arms open for me. I gave her a loose hug, surprised when she tightened the embrace.

"The ceremony was lovely," I said in her ear, meaning it.

She actually smiled at me, not through me, for a change. "Thank you, Melissa. I know how close you and Mitch are. Your being here makes everything perfect—for both of us."

Wow, maybe Beth was right. Maybe I should cut Ann a little slack. "There's no way I'd miss this. You two deserve nothing but happiness. Congratulations."

Ann teared up and reached for Mitch's arm. They cuddled for a moment, and I blew them a kiss before heading to the tables, happy for them and proud of myself. I'd left everyone smiling—except Tricia. Mission accomplished.

I chose a seat at an unoccupied table far from the dance floor and sat down with a deep sigh. My feet begged to be free, but if I took off my shoes I wouldn't be able to get them back on. At least I'd brought sneakers and jeans for the trip home.

The scent of flowers distracted me from my aching dogs. Every table around me had a unique bouquet in the center, each featuring a different type of flower. I spied orchids, hydrangeas, peonies, and even tiny daisies, all ranging in shade from a faint amethyst to a deep violet. Only my favorite was missing, but I doubted carnations were expensive enough for the occasion.

Slowly the chairs around me filled, and I was pleasantly surprised when Beth collapsed into the seat next to mine. She nodded toward the bridal table, and after a moment's hesitation I looked. Todd was alone on the platform, scratching his chin as he tried to discern which seat was his. He pulled out one chair, only to be directed to the next one over by a red-headed bridesmaid.

A couple of college-age guys meandered over and introduced themselves as Ann's friends from USC. When they asked if we liked Trojans, Beth choked on her water and I rolled my eyes. I was about to comment on the success of USC's football program when an older couple pointed to the empty seats at our table. Beth waved them over, welcoming the two, who turned out to be Ann's cousin and his wife.

I'd expected dinner conversation to revolve around the bride, since everyone else had connections to her, but it soon shifted to Mitch. Beth and I were interrogated about everything from his favorite color to how he picked up a hobby like steer wrestling. By the time the main course was served, I decided I'd rather do the asking than the answering.

"Mitch has spent every weekend down here for months. Why haven't you guys asked *him* anything?" I pointed the question at Trojan Number One, sitting next to me.

He picked at his filet mignon. "Mitch isn't the easiest person to get to know."

"What?" I gawked at him. "Once you get him started, you can't shut him up. He's one of the most outgoing guys I know."

Beth nodded in agreement.

Ann's cousin, Dean, I think, pursed his lips, hiding a smirk. "Sometimes it's starting the conversation that's the problem. Mitch's size makes him somewhat…unapproachable." The glint in his eye and the pink on both Trojans' cheeks explained a lot.

"You guys are afraid of Mitch," I guessed, grinning.

"Uh, yeah. The guy's two hundred pounds of 'don't mess with me,'" Trojan Number Two chimed in.

"Two-ten," I corrected.

"And more than a little protective around Ann," Trojan Number One said, then leaned toward me. "Doesn't he intimidate you?"

Beth laughed out loud. "Melissa? Not on your life. If anything, Mitch is afraid of *her*."

I knew exactly what was coming next and squirmed. "Beth, I don't think—"

"Mel KO'd Mitch the first day they met," she crowed.

The chatter and clinking of silverware around us got sucked into the silent void of our table for a long second. I stabbed a spear of broccoli, wishing I had some place to hide.

"No way. You couldn't even reach his jaw, let alone knock him out," Trojan Number One said, leaning back and crossing his arms.

"Oh, she didn't punch him," Beth said. "She kneed his you-know-what's into next week. He went down faster than a—"

"It was a misunderstanding," I interrupted. "I was young, Mitch was tipsy, and things got a little out of hand."

The other woman at the table gasped. "Mitchell didn't do anything *inappropriate*, did he?"

Beth's mouth opened, but I elbowed her. "No, of course not."

"He just couldn't take no for an answer," Beth interjected, and I dropped my fork. Mitch would be so happy to know I'd painted him as a sex offender at his wedding. Talk about a gift that keeps on giving.

"It wasn't like that, and you know it," I said to her, then turned to the gaping faces around me. "Do you really think I'd be sitting here if anything remotely offensive happened?"

"What did happen, exactly, Melissa?" Dean asked quietly.

I glared at Beth. She got us into this awkward mess—she'd better find a way out. "Well?"

"Um, well, I don't really know exactly what he said to you in the bar," Beth said slowly. "I just know he followed you out to the parking lot. You *did* look scared."

At the time, I'd been terrified, but not because of Mitch. Okay, not *just* because of Mitch. "Only because I didn't know him or any of the other guys that followed *you* outside."

"Oh. I never thought about it that way. Sorry, Mel." Beth's expression darkened when she finally realized no one was smiling back at her. "It really wasn't bad," she said. "It's actually pretty funny."

She explained how I'd met Mitch and the team at the local watering hole after my first rodeo, and how he'd taken a shine to me. She didn't go into detail about Mitch's past reputation for chasing skirts, but I remembered exactly when he'd caught me in his sights.

I'd been surprised he'd seen me at all, considering he'd spent most of the night grinding all over a double-d airhead he'd met at the bar. I'd decided I had more than enough background for my article and was calling it a night when he ditched Barbie and found me.

"How about a dansssss before you go, Melissssssa?" he said, swinging his hips suggestively.

"First, I don't dance. Second, I think your top-heavy friend is going to tip over without you," I said. When Mitch turned to check on D-Debbie

D-D Cup, I flung myself out the door. I was almost to my car when he caught my arm and spun me around.

"Come on, Melissa. Juss one sssong." He peered at me and snickered. "Ya know, you're purty when you're pissssed."

"Get your hands off me," I snarled, twisting out of his grasp.

He staggered back a little. "Come on, it'll be fu…fun. Didja haf a goo time with me today?"

That's when Beth and a few of Mitch's buddies appeared.

"I did. Don't spoil it by being a jackass."

"Aw, Mel, don't be like that. Juss one dink ana dance. It'll be fuuuun," he repeated to the drunken delight of his posse.

"Are you okay, Melissa?" Chase said, pushing his way between two of his teammates.

Sober and serious, his presence was a welcome sight.

"She's fiiiiine, aren't you?" Mitch said. "We're juss talkin' here."

Mitch's hand came up to my shoulder, but I backed away again. One of the other guys shouted, "Go for it, Mitch," earning him a punch in the shoulder from Chase.

"Shut up, dickhead," Mitch growled and took a step closer. "Kay, juss the dink then," he mumbled. "Dansssing doesn't sssound good anyways." The alcohol on his breath wafted toward me, burning my nose.

A strong, sure voice echoed in my head. My father's voice. *Distract and escape, Melissa. Protect yourself.*

"Leave her alone, Mitch. She just wants to go home," Beth yelled, shooing the guys back inside with Chase's help.

"What if I asssed niiiice?" Mitch hissed.

"Don't make me hurt you," I warned, hoping he'd removed *all* of his protective gear before he'd left the arena.

The guys stopped at the door with a low *ooooo*.

"*You* hurt *me?*" Mitch laughed and looked over his shoulder at his friends.

That's when my knee met his crotch with the force of a major league line drive, sending the champion bulldogger to the ground in a whimpering heap.

"You have to understand that he really did only want to dance—nothing else," I said quickly, ending Beth's story before she got to the part when I pulled my pepper spray on Chase by accident.

"Sounds like he deserved it," Dean's wife murmured.

I shook my head. "It was a very long time ago, and it wasn't as bad as it sounds. Mitch is a great guy. Even Ann agrees I overreacted."

That Ann knew about Mitch's antics pulled the woman up short. I didn't have to be a mind reader to see she'd been planning to go straight to the bride with this little tale.

"You *were* the first one to apologize," Beth added, finally understanding the disapproval on both Dean's and his wife's faces.

"*You* apologized?" the woman asked, her question more like an accusation.

"Like I said, my reaction was a little over the top. I sent him a get-well card and a little gift."

I'd woken up the next morning panic-stricken. What if Mitch called my editor and had me fired? I was supposed to write about assault and battery, not commit them. I'd been convinced I'd ended my career on my very first assignment. Thankfully, Mitch tracked me down and offered his own apology a day later.

"Tell them what you gave him," Beth demanded. Her lips puckered, waiting for me to finish the story. When I didn't answer fast enough, she bounced in her seat. "Mel sent him a bag of frozen peas!"

Like a spell being broken, relieved laughter rippled around the table.

"I've heard they're better than an ice pack," I added with a shrug.

Seizing the opportunity to change the subject, I drove the conversation with short, interview-style questions while we finished the meal. The Trojans boasted they'd been accepted into the graduate biology program and made some crack about looking for participants for their upcoming pheromone experiment.

Ann's cousin and his wife were conversant in a much wider range of topics. When the subject of jobs came up, Dean passed me his card.

I politely took it, not sure why he, an internet consultant, would be giving it to me.

"I have several clients in the online news business," he said. "When you head into the job market, I can put you in touch with some good people."

"Wow, I don't know what to say." I'd just met the man and he was ready to recommend me for a job?

"You obviously know how to hold your own, so I doubt you'll have any trouble finding work," he said. "But should you need anything, feel free to give me a call."

I fished out my last homemade business card and gave it to him. "Thank you." I was expecting an offer for a fall internship any day now, but if that fell through, Dean could be a lifesaver.

He pocketed my card after a quick inspection.

Beth nudged me and gave a thumbs up.

I stifled my grin and turned my attention toward the front of the room. Again. More often than I'd intended my eyes had drifted to the bridal table. Throughout dinner, I'd told myself I was checking on Mitch, but somehow I always ended up staring at Jason. Engaged in a deep discussion with Chase and Linda, he rarely acknowledged Tricia, much to my delight. She was fuming from the lack of attention.

Desperate, Tricia tipped the last of her champagne onto Jason's hand. He nodded to her but turned away quickly, extracting his hand from her napkin.

Wiping his hands on his own napkin instead, Jason scanned the crowd.

He's looking for me! Fighting the irrational, hopeful voice in my head—and the very nerdy urge to wave—I watched him inspect the tables one by one.

The moment he saw me, his eyes brightened, catching me in their spotlight. His sly smile sent a delicious tremor through me. *Told you!*

We stared at each other, locked in a silent closeness that excluded the roomful of people around us. When he broke our connection, I gasped for air, unaware I'd been holding my breath.

Jason turned his attention to a man in front of the platform who handed him a long, black cylinder. At our table, a regiment of waiters moved in, blocking my view while they cleared dishes and refilled glasses. The music faded, replaced by the clinking of metal on glass.

The tinkling sound became deafening as everyone joined in, banging forks and spoons against their glasses, demanding that the bride and groom kiss. With a flourish, Mitch captured his wife and sealed his lips to hers. Amid the cheers Jason stood, his glass in one hand, a microphone in the other.

He cleared his throat, and the room quieted. "Could the bride and groom please stand and hold hands?" he began. Mitch held one hand open to his new wife as they rose, and she easily fit both of hers into it. He covered them possessively with his other hand and looked at Jason.

"Excellent. Mitch, I want you to remember this moment fondly for the rest of your life." He bobbed his chin toward the couple's intertwined fingers. "This is the last time you'll ever have the upper hand." Ann and Mitch looked down and chuckled along with the crowd.

When the laughter died down, Jason continued, perfectly at ease in front of the crowd. "Thank you for inviting us all to witness the love you two share and to celebrate the final joining of your souls. It was obvious when you first met you were made for each other—at least it was obvious to Mitch. Ann, did you know that after your first date, Mitch called and gushed over you for hours?"

Another laugh erupted, and Mitch nodded at Ann, whose eyes had widened in surprise. "That's what I thought he was talking about, anyway. I kind of fell asleep in the middle. He kept me up till five in the morning with his blabbing." The laughter continued.

"I knew then you were special, Ann, and wasn't surprised when Mitch told me he was going to ask for your hand. He was so sure you'd turn him down. Little did he know you'd called me the day before, asking if I thought he was ready to propose." Mitch's mouth dropped open and Ann beamed. "So really, this toast should be to me, right?" Jason grinned widely.

Mitch and Ann picked up their crystal champagne flutes and tipped them to him, mouthing "thank you" as they did.

Waiting for the crowd to quiet again, Jason raised his glass high.

His voice, brimming with love for his brother and new sister-in-law, filled the room. "May the best day of your past be the worst day of your future. To the bride and groom."

"To the bride and groom," we responded and drank. Lowering his glass, Jason's gaze immediately met mine. Even from across the room I could see the blue in his eyes flare, and I found myself drowning yet again. Unfortunately, a tap on my shoulder freed me.

"Miss, this is for you."

I turned to see a waiter with his hand out.

"Thank you," I said and looked down. He'd given me a purple napkin with *Congratulations Ann and Mitch* embossed on it. Below the gold script was the faint impression of handwriting. I flipped the napkin over and found a note written in a smooth, swooping hand.

Melissa,
It's been too long. Will you save a dance for me?
Jason

My heart flew to my throat. I looked up at Jason, who tipped his glass to me and bobbed his head in my direction. *What could he possibly be thinking?* I tilted my glass with a small smile, and we sipped in unison. As I sank back into my chair, his unwavering stare flooded me with an unfamiliar contentment. The vision of Jason kissing me—*really* kissing me—returned, stoking my desperate glimmer of hope into a small flame.

My flight of fantasy came crashing down to earth when Tricia pulled Jason into his seat, her bright purple fingernails caressing his cheek, coaxing his face toward hers. My fingers closed around his note, crushing it, along with the happiness I'd briefly enjoyed. Tricia aside, an icy truth quenched my unrealistic hopes.

As Mitch had learned years ago—painfully—I didn't dance.

Four

After the toast, Mitch and Ann took turns at the mic, making short thank-you speeches. I refused to look at Jason and Tricia, but I couldn't concentrate on anything else. The soft, sexy way he said my name swirled around my head—along with Tricia's shrill retorts—effectively drowning out everything the bride and groom said. Just when I thought things couldn't get any worse, the DJ shouted my five least favorite words: "The dance floor is open!"

Dean and his wife rose immediately to join the swaying mass. I caught a passing waiter's eye and indicated my empty water glass. My intention was to stay as far away from the dancers as possible—both for their safety and my own. I had about as much rhythm as a heart attack…or a seizure.

The two Trojans tossed their napkins on the table and slid their chairs out with a loud screech.

"So, ladies," the braver Trojan, Number Two, started, "shall we?"

The waiter chose that moment to step between us to fill my glass.

"Gee, dance with them, or with *him?* Not much of a choice is it, Mel?" Beth whispered, pointing at the white knuckles on my left hand. My fist was still clenched around Jason's note—had she been reading over *my* shoulder?

"You little snoop," I scolded.

The waiter moved aside, and Trojan Number One quickly wiped his impatient grimace away. He wiggled his eyebrows and offered me his hand.

"No thanks," I said. "Beth is the one who tears up the dance floor."

Trojan Number Two's face lit up like a kid on Christmas morning, and Beth pinched me in the side.

"Sorry, I'm with him," she said firmly and waved at her approaching boyfriend. The grim scowl on Todd's face sent both Trojans scurrying away.

"Good luck, Melissa," Beth said, then disappeared, wrapped around Todd.

I debated venturing into the crowd milling around the edge of the room. Mitch's parents weren't too far away; striking up a conversation with them wouldn't be hard. A casual "I didn't know Mitch and his brother looked so much alike" would be all it'd take to steer the conversation toward Jason.

An arm raised in my direction. I'd been staring at Mr. and Mrs. McAlister, and the guy next to them must've thought I was looking at him. Not more than eighteen, his expression was one of naked shock.

He pointed at me, then back at himself, and swung his arms and hips in a vague dance-like motion.

You've got to be kidding.

I let my hands fly around in front of me, feigning sign language. Ending with a silent "Sorry," I shrugged.

The kid's mouth opened, closed, then opened again like a suffocating goldfish. I made a few more spastic gestures, and he blushed. With a feeble wave, he sped off into the crowd. Snickering, I took a sip of water. I should've been flattered by the interest, but I wasn't that desperate.

My eyes automatically found the head table and Jason's empty chair. Was he on his way to find me? I hazarded a glance around the room. His spellbinding eyes and tantalizing hair were nowhere to be found; why didn't that make me feel better?

I picked at my fingernails nervously. What would I say to him? Somehow I knew I couldn't turn him down, even though it would mean complete humiliation for me. The thought of having him hold me drew my eyes around the room again, this time with more anticipation than fear.

Just when I realized Tricia had disappeared too, the worst of the unattached targeted my table. My stomach lurched when the wrinkled suit of the eighties guy I'd bumped into outside stalked toward me. Not surprised or angry—thank goodness—he had a confident, almost predatory walk. His smile didn't convey excitement or happiness but voracious greed, his lips rising to fully expose his canines in a wolf-like grin. He was, in a word, creepy.

That's it. Gotta go. I reached for my purse, but the strap caught on something. I'd just untangled it when I felt a heavy hand on the back of my chair.

"Hi. Would you like to dance?" he asked in an oily voice.

"No, thank you. I don't dance." *Still.*

"How about I join you, then?" he asked and promptly sat in the chair closest to me. "I was rude when we ran into each other earlier. I'm Ron."

Was that supposed to be an apology or a pick-up?

"What's your name?" he asked, ignoring the fact he hadn't let me answer his previous question.

Showing him the same level of courtesy, I scanned the crowd, searching for a lifeline. Chase and Linda were busy talking to his parents several tables away. Beth and Todd were dancing; Mitch and Ann were across the room, laughing; and neither Tricia nor Jason had reappeared. *Welcome to wedding reception hell.*

I picked up my water glass and considered dumping it in Ron-the-creep's lap, but that would mean getting closer to him and his smelly suit. Instead, I took a long drink and inspected the five-tiered wedding cake in the far corner, avoiding his eerie stare. Would he get the hint if I refused to acknowledge his existence?

"So, are you a friend of the bride or the groom?" he asked, unfazed.

"Groom," I nearly shouted, hoping this guy was as intimidated by Mitch as the Trojans were. "*Close* friends." None too subtly I clutched my purse, thankful I'd remembered to slip my pepper spray in the tiny bag. "I should probably go congratulate him." I tried to inch my chair away, but Ron held it fast.

"He's busy with the other guests." His head turned slightly, toward the newlyweds I assumed. "I'm a friend of a friend of the bride. She's quite beautiful, isn't she?" The covetous smile reappeared.

"Yes, she is," I said. Coldness enveloped me when I realized all the tables around us were empty.

Options…I need options. The door closest to me was marked WOMEN—that'd do nicely. I tensed, planning to make a dash for the bathroom should Ron's hold on my chair loosen even for a second.

He scrutinized me with hungry eyes. "Hey, let's get out of here and take a walk in the garden. There's a trail that goes down to the beach. I doubt a little hike would wear you out." A cold finger grazed my back. Was he touching the ends of my hair?

I jerked forward, away from his hand, still unable to budge my chair. Ron was exceptionally bold, quickly moving from creepy to frightening. My thoughts turned from flight to fight.

"No thanks. I wouldn't want to miss the action here." I repositioned my purse in my lap so I could reach the zipper. As I did, the table moved—and another path appeared: tip the table and make a scene. Could I ruin Mitch's celebration? What if I was misinterpreting Ron's eagerness?

"Aw, come on, this stuff is boring anyway. It doesn't look like anyone will miss us," he pressed. "It'll be a treat."

A treat? I had to get away from this guy! Like a song stuck on repeat, the possibilities raced around my brain, along with an adrenaline-enhanced list of Ron's weaknesses. *Run, scream, fight, spray. Ribs, eyes, knees, groin.*

Summoning all my courage, I gripped the edge of the table. Thankfully, Chase materialized beside me before I tipped it over.

"Hi. I've been looking for you." He carefully avoided using my name, somehow sensing the fear surging through me. "We're dancing as a group over in the corner. Come join us."

I didn't hesitate. "Okay." Without a second glance at Ron, I pushed myself away from the table, catching my captor off guard.

In a flash, Ron wrapped his clammy hand around mine and squeezed it hard—too hard. I flinched, still trapped in my chair.

"She doesn't dance," he said, his nostrils flaring. I tried to free myself, but his fingers became a vise, tightening as I struggled against them.

"Get your hands off her!" someone snarled. Ron's head whipped around, looking for the new speaker.

I took advantage of the distraction and ripped my hand out of his, jumping up so fast I slammed into Chase. He caught me, automatically wrapping a protective arm around my shoulders.

Ron rose to face him, his hands bunched into fists. My new savior intervened, equally incensed: *Jason McAlister.*

I peeked up at him, my breath catching at the wrath darkening his features. His tight eyes and clenched jaw left no doubt that Jason ached to tear Ron to pieces. Fearsome and furious…and protective of *me.*

I'd never seen a more beautiful sight.

Ron, however, didn't give up in the face of such obvious opposition. "We were having a *private* conversation," he said. He reached out, attempting to angle his shoulder between me and Jason.

I shook my head violently and backed away. "I don't know who he is, and he won't leave me alone," I said in defiance.

In an instant Jason caught the outstretched hand, and with startling speed, twisted it behind Ron's back. At the same time, Chase swung around, making himself yet another barrier between me and my unwanted admirer. He drew himself up to his full height and glared down at Ron.

"Who are you?"

Ron didn't back down, glaring up at Chase while he struggled weakly against Jason. "An invited guest," he sneered, producing a tattered lavender card with his free hand. "How dare you treat me like this!"

Jason tightened his hold and Ron grunted. "Is that better? If you hurt her—"

Chase cleared his throat, interrupting Jason's threat. "Guest or not, it's time for you to go," he commanded and snapped his fingers over his head.

When three additional tall, muscled groomsmen arrived, Ron wilted, becoming more interested in the doors than me. Ropers Todd and Alex and bronc rider Dave had answered their rodeo teammate's call to arms, each quite capable of teaching Ron a lesson he wouldn't soon forget.

"Get out," Jason growled. He viciously pushed Ron toward the nearest exit.

Ron stumbled, narrowly avoiding falling across a chair. He righted himself and looked back at me, straightening his rumpled tie.

"Another time, then." An evil grin crept across his lips until Jason took a threatening step toward him. Red-faced, Ron glanced one last time in my direction before slithering away, followed closely by Dave and Alex.

"Thanks, guys. That was spooky," I said, my voice wavering.

Todd tipped an imaginary hat, and with a nod from Chase, returned to the dance floor. The few onlookers that had gathered dispersed as well, leaving my corner of the room quiet again. Jason didn't turn around immediately. When he did, all evidence of his fierce anger had disappeared. He inspected me closely, looking confused. Chase's arm was still wrapped tightly around my shoulders.

"Melissa, you're shaking. He really scared you, didn't he?" Chase said, loosening his grip.

The image Linda and I had laughed over reappeared—only I was the one in the bloody bridesmaid's dress and Ron was the one wielding the knife. No longer finding it funny, I trembled harder.

"Yes, he did. Can you sit with me for a few minutes?" I looked at Jason.

He moved my chair to face the one next to it and invited me to sit down. I steadied myself against the table as I took my seat. Chase pulled up the chair Ron had been in and sat behind me; Jason took the seat facing mine, frowning.

"Are you hurt?" he asked, carefully lifting my left hand. Finger-shaped red lines marked where Ron had grabbed me. Jason gently traced the back of my quivering hand, watching my face for any reaction.

Mesmerized by the gentleness of his touch, I had to repeat his question in my head before I could answer.

"It's a little sore, but I'll be okay," I said, trying to keep my voice steady. A bag of frozen peas sounded really good right about now.

I inhaled slowly, but the trembling didn't wane. The sting of fear, mixed with the same pleasing sparks I'd felt when Jason touched me earlier, made a very shaky cocktail of my insides. The adrenaline coursing through me scrambled all my responses; I wanted to laugh *and* cry *and* scream, all at the same time. I blinked back the tears welling in my eyes and swallowed hard, trying to regain some kind of control over myself.

"May I see your other hand?" Jason asked. Too frazzled to question why, I held out my right hand. He turned it over and massaged my palm, his thumbs repeatedly traveling from my wrist to my fingers with slow, soothing pressure. "Just relax. It's all right now. You're safe," he chanted, his voice as comforting as his touch. After just a few strokes the shaking ceased, and I managed to take a deep breath. His simple motions and calming words infused me with peacefulness.

My breathing slowed, and along with it, my heart rate. "How are you doing that?" I asked, amazed.

He smiled at my hand, stroking it for the last time. "Acupressure. My mom tends to get a little stressed with me living so far from home, so I took a class and taught a few techniques to my dad. Do you feel better now?"

"Much." This time my body responded appropriately, and a fiery tingle raced up my arm when he followed the lines of my palm with the tip of his finger. Jason's chest expanded, and he leaned back, releasing a quiet sigh. The massage seemed to have relaxed him too.

Something brushed my arm, and I was startled to see Chase holding out my purse. I'd forgotten he was here.

"I was serious about you joining us, Mel. We've ditched Ann's pedestal of a bridal table and commandeered one by the bar. How about I get you a drink?" he asked. "You, too, Jase," he added.

"That sounds great," I replied, pleased that "us" would include my masseuse.

Chase led us on a winding path through the tables to the other side of the room. Jason followed me, his reassuring hand finding the small of my back whenever we came near anyone.

He's just being polite.

Linda jumped up when we circled the last table.

"Are you okay, Melissa? You don't look so good," she said, looping her arm in mine and guiding me to the seat next to hers. "Who was that slimeball?"

"I have no idea. But if Chase hadn't shown up when he did, I think the reception would be suffering from eau de pepper spray." I managed an empty laugh, pretending I was joking.

I reached for the chair, but my hand landed on Jason's; he'd already started to pull it out for me. My fingers lingered on his silky skin as I took my time sitting down.

"As soon as I saw that guy with you, I knew something was up," she said, glancing back at the corner. "Chase agreed he was *not* your type."

"Thanks. I owe you both," I said, trying to erase Ron's repulsive smile from my memory.

"What'll you have, Melissa?" Chase asked, changing the topic.

Something strong. "A kamikaze, please."

Linda just winked; Chase already knew what she wanted.

"Allow me," Jason said. "I'll get some ice for your hand too."

I grabbed his arm, finally comprehending what he'd done for me, a stranger. "Thank you," I said. It took every ounce of strength to make my head turn to find Chase standing behind him. "To both of you," I added.

"No problem, Mel," Chase said.

Jason ran his hand along my arm, catching my fingers in his. "I'm sorry I didn't get there sooner," he said. He brought my sore hand to his lips, tenderly kissing the fading red marks.

I gulped.

"I'll be right back," he promised, slowly lowering my hand.

He and Chase trooped off, sharing a handshake as they went. Chase clapped Jason on the shoulder and got a tired nod in response. My drama must've taken more of a toll than he'd let on. Perhaps he'd take this opportunity to escape. I wouldn't blame him—*bodyguard* hadn't been part of the best man's job description for centuries.

"He's really something," Linda said, watching the guys walk away.

"Yes, he is."

Linda spun around. The crease between her eyes meant I had to take evasive action fast or get razzed about Jason.

"When are we going to do this for you?" I said, waving at the elaborate decorations around us.

The diversion worked; she bit her lip and her cheeks pinked. "Soon, I think. I have a feeling Chase may be asking me a very important question tonight."

The excitement bubbling in her voice brought a smile to my lips. Should I tell her what Chase had said earlier?

"I don't know, Linda. I think he already has a new roommate picked out."

Her face fell. "He does? Did he say who? God, I hope it's not that idiot Mike. The guy's dumber than a stump."

Glad I could pay Chase back in this tiny way, I kept her guessing. "Could be. He told me not to tell you, and you know what that means."

"Yeah, he thinks I'll get mad. Darn, I was so sure." She crossed her arms. "We'll be having a chat about that later."

"What made you think he was going to ask you something else?" I didn't want her angry with her boyfriend. A proposal would definitely explain his cryptic comments.

"Watch." She nodded toward the line at the bar. "In a second he'll reach inside his jacket. He's been doing it every five minutes."

Thirty seconds later Chase patted his coat. His hand darted inside, and he got the silliest expression on his face.

"Now he'll look around until he sees me. Three, two, one…"

At that moment he spotted us and yanked his hand out of his jacket. With a sheepish grin, he jerked when the bartender passed him two glasses.

Linda sighed. "I guess I just figured it was a ring."

"Maybe it's more pictures for Mitch's phone. He looks a little guilty to me." Scared to death was more like it. Linda's first guess had to be right.

She grinned. "That's probably it. He did say something about making arrangements with the limo driver. They're probably booby trapping the video player or something."

"Booby trapping?" I repeated slowly. "Nice!"

Linda's blank look lasted only a second before dissolving into her trademark snorting laughter. "Shhh," she hissed, seeing the guys on their way back.

"Here you go, sweetie," Chase said, setting Linda's drink on the table with a flourish before taking a seat next to her.

Jason was right behind him. He passed me one glass before setting another and a napkin full of ice on the table.

"Now, may I have another look at your hand, please?" Jason's voice took on a clinical seriousness but wasn't cold or unfeeling. I could easily imagine him wearing a crisp white lab coat with a long stethoscope dangling from his neck. The picture was sexy enough I had to look away or start drooling.

"It's fine, really," I said, but I offered him my injured hand. His skin was so smooth and surprisingly warm—nothing like Mitch's rough calluses.

Jason manipulated my fingers, testing each one before having me make a fist. His movements were confident and graceful—were his fingers really that long?

"You don't feel any pain?" he asked.

"Not much. I'll probably just have a little bruising tomorrow, that's all."

He picked up the napkin. "That's what this is for." He set the makeshift ice bag on the back of my hand.

I inhaled sharply when the coldness hit my skin.

"It'll feel great in just a minute, promise." He looked up and smiled, then leaned forward. My heart skipped a beat when his cheek brushed my hair. "I guess I get to play doctor with you after all," he whispered.

With those words, the discomfort in my hand disappeared, erased by an embarrassed hot flash. Was my face burning because he'd remembered my tasteless emails or at the thought of *really* playing with Dr. Jason?

"Yeah, about that." I cleared my throat. He was still hovering at my ear, so I tried not to shout in his. "I was just kidding, you know. I never thought—"

"You never thought we'd meet in person," he finished. With those words he extinguished my fire faster than ice ever could. He was already two steps ahead; he'd recognized that the real me didn't live up to my online persona. I bit my lip. I wouldn't wait for him to fabricate a reason to go find "Tee."

"Yes, I guess so. You know, my hand is fine now. You don't have to—"

Before I could finish, he pressed his lips closer to my ear.

"This wasn't the kind of doctor I was suggesting, you know." His seductive lilt and hot breath catapulted me back into my fantasy. In my vision, his lips started at my ear, traveled down my neck…across my collarbone…down to my…

Jason pulled away and stared at my frozen face, analyzing the idiotic expression that surely filled it. At first he scowled, then broke into a wide grin as my heart raced out of control.

Having been caught indulging my erotic imagination, I ducked my head and stared down at the drippy napkin between us. That's when I saw his fingers under my wrist.

He's reading my pulse! Cheater!

"Melissa, we're going to dance. Have fun with the good doctor, okay?" Linda said as she and Chase rose.

I looked up to find Jason shaking with laughter. "Okay," I said, giggling too.

"Did I shock you?" he asked when Chase and Linda were out of earshot. His smile faded a bit, and I saw just a hint of regret in his eyes.

"No…well, yes, but not by what you said…exactly." I chewed the side of my mouth, having given away too much.

He moved a little closer, his eyes wide, expecting an explanation. It seemed I was destined to humiliate myself in front of him, and here was the latest opportunity. Would he vanish in a puff of smoke like every other dream?

"It's just that…" I stopped, too ashamed to continue.

He stroked my palm, but it would take more than that to calm me this time.

"What? You can tell me. I'm not going to disappear, I promise."

Can he hear what I'm thinking? I grabbed my drink and took a swig of the lime-flavored vodka. *Fine, might as well get this over with.*

"It's just that you said it to *me*."

I avoided his eyes, waiting for the "I was just being funny" line, but it never came. Instead, Jason pursed his lips and removed what was left of the ice from my hand. He took a fresh napkin and dried my skin, repeating his gentle massage. "There, how's that?" he asked quietly.

"Wonderful," I sighed, and his gorgeous smile returned.

My hand stayed in his until the waiter came to collect the empty glasses and dirty napkins. Before he did, he tapped Jason on the shoulder and spoke in his ear. I busied myself with my drink but didn't miss the note that changed hands, along with a small, white piece of plastic—a hotel key.

Jason nodded and the waiter subtly pointed at a table occupied by one of the women who'd sat next to me during the ceremony. When Jason's eyes followed his arm, she immediately gave him a cute little wave and batted her eyelashes. He smiled briefly, pocketing the card and tipping the waiter.

As I'd suspected, Jason wouldn't be sleeping alone tonight. Even if Tricia had managed to drop off the face of the earth—*if only*—the line behind her had already formed. I wanted to crawl under the table, tired of my emotional rollercoaster ride.

The waiter left, and Jason faced me again.

"So how many of those do you have?" I asked, trying to sound nonchalant.

He inspected the tablecloth and actually blushed. "Do you really want to know?"

Is he embarrassed? How could he be after that display?

"Yes. No-nonsense, remember?" It would be better to end this delusion now, before it went any further. I'd already considered checking into the hotel, just so *I* could hand him a key. I was pathetic.

Jason reached into his right jacket pocket and retrieved not one, but *four* keys—and a handful of notes, which he crumpled into a tight ball.

Damn. I'm such a loser.

"I see. So how do you know which key goes with which note?" I asked flatly. The number of propositions shouldn't have surprised me; a girl would have to be both blind and deaf to not be attracted to Jason. His frankness with that fact did surprise me.

"I don't care. I have no intention of ever contacting any of these women." He set the ball of paper on a passing busboy's tray and re-pocketed the cards. "I'll drop these off at the front desk." He looked at me again, anticipating the next question.

"So what's in the other pocket—underwear?" My words came out unnecessarily sharp, and I immediately slapped my hand over my mouth.

Jason's eyebrows rose, along with the corners of his perfect lips.

"I'm sorry. That was rude. There's no delete button in person, is there?" I shook my head and clamped my mouth shut before I could say anything else obnoxious.

He laughed. "No, I guess not." Jason's smile shrank, and he captured my gaze with his. "I only put important things in my left pocket," he said, his smooth voice challenging me.

Now my eyebrows crept up. "Really…" The sarcasm slipped out before I could stop myself.

"Would you like to see?" He stretched his jacket toward me, inviting me to put my hand in and check for myself. I rolled my eyes when he waved the coat seductively.

It didn't take long for curiosity to get the best of me, and I carefully reached into his pocket. I couldn't feel a thing—it was empty. His hand followed mine into the space, weaving our fingers together and sending my heart to my throat. "Only things I care about go in this pocket," he murmured and gently pressed my hand a little farther in.

Again I had trouble breathing.

Before I could respond, Chase's voice startled me. "Jason, the DJ says he's ready when we are," he said from behind me. Jason nodded and slowly released my hand.

"I'll be back for that," he said, his eyes flickering to my hand, still suspended where he'd released it. "Stay right here, okay? I'll just be a minute or two."

"All right," I croaked.

Chase said something and pulled out the chair next to me, but I was too busy pinching myself to pay attention. I had to be dreaming. This couldn't be real.

"Hurry back," Linda said as she sat down, making me jump—again.

"What's going on?" I asked after deciding that if I was asleep, waking up was a really bad idea.

"We have a special gift for Mitch and Ann. You'll see," Chase said, smiling at Linda. He caressed her cheek with one finger before following Jason across the dance floor.

Smugness shadowed her face like a veil; she knew what they were up to. She just pointed after the guys, refusing to speak.

Next to the DJ's table a polished baby grand had gone untouched until Jason propped open its lid. He settled himself at the instrument and gently tapped on the microphone mounted in front of him. A guitar appeared in Chase's hands, and he picked a few notes. With a nod to Jason, he gave the DJ a thumbs up.

The music died, and the DJ's voice boomed over the speakers. "At this time, I invite you to clear the dance floor for the bride and groom. Mitch and Ann, could you please take center stage for your first dance as husband and wife?"

The crowd parted for the newest Mr. and Mrs. McAlister. Striding to the center of the floor, Mitch twirled Ann under his arm before catching her waist.

With that, Jason began playing. A murmur rolled through the room, followed by quiet applause. Mitch took Ann in his arms, and after one tentative step, they fell into a steady rhythm. Then Jason began to sing.

Stunned by his talent, I shrank in my seat. What other hidden abilities did my protector possess?

After the first verse of the ballad, Chase started playing, adding a complex harmony. I'd heard the song before, but never really listened to the lyrics. They chronicled the life of a man, celebrating how he found his soul mate and shared a century of love with her. It was my fantasy repeated, narrated musically by the object of my desire.

Object? Jason was anything but an object. Smart, funny, caring, and strong, he was so much more than his handsome face and virile physique.

As for desire…that was *exactly* the right word. But what was it I really wanted?

Mitch and Ann spun around the floor, entrancing the crowd. They laughed and kissed, truly as one. Was *that* what I wanted? With Jason, the man I imagined to be my Prince Charming? *Grow up, Melissa!*

Rather than watching his sister and brother-in-law, Chase stared at Linda. He mouthed the words along with Jason, and at the mention of family and children, tears streamed down Linda's cheeks. I had absolutely no doubt she and Chase would be sharing a similar dance in the near future.

Somehow I knew Jason wouldn't be watching his brother either, but I expected he would have to check his music, his hands, or something as he played. Instead, I met his gaze as he sang of encountering a fiery love at the age of twenty-two, and we hardly blinked as the world closed in around us. It was as if Jason sang only to me, his eyes swallowing me until he ended his musical tale at the age of ninety-nine, wishing only to join his love, wherever she was. Could he see the same fantastic future I did?

It's just my imagination, I told myself as the final notes drifted into nothingness.

The crowd whistled and hooted when Mitch dipped his wife dramatically. If they only knew how many hours he'd spent at the rec center practicing his waltz with a mop. Clapping carefully, I joined in the enthusiastic applause.

Jason stood, shook Chase's hand, then started toward Ann and Mitch. He glanced back at me, putting his hand in his left jacket pocket and giving me an expectant smile. The memory of his words rang in my ears, and my hand twitched involuntarily.

"I'll be back for that…"

Five

After congratulating Mitch and hugging Ann, Jason turned his attention back to me. Even from across the dance floor the sincerity in his smile wrapped itself around me, and I started to rise, pulled to him by some irresistible force. I couldn't detect any flaws in this blue-eyed wonder, which made his interest in me that much more unbelievable.

Jason managed only one step toward me before Mitch put a restraining hand on his shoulder, frowning in my direction.

The DJ scolded Jason loudly. "Oh no you don't, Best Man. Can I have the rest of the bridal party front and center? Mitch, would you like to dance with your mother, and Ann, with your father?"

Jason jerked out of his brother's grasp, but he sighed and didn't move again.

"Gotta go," Linda said and jumped up. Chase waited for her on the dance floor with open arms.

Alone again, I watched as the black and purple filed onto the floor. Jason scanned the group briefly before looking at me and shrugging. For a split second I thought he'd been given a reprieve, but then his partner clicked past me...the maid of honor.

Tricia stalked toward Jason like a lioness on the prowl. She crossed the floor quickly, the sway of her hips bouncing the chiffon ruffles like pom-poms while her stare remained fixed and unwavering. She must have said something, because Jason's head turned in her direction. My heart dropped to my stomach when he smiled and took her hand in his.

The music started again, and Tricia wrapped herself around Jason, forcibly spinning him so he couldn't see me. She returned my sneer and tightened her grip on his shoulders. The message was crystal clear: *He's all mine now.*

My social inabilities came into sharp focus while watching Tricia effortlessly match Jason's movements. I couldn't dance, wasn't much for small talk, and stuck out like a weed in the garden of beautiful people twirling in front of me. Jason was obviously accustomed to floating in high-class circles—what could possibly have possessed me to think I could keep up with him?

I sighed, sad but sure the fantasy was over. Behind me, the bar tempted, but my head was still buzzing from my last drink. With a four-hour drive ahead of me, I couldn't risk any more alcohol. I enjoyed the view of Jason's broad shoulders instead—until Tricia brought her face to his ear. Her long hair hid the contact, but I doubted she was giving him stock quotes. He stiffened; apparently her ministrations were having the desired effect. Without another thought, I grabbed my purse and headed for the nearest door.

Outside, the breeze had turned cold, ushering in the summer fog. "June gloom," the locals called it—a name that fit my mood exactly. Hugging myself, I couldn't help but wish other arms were protecting me from the chill.

Stop it. Wake up, already! So I'd had a nice little daydream and a quick—albeit steamy—conversation. That didn't mean I had any feelings for Jason. *Then why do I feel like I just lost something precious?*

With a start I realized I'd wandered into the garden where the reception had started—and where I'd run into Ron the first time. Remembering his evil face and frightening grip, I whirled around, thankful to find myself alone. I hugged my purse tightly, keeping my only weapon close at hand. Hopefully he'd crawled back under his rock; all my protectors were quite out of reach.

The path I followed wound between tidy flowerbeds and neatly trimmed topiaries, but their manicured beauty did nothing to ease the stormy ache inside me.

Infatuation—that's it. Nothing more. I'd stamped this Prince Charming image on a man I didn't know—a man I'd never know. In a few hours I'd make the long drive home, and he'd be a fleeting memory. Mitch had graduated, Jason would go back east, and I wouldn't have contact with either one of them ever again. This cold shower of reality washed away the last vestiges of my fantasy like so much dirt off Jason's shiny shoes. Prince Charming could only be happy with a princess, not with me.

Pangs of sorrow rippled through my chest. I squeezed myself tighter, trying to crush the memories of how Jason had briefly touched me, teased me, kissed my cheek. My eyes burned in the icy wind.

Stop being such a wuss! He could be a psychopathic killer for all I knew.

The brick wall at the end of the garden halted my march. The view of the waves crashing fifty feet below should have been awe-inspiring, but apathy was the best I could muster. In the distance, Catalina was slowly becoming shrouded in fog—disappearing, just like Jason would. I rested my arms on the waist-high barrier as I tried to erase the dramatic drivel in my head. I should be happy I'd met him at all.

The sounds of the party drifted out to me. Some friend I was, whimpering in the dark when I should be celebrating this huge milestone in Mitch's life. The music inside changed to a lively country song—one of his favorites—but all I could think about was Tricia rubbing herself all over Jason.

I vowed with a shaky breath that I wouldn't cry. Mitch had found that elusive joy only a soul mate could bring, and he deserved my happiness and support, not my morose self-pity. This was *his* day.

I steeled myself with a lung-full of cold air. Only a few events remained before Mitch and Ann's departure: the cake cutting, the bouquet toss, the garter, the send-off. How long could that take? Tricia would guarantee Jason was distracted, and I could stay on the fringe of the crowd.

It won't be so bad. But my traitorous eyes started to well.

Before I could get my feet moving, I heard a rustling behind me and tensed. Out here I didn't have to think about my response. I shifted my purse, ready to draw my pepper spray…

"There you are," Jason said, sounding relieved.

My heart somersaulted in my chest, but I beat it back, not daring to turn around. I expected a choice taunt from Tricia, but heard nothing. Maybe her tongue was still tied up in his ear. The wind whipped my thin blouse, and I shivered.

He must've noticed. "It's freezing out here. Come back inside."

I glanced over my shoulder to see him standing there, alone and concerned. I turned away before any tears could betray my confusion. *Why is he here?*

"Melissa," Jason pleaded, still playing the chivalrous knight.

I swallowed hard, trying to remember I was an adult, not a star-struck schoolgirl. "I'm fine. You go ahead. You know I'm not into dancing." My voice almost sounded normal. *Maybe I'll skip the rest of the reception. I could write Mitch a nice long letter instead.*

There was more swishing behind me, and the tear I'd sworn wouldn't fall dripped off my chin. I heard footsteps, then nothing. He was gone.

At least that's what I thought I heard.

I jumped when Jason wrapped his jacket around my shoulders, followed by his arms. "Why are you crying?" he asked.

When the shock had subsided, I dug through my purse for a tissue. "It's just the wind," I said, sniffling. "You need to get back. Here, I'll get my jacket out of the car." I tried to wiggle out of his arms, but they didn't budge. If I could get to my car, I'd go, and he wouldn't have to feel responsible for me anymore.

"No, I *don't* need to get back," he said sternly, but followed it with a quiet, "I'm sorry." His voice lost its edge, becoming a whisper. "What's wrong, Melissa? Please tell me what's bothering you—it's killing me to see you sad. Did I do something to offend you? Is that why you left?"

How could I tell him what I was feeling when *I* didn't even know? I wiped my eyes and turned around, still in his arms. Rubbing my nose with the tissue, I didn't look at him, but at the ground.

"You didn't offend me; that's absurd. I'm…I'm just going to miss Mitch." My lie was so lame even I didn't believe it, and Jason actually snickered. I pinched my eyes shut, trapping another fat tear. *How far is it to the car?*

"I'm sorry, but you're a rotten liar." He touched my chin and eased my face up, but I refused to open my eyes. "Did you think I wouldn't come back to find you?"

I didn't move.

"Melissa, please talk to me. What happened to the no-nonsense woman who swept me off my feet?"

My eyes popped open. He was staring at me; his face so close it filled my vision. "What did you say?" I asked. *Who swept whom?*

"You heard me. I thought I'd made myself clear earlier as well." He scowled, whether at me or himself, I couldn't tell. "Maybe I misread you."

I blinked my eyes in disbelief. This couldn't be happening—the fantasy ended already, didn't it?

"Jason, exactly why are you out here?"

He inspected me closely, tiny wrinkles appearing at the corners of his eyes. He carefully cupped my chin in his palm and brushed my cheek with his thumb. The tips of his fingers caressed my ear lightly. *Are his hands always warm?*

He took a slow breath before he spoke. "I'm here because this is where you are. From the first moment I saw you, this is where I wanted to be.

It's embarrassing actually; I feel like a schoolboy." His voice faded. His face became vulnerable, almost child-like, and—if it were possible—even more attractive. "But if you want me to go, I will."

"No. Don't go." *Ever.*

With those words, the warring voices in my head disappeared. Like a switch had been flipped inside my brain, everything became clear and bright. My shadowy, whiny self-doubt evaporated. Jason had come looking for me. He was here, touching *me!* The whys didn't matter anymore, only the now. The sheen on his lips, the breeze mussing his hair, the smooth stroke of his thumb across my cheek—that's all that mattered.

One last warning, *this can't be real,* faded away in the cry of a seagull.

Without thinking, I dropped everything, my purse, the tissue, anything that kept me from touching him. My right hand found his cheek, turning his face back to mine.

"How did you read me, exactly?" I asked, locking my eyes on his. My hand followed the strong lines of his jaw, rising until it grazed his velvety earlobe. My fingers wove themselves into his hair, verifying it was even softer than I'd imagined.

"You are a beautiful, intelligent, sensitive woman with a fantastic eye for detail and an amazing talent for flirtation," Jason said hoarsely, bringing his other hand to my face. My heart tried to leap out of my chest as he moved closer, his hot breath tickling my chin. "But I sensed there was something more than playfulness lurking in your sexy looks across the room. I'm hoping you feel the same attraction I do." He stopped, his lips just inches from mine, his sea-blue eyes filled with a tide of want.

"I do," I barely whispered and guided his face down.

His eyes held mine until the last possible second. He barely touched his lips to mine, a tease…or a taste? My mouth opened slightly, and we shared a breath. Not really a kiss—but so sensual my head began to spin.

The faint aroma of alcohol tickled my tongue, and I sighed, disappointed when he didn't linger.

"Mmmm," he purred, his lips brushing across my cheekbone. I sucked in a breath when he leaned closer and teased my ear with the lightest touch of his mouth. "I've wanted to do this all afternoon," he breathed.

"Jason…" He hadn't even kissed me, and I was already weak-kneed. Whether this was real or not, I didn't care anymore, and my eyes closed as he softly exhaled in my ear. His hand slid down my arm and wrapped itself around my waist, his fingers caressing my back like they'd caressed the piano keys. His mouth moved to my neck, titillating me with feather-like nips from his warm, moist lips.

I shivered again, but not from the cold.

"Do you…have any idea…what that does…to me?" I croaked. He had to notice I was quaking in his arms.

"Would you like a no-nonsense answer, or shall I let you guess?" he asked with a low, sultry chuckle.

Jason inhaled deeply and my hands, still out of my control, moved to his chest and closed tightly on his shirt.

"You smell amazing," he said in a throaty whisper.

"Ahhh…" Incapable of speech, I clung to him, hoping I didn't fall over.

As if sensing my loss of balance, Jason slid his other hand behind my shoulders, knocking his jacket to the ground. He tilted me back slightly, easily supporting my weight, still sampling my neck. My head fell back, giving him easy access as his mouth made its leisurely return to my chin.

"Your allure defies description," he said against my skin. "Beautiful, enchanting, captivating…they aren't enough."

The words seeped into me, steaming me from the inside out. If he didn't kiss me soon, I was going to explode.

His lips traced my jaw, becoming firmer and more demanding as he neared my mouth. Jason pulled me even closer, crushing my chest to his. A low rumble rolled through him—more a growl than a laugh. I realized my thin bra and blouse did little to mask how much my body craved his.

Finally his lips found mine. Both my hands slid into his wavy hair, preventing any escape. No longer interested in tantalizing, he devoured me, supping on one lip and then the other before sealing his mouth to mine. I returned the kiss with equal fervor, reveling in the sweet taste of rum and Coke lingering on his breath. Our tongues finally met, barely touching as they circled and danced, exploring each other. Like a bundle of live wires, every nerve in my body crackled with erotic energy. Wordlessly we conversed: giving, taking, chasing, hiding—delving deeper and deeper into each other. I ached to be even closer.

Starved for air, I broke away. After a quick gasp I sought him again, consuming him. As I delighted in the ambrosia of his wet, powerful kiss, I imagined his tongue elsewhere on my body, kindling a fire that raged across my skin and settled low in my hips.

I wobbled in his arms again, but he held me securely and straightened up. Ever so slowly he finished the kiss, ending with one last, light brush across my lips. I couldn't move; I couldn't lose this feeling.

I didn't want to open my eyes, sure he'd vanish the second I did. Reluctantly, I cracked an eyelid and with a glorious sigh, took in his adoring face.

"Wow," we whispered simultaneously, then laughed, our bodies jiggling as one.

Jason suddenly tightened his grip around me.

"What the hell do you think you're doing?" a deep voice growled.

My cheeks burned as I awkwardly removed my hands from Jason's hair. I twisted around to face a seething Mitch.

"I can explain," I said, afraid to look him in the eye.

"Not you. *Him*."

Jason kept his arms locked around me. "What does it look like?" he asked, the venom in his voice unmistakable. He tried to edge past me, but I elbowed him back.

Mitch took a step toward us. "Why can't you leave her alone? She's not a side of beef you can hook up with, then leave behind."

Throwing one hand toward Mitch while keeping my body pressed against Jason, I glared at the elder brother. "Did you just call me a cow, McAlister?"

Whether it was my question or my leer, Mitch stopped his advance and blanched. "No…that's not what I meant, Mel. I'd never—"

I pointed at him, my finger level with his nose. "I'm perfectly capable of taking care of myself, as you well know."

Mitch's hands came together below his belt, shielding himself. Jason snorted, but wisely remained silent.

While Mitch's defense was flattering, I wondered what brought him outside. "Are you here just to check up on me, or was there another reason?" I had a hard time staying angry, seeing the huge lug cowering in front of me.

"I just wanted a minute with my *best friend*," he said, glaring over my shoulder at Jason.

Hoping I hadn't irreparably damaged the bond Mitch shared with his brother, I lowered my hand and tried to wiggle out of Jason's arms. They'd want some privacy, and I needed a chance to figure out what'd just happened.

"If you'll let go of her, that is," Mitch added.

My head snapped up. "Me?" I asked timidly, and Mitch opened his hands.

Jason loosened his hold on me, but didn't smile. "You can have her for a minute, I guess." He gently stroked my cheek before releasing me.

Mitch gathered me in his arms. "I know you can take care of yourself, Mel, but I still worry about you." His head rose and he looked over my shoulder. "I'll *always* worry about you," he said loudly.

Jason didn't respond—at least in a way I could hear.

"Don't you trust your own brother?" I asked.

Mitch looked down at me, then back at Jason. He chewed the side of his mouth while he stared, his expression stony.

Remembering the pocket full of room keys, my own doubts resurfaced. What was it about Jason that worried his brother? "Mitch?"

"I do trust him," he said with a sigh. "But you two just met. To see you out here…making out…Just be careful, okay?"

I put my hand over his heart. "I will."

Without warning, he hugged me hard. "I won't be around to kick his butt if he hurts you, even by accident," he added, his voice cracking. "I'm going to miss you, Mel."

My vision blurred as the tears welled again. This was the farewell I'd been dreading.

Swallowing loudly, his voice strengthened as he began to speak. "All the time you spent with me these past years was priceless. You know, before I met you, I had no idea how to behave properly around a woman. Even though I treated you just as bad, you decided to hang around and throw my crap right back in my face. You taught me more than I learned in any class, Melissa—you taught me how to be myself, to be a real man, not just an insensitive jackass."

"Thank God," Jason murmured behind me. Mitch shot him a dirty look.

I sniffled again. "Mitch, no, that's not true—"

Before I could finish he put a rough finger over my lips and smiled.

"Don't interrupt. I worked hard on this speech. Please let me finish." He paused, refocusing his dark eyes on mine. "You made me think, you made me listen, and most of all, you made me laugh like no one else ever has. And if you hadn't, I would never have ended up with my Ann."

His expression changed, and another emotion flashed across his face. "I know you and Ann never really clicked, but you supported my decision to marry her, even still. I wish I could tell you how much that means to me. I love you, Melissa."

I tried to blink back the tears, but one escaped. "Aw, Mitch, anyone can see how happy she makes you. That's all that matters."

He released me, his eyes glistening. "You're an amazing woman. Don't you *ever* forget that." He kissed the top of my head and then turned to Jason. "And don't *you* forget it, either." The laser glare returned.

Jason didn't flinch, but he didn't return the animosity either. "Never," he said fiercely. His expression softened into a devious smile. "Frankly, I'm stunned you didn't snap her up first."

Jason hadn't budged since I'd let go of him, and his hand twitched toward me impatiently.

Understanding spread over Mitch's face. "Somehow I knew she wasn't for me."

I shuffled my feet, caught between flattered surprise and impending loss. "You and Ann were made for each other, and you're going to make each other very happy for a long time. Thanks for being *my* best friend, Mitch. I love you too," I said around the gravel in my throat. I stretched up and kissed him on the cheek.

With a big sniffle, he swiped his nose with the back of his hand and smiled. "'Course, if we can't have kids, I'm blaming you," he said, tugging on his trousers.

I laughed. "Sorry about that, but you did bring it on yourself."

Mitch gently pinched my cheek and then stepped over to a confused Jason. They embraced, and Jason laughed when his brother suggested he keep his cup handy. I tried not to eavesdrop, but I caught a hoarse "Love you, bro" before Mitch slapped Jason on the back.

"You two need to come in. We're cutting the cake in a minute." He took two steps toward the ballroom, paused, and looked back at us. One side of his mouth turned up in a cocky grin. Without a word he turned and left.

A few other people had wandered into the garden, so Jason picked up his jacket and handed me my things. He draped his arm across my shoulders. "Shall we?"

My arm wound its way around his waist, and he gave me a squeeze. Slowly, the rational part of my brain started to come back on, shocked at what had just happened. He kissed me…*me*…

When we stepped inside I stopped, remembering what had driven me outside in the first place.

"Did we forget something?" Jason asked.

"What about Tee?" The last thing I needed in my current emotional state was another round with that snake. It was unlikely she'd given up on Jason. I expected her to be lying in wait, sharpening her purple claws.

"Oh, I think she's quite occupied," he said and pulled me a little closer. He tilted his head to the left. In a dim corner I barely made out the top of Tricia's head, glued to a dark-haired guy in an expensive suit.

Jason kissed my hair. "I was never *with* her. You know that, right?" he whispered.

I lifted my face to his, hoping he could see truth in my eyes. "I do now."

He smiled and touched my cheek, running his thumb over my lips. My heart skipped a beat, and a single, satisfied thought raced through my head:

Hasta la vista, Tee.

Six

We'd just arrived at our table when the DJ announced Mitch and Ann would be cutting the cake. After our walk in the cold evening, the ballroom was stifling, and Jason decided to leave his jacket off. The dim light highlighted more details of the well-defined physique hiding under his thin tuxedo shirt, which did nothing to cool me off.

After hanging his coat on his chair, Jason removed his tie and tucked it in an inner jacket pocket. I was about to comment that his tie must not be *that* important when, to my delight, he started to work on the top button of his shirt.

I set my purse down—on the table, I think—I was too busy fighting back drool as I waited for even the smallest patch of Jason's chest to be revealed. I almost cried out when he released his collar, still tightly fastened.

"Could you help me with this?" he asked with a frustrated huff.

Me, help undress you?

"Sure, no problem," I said. His smooth chin and neck were so inviting that I had a hard time focusing on the tiny top button. Words from our lewd emails flashed through my mind as my hands rose. It was my taunting I recalled first.

> Doctor doesn't sound as exciting as a roll in the hay with a hot bull rider.

He'd responded shamelessly:

> I'm sure I can make your pulse race, and I guarantee it'll last longer than eight seconds.

My email alter-ego! *That's* who'd taken charge and run rampant over my common sense.

Still in control, the wicked me placed a hand on his shoulder and slid it up to his collar. As I listened to what my devious side planned, I looked around, happy to see that for once Jason wasn't the center of any other woman's attention.

He innocently waited for my help, unaware of the naughty creature that had been unleashed in me.

Calmly, steadily, I slipped a finger between his collar and his neck, slowly dragging it all the way around to the front of his shirt and the uncooperative button. My other hand traced the tight pleats covering his chest, rising to assist with the stubborn disk.

His heart pounded under my touch. "Melissa," he hissed.

Am I making him nervous? I couldn't hide my smug smile. "Just breathe normally," I said, imagining myself in a nurse's uniform—a low-cut, very short-skirted nurse's uniform. "What seems to be the problem?" I teased.

He was right, playing doctor was fun.

"The *button*, Melissa," he said through his teeth.

With a petulant sigh, I went to work. The button *was* stubborn, but finally it came unfastened. I ran both index fingers down the silky, tanned V of skin peeking out of the opening in his shirt. When they met at the first black stud holding the fabric closed, I looked up and grinned. Jason's eyes shone like blue fire as I rested my hands on either side of the black dot, and my smile grew. My fearless online personality had completely taken over—and I liked it.

"Shall I continue, Doctor?" I asked coyly. I wiggled the shiny black dot with the tip of my finger.

In an instant, Jason's hands locked around my wrists, separating them slightly. He whispered in my ear, his hot breath sending a spasm through me. "Later, Naughty Nurse Melissa. Later."

The snicker on my lips disappeared and emerged as a gasp instead. The thought of repeating this exercise *later*—and finishing the job—had my fingers tingling.

Jason leaned back with a devilish grin on his face, while mine baked with a blush that must have reached my toes. *How could this be happening to me?*

Abruptly, he dropped my wrists.

"You guys coming?" Alex asked, completely unaware of the steamy atmosphere he'd entered. "I think Linda's looking for you."

I took a breath, trying to cool my cheeks.

"We're on our way," Jason said. "And thanks."

The two men shared a meaningful look, and I remembered Alex had been another of my rescuers. Before I could offer my own thanks, he'd wandered off in the wake of one of the prettier bridesmaids.

Jason waved his hand toward the gathering crowd. "I think we should go," he said. Instead of offering me his arm, he placed his hand against the small of my back and guided me through the people toward the cake table.

We stopped next to Chase, who had Linda tucked under his arm.

"Where were you guys?" she asked, cocking an eyebrow.

"Melissa got hot and stepped outside for a sec," Jason said.

I poked him in the ribs, then cozied up next to him.

Chase gave him a sidelong glance and snorted.

Linda continued to stare, squinting as she processed his statement. Her mouth formed a perfectly round O as she caught on. "It's about time you got hot with someone, Melissa," she said with a giggle.

"Ready?" Mitch called. Ann picked up a long silver knife, and he wrapped his hand around hers. Amidst flashing cameras, I assumed the knife pierced the frosting-covered masterpiece, but I'd never know. Jason chose that moment to pull me in front of him. Warm, happy, and wrapped in his arms, the earth could have swallowed us up and I wouldn't have cared.

Everyone laughed when Ann crammed a huge piece of cake in Mitch's mouth, waking me from my trance.

"Duh akes ood," Mitch sputtered. He wiped the frosting off his cheeks with a devious grin.

The crowd ooo'd when Mitch picked up a crumbly piece and eyed his new wife. She confidently leaned toward him, opened her mouth part way, and closed her eyes. Men all around me groaned at the sight; even I had to admit she looked incredibly sexy.

Jason ran his hand through my hair, combing it back from my ear. "Ann told Mitch if he got one speck of frosting on the dress she'd never touch him again," he whispered. His lips brushed my ear as he spoke, bringing back the memory of our kiss in the garden.

My pulse thundered in my ears, drowning out the comments around us. I interlaced my fingers with his, tying us together and preventing my naughty side from whirling around and kissing him right in the middle of the crowd.

Mitch carefully scooped up a tiny bite of cake and frosting on one fingertip and gingerly lifted it to Ann's lips. She meticulously licked every bit of the confection from his finger, drawing another moan from the crowd—and a cough-laugh from Jason. When the entire length of Mitch's finger disappeared between her lips, his cheeks glowed crimson, and he adjusted his belt. The spectacle ended with a spirited round of applause, but I was daydreaming about how Jason would look if I did that to him.

We meandered back to the table, hand in hand.

"Would you like me to get you some?" Jason nodded toward the line forming for cake.

"No, I'm fine. Maybe later," I said. "But feel free." I waved my hand toward the line without enthusiasm. While the prospect of feeding him dessert sent my pulse into overdrive, I'd much rather he stayed with me.

Jason caught my fingers and brought my wrist to his mouth. He feathered his lips across my skin like before, this time adding the warm, wet touch of the tip of his tongue.

Stunned, I looked around nervously. People filed past, ignoring us, but when I saw Linda heading our direction, I panicked.

"What are you doing?" I whispered. I tried to tug my hand out of Jason's grip, earning another nerve-tingling kiss at the base of my palm. I grabbed a napkin with my free hand and started fanning myself. What would Linda say if she saw this? She couldn't possibly understand how or why Jason and I had clicked—hell, I didn't understand!

Jason looked at me with a satisfied smile, setting my hand down on the table and sinking into the chair next to me. "You've got quite the Jekyll and Hyde thing going, don't you?" he said, keeping one eye on Linda as she closed in. "One minute you're a shy, tearful, innocent girl, the next you're trying to take my shirt off in the middle of a room full of people. Now it's back to nervous and self-conscious. It's hard to keep up, you know?"

"Well, that's the thing about flirting, right? The mystery?" I babbled.

Jason raised a disbelieving eyebrow.

"I…well…you know…" With Linda only a couple of tables away, I couldn't even compose a whole sentence. "Um, later? Please?" I begged.

"*Later?* Definitely," Jason said. He straightened his collar and gave me a cocky smile.

All I could do was stare, my mouth hanging open.

Linda set a piece of cake in front of me. "Here you go, Melissa. I thought you and Jason might like to share," she said. She sucked a dollop of frosting off her thumb.

Can everyone read my mind now?

"Thanks," I said after a long pause. I pushed the cake over to Jason. "It's all yours."

Eating was out of the question; my stomach was already churning. Manufacturing a plausible explanation for my totally irrational mood changes wasn't going to be easy. I could go with the PMS excuse, but somehow I knew Mr. Pre-Med wouldn't buy it. *I* wasn't even exactly sure what was triggering my erratic behavior. Apparently Jason's presence disabled all my internal filters; all my dirty thoughts just shot out of my mouth like darts. *He must think I'm certifiable.*

"…messing with Mitch's limo, okay?"

I hadn't realized Linda was talking to me. I looked to Jason for help.

"Sure, Linda, stay as long as you'd like," he said, his eyes not leaving me. No doubt he was questioning my sanity.

I reached for my water, but only managed to demonstrate how hard my hand was shaking when I sent the ice clinking against the sides of the glass.

Even Linda noticed.

"Melissa, are you all right?" she asked. "You're turning white."

No, I'm not all right. My newly discovered multiple personality disorder is tearing me apart.

"I'm fine, really." I forced my lungs to expand and tried to think about something benign, like global warming. I set the glass down carefully, using both hands.

"May I?" Jason asked, taking the hand closest to him. He slid his fingers to my wrist, checking my pulse. I took another slow breath, chasing away most of the butterflies, and tried again for a drink. "Do you feel dizzy?" he asked, shifting back into physician mode.

"No, I'm okay," I said. I got the glass to my lips without shaking this time, and the cool water helped immensely. "Just a little overheated, I think." *Because of you.*

"Her color is returning," he said to Linda. "Just take it easy for a few minutes, Melissa." He was still serious, but his tone struck me. It carried more than just friendly concern; it was filled with obvious affection. I glanced at Linda, wondering if she'd heard it too.

She didn't react but continued to peer at me. I gave her a reassuring nod, my episode hopefully over.

"It's awfully convenient having your own personal physician around, isn't it?" she teased.

"You're not helping," I said under my breath.

Chase appeared behind her, saving me for the second time this evening. "If you're done eating, want to dance?" As he spoke, the music started and Linda's eyes lit up. They skipped away with a chorus of "See you later!"

Ignoring the screaming guitars, Jason continued to observe me out of the corner of his eye. I, in turn, watched him eat the cake, listening to so-called "Naughty Melissa" rattle off the play-by-play in my head.

With delicate precision, his elegant fingers angled the fork sideways and cut a perfectly square bite. He balanced the piece on the tines and raised it to his mouth, his rosy lips parting to receive the sugar-coated cake. His hand froze in midair and his mouth closed, then opened again.

"Are you sure you don't want some?" he asked. He held the fork out, offering me the bite. "You look hungry."

"What? Uh, no…" I stammered, realizing too late that my mouth had mimicked his, like a mother feeding her baby. "I…uh…prefer chocolate."

Forget the cake. It's you I want to taste.

Literally biting my tongue, I tried to settle the lumps of embarrassment twisting in my stomach.

Jason may have hidden his smile by pursing his lips, but his eyes betrayed him. I forced my gaze down to the centerpiece. *Tulips. How appropriate.*

"Yup, your color is definitely coming back," he said, touching my blazing cheek.

I rolled my eyes, and the fork finally made it into his mouth. Trying not to gawk this time, I watched him slide it out between moistened lips. *Lucky fork.*

Jason ate the rest of the cake with the same deliberate care. Each time his eyes flitted to mine I busied myself with my napkin, folding and refolding it, pretending to ignore him. On the last bite, he moved even more slowly, drawing out the torture even further when he raised the empty fork and licked it like a lollipop. I looked away, fearing I'd turned pale again. What I really wanted was to sample the frosting lingering on his tongue.

Jason's display of dining technique had turned me into a complete basket case. I knew almost nothing about him, yet his slightest movement made me hyperventilate. *It's just a physical response. I'm lusting after him, that's all.*

The DJ put on a slower song and the lights dimmed. I'd just finished my origami swan when Jason touched my shoulder. "Feeling better now?"

"Uh, yeah." *You have no idea.*

"Come on." He offered me his hand.

Hoping we were heading back out to the garden, I took his hand, realizing much too late he'd led me to the edge of the dance floor. Terror froze me to the spot.

"Are you trying to give me a coronary—I really don't dance. I *can't* dance," I wailed in his ear.

"That's Nervous Melissa talking. I bet Naughty Melissa loves to dance," he coaxed, leading me into the writhing mass of bodies.

My breathing became shallow as I desperately tried to find Naughty Melissa and her boundless confidence. Jason turned to face me, guiding my hand to his shoulder before encircling my waist. I stumbled as he moved against me, slowly pacing out a simple pattern. "Just relax. It's easy," he said and began the steps again.

By the third time through I was getting the hang of the dance, mostly by following the sway of Jason's hips. When I'd completed the set without stepping on his toes, he pulled me even closer, and I felt…happy?

He's right. I am enjoying myself. How did he know? And in such a short time?

"You do realize you're smiling," Jason said in an I-told-you-so tone.

I pinched his earlobe. "I guess you were right. Naughty Melissa decided this is pretty nice."

His eyes lit up, and he grinned triumphantly. We passed Linda and Chase, who had become statues, watching me. I could feel their dumfounded stares as we glided by, but I was too focused on staying in step with Jason to laugh.

The music changed, and for a moment I panicked, but the next song was another slow one, and I relaxed again.

Jason sensed my momentary lapse into nervousness. "Can you please give me some clues into your seemingly incompatible personalities?" His tone was sincere, not judgmental.

I tried to come up with something coherent while pushing aside the thrill of his lips so close to my face. He placed his cheek against mine as we danced, waiting for my explanation, distracting me again.

My heart rose to my throat as I spoke, but the warmth of his skin against mine encouraged the truth to come out. "Actually, I am the shy, nervous girl—or at least I *was*—until I met you. You seem to bring out very intense feelings in me and"—I took a breath—"the fact that I can't seem to control them scares me. I'm sorry, I've never reacted to anyone this way before." I buried my head in his chest, completely embarrassed. "I'm a lunatic," I murmured into his shirt.

"So you're saying *I* bring out the Naughty Melissa in you?"

I bit my lip, glad my hair had fallen across my face. "I apparently lose my ability to think rationally around you. I'm sorry. I should let you go find someone sane." Nervous Melissa was making a big comeback.

Before I could move, Jason squeezed me tighter. "No way, and no more apologies. I like this two-for-one Melissa. The packaging is exquisite," he said, pushing my hair to the side so he could kiss my forehead.

The music changed again, and the crowd around us shifted into a rhythmic bounce, matching the loud bass beat. I stopped dancing and shook my head at the couple next to us grinding their hips together. *Are they dancing or dry-humping each other?*

"Even Naughty Melissa doesn't do that kind of dancing," I said.

"Maybe later," Jason said, grinning. "How about another kamikaze?" he asked and stepped out of the crowd near the bar.

"No thanks, but a Diet Coke would be great." He flagged down the bartender, giving me a view of his watch. *It's after ten already?*

There wasn't going to be a later, I realized, and let out a long, slow breath. My Cinderella-inspired evening was almost over, and soon I'd have to leave Jason behind. The memory of his lips caressing my skin would make the drive back to Santa Lucia tough. I still couldn't believe he'd actually done that to *me*.

Fantasy. This is just one big fantasy…and it's ending very soon.

Jason caught me checking the time, and his eyes immediately narrowed. "What is it?"

"Well, it's just that the party is almost over…and then I'll have to leave," I said, confused.

"Why?" he demanded.

I gaped at him. *What does he expect to happen after the reception?*

"I have to get back and finish emptying out my apartment. If I don't turn in the key by noon tomorrow, it'll cost me an extra two hundred bucks. There's no way I can make it unless I leave tonight."

Jason pressed his lips together so hard they turned white.

"It's an easy drive. You don't have to worry about me," I added quickly. Mom nagged me about driving at night—wearing a similar expression, actually—but I enjoyed it. No traffic, loud music, and lots of caffeine made for a fast trip.

Still silent, his face contorted again into a grimace.

"What's wrong, Jason?"

Leaving our drinks behind, he rushed me into a dark corner. "First of all, I *will* worry about you. I won't have you driving halfway across the state in the middle of the night, alone."

His uncompromising glare and commanding tone triggered a new response in me: anger. I thrust my chin up at him defiantly. "Don't tell me what—"

"I'm not finished," he said, putting his hand over my lips.

My teeth snapped shut, and I backed away, bumping into the wall. He'd trapped me.

Fuming, I shook my face out of his hand and turned away, refusing to look at him. If he was going to treat me like a four-year-old, I might as well act like one. However, as much as I wanted to continue my temper tantrum, a small part of me was rejoicing. The fact he cared so much about my safety fed the Prince Charming fantasy I'd created.

Jason closed the small gap between us, placing his lips tantalizingly close to my ear. "Second, I won't have you walking out of my life like Cinderella." He backed away just enough to peer down at my shocked face.

"Cinderella?" *How does he keep reading my thoughts? Does he know all of them?*

He flushed, but didn't shrink away. "I don't want you to leave, Melissa. I want you to stay. Please stay," he implored. "Please stay, with me."

My anger melted under his scorching gaze, leaving me speechless.

Jason continued, becoming more earnest with each word. "You know the effect you have on me, but it's much more than that. The things that keep flashing through my mind when I look at you—I can't explain it. I've never felt like this before, either."

My mind reeled as he recited my own thoughts back to me. This couldn't be happening, not to *me*. I'm not a fairy-tale kind of girl. But I could easily see myself staying with him—*I had seen it*—and for much more than one night. Staring at his shoulder, I tried to make some sense of what I'd just heard.

Jason was nearly panting now, and his words came out in a rush. "Please don't go, Melissa. Not tonight. Stay here with me. I'll take care of any inconvenience, I promise. And no expectations, okay? We can talk and laugh, and you can sleep safely alone. *Please.*"

I looked up and lost myself in his eyes, trying to read *his* thoughts. Did he really see himself as my prince, chasing after me into the night? The idea was ridiculous. Yes, we'd found a physical connection, but we'd only shared one kiss. How could he want me so much after such a short time? The depth of the need darkening his features scared me.

My insecurities tried to overwhelm me again, but when I opened my mouth to answer, it wasn't Nervous Melissa who spoke.

"If I stay, I certainly hope I won't be sleeping alone." My hand came up to my mouth with a slap, but I couldn't take the words back, even if I'd wanted to.

Jason's face changed in an instant, his eyes lighting up like candles. "Deal," he said.

What have I done?

He put one hand on the wall behind me and the other around the back of my neck, pulling my lips to his. Without hesitation I slid my hands under his arms and molded myself to him.

You want this. You need this.

Jason leaned into me, pressing me against the wall. I inhaled sharply at this preview of what he had in store for me.

As intense as our first, this kiss sent one tremor after another down my spine. Jason's touch seemed to be everywhere: buried in my hair, stroking my neck, grasping my shoulder, fondling my waist. Our lips separated and I gulped in air, my heart pounding in time with the music blaring on the other side of the room.

With our foreheads touching, I gently ran my fingernails across his back, feeling the heat of his skin through his shirt. *Was I really doing this?*

He slowly stretched his head back with a low, inviting *mmmm*. When my fingers stopped, his began to move, slowly creeping up from my waist.

His fingertips tickled my ribs, slipping over the smooth fabric of my blouse. The higher his hand rose, the larger his eyes became, questioning me. His fingers lingered, caressing the side of my breast. When his hand stilled my mouth fell open, and I stared up at him with a new, intense desire. *I want you…*

Recognizing my unspoken plea, he dove for my lips again, devouring me. Sensible Melissa vanished, leaving only fiery lust in her wake. I'd never wanted a man's touch the way I wanted Jason's. I wanted, no *needed*, to feel his skin against mine. He continued to tease the edge of my breast, and all I could think was *more*.

Read my mind now, Jason.

On cue, his hand slipped between us, drifting over the center of my breast. I pulled my lips from his, the air whistling through my clenched teeth. My head found the wall with a *thud*.

"Is that what you want?" he whispered, fingering me again. I nodded once, then bit down on my bottom lip, trapping the groan growing in my throat. I embraced the deep fire his touch ignited in me, savoring how it raced around my body, growing in strength the longer he teased.

His breaths came fast as withdrew his hand. We were so close his voice seemed to rumble from within me. "The things I want to do with you," he said, catching my earlobe between his lips. His hips rocked ever so slightly.

"I'm yours," I promised. *Take me now.* I wished he'd sweep me up in his arms and march me to his hotel room. A bead of sweat formed at my temple, anticipating how we'd continue what we'd started, minus our clothes. I searched my thoughts, listening for that warning voice—my rational, nervous self—but it was quiet. All my limits had disappeared, leaving only Naughty Melissa behind. As proof, my hand drifted down his back, past his waist, and gave his glutes a hard squeeze.

Jason's head jerked up, but it wasn't surprise I saw. His weren't the eyes of a stranger any longer, but of an intimate lover, burning with passion. He eagerly leaned in for another kiss.

Just then the music stopped, the lights came up, and we both froze. The DJ's booming announcement interrupted the party. "For some reason, the bride and groom are anxious to start their honeymoon. So, without further ado, could all the single ladies join me on the dance floor for the tossing of the bouquet?"

"Damn it," I said under my breath, and Jason groaned, reluctantly separating himself from me. I caught a glimpse of his straining pants before he turned toward the plant beside us and took a few slow, deep breaths. I tried not to think about what lay beneath his tailored slacks.

"Are you going to be okay?" I asked quietly, taking a deep breath of my own. "Or shall I grab your jacket and bring it over?" Naughty Melissa teased.

"Oh, I think you need the jacket more than I do," he said with a lofty quirk of his lip, his eyes drifting down to the two obvious protrusions in my blouse.

I quickly crossed my arms. "Touché."

We stood together silently for another minute before Linda came bouncing over. "There you are, Melissa," she said, grabbing my elbow and dragging me toward the crowd of women in the center of the room. "Looks like you've been busy," she snickered, looking at my arms still folded in front of me.

"Have you and Chase been enjoying the porn in the limo?" I held up her left hand. "Hmmm, I wonder if this finger will always be naked."

She blushed deeply and her voice dropped. "No, it won't. I've done a little investigation of my own, and porn isn't involved. Chase won't tell me where we're going after the reception. That's when I'll find out what's up his sleeve."

"Don't you mean in his jacket?" I asked with a wink. "You'll call me tomorrow with the details, right?"

"I promise," she said, crossing her heart. "But don't expect an early call."

We reached the crowd of women milling around the dance floor, and Linda let go of me, saying something about the bouquet and insurance. She jogged straight to the front of the pack, but I stayed behind; I didn't want to be in the line of fire. Linda could be a dangerous woman when she was motivated, and she definitely wanted that bunch of flowers.

Unfortunately, I found myself next to Tricia.

"Having fun tonight, *Mel?*" she scoffed.

"Yes, *Tee*, it's been quite an evening," I said, taking a keen interest in the light fixture across the room.

"How's Jason treating you?" Her voice was smug.

I didn't trust her feigned innocence. "He's a perfect gentleman," I said. She *so* didn't deserve him.

"That's what I thought…at first." She paused dramatically as Ann strode past. "But when I found out he was engaged, well, I moved on to a more *available* man." She batted her lashes and blew a kiss at her latest conquest standing at the edge of the dance floor. I didn't check to see if he responded.

I tried very hard not to let my disappointment show, but I couldn't help but grit my teeth.

"Did he fail to mention that to you too?" Tricia said with a malicious laugh. She slithered into the pack of clamoring women and disappeared.

I stood rooted to the spot, trying unsuccessfully to erase what she'd said. Jason *was* too good to be true.

Ann peeked over her shoulder, a small, informal bunch of my favorite carnations in her hand. The DJ began a countdown the audience picked up. "Three, two, one!"

She flung the flowers over her shoulder. The mass of women in front of me lurched toward the projectile, but a flying curtain of black hair beat them to it. Shouts of "hey!" and "ouch!" and a quiet murmur of "bitch" rippled through the group. Linda jumped up and down, her tattered prize raised triumphantly in the air.

I turned on my heel and walked back toward Jason. Consider the source, I reminded myself, unable to return his dazzling smile.

"Guys, get ready. It's your turn next," the DJ called.

Jason's welcoming expression faded as I approached our table. "Did someone stomp on your foot?" he asked.

"No. I ran into Tricia," I said.

Jason chuckled. "Literally?" When I didn't even smile at his joke, he frowned. He searched the dance floor, looking for the source of my discomfort.

"Gentleman, please join me on the floor while Mitch removes the garter," the DJ said.

Jason ignored the people stirring around us. "Melissa, what's wrong?" he asked.

"Get your butt up here, little brother," Mitch called, but Jason didn't move.

"Tricia just mentioned your fiancée, that's all," I said, my eyes glued to his.

The blood drained from his face. I waited for a denial, but heard none.

Chase walked up and grabbed Jason's arm. "Let's go, *brother*," he said.

Jason stumbled toward the group, trying to free himself, but Chase held him tight. I guessed Jason assumed I'd walk out again, but this was one story I wanted to hear. Maybe then this unreasonable infatuation would go away and I could go home without regret. The thought of leaving him, even if Jason was a two-timing lout, still caused an icy emptiness in my chest.

Jason stared back at me from across the room. He mouthed the words "Don't go."

To demonstrate my intentions, I made a show of sitting down at the table, crossing my legs and flagging down a waiter. My attention shifted from Jason's brooding features to his elder brother's facetious grin. Mitch held a chair for his wife in the center of the floor. She sat down gracefully and smoothed her skirts like a monarch holding court.

"All right, I think you know what you have to do," the DJ said. Mitch knelt at his wife's feet, his hands at the edge of her dress. "Any suggestions, guys?" called the DJ.

Quietly at first, the eager men's chant of "teeth" grew steadily louder. Mitch looked up at his wife before proceeding. With an exaggerated sigh, she gave her approval.

His head disappeared under her skirt, leaving his ass pointing at the tables. I welcomed Beth when she sat down next to me.

"I'd never let my husband do that to me," she said, shielding her eyes with her hand.

"Yeah, she really looks like she's suffering," I replied, watching Ann's face contort. Mitch seemed to be making things quite pleasant for her.

Beth smirked and angled her chair toward me. "I think Mitch did say something about the garter in his notes this morning. So what have you been doing, Melissa? Having fun?"

"I was." I glanced toward the guys watching Mitch's antics. Jason hadn't taken his eyes off me since his brother disappeared under the white satin.

"Jason McAlister is really nice, isn't he?" Beth asked, following my gaze. "He was very funny last night at the rehearsal dinner."

"Was he." The comment came out flat—a statement, not a question. But my curiosity was piqued, nonetheless.

"Mitch, you need to actually *remove* the garter, my friend," the DJ said, drawing a laugh from the crowd.

I tore my eyes away from Jason and turned to Beth. She was a wealth of information.

"Yes. We sat next to him all evening. He kept us in stitches with stories about Mitch. They're really close, you know."

"I know." Surely Mitch would have said *something* about a fiancée when he caught me in Jason's arms.

"So, which is it?"

I stared at her cryptic grin. "What?"

"Which does he prefer, blondes—" Beth tugged a lock of hair on the left side of my head "—or brunettes?" She slid a finger through the hair on the other side of my head. "You must have talked about something while you were dancing. When I saw you out there, I about fell out of my chair."

With a shake, I freed my hair from her hands. "I don't know. He didn't tell *me* any stories. I was just trying not to step on him." *Does she know about his engagement?* "What did you guys talk about last night?"

Beth's expression turned suspicious. "You know he's studying to become a doctor, right? In his spare time he plays piano with the symphony. I didn't know he sang, though." She paused to check Mitch's progress and scowled. "How long is he going to stay under there?"

I chewed my lip trying to figure out how to steer her back to Jason. "Maybe until his brother gets married."

Subtle, Melissa.

"I doubt that," Beth snorted. "Jason's going back to Michigan tomorrow. He only has a couple of classes left before he graduates. As if being handsome and talented wasn't enough, the guy's incredibly smart," she said. "He's getting his bachelor's degree nine months early."

"Ah." So no matter what happened, my little jaunt with Jason would be short, assuming it wasn't over already.

"You're smart, too, Mel. I wasn't saying…"

"No, of course not. What else did Jason say?"

Beth looked at me curiously. "What are you fishing for, Mel? What is it you really want to know?"

I pinched my lips together. "Well…" I peeked back at Jason. He couldn't be that much of a cad, could he?

Mitch finally emerged from Ann's dress with the garter dangling from his mouth. She looked like she needed a moment…or a cigarette. Jason still stared in my direction, ignoring his brother. I turned back to Beth.

"I heard Jason was engaged," I said. I tried not to let the betrayal show, choosing instead to crack my knuckles one by one.

I was taken aback when Beth laughed. "Oh, that." I made a fist under the table, barely repressing the urge to shake the story out of her. "Last night we were talking about how Mitch met Ann, and Mitch started needling his brother about how he needed to get busy and find a wife. Jason said, 'I already did. I'm engaged, remember?'"

A waiter stopped at our table, interrupting Beth to put down my soda and ask if she'd like something to drink. A cheer went up, but I ignored it.

Finally, the waiter left, and I looked at Beth again. "You were saying," I coaxed.

Beth looked around for a minute, then back at me. "Where was I? Oh yeah, Jason announced he was engaged. Well, I didn't think anything of it at first, other than wondering how Mitch could have forgotten something that important. But then he asked, 'How *is* Sandra?'"

"'She's due in about a month,' Jason said, and I about spit my drink on Todd." Beth waved to someone behind me. "Over here!"

Todd joined us, sporting the garter on his arm. "Look what I got! You know what that means," he crooned.

"All in good time, sweetheart," Beth replied. She was adamant about staying single until she became a practicing psychologist, contrary to her boyfriend's plans. But I didn't care so much about that at the moment.

"Beth, is Sandra pregnant?" I tried to get her back on topic before Jason returned. I scanned the people around us, but didn't see him.

"Hmmm? Sandra? Oh yeah, she's *very* pregnant." Beth's head bobbed up for a moment. "She's over there."

"She's here?" I asked, my voice rising two octaves. Two tables down sat a lovely young woman, obviously in the final weeks of pregnancy. Even with her large belly she was gorgeous, with long black hair and sun-kissed skin. Her huge diamond ring sparkled in the light as she carried on an animated conversation with the man sitting next to her.

No, this can't be—no one could be that crass. Leaving his pregnant fiancée to feel up a total stranger? No way!

If Jason was that much of an asshole, Mitch would've blown a gasket in the garden and beat the crap out of him, brother or not.

But why didn't Jason deny it? Was there something to the story? In any case, Tricia was somewhere out there, laughing.

If I'm the butt of her joke, what's the punchline?

Before I could glean any more information from Beth, Jason sat down next to me.

"You're still here. I'll admit I'm surprised," he said carefully.

Before I could answer, Beth chimed in. "Jason! I was just telling Melissa the story of how you proposed to Sandra in the third grade. We were still laughing about it this morning."

And there it is. Cue rim shot.

For the first time, Jason's stare felt uncomfortable. I licked my teeth and turned away.

"Todd, the photographer wants to see you for pictures with the garter," Jason said.

I refused to look at him, concentrating instead on swirling the ice in my glass with my straw. Only by amusing myself with images of Tricia's hair on fire did I keep from beating my head against the table. *I'm an idiot.*

Beth left with Todd, and Jason slid his chair close to mine. His voice carried a hint of disappointment. "You didn't really believe her, did you?"

I really wanted to say no, but it would've been a lie. I took a deep breath. "Yes, I did. The expression on your face seemed to confirm it. You turned white, and when you didn't say anything, I didn't know what to think."

"That was about the last thing I expected you to say. I was about to explain, then Chase showed up…" He put a hand on my knee. "Did you get the whole story from Beth?"

"Yes, and I feel completely stupid. I owe Tricia for that one," I spat.

"Hey, it's all right." Jason traced my jaw with one finger, turning my head to face him. "I'm sorry for the confusion."

"It's not your fault, really. I should've figured it out when Beth pointed out Sandra sitting over there, ready to pop."

The corners of his mouth curled into a tentative smile, and we both laughed.

"We have a very open relationship," he joked, letting his hand creep a little further up my leg. I quickly covered it with my own.

My inner reporter wasn't quite satisfied. Something about Tricia's comment had rattled Jason, and not just the unexpectedness of it. "I realize this is a little late in the game, but is there anyone else I should know about?"

This should have been the first question I asked him. 'Course, it should have been over coffee or lunch, not *after* I'd agreed to sleep with him.

Jason picked up my Coke and, with my silent approval, took a drink. "No, there isn't anyone, unless you count my parents' next door neighbor. We used to go out to lunch together and split a Happy Meal every—"

"Seriously," I interrupted.

Jason looked deeply into my eyes, and the smile left his lips. "Seriously, there's no one. I've had girlfriends—and I *did* almost propose to one—but it wasn't meant to be. I've spent my Friday nights with my lab partner for the last six months, and he's not my type." His hand inched up a little higher under mine, and I didn't stop it. "And what about you? How many cowboys are sleeping in your barn?" He smiled, but his eyes tightened.

"Truth be told, I've never slept with a cowboy—never even dated one. There isn't anyone tucked away in my apartment, either, and there hasn't been for quite a while, I'm sorry to report."

"Why's that?" he asked, much to my embarrassment.

"Well, other than being pretty much invisible to the male population, I've been busy with school. Friendship's been enough, I guess."

My lack of romantic relationships hadn't been a problem, and I was proud to be a self-sufficient, independent woman. Looking at Jason, though, the concept of such a solitary life lost its appeal.

"While I think the rest of the male population are idiots, I'm not complaining," he said, and planted a kiss on my cheek.

I took a deep breath and decided to let Naughty Melissa have free rein. "Do you think Mitch would mind if we left before he does?" I whispered.

Jason shot a glance at his brother standing across the room, and his grin returned. "No." Without hesitation, he stood and offered me his hand. "Let's go."

Seven

The nearest exit was just behind the bar. I squeezed Jason's hand, ready to make a quick getaway.

When he steered me toward the crowd, rather than the doors, I balked.

"Mitch," he said. "He'll kill me if we just disappear."

"Oh." I'd already said my farewell to Mitch. Maybe I could meet Jason outside and…

Jason touched my cheek. "No one knows our plans," he said. "Don't worry. I won't embarrass you."

"Okay," I said, doing my best to look relaxed and innocent. I'd been the one to suggest our tryst; trusting him with my reputation should be a no-brainer.

His warm, consoling smile did nothing to ease my nerves, however.

The party was starting to wind down, and people were scattered all around the room. I scanned the crowd for the happy couple and swallowed hard when I saw them. Directly between us and Mitch were Jason's parents. How would he explain me to them?

Thankfully, Jason took a different path, taking us through the corner of the dance floor instead.

All the lights in the room seemed to point at me as we made our way across the room. We were almost to the bride and groom when Beth caught my eye. She gave me a thumbs up, and I about fainted.

She doesn't know we're leaving, I told myself, remembering Jason's promise. I mirrored the gesture with a weak smile. When Beth went back to dancing, I went back to breathing.

A few feet from our destination an older man stopped Jason, which gave me another coronary. He asked about Jason's studies, giving me a sideways glance. Ever smooth and diplomatic, Jason kept the conversation short and left the man with a handshake and a smile. He didn't introduce me, which was just fine.

"Friend of Dad's," he murmured. "This way." Finally the crowd thinned, revealing Mitch and Ann.

The closer we got, the weaker my naughty side became. What *would* I say? *Have a nice honeymoon. We're off to do the horizontal mambo.*

I had nothing to be ashamed of; I was an adult capable of making my own decisions. If your mother could see you now, Naughty Melissa taunted. Internally I cringed but marched forward on Jason's arm.

"Hey, bro," he called, getting Mitch's attention. They met with a firm handshake. Mitch's smile didn't change—either he'd decided it was okay that Jason and I were seen together, or he was just happy we weren't sucking face in front of him anymore.

Jason gave Ann a quick hug, chuckling when she whispered in his ear. "We just wanted to wish you a great honeymoon," he said. "You'll call when you get back to let us know you survived, right?"

Us? He didn't mean US us—as in him and me—did he?

"We will. You taking off?" Mitch asked, glancing at me.

"Yup. I think we've gotten all the entertainment we're going to get out of you," Jason said, the corner of his mouth quirking up.

Mitch's stare intensified, his eyebrows rising at the plural "we" his brother used. "Do you have a place to stay, Melissa?"

I don't know how my face looked, but my stomach dropped to the floor. Mitch grimaced, and I was sure we were busted. "You are *not* driving back to Poly tonight, are you?" His voice carried the same commanding tone Jason had used earlier.

I sighed, relieved he hadn't guessed the truth, but I *again* resented the child-like treatment.

Naughty Melissa had had enough, too. "No, Mitchell. For your information, I'm going up to your brother's room to have wild sex. Have a nice honeymoon, okay?" I deadpanned.

Out of the corner of my eye I saw Jason's head snap around, his face the color of paste. I tried to keep my expression blank, unreadable, hoping Mitch didn't see his brother's reaction. I didn't dare look at Ann.

Mitch blinked at me four times and then burst out laughing.

"Mel, you almost had me there. Have fun with the girls." Without another word, he gave me a quick hug.

Jason leaned over and whispered, "I take back what I said about you being a bad liar. Remind me never to play poker with you." He could barely keep a straight face as he gave his brother a one-armed man-hug and wished him a safe trip.

Ann seemed less convinced, her eyes darting between me and Jason. She pinched her lips together, like she was trying not to say something.

Afraid she suspected the truth, I hugged her quickly and whispered, "There's a box covered in cupids in the gift pile. You might want to take it with you tonight."

"What did you get us?"

"Just a little leather and lace," I said, releasing her with a wink.

She smiled back wickedly. "Thank you, Melissa, for everything. I hope we'll see you again after we get back."

I wish. "Have a great trip," I said, my mouth dry. Ann's well-wishes brought reality into painful focus for me. Tonight would be all there was for me and Jason. Just like his brother, tomorrow he'd be on a plane heading out of California and out of my life.

Then you'd better make the most of it. Naughty Melissa jerked me back to the present.

Jason draped his jacket over my shoulders, followed by his arm. I automatically hooked my arm around his waist, and we strode out the front doors. I wasn't even tempted to look back.

Seeing the cars in the parking lot, I angled him in that direction. "I need to grab my bag and coat out of the car."

"Which way?" Jason squeezed me a little tighter as the fog descended, creating a halo around the few street lights. I pointed to the left, and we easily fell into step. As we passed the first row of cars, a *slam* brought me to a halt.

"It won't start."

I recognized the oily voice and pulled Jason between two SUVs.

Ron's still here?

"What is it, Melissa?" Jason said, startled.

I held my finger to my lips.

"Once the limousines are gone, I'll be happy to call a tow truck for you," a woman promised. "It shouldn't be too much longer."

"Maybe when the party's over *you* could give me a ride to the gas station."

Ron's propositions hadn't gotten any better, and I shivered, hoping the woman knew better than to go anywhere with him.

"Is that…?" Jason whispered.

I shushed him and nodded.

"It's against hotel policy for me to leave the property while an event is in progress," she—the wedding liaison, I realized—replied smoothly.

Thank goodness.

Her heels clicked on the asphalt, coming closer.

Jason pressed me against the SUV, angling his body to shield me from the pair. Peeking over his shoulder, I barely made out Vanessa's green dress—she'd draped some kind of sparkly scarf or shawl over her shoulders. Ron was a dark blob next to her.

"Well, I guess I'll just have to wait with you," Ron said, his voice as cold and clammy as the fog hiding him.

"He's got some nerve hanging around here," Jason snarled.

Vanessa said something else, but I couldn't make it out. When more voices joined hers in the foggy darkness, we emerged from our hiding place. If Ron knew what was good for him, he'd make himself scarce.

We walked the rest of the way to my car in silence. I popped the trunk, thankful I'd cleaned it before I'd left home. With the compartment unobstructed by the normal mishmash of papers and empty fast food bags, my coat took up most of the space. Jason picked up my overstuffed messenger bag.

"Here, take this. You must be getting cold," I said and slid his jacket off my shoulders. He paused, but then put it on.

"Mmmm, pre-warmed, thank you. Allow me." Like a butler, he held my coat open and helped me into it.

Looping his arm through mine, he took the lead, guiding me up the path to the hotel. The fog thickened, and I snuggled closer. I was almost sad when the hotel appeared in the dense, hazy air and his grip loosened.

I reached for the door, but with a *tsk*, Jason beat me to it. As if he wasn't perfect enough, his manners were impeccable. His other hand never left my waist. He steered us past the registration desk, dropping the handful of unsolicited cardkeys in the check-out box. The busboy held the elevator for us but didn't step in. Seeing our reflection in the polished chrome interior, I abruptly realized what I was doing.

I was about to let this stranger—this beautiful, smart, sexy stranger—have his way with me. This wasn't really me, was it? How could I do this?

Naughty Melissa remained ominously quiet.

By the time the elevator doors opened, my heart was thundering like a stampede of cattle. With a gentle nudge, Jason said, "This way," and turned us to the right. I tried to swallow, but my throat was closed for business. Here I was, having an anxiety attack while Jason remained completely calm. He kissed the top of my head before stopping us in front of a set of double doors, complete with a doorbell.

Why does a hotel room have a doorbell?

He slid his key into the slot, and the green light on the electronic lock flashed three times. Jason swung the door open with a flourish and a dignified "My lady."

I crossed the threshold and froze.

What greeted me wasn't a normal hotel room, but a living room. On the left, a bar—complete with a sink and three stools—stretched across the wall. Where I'd expected the bed to be, two couches cornered a low glass table. The largest plasma TV I'd ever seen hung over a marble fireplace beyond them. The curtains on the wall opposite me had been left partially open, revealing inky black; not even the stars could pierce the thick fog. On a clear day, the view of the Pacific must be stunning.

"Where's the bed?" I asked stupidly.

Jason raised an eyebrow at me. "Anxious, aren't we?"

"No…yes…well, aren't *you?*" My cheeks roasted, and I was only slightly comforted to see the color rise in his face. I stalked over to the windows and stared out at nothing.

With a quiet chuckle, Jason laid his jacket on the back of the couch. As he had in the garden, he engulfed me in his arms, scattering my thoughts. We fit together so naturally. My anxiousness slowly gave way to anticipation.

Using the window as a mirror, I watched him answer the question I hadn't voiced. "As part of the wedding package, the hotel provided a room for Mitch and Ann. They let me use it since their flight to Tahiti is at something awful, like seven in the morning. They're staying at a hotel near the airport instead."

"So this is the honeymoon suite?" I squeaked.

"Technically." He smiled and backed away, catching my hand. "Come on, there's more." He led me past the fireplace to another door I hadn't seen and ushered me through.

I came to a halt in the middle of a thick, white throw rug at the foot of a king-size, four post bed.

"Oh, there it is," I mumbled. The red satin coverlet had been neatly folded over, revealing a bevy of monstrous white pillows. Balance on the center of one were golden cubes—more chocolate, I guessed. My nerves returned with a vengeance, my hands trembling with the pressure of unspoken expectations. Everything was happening so fast. Could I actually go through with this?

I jumped when the fireplace blazed to life behind me.

"What do you think?" Jason asked softly, his fingers meandering down my arm.

"It's lovely." I chewed my lip, trying unsuccessfully to picture myself in the bed with him.

He stepped between me and our sleeping accommodations and waited until my eyes rose to his. "Are you all right?" he asked.

"Just a little nervous." *Okay, a lot nervous.* "I've never done anything like this before."

His brow creased, then his eyes bugged out of his head. "You've never..." his voice trailed off.

I started at his response. *You've never...* I gasped. *He thought I was a virgin!*

"No, no, *no!* I mean...I've done *this*...but not...UGH!"

Mortified, I banged my head against his chest.

He held me close and stroked my hair but didn't say anything. I tried again. It was much easier to think when I wasn't looking into his infinite eyes.

"What I *meant*," I said into his shirt, "was that I've never had sex with someone on the *first* date." This wasn't even a real date—we'd only laid eyes on each other a few hours ago. And a few hours from now, this date...encounter...affair...*whatever* would be over.

"Neither have I." He kissed the top of my head.

I looked up at him, feeling some of my confidence return. "I never wanted to...before now." I reached up and traced his lips with the tip of my finger before resting my head on his shoulder and hugging him.

"Me neither."

We held each other silently in the firelight, and I finally started to relax. Just as I lifted my head to find his lips with mine, the doorbell rang, muffled by the bedroom door. Now I understood—a knock would have gone unnoticed.

"Great," Jason groaned, then released me. "Stay here for a minute," he said, kissing me lightly.

He headed to the front room and peered through the peephole. I stood by the bedroom door, and it dawned on me why he wanted me to stay behind. What if it was Tricia—or one of the other girls who'd been drooling over him?

No, we were past that—weren't we? *Wasn't I?*

I continued to argue with myself, trying to contain my completely juvenile jealousy while Jason spoke to the intruder. After a few words, he put his left hand in his pocket and opened the door wide.

I was surprised to see a waiter in a vest and tie roll in a cart with an ice bucket and a covered dish. He pushed it out of my view, and after some rustling and a *woof* I recognized as the fireplace being lit, he asked, "How's this?"

"That's perfect. Thank you," Jason replied. He walked the waiter to the door, passing him a tip on the way.

Curious, I stepped out of the bedroom.

Jason's face lit up when he turned and saw me. "A gift for you, Mrs. McAlister," he said, pointing toward the couches.

"Ummm…" *What did he just call me?*

It's a joke. Get a grip! I followed his finger to the coffee table.

In the center, two glasses of champagne, each with a strawberry bubbling away inside, caught the firelight. Next to them another flame danced: a tealight, tucked under a ramekin of melted chocolate. Skewers, napkins, and a tray of assorted items—to dip in the chocolate, I realized—rounded out the spread.

Jason caressed my back, encouraging me toward the couch. "You said you preferred chocolate," he snickered.

We sat, and I finally found my voice. "What's all this?"

"As part of the honeymoon…experience…the hotel provides chocolate fondue and champagne to the bride and groom. They assumed the happy couple would be here…" He picked up my hand and brought it to his lips. "And they were right."

"Ah, that's why the Mrs. McAlister." *Duh.*

He grinned mischievously and handed me a flute of champagne. He raised his and toasted, "To the bride and groom."

"To the bride and groom," I repeated, and we touched glasses with a smile and drank. Remembering our last shared toast across a crowded room,

I slipped my shoes off and cuddled up next to Jason. I took another sip of champagne, content to watch the fire through the bubbles.

We sat in comfortable silence until the aroma of chocolate wafted over, tempting me. I slowly slid onto the floor.

Fondue fork in hand, I inspected the tray of fruit and sweets. "Hungry?"

Jason planted his elbows on his knees and surveyed the food. "Mmmm, definitely."

"What would you like to try first?" I asked. The mirth vanished from his eyes, replaced by a fiery gleam. "From the tray," Naughty Melissa added. I rested the end of the fork on my lower lip.

Jason's Adam's apple bobbed. He kicked off his shoes and joined me on the floor. "In that case, strawberries are *my* favorite," he said.

"All right." I skewered a large strawberry and dunked it in the chocolate.

His eyes followed it as I twirled the fork, letting the excess chocolate drip back into the bowl. His mouth opened when I lifted the berry between us.

Peering directly into his eyes, I brought it to *my* lips and took a bite.

"Hey!" he exclaimed, putting on an incredibly sexy pout. I shook my head. With my free hand I grabbed his shirt and pulled. His irritation turned to astonishment as our lips came together, sealed by warm chocolate. I opened my mouth and passed the juicy bite to him, bathing our tongues in sweetness. The kiss ended with one last taste of chocolate from his lips.

His expression didn't change when I reached for a napkin and wiped a drop of chocolate off his chin. He slowly chewed the bite of strawberry, the shock finally leaving his face. I blotted my own lips, and he slid an arm around me.

"You're the sexiest woman I've ever met," he whispered, gazing at me from under full, dark eyelashes.

"Oh, I don't know about that." To prove my point, I stuffed the rest of the huge strawberry in my mouth and struggled to chew it.

Jason rolled his eyes, and I barely got the napkin to my face before my laugh turned into choking.

"Are you all right?"

Nodding, I managed to swallow the last of the strawberry. "Still think I'm sexy?" I asked with a cough. A long sip of champagne helped clear my throat.

Jason waited until I finished drinking, then wrapped both arms around me and pulled me toward him. I thought he was going to put me on his lap, but his legs opened and I found myself tucked between them with my back against his chest.

"I *know* you're sexy," he murmured, tickling my neck. He moved my hair to the side with one hand. The other rested tantalizingly against my waist. "And amazingly beautiful," he breathed. With one finger he traced the collar of my blouse, reminding me how I had teased him earlier.

Me, beautiful? I frowned at the fire. "You might want to see someone about your eyesight." Considering the crowd we'd been in tonight, "pretty" would be a more than adequate compliment.

I sighed as his finger made it to the front of my blouse and descended to the first button.

"Melissa, *you're* the one who needs a vision adjustment. How can I persuade you?"

His finger reached the button and circled it. At the same time he teased my ear with his lips, lightly exhaling, sending cool chills down my back. "Shall I continue?" he asked, mirroring my words from earlier.

My pulse rocketed as his hand hovered expectantly over my chest. "Please do."

With one quick flick the button flew open, and his finger progressed down to the next one. My fingers tensed, latching onto his knees. He wasn't just undressing me with his hands; he was undoing me with his words.

"You're lovely, Melissa. Your eyes are so clear and deep. They swallow me up. Then there are your lips. Sweet as candy, but as addictive as any drug."

He reached the next button and with another flick released it. He slipped his hand under my arm, lightly brushing his fingers across my chest as he sought out the next one. I inhaled sharply as he traced the edge of my ear once with his tongue.

"During the wedding, you would lick your lips every so often. Talk about arousing…if I hadn't turned around when I did…." He let the words hang while he traced the open edge of my blouse and the skin underneath. "What were you thinking about?"

I had trouble comprehending his question as his fingers moved lower and undid the next button. With little to keep my blouse closed, my bra came into view, and *he* inhaled audibly.

"That was when I figured out who you were," I whispered as another button came free. *One more…* "And that I'd made a complete fool of myself with the emails I'd sent." My voice cracked when he grazed my earlobe with his teeth.

"Mmmm, you teased me even then. I was quite envious of Mitch—having such a…*creative* friend. When he said you'd be here, I hoped to finally meet you."

His lips began a trail of kisses down my neck while he worked on the last button. His voice was smooth, each word more persuasive than the last.

"When we were introduced, I couldn't believe the gorgeous woman in front of me was the same smart, sexy woman from my inbox. You're so much more than I ever imagined."

His fingers captured the edges of my blouse and slowly pulled it open. I turned my face away from his, suddenly self-conscious. Practical to the core, my underwear was less than exciting. His breath tickled my shoulder, and I imagined him frowning at my plain black bra. I'd never seen the need for lace until now.

"No, I'm not," I argued. "See, I'm just plain, practical Melissa." I tried to close my blouse.

"You still aren't listening to me," he said with a seductive firmness. His hands blocked mine, baring more of my skin in the process. "You're beautiful no matter what you wear. Your skin alone is so perfect."

He slid one hand across my belly, letting his pinky slip under another button—the one holding my slacks closed. "And the more I see, the more I like it."

My breaths came in bursts as his other hand swept across the exposed skin above my bra. He paused and held me very close, his palm over my heart. I thought it might jump out of my chest into his hand.

"I still think your vision is flawed," I said breathlessly, not arguing so much as encouraging him to continue. None of the men I'd dated had ever detailed how I appeared to them. Jason's voice was as stimulating as his touch—but of course he saw right through me.

"Hmm, you don't sound quite so sure anymore," he mocked playfully. "You do know that actions speak louder than words." He shifted his hands so that each cupped a breast. My body responded immediately, rising to his touch. "Cold?" he snickered, lightly circling my well-defined nipples.

I scooted off his lap, and he held up his hands, panicked. "Melissa, I'm—I didn't mean—" he said, scrambling for words.

Before he could finish apologizing, I spun around and let my blouse fall to the floor. His mouth hung open as I settled into his lap—facing him.

"You've teased enough," Naughty Melissa scolded.

Without another word, our lips met, the heat of the kiss rivaling the flames behind me. Deeper and deeper my tongue reached into him, and with each sweep my hips bucked against his. His body responded, and through all the layers of fabric, I felt him rising to meet me. My bare back tingled while his fingers stroked my shoulders, encouraging the straps of my bra to slip down.

Too many clothes! My hands moved to his shirt and found the small stud I'd played with so long ago. In no time his shirt was open, and I explored his muscular chest, fingering every contour from his collar bone to his navel. His skin was so smooth and taut, and as my fingers crossed his sculpted abs, he giggled! I slowed my hands over his heart, reveling at how the rhythm matched my own excited pulse. Our lips still hadn't parted, which distracted me from removing his shirt.

It took three tries to slide his shirt off without breaking the kiss. His hands left my back for the eternity of a second, but then his bare arms encircled me. Having so much of his skin against mine was euphoric—and yet not nearly enough. One piece of clothing kept us apart…from the waist up, anyway.

Jason brought our kiss to an end and gingerly pushed me back. He held me just far enough away to look down at the black fabric covering my wide-awake breasts. With the dexterity of a surgeon, he unhooked my bra and watched with hungry eyes as it joined the growing pile of clothes on the floor.

The temperature of the room around me plummeted as he drank in my appearance. I resisted the urge to cross my arms. Pressing them against my sides instead, I inspected the patterns woven into the couch behind him.

I might as well be a virgin. What do I do now? All my previous sexual encounters had been quick and in the dark—ending with a sigh or grunt. It was clear Jason had no intention of rushing this experience. He raked his eyes over every inch of my nervous body.

Jason licked his lips, and his gaze rose to my face. "You *are* beautiful, Melissa. Never, ever doubt that again." Like molten lava, his voice sizzled over me, scorching away any argument.

Without looking away, his hands slid up my arms, hesitating for one long, tantalizing second before they began their slow descent.

"So soft, like silk," he marveled, fondling each breast, eliciting gasps and moans whenever he touched me. The longing returned to his eyes, and he dipped his head.

Oh yes. His breath tickled the top of my breast. With feather kisses that sent surges of delicious pleasure through me, his lips followed the path his fingers had taken. He found my erect nipple, circling and fondling it with his tongue. He inhaled sharply before surrounding it with his lips.

I couldn't quiet this moan or suppress the spasm that accompanied it. I latched onto his shoulders, grinding my hips into him. He relentlessly sucked and teased, answering my wanton cries with a groan of his own.

"So perfect," he said, his words tickling my skin.

I wanted him so much it was almost painful, but he wasn't finished. As he moved from one side to the other, he tilted his head so his soft hair brushed across my chest. My vision blurred. *How long have I been holding my breath?* Intense need overwhelmed me. It wouldn't take much more to send me into climactic oblivion.

Jason performed the same sensual ritual on my other breast, drawing an even louder moan. My fingers buried themselves in his hair, reluctantly letting him tip his head up when he finally released my granite nipple.

"There aren't words to describe how enticing you are, Melissa," he said.

As I lost myself in his eyes, the rest of the world faded away. "Then show me," Naughty Melissa commanded.

Jason squeezed me to his chest. Our mouths met, and the kiss wasn't the only thing that was wet.

Before I knew it, he'd lifted me off the ground, sending another jolt through me when his erection rubbed against my core. As he stood, my feet automatically locked together behind him. He placed one hand on my back, while the other cradled my ass.

He took a careful step forward, and I realized he couldn't see where he was going as long as my mouth was glued to his. Well, there were other places I could put my lips.

We'd made it to the bedroom by the time I'd reached the hollow over his collar bone, and when I tickled the perfect indentation with my tongue, Jason actually growled.

He set me down on the edge of the bed, admiring the view of my chest before letting his hands fall to the waistband of my pants.

"No, you first this time," I said slyly, pushing him away. He stood motionless before me while I ran my hands down the outside of his legs. The firelight illuminated every curve, every ripple of his muscular body—making an especially long, straight shadow across his trousers. His pants twitched when I reached his knees and started back up his legs, my thumbs skimming a leisurely path up his inner thighs.

At the top of his legs I paused, earning a grunted "Oh, God."

"These look a little tight," I teased, running my hands along the thick, hard bulge that was *him.*

I couldn't tell if he actually voiced the "yes" that formed on his lips. My fingers slipped between his pants and skin. His eyes closed, and his mouth opened slightly in obvious pleasure. The button on his pants came open easily, and following his example, I lowered the zipper as slowly as I possibly could.

"Oh, Melissa," he groaned. Five excruciating seconds later, his pants fell to the floor, revealing a wondrous sight. His briefs were exactly that—brief—with only the waistband connecting the small amount of black fabric in the back to the even smaller piece in the front. There was barely enough material to contain him.

"Oh my," I whispered, and he opened his eyes. I looked up at him in awe, and my lightheadedness returned. My fingers rose to the trail of dark hair leading from his belly button into his briefs, but they were shaking so badly I couldn't control them.

Jason caught my hands in his and held them securely. "How about if I do this part?" he said. I nodded, and he bent down and kissed me again, our tongues tangling as we panted together. He kissed each hand before releasing it, then lifted the edge of his briefs. He paused and smiled.

Stepping out of his pants, he turned his back to me. The midnight briefs slid smoothly to the floor, giving me full view of the most perfect ass I'd ever seen. His socks disappeared with the briefs, and he straightened up, glancing at me over his shoulder. Just a hint of pink tinted his face.

"You're breathtaking," I assured him with a stab of guilt. I hadn't said a word about how fabulous *his* body was. "Perfect."

When he turned around, my heart stopped.

Without an ounce of shame, my eyes drifted down, drinking in every inch of him. He *was* perfect, and so hard, curving slightly in anticipation of completing me. The sight sent another tidal wave of hot lust rushing through me, pooling between my legs.

Jason held out his hand. "Your turn, beautiful," he said, pulling me to my feet. I swayed for a moment, but he caught me, steadying me against his body. His tip was moist against my stomach, and I gasped again. I shuddered at the thought of how he would feel inside me.

"I told you how you affect me," he said, then kissed me deeply, swallowing my surprise.

When he backed away, he raised his eyebrow at my slacks. "You seem to be a little overdressed. May I?" he asked with a twinkle in his eye.

"Yes," I barely breathed. He copied my movements, bringing his hands slowly down the outside of my legs, then back up with his thumbs pressing firmly along my inner thighs. He didn't hesitate at the top, immediately finding the source of the hot desire flowing from me.

Pressing his thumb against the center of my moistened slacks, he slowly dragged it forward. The other thumb followed close behind, taking with it my ability to stand. I reached for Jason's shoulder to steady myself. Suddenly my slacks fell to the ground. While I concentrated on staying upright, Jason leaned over and freed my feet from the pants. As he did, his hair—his luscious, thick hair—brushed my thighs.

I wavered, unable to feel my toes.

He leaned back and caught my hands. "Are you all right?" he said, turning his face to mine.

"Oh, God, yes," I whispered and bent down to kiss him. As our mouths met, his hands released mine and found their way to my lower back. His fingers slowly slid down, catching the edge of my plain, black bikinis and sending them to the floor. He ended the kiss, and I realized he'd captured my hands and was silently urging me to straighten up.

I tried to bring my hands down and together to hide myself, but Jason held firm and scanned me from head, to chest, to hips. His gaze traveled lower, but I stared at the floor, suddenly insecure.

"Magnificent," was all he said, and I managed to peek at him. The flames that danced in his eyes may have been echoes of the fire across the room, but they matched the desire burning in his voice. "Come here," he coaxed.

Jason slid himself between the sheets, giving me a gentle tug before releasing my fingers. With a single sweep of his arm, he banished the extra pillows and candies to the floor.

I climbed in after him—and promptly got caught in the covers. It took some embarrassing squirming to untangle myself.

Avoiding further awkwardness, Jason guided my arms around his neck. For a silent moment he held me close, then gave me a careful kiss.

Guessing at what he was about to ask, I hitched my leg over his. "I want you, Jason," I whispered against his lips. "So much it hurts."

No more questions. No more doubts. I stroked his calf with my foot, opening my hips to him.

With renewed intensity, he kissed me—no, *consumed* me. One hand at my back, one at my neck, he held me so tight I couldn't tell where he started and I ended. Only one match was yet to be made, one last connection.

His fingers roamed down my back and over my hip, lingering, squeezing, teasing.

So close. He paused, so I moved against him, delighting when he grabbed my ass in response. More than naughty, I sucked in his earlobe, letting it slip out between my teeth.

"You promised me more than eight seconds, remember?" I breathed.

"Holy hell, woman," he croaked. His hand slipped lower, his fingertips sliding smoothly through the welcoming wetness. With a high-pitched gasp, every cell in my body exploded in an inferno of tingling pleasure. His fingers moved steadily back and forth, matching the rhythm of his body. When he slowed, I moaned, "No," and he slid his fingers back—then inside me.

With a quiet scream I arched my back, driving my chest to his face. He withdrew his moistened fingers, and I cried out again. Jason's ability to tease and arouse me at such a slow pace was gloriously frustrating. His fingers repeated their erotic slide, and as he entered me, his mouth caught my breast. My entire body spasmed, and the first hints of the coming orgasm burst through me.

His fingers retreated, and he released my nipple.

"Jason…" I begged.

"Melissa," he whispered hoarsely. "What is it you really want?"

Answering his question with my touch, I sent my hand down his chest, over his abs, and through the stiff curls at the base of what I wanted. His fingers stilled, allowing me to concentrate as my hand drifted lower, cupping the delicate velvet between his legs.

"Soft," I whispered, carefully fondling his vulnerable sac. Moving higher, I wrapped a finger and thumb around him and thrilled at how his whole body stiffened. I slowly stroked his solid, silky length once. "And oh, so hard."

"Please," he begged through his teeth. "I want you, Melissa, so much."

I wrapped another finger around him, stroking him a little faster this time, and he drove his hips against my hand with a deep, unrestrained growl. I stroked him one last time, grasping with my entire hand, and he threw his head back, barking my name.

"Jason, make love to me," I pleaded.

His lips met mine before I finished speaking, his kiss scrambling my thoughts. The rattle of foil registered in my brain somewhere between *I hope I remember how to do this* and *Take me now, damn it!*

My legs opened eagerly when his fingers returned, stroking me with such a tantalizing lightness that he brought me right to the edge of climax. My teeth snapped together in a desperate attempt to hold back the wonderful finale.

"Now!" I cried.

Effortlessly, Jason rolled on top of me, and with a shared moan our bodies became one.

The shock of his invasion—and his size—interrupted my pleasure for one distracting second, reminding me just how long it'd been since I'd had sex.

He froze, his eyes locking on mine, questioning.

"Jason, I want this. I want *you*," I whispered earnestly, and contracted around him.

The uneasiness vanished, and we lay motionless, filled with the completeness of becoming one. I kissed him as deeply as I could, hoping to convey the desire words couldn't.

Slowly, Jason pulled his lips away. "God, Melissa, you feel so good," he breathed as his hips began the one dance I did know. With long, slow, deliberate passes he filled me over and over again, refusing to surrender to the eminent ecstasy. At first I rocked with him, matching his movements, but as the intensity increased, I stilled, giving him complete rein over me. His eyes closed tightly, and the tenor of his movements changed. *Faster*, I thought, *deeper*…and his tempo increased without a sound.

Beads of sweat covered my skin as I focused on reaching that one delectable goal. I pinched my eyes shut and held my breath, willing myself over the edge. With a muffled cry I came first, arching into him. In that blissful, eternal second, there was only Jason; all my senses filled by him, all my being was his. His last strokes held my climax for a few more glorious moments, and then he joined me in orgasmic ecstasy, pulsing deep within me. I whispered his name as he lowered his body onto mine, resting his head on my shoulder.

I wanted to speak, to tell him…but there was no way to describe what he'd just given me. Instead, I buried my face in his hair and lightly rubbed his back, clinging to the bliss for one more second.

Jason lifted his head and gazed at me, bathing me in such deep affection that I was overwhelmed. A tear escaped from the corner my eye.

He caught it with his finger. "What is this?" he asked, his expression fading into concern.

"You're so *amazing*," I whispered. "There aren't words."

He peered at me, ready to argue or complain, but I touched his lips, shaking my head. I traced his mouth, his cheek, his eyebrows, letting my finger wander his face. A few strands of hair had flopped down over his forehead, and his eyes closed as I carefully pushed them back into place.

With a purr, Jason smiled, pecked my hand, then ducked his head to mine. One last tremor shook me as our languid lips touched, a final taste of the rapture we'd shared.

The vision I'd had when I first saw Jason reappeared in my head, mirroring what had just happened. I couldn't believe how much of the fantasy had come to pass. At this moment I was closer to Jason than I'd ever been to anyone in my life, and yet he was still largely a stranger to me. Could more of the fantasy come true? What was it about him that drew me in?

Jason returned his head to my shoulder, and I decided it didn't matter. He sighed serenely as I ran my fingers through his hair, and I knew he was falling asleep.

Unable to resist, I pressed my lips to his forehead. The sweetness of his shampoo mixed with the pleasant saltiness of his damp skin. Though I was tired, my eyes stayed wide open. I wouldn't waste the little time I had left with Jason by sleeping.

Tomorrow he'd be gone.

Eight

_J_ason slept so deeply I could barely tell if he was breathing. I rested my head on his chest, listening to his slow, steady heartbeat. I still couldn't believe he'd discarded offers from a dozen attractive women and chosen me…and that I'd actually come with him.

Literally.

My thoughts drifted back, reviving every memory Jason had given me over the last few wonderful hours. I couldn't stop the smile that spread across my face, or the blush, as I remembered his sly looks and coy comments. As happy as I was, one thing was missing. I slid carefully out of Jason's grasp and rested my chin in my hand so I could see him.

What was the word he'd used? _Magnificent._ Now I was complete.

He didn't wake when I stirred, but he unconsciously pulled the sheet up to his chin and turned his head toward me. Asleep he was the picture of peace, his eyes fringed with thick, dark lashes; his lips full and pink. His mussed hair danced around his face playfully, giving him an innocent, wholesome look. My fingers twitched, dying to stroke his cheek, but I resisted, afraid to wake him. Or was I afraid if I touched him he'd vanish, a figment of my imagination?

No, my imagination has never been this good.

I'd given up on miracles a long time ago, but lying next to Jason, I had to admit they existed. He'd tried to persuade me I was beautiful with his words, his kiss, his touch; and for a brief moment I did believe. In the flickering light of the fire, I _was_ beautiful to him, just like in the fairy tales. But now the fire was out. This miracle would last only one night, and unlike Cinderella, there would be no shoe left behind. My handsome prince would be riding off to medical school, not after me.

With that thought, I rose. I couldn't lie next to him and think about the coming end—but I couldn't erase the worry, either.

I went to the closet, cringing when it squeaked open. Searching for a robe, all I found were empty hangers and Jason's suitcase, propped open on the luggage rack. There was just enough light for me to make out a wad of clothing on top of the folded sets below, and I realized I'd found his regular nighttime wear—light knit pajama pants and a t-shirt.

Standing in the dark, naked, I lifted the t-shirt and held it close, inhaling the scent clinging to it. Hints of his woodsy cologne reminded me of the kiss he gave me in the receiving line and the gleam in his eye when he learned my identity. I glanced back toward the bed, but Jason hadn't moved. A strange urge filled me, and I quickly slipped the shirt over my head. It felt so right…like I belonged to him.

Jason coughed and rolled over, and I froze. What would he think, seeing me wearing his clothing?

He'd want it back. Naughty Melissa was awake, and I covered my mouth, stifling a giggle.

Jason resumed his even, nearly silent breathing.

I'd never indulged my reckless side before, and I felt amazingly satisfied, even powerful, having done so. Unfortunately, before I could celebrate my freedom, Nervous Melissa woke up too.

Yes, last night was fun, but now it's over.

The words thundered through my head as I stood beside the bed. I tried to sort out the conflicting voices: one begging me to rejoin Jason, wake him, and find ecstasy with him again; the other advising me to distance myself, reminding me I didn't know him and that in a few hours he'd be gone forever. It was the second voice I heeded.

I found my bag stashed next to the door and fished out the extra set of clothes I'd planned to wear on the trip home. I donned a fresh pair of underwear—thanking my mom for urging me to "always be prepared"—and jeans. Tiptoeing into the living room, I intended to leave Jason alone for the rest of the night.

The fire had died in here too, but the room wasn't dark. A ghostly white glow emanated from the few visible windows. The fog had flattened itself against the water, reflecting the rising moon's bright light. But it was the clothes strewn across the floor that caught my eye.

I picked them up, one by one, in the order they'd been tossed aside. My blouse, his shirt, my bra—each piece evoked a different erotic memory. Who knew how sexy buttons could be? I felt like I watched someone else as the images passed through my mind's eye—surely it wasn't me who said those things, who *did* those things?

But it *was* me. My original vision reappeared—that intense flash-forward to the future. This time I paid closer attention to the rest of the story, having already experienced the first part. I watched an imaginary Jason slide a diamond-studded band on my finger…hold a SOLD sign high above his head…cradle a pink bundle gently in his arms, tears streaming down his face. I saw every girl's happily ever after.

The dream wasn't new, I realized. I'd had it many times as a child. Prince Charming didn't have a face in those days; he'd just been a blurry image, a hope. I'd been sure he would come for me, that I would get *my* happily ever after. When my fairy-tale life had turned tragic, I'd discarded my dreams…or so I'd thought.

The movie in my mind shifted from PG to R as the Jason of my fantasies appeared again, rolling me on top of his eager, naked body. No, this Jason wasn't a dream—far from it—and he'd given me *that* extremely happy ending. The dream was that we'd have anything more than sex. Granted, it was intense, mind-blowing, and-the-angels-wept sex. Sure, I'd want more of *that*. Who wouldn't?

If only I could truly believe the fantasy was just lust. While waking Jason and having my way with him was appealing, what I really wanted was to curl up in his arms and stay that way. Tonight, tomorrow, the next day…I wanted to know he'd always be there, next to me.

This is bad. Really, really bad.

As I stood in front of the windows, bathed in moonlight, the real future unfolded before me, minus the happy ending.

Jason would return to Ann Arbor tomorrow—no *today*—to start the summer session. After he graduated in the fall, he'd attend medical school; would that be in Michigan too? It was obvious he was anxious to move through his studies and begin practicing medicine. It was equally apparent he was going to be a great physician. He wouldn't have the time—or probably the inclination—to see me, even if he were close enough to do so.

My future was much less interesting. I'd drive home, collect the few remaining things at my apartment in Santa Lucia, then head for my mom's house. Our last summer together would consist of a short trip to the Northern California wine country and a part-time summer job for me. Next fall I hoped to start an internship at a real newspaper; I had applications submitted at ten different papers up and down the West Coast. Following that would be a few more months of school, then I'd start my career.

Who knows where I'll end up…

I caught my gloomy reflection in the window. As much as I wanted to be with Jason, I knew it was impossible. And the more attached I became, the harder leaving would be—for both of us. We'd each built our own lives, and they only intersected at this one place, at this one small point in time. I couldn't give up my hopes and plans, and I certainly wouldn't expect him to make such a sacrifice.

I argued with myself, feeding the despair that was eating me from the inside out. All the relationships I'd been in had ended the same way: with the guy eventually disappearing, usually with the words "I'll call you sometime." I'd given up, accepting my fate as everyone's dependable friend. I was happy with my uncomplicated life—at least I used to be.

But Jason didn't deserve to be strung along. I should make it easy for him to go; he didn't have any choice *but* to leave. That we knew so little about each other meant our tryst held no lasting ties. He'd be free to find the one who'd drop everything and follow him as he pursued his passion.

Even still, my heart yearned to hear him ask *me* to stay, to find a way to be together, but I knew those words wouldn't come. He deserved better than me: an invisible loner who spent more time writing about other people's lives than living one of her own. My prince deserved a proper princess.

Nervous Melissa urged me to run. If I left while he slept, I could save him the messy sendoff and the empty promises that would come with it. If I walked away now, he could go back to Michigan with a nice memory and a clear conscience. I could go back to my life and this amazing night would fade into the past—wouldn't it? Would Naughty Melissa accompany me home, or was she only for Jason?

Turning, I looked at the front door, outlined in creamy brightness, and realized I couldn't do it. I couldn't just slink away into the night. Pride said I wasn't that much of a coward, but in truth, if I'd been able to run from him, I wouldn't be standing here now. I had no remorse for having spent the night with him; on the contrary, I savored the glimpse of heaven he'd given me. No matter the consequences of this night, I wouldn't change a thing.

Jason had been such a gentleman. With every word and action he'd considered me first—so concerned about my feelings, both emotional and physical. I owed him the same courtesy. He deserved a face-to-face farewell before I left, a closure. I didn't want him to feel like he *had* to stay in contact with me—another email exchange would be pointless. The last one had only made it a few weeks before it evaporated.

Long-distance relationships didn't live long, that I knew. Summer vacation had killed the last relationship I'd been in, and that guy had only lived in the next county. Michigan was more than two thousand miles away. Jason had to know I understood this one night was all we had.

Just one night? It's not enough.

I felt like I was losing a lifelong friend, not a recent acquaintance. I squeezed the clothes in my arms against my chest and against Jason's shirt, wishing it was him. What would I say?

Sappy, meaningless phrases paraded through my head. *You're a dream come true…last night was amazing…thanks for the memories…* it was all crap. How could I tell him how wonderful he was? That he deserved so much more than I could ever give him?

My life changed the moment I saw you… No, no, no. It can't be that way. *Farewell, my prince.*

I let the clothes fall and buried my face in my hands. The pain welled up—like my heart had grown spines and was stabbing me from the inside. All I could see was a big, silver plane and Jason's face, smiling happily in one of the small, oval windows. The plane taxied and took off, becoming a smaller and smaller dot in the sky until it disappeared completely.

A familiar emptiness enveloped me, an ache I hadn't felt in a long time. Why was I feeling this…this *loss?* It wasn't like Jason was dying, and yet it was the same pain I'd felt years ago when Dad—

"Couldn't sleep?"

I jerked my head around.

Jason stood behind me, clad only in his pajama pants. He grinned, seeing his baggy shirt hanging on me. When his eyes drifted to mine, his approving smile faded.

"No, I couldn't. I'm sorry if I woke you," I said. I turned back to the windows, mad at myself for letting him catch me like this. It was no surprise when his arms appeared around me.

"I was wondering where my shirt went," he whispered, and I tried to fight the sizzle his closeness sent through me. "Did you get chilly?"

"No." I struggled to find something else to say, but had nothing.

"Why did you get dressed?"

"There wasn't a robe." *Lame.*

He traced my arm, his breath cool on my neck, raising goose bumps all over my skin. "Come back to bed, Melissa. If you can't sleep…" He finished the sentence by kissing the nape of my neck.

Naughty Melissa made a feeble attempt to comply with his request, but she lost the battle for control of my mouth, for once.

"Maybe in a minute," I said.

As much as I wanted to take him up on his offer, I knew it would only make leaving that much harder. My throat tightened, and I closed my eyes, trying not to think about what he had in mind.

Jason abruptly let go of me. "What's wrong, Melissa?" His voice cut through the air, laced with something dark. Dread?

"I just need to think, that's all. Go back to bed. I'll be there in a sec." Now was not the time to be discussing this. *What is it, three thirty in the morning?*

Jason stepped around me and lifted my chin. He searched my face. "What are you thinking about out here, all alone?"

I took a deep breath, realizing this *would* be the time after all, and after our talk I'd be leaving. *At least I'll get back home in time to turn in my key.*

Dismissing my disturbing practicality, I sighed. "I was thinking about you," I said.

Jason remained motionless, waiting for more.

"And how I would say…" My throat burned on the last word, and I tried again. "How I'd tell you…" Dark, unwelcome images flooded my mind before I could finish, and I gave up. "How I'd let you go," I said instead.

His jaw tensed, and his eyes narrowed as if preparing for a fight. "Why?" he asked, and I cringed.

"You know why."

"Because you regret what happened," he said somberly. His hand fell back to his side, and he shrank away from me. "I'm sorry, Melissa. I shouldn't have forced you to come here."

The sadness in his voice brought a huge lump to my throat. *Regret?* That was about the only emotion I *hadn't* felt in the last twenty-four hours. I exhaled loudly, not knowing how to explain.

"No, I have absolutely no regrets, and you didn't *force* me to do any-thing. I can't imagine experiencing anything more perfect. I can't begin to describe how you make me feel, Jason," I rambled, frustrated. He could read every other thought in my head, why couldn't he read this one?

He turned back to me slowly, and I could see something else filling his eyes. Anger, I guessed. "Then I don't understand. Why are you trying to say goodbye?"

That word…

I looked away. Regret tempted me now; maybe I should've just left.

"Why?" he demanded impatiently. He used the same patronizing tone that had infuriated me before. It had the same effect now.

My jaw flexed as my head snapped back to face him. When I opened my mouth the words came crashing out. "Because you live in Michigan, and I live in California. Because I'm invisible, and you're amazing. Because you deserve so much better than me. Because we live in the real world, not some fairy tale." I blinked back the sting in my eyes. *Why can't he see the truth?*

"You think I deserve better than you?" His eyes deepened to an ominous cobalt as he barely restrained himself from shouting. "What exactly *is* better than you, Melissa? Because I can't quite figure that one out!"

"A lot of women," I said, the bitter truth puncturing my anger. "I was trying to figure out how to make this easy for you, and I've failed miserably. Maybe I should get my things now. It'll be light soon." My heart twisted in my chest as I picked up the clothes at my feet and started back to the bedroom.

Jason held his arm out, blocking my path. "No, don't go." His tone quieted, the irritation giving way to desperation. "Tell me one thing. Why did you stay with me?"

My heart stopped. How was I supposed to answer that? My sarcastic side instantly replied with a quiet *duh* in my head, but I suppressed it. I stared at his feet. "I was being selfish. I'm sorry."

"That doesn't make sense. I practically begged you to stay," he said defiantly.

"And I should have said no. But when you talked about disappearing like Cinderella, it was like you were reading my mind. I thought I could pretend to be her for one night." *How stupid does that sound?* I brought one hand to my face and pinched my eyes.

"Ah, so I was just a one-night stand," he said sourly. "You're right. You *are* selfish."

Shit. He'll probably throw me out now. "No, damn it. That's not what I meant," I snapped. Frustrated, I rubbed my eyes, unable to stop the tears that had been building. When did I turn into such a crybaby?

Turning my words around, I tried one last time. "I definitely don't deserve you. You had beautiful women falling all over you at the reception, but for some insane reason you chose me, and I'll never understand why."

His fingers flexed, but he didn't interrupt.

"You don't know me from Eve, and yet you picked me. How could I *not* come with you? From the first time I looked in your eyes…" I clamped my hand over my mouth. The last thing he needed to hear how ridiculous my imagination could be.

The deafening silence wore on, neither of us moving or speaking. As tempted as I was to look up at him, to see the confusion and disgust in his face, I didn't. I continued to inspect his toes instead, noting that they too were perfect, just like the rest of him. He finally spoke.

"Tell me, what *did* you see, Melissa?" he whispered.

I shook my head. There was no way I'd tell him.

"It was in the church, before you took my arm, wasn't it? Shall I guess?" he pressed.

I didn't answer, wringing the clothes in my hands while I waited. Part of me wanted him to know exactly how I'd envisioned us together. But he couldn't know; it was just a daydream, after all.

I forgot he could read my mind.

He lowered his arm and took a deep breath. "You saw us, didn't you?" He placed his finger under my chin and lifted my face to his. Staring into my eyes, he could see the answer. "What if I told you I could see the same thing?" A tiny smile crept across his lips. "I may know you better than you think."

I struggled to understand what he was saying. How could he know me? "But it's only been hours," I reminded him—and myself.

Jason snickered, apparently at some joke I wasn't privy to. "True. And yet I'm drawn to you in ways I can't explain," he said. He focused on his fingers and wiped my tears away, considering his next words. His hand dropped from my cheek, and he took a deep breath, like he'd made an important decision.

I locked my jaw, expecting the worst.

His words were quiet, yet determined. "It's completely foolish, I realize that. But how's it supposed to feel when you finally find the one who makes you whole? Does it have to take weeks or days to figure it out, or can it just take minutes, or seconds?"

I couldn't speak, I was so stunned. Was he saying what I thought he was saying?

Jason relaxed as he surveyed my expression, and his voice became the soft, silky croon that made me melt. "I've tried all night to tell myself you can't mean that much to me after just a few short hours, but it actually took much less time than that. Somehow when I first saw you, I knew." He traced my jaw with one finger. "And you already admitted you feel it too," he reminded me.

My heart spoke for me. "I guess I did."

I did feel it, the completeness. I even saw it—and chalked it up to lustful fantasy. But what if I'd misinterpreted the vision? If it wasn't carnal desire and it wasn't childish infatuation, then…

The look on Jason's face only strengthened his assertion. His expression conveyed a single emotion, but I hesitated to put a name to it. I realized I'd been avoiding the word since I laid eyes on Jason; love at first sight was something for hormonal teenagers and weary housewives. It didn't really exist…did it? But as I gazed at his face, I could only find one word to describe what I saw: love.

Jason's expression changed quickly, leaving me even more confused.

"Then why do you keep running away from me?" he asked, his voice sharp.

I opened my mouth, but nothing came out. He wanted *me*. I obviously wanted him…Why *was* I running away? My mouth closed, and I focused on his chin as I tried to think. He'd all but said he loved me—how could that be? Did I feel the same way about him?

As I thought about Jason, a warm tingling filled me. It was followed by the sensation of drowning in cold water, though, and I finally understood why I was trying to run. If *I* left *him*, the separation didn't seem so final. If I walked away first, the last thing I'd see would be his face. I could always pretend that if I turned around, he'd be waiting for me. For some reason I couldn't handle the thought of him walking away from me; there was a permanence to the idea I couldn't explain. Horror filled me as I imagined him doing just that.

He sensed my panic and put his hands on my shoulders. "It's okay, Melissa. You can tell me. I'm not going anywhere," he reassured.

"But you *are*," I choked. My hands balled into fists as I voiced the hard truth. "I'm terrified—having fallen so fast for you, knowing you'll be gone in a day. If I stay until you leave, I'm afraid you'll ask me to come with you, but I'm also scared you won't. I don't know what to do." The stress of my paradox bubbled to the surface in another wave of tears.

Jason's damp eyes sparkled in the moonlight, and my heartache grew. He seemed to want to hug me, and I felt his hand tighten on my shoulder briefly. I didn't respond, clinging to the clothes in my arms like they were some kind of armor, keeping my heart from falling out of my chest.

He ran one finger through my hair as he spoke. "Melissa, I understand, and I'm scared too." A single tear rolled down his cheek, and for some bizarre reason the sight comforted me. "I'm not ready to give up, though. When I said I wasn't going to disappear, I meant it," he whispered. He took a deep breath and a new sense of purpose filled his gaze.

"But how can we—" I started, but his finger moved to my lips. The familiar shock of his touch flashed through me.

Jason's voice was soft, soothing. "I don't know how. But isn't it worth *some* effort? Can we at least take some time and try to figure this out together? Let's not make any decisions tonight, all right?" He managed a small smile.

He wasn't making any promises, just asking me not to throw away what little time we had left. I nodded slowly, and his smile widened. Jason held out his hand. *Trust me,* the gesture said, and I couldn't resist.

I put my hand in his and tried to let go of my fears. He pulled me close, wrapped his arms around me tightly, and brushed his lips across my forehead. As he enveloped me, the feeling of belonging returned, and for once I didn't fight it. For this brief second, I did belong to him, with him, and nothing had ever felt so good.

Another tear fell from my cheek onto his bare chest. "This isn't going to be easy, is it?" I asked weakly.

Jason squeezed me a little tighter, and his hand came up to my cheek. It was so warm and soft, I automatically leaned into it. "I don't know. From the moment I realized who you were, I knew that this would be…different. I'm sorry *I* was too selfish to just leave you alone," he said.

I grimaced; he thought *he* was selfish? He was right the first time—he was foolish.

He kissed my hair before continuing. "Can you just do one thing for me? No more thinking about goodbyes, okay?"

I sniffled loudly and swallowed, thankful to find that the lump in my throat had shrunk to nearly nothing. Hope crept into my heart, filling me with a dangerous contentedness. *Could there be a way?*

"All right," I said. I turned my face to his, pleased to find his lips waiting for me. As we kissed, all the drama faded from my consciousness. The ache in my chest disappeared completely when Jason's tongue found mine, and I shuddered in his arms. Lightheaded, I pulled away, trying to catch my breath.

"Come to bed, Melissa."

I nodded slowly, covering the yawn I couldn't contain. He smiled at me—lovingly—then swept me up in his strong arms and carried me into the bedroom. My head drooped onto his shoulder, and Jason's grip tightened. No matter what else I felt, right now I felt safe.

"Let's get some sleep," he said and gently set me down on the bed. He took the clothes out of my arms, and I wiggled out of my jeans. I rolled onto my side, thankful for his T-shirt under the cool sheets.

A random thought fluttered through my mind as he curled up next to me, molding his body to mine. "I may know you better than you think," he'd said. But then his lips touched my cheek, and I drifted to sleep.

Nine

"How long will you be staying here at the Mission?" Ann asked in a sweet, sing-song voice. She held out a huge bouquet of white roses for me.

"Not long," Jason said, his eyes bright. He was dressed in a charcoal gray morning suit, low-cut silver vest, white shirt, and wide, striped tie. As he crooked his left arm, I saw a gold band gleaming on his third finger. "Are you ready?" he asked.

I shifted the heavy bunch of flowers and straightened the skirt of my long satin gown before taking his arm.

"Definitely," I replied. Behind his adoring face, I recognized the white adobe walls and brown, high-beamed ceiling of the sanctuary at Mission Santa Lucia.

This is odd. I'm not Catholic.

"Good luck, Mel," Mitch called behind us.

Jason squeezed my hand with a flex of his bicep and smiled at me again, his teeth flashing in the light filtering through one of the few tiny windows. My shoes echoed through the church as we passed pew after empty pew. Ahead of us towered the huge wooden doors that led outside—that led to our future. When we reached the end of the seats, Jason stopped.

He lifted my hand to his lips, kissed it lightly, and said, "Congratulations." The doors swung open silently, and he encouraged me toward them. When his hand slipped out of mine, panic swept through me. Jason stepped to the side and stood next to Tricia. He kissed her on the lips before waving to me.

"Good luck, Melissa," they both said.

A silhouetted figure stood in the doorway, his arms stretched wide. The bells of the church tolled, and the man took a step toward me.

I recognized him and started to scream.

"You're all mine, now," Ron said.

I woke with a start, but the bells in my head remained. *Ding dong, ding dong.* Confused, I opened my eyes. Seeing only white, I squeezed them shut again. It was a dream, it was a dream, I chanted silently. With careful fingers, I stroked the fabric around me, finding not satin, but cotton. Sheets…I was in bed.

It wasn't *real.*

"Good morning, beautiful," Jason whispered. He held me close to his chest, spoon-style, his breath tickling my ear as he spoke. *This* was the dream I didn't want to end. The nightmare faded, leaving only an aftertaste of anxiety. When I ran my hands over Jason's ring-less fingers, my fear dissipated completely.

I tried again to see, blinking to adjust to the bright morning light. Rubbing my eyes, I rolled onto my back. "Good morning, handsome," I said, my voice sounding like rocks in a cement mixer.

"How are you? Feeling better?" His voice was clear and smooth; he'd been awake for a while, I guessed.

My vision cleared, and I was rewarded with the sight of his vibrant blue eyes and inviting lips. His hair stuck out in every direction, and I couldn't resist mussing it a little more. I could wake up like this every morning. The voice in my head whispered, *if only*, but I ignored it. "Yeah, I feel great."

The sun shone in his smile as he brushed a wayward lock of my hair out of my face and tucked it behind my ear. Remnants of our last conversation darted through my mind, but then the chime—the doorbell—rang again, and Jason swore.

He planted a soft peck on my forehead before climbing out of bed. "This'd better not be one of Mitch's pranks," he muttered.

After dragging a hand through his hair, he stretched his arms toward the ceiling, giving me full view of every sculpted muscle from his chin to the top of his very low-slung pajamas.

Realizing I was gawking, I quickly stretched too, thankful again for the t-shirt I'd borrowed last night. I tried not to think about what *my* hair looked like. "What time is it?" I asked and pushed the sheets down.

"Almost ten." He paused at the door and looked at my chest with greedy eyes. "That color suits you. Maybe you should consider transferring."

"What?" *Transferring?* I looked down. In the dark I hadn't realized I'd put on his navy blue Michigan t-shirt. The huge, gold M GO BLUE was plastered directly across my breasts. I rolled my eyes and received a sexy half-smile in return. The doorbell rang again, accompanied by a loud knocking this time.

"Coming," Jason yelled at the front door, then winked at me. "Stay here. I have plans for that shirt." He slipped out, grumbling about paying his brother back.

I snuck to the bedroom door and opened it a crack, just like I had last night.

Jason hiked his pajamas up after looking through the peephole. I could just make out surprise on his face as he undid the locks.

"Yes?" he said. I couldn't understand the low voice coming from the hall, but the tone sounded inquisitive. "Yes, she's here. Why? Did my brother put you up to this?" The speaker continued and Jason stiffened.

"Of course, please come in," he said.

Jason held the door open, and a man in a coat and tie entered, followed by a uniformed police officer. Jason waved them to the couches. "I'll get her, but it'll be a minute."

"Can she at least confirm she's here?" the man in the suit asked.

"Um," Jason stalled, probably trying to find a polite way to explain I wasn't completely dressed.

I pulled my hair back, hoping to look slightly less bedraggled, and stuck my head out the door. The rest of my scantily clad body stayed safely hidden. "Are you looking for me? I just need a minute to change. Okay?"

The man in the suit took a deep breath and nodded to his companion. "Yes, that's fine. Thank you, Ms. Williams. Please, take your time."

Jason said something else to the men, but I shut the door and grabbed my jeans off the floor. He came in as I was pulling a green *Mission Daily* T-shirt out of my bag.

"What's going on?" I asked.

"I don't know. Our visitors are from the sheriff's office. They only asked about you." He rubbed the stubble on his chin, his eyes locked on me in a pensive stare.

"Did they say why they needed to see me?" I turned my back to him and prepared to change shirts.

"No. The one guy seemed awfully worried about you, though. Do you know him?" he asked. Surprising me, Jason spun me around and caught me in a hug.

"No, I don't think so." I kissed his cheek and then tried to wiggle out of his arms. "I need to finish changing."

"May I have my shirt back?" he whispered, an impish gleam in his eye.

"Jason, there are two cops waiting for us in the next room," I said nervously. Even though the bedroom door was closed, I knew they'd be listening. The sunshine streaming through the thin curtains didn't help. It added to the feeling of being trapped in a very bright spotlight.

"*They* can't see you," he argued and lifted the bottom of my shirt.

I pushed it back down, embarrassed. Jason may have explored every inch of me in the dim firelight last night, but that didn't mean I wanted to be put on display like a pin-up calendar. "You must have other shirts in your suitcase," I said through my teeth.

"Yes, but none of them smell like this," he murmured, nuzzling my neck.

He nipped his way to my lips, and my grip on the fabric loosened. The shirt slipped a little higher.

In one last attempt to prevent him from ogling me, I slung my arms over his shoulders and smashed my chest against his. He continued to tug on the shirt, chuckling when the material rubbing across my breasts elicited a gasp.

"You're incorrigible, you know that?" I said, clinging to him. He held the shirt at my shoulders, waiting for me to give in. The feeling of his skin pressed against my bare chest was intoxicating.

"Yeah, I've heard that." He kissed my ear before whispering, "You know the longer you resist, the harder it gets." A warm hand slid down my bare back and pulled my hips into his, demonstrating his point.

"*Jason,*" I scolded, but Naughty Melissa was ready to give in.

Hearing a loud hiss from one of the cops' radios, I glanced at the door. My curiosity proved an effective defense against my lusty, naughty side. Only something newsworthy could've brought the police here—and I had a feeling they'd be storming the bedroom if I didn't show up soon.

"They're going to wonder what's taking so long," Jason warned.

Dirty mind reader!

"Fine," I grumbled and raised my arms.

He slipped the shirt over my head, grinning like a kid who'd just beaten his favorite video game.

"Happy now?" I snipped, spinning around and throwing on my bra.

"Very." He slapped my ass on his way to the closet.

I tried to tame my hair while watching him change, but I dropped the brush twice when he stripped off his pajama pants and donned a pair of form-fitting boxer-briefs.

"Now who's staring?" he teased, slowly buttoning up his jeans.

Before I could answer, my stomach growled.

Jason reached for the phone, leaving the top button undone. "I'm calling room service. What would you like for breakfast?"

"Whatever," I said, juggling my brush a third time. "I'm pretty easy." After the words left my lips, I froze.

Jason snorted, but didn't say anything.

"May I *please* have some coffee?" I asked, then sprinted into the bathroom. The door closed behind me before he could answer.

I had better luck brushing my hair alone and tied it up in a simple ponytail. Jason's shaving kit was open on the counter. His toothbrush stuck out of the case, tempting me. I couldn't bring myself to pick it up, reaching instead for the toothpaste next to it. I squeezed a dab onto my finger and ran it around my mouth. I replaced the tube and thought about checking out what else was in his kit.

My mother's stern voice rang in my mental ears. *Would you want him to look through your toiletries?*

With my shoulders set in a guilty slump, I opened the bathroom door.

Jason and I swapped places, and while he cleaned up, I made a pass around the room to collect my clothes. I crammed everything into my bag, thinking about our visitors. Why would they be looking for me? My mother didn't know I was still in L.A., so she couldn't have sent them. *Has something happened to my car? Who else knows I'm here and not in Santa Lucia?*

Questions raced through my brain like wild horses as I zipped open the side pocket of my bag. Next to my laptop was a pad of paper, which I snagged along with a couple of pens and my media pass from last week's baseball game. A little credibility might come in handy.

Jason, dressed in the shirt I'd just been wearing, reappeared. "I guess we shhh—"

The last word hung on his lips as his mouth fell open. He leaned toward me, staring intently at my face.

"What?" I rubbed my eyes, feeling around for what must be a Volkswagen-sized blob of sleepy goo stuck somewhere. "Did I get it?"

"Get it?" Jason blinked furiously. "No, it's not that. You're fine." He gently tilted my face toward the windows. "I could've sworn your eyes were blue."

"Oh, that." Relieved, I smiled. "My eyes like to mimic my shirt. I suppose they're technically hazel, but they vary quite a bit." My grin widened. For once, I'd caught him off guard. "Weird, I know."

He held a hand in front of my nose, testing my explanation, I guessed. "No, definitely not weird." His fingers returned to my chin. "More like incredible," he said, rekindling the fire that made my whole body sizzle.

"We really should go," I whispered.

He nodded slowly, gave me a soft kiss, then opened the bedroom door.

I almost turned right back around when I saw the two cops eyeing the nearly untouched fondue from last night. Of course they knew what'd happened—the fondue told them nothing my initial disheveled greeting hadn't already revealed. *Get over it, Melissa. You're an adult, after all.*

Jason invited them to sit, offering them the nearest couch.

"Good morning," I said a little too jovially. I sat on the adjacent couch and set the pad on my lap. Jason joined me, resting his hand on the back of my neck.

"Good morning, Ms. Williams," the suit said. "I'm Detective Clark, and this is Officer Rodriguez. We're from the L.A. County Sheriff's office. We're investigating an incident that occurred on the premises last night. Your car was found in the lower parking lot this morning, and since you're not a registered guest, we became concerned for your safety."

During his speech, the detective discreetly examined us, taking in my appearance from head to toe before giving Jason the onceover. Officer Rodriguez hardly gave me a second look—he busied himself inspecting Jason's hands.

Swallowing a number of snide comments, I chose a more polite reply. "Thank you, Detective, and as you can see, I'm fine. What happened?"

He ignored my question. "We're interviewing everyone who was at the reception last night. Beth Miller mentioned you might be in the company of Mr. McAlister. Have you been together all night?" His eyes locked onto Jason's. It was clear I was no longer the subject of the conversation.

I tried not to blush as I answered. There was obviously more than voyeuristic curiosity in his question. "Yes, I have, Detective. Is that of particular importance?" I asked. My pen hovered over my paper.

Detective Clark looked at the notebook in my lap and frowned at the paper screaming PRESS sticking out from under it. "May I?" he asked, motioning for the old pass. He looked at it closely before handing it back. "You're a reporter?"

"Yes. Can you please tell us what's going on? What is it about Jason that has you so interested?" I wouldn't let him worm away again.

Detective Clark returned my stare, undaunted, but the other officer shifted in his seat. After a long minute, the detective tilted his head to one side and evaluated me again, pursing his lips. I assume I passed muster, because as he straightened back up, the tiniest hint of a smile crossed his lips before he answered.

"Early this morning, a woman was found dead in the garden near the ballroom. She was present at the reception for your brother, Mr. McAlister," the detective said evenly.

Jason inhaled sharply.

My heart skipped a beat, and I swallowed, unable to stop the next thought. *A murder is big news.*

"Who was the victim, Detective?" Jason asked.

I bit my lip, guilty for my callous thoughts. What if it was one of my friends? Beth was okay, but what about Linda? Or…Ann?

The detective nodded at Officer Rodriguez, who opened the folder he'd been carrying. "Ms. Vanessa Trammell. Do you either of you know her?" Rodriguez removed a sheet from the file and passed it to me.

The page contained a fax copy of a driver's license. The grainy enlargement of the photo distorted her features, but there was no mistaking the blond hair and big smile of the wedding liaison.

I looked back at Jason and held up the paper.

His jaw fell slack as he stared. "Oh, no," he breathed.

"So you *did* know her?" Officer Rodriguez accused.

"No, not really. She worked for the hotel. She is…*was*…the wedding coordinator." Jason's voice was hollow, distant. He had to be thinking what I was—that maybe we could have done something to prevent whatever happened to her.

Whatever Ron did to her.

No, don't jump the gun. The guy may have been a creep, but that didn't mean he was a killer.

"Ms. Williams?" the officer asked impatiently.

"No, I didn't know her either, but she was working at the reception. How did she die?"

The detective hadn't moved, cautiously gauging our reactions. "She was strangled."

Ron's skinny tie would have made an excellent murder weapon, and he definitely had the strength to strangle someone. "I'll have to wait with you," he'd said to her, in the same eerie, possessive voice he'd used with me—and now she was dead. *Had she taken my place?*

Jason must have sensed my horror, because he brushed his lips against my hair. "You're safe here," he whispered.

I nodded, and the detective's stare intensified.

"Do you have any suspects in custody yet?" I asked. *Please say yes.*

"We have suspects, yes," the detective said, returning his gaze to Jason.

"Mr. McAlister, did you wear a black tuxedo yesterday?" Officer Rodriguez asked, reaching for the photo in my hands.

"What?" I blurted. The question caught me by surprise—they didn't think Jason was involved, did they?

Jason didn't catch the implication. "Yes, I did. All the groomsmen, the groom, and both fathers did," he said.

"Did you wear a bow tie?" Detective Clark queried. Shock registered in Jason's eyes when he realized "suspects" included him.

Ron's tie must not have been the one found.

Jason's voice became defensive and tight, and the color drained from his face. "None of us could have—" he started.

The detective held up his hand dismissively. "May we see it, please?"

"Of course." Jason's jacket had fallen off the back of the couch, and he walked around to pick it up.

Officer Rodriguez fingered the speaker-mic clipped to his shoulder, clicking it three times. I recognized the signal—he was warning someone.

I put my hand over my mouth. There had to be more cops outside, preparing to stop anyone who stepped out of our hotel room. They were afraid Jason might run. The detective's brow wrinkled. "Is there a problem, Ms. Williams?"

I shook my head once, reluctant to explain how I knew what was going on. "Have you talked to all the other groomsmen already?"

"Almost," he said, then directed his attention behind me.

"Well, here's *my* tie," Jason said and stuck his hand into the inner pocket of his jacket. He felt around, frowned, then swiftly went through his other pockets. His face faded to a snowy white when his hand came up empty time and again.

"I took it off during the reception and put it in this pocket." Jason pointed at the empty jacket, his eyes wide. "It's…it's…gone. I…I don't know what happened to it," he stammered.

"Have a seat, Mr. McAlister," the detective commanded.

Jason slumped back down next to me. My hand found his knee and squeezed it, trying to reassure him.

I looked directly into the detective's eyes. "Jason hasn't left my presence for at least the last fourteen hours—the hotel security system should be able to prove that," I said, matching the detective's tone. "He has nothing to do with this."

Detective Clark's guarded expression didn't change. "I'm not accusing anyone, Ms. Williams. I'm just trying to sort out the facts. When was the last time either of you saw Ms. Trammell?"

I shot him a disbelieving glare, but maintained my professional demeanor. Jason's color had started to return, but he didn't look like he could speak.

"*We* saw her at about ten thirty last night when we left the reception together and walked to this hotel room," I answered. "She was in the parking lot with a man named Ron. He's the one you need to question."

"What were they doing?" Officer Rodriguez asked.

"He said his car wouldn't start. I heard Ms. Trammell offer to call him a tow truck."

Jason nodded in agreement. At the mention of Ron's name, he put his arm around me.

I wondered if the whole story about Ron's car was just a setup. Would he have used the same ploy on me?

"You didn't see anything else?" the officer asked.

"No."

Jason shook his head, mirroring my denial.

Detective Clark had been taking notes while the officer questioned us. "How do you know his name is Ron?" he asked.

I took a breath, and Jason's grip on me tightened. "Earlier in the evening, Ron approached me and asked if I would join him outside. When I said no, he wouldn't leave, and my friends confronted him. Ron grabbed my hand and probably would have broken it, if not for Jason." I turned my right hand over, lightly touching the faint marks on the back.

"Can you describe him?"

As Jason detailed the plain man with greasy hair and mud brown eyes, things began to fall into place: Jason had twisted Ron's arm, humiliating him; somehow Ron had gotten Jason's tie to implicate him as revenge. But when could he have taken the tie? Without that crucial detail, convincing the cops would be difficult, if not impossible.

I doodled the word FRAMED on my notepad.

"You think this Ron took Mr. McAlister's tie to cast suspicion on him?" the detective asked, reading my notes.

"Maybe. Ron may have seen us in the garden, Jason."

Jason's eyes narrowed.

"What happened in the garden?" the detective asked.

"We talked, and I kissed Melissa," Jason said, without inflection.

You kissed me, all right. I picked at the edge of my notepad, trying not to indulge in the memory. Jason rested his cheek against my hair.

"Have you two known each other long?" the detective asked. His keen eye hadn't missed a single detail of our interaction.

"We met online about nine months ago," Jason answered.

I didn't look at him. What he said was true, though misleading.

"I see," was the reply.

The two men spoke quietly together, and Detective Clark took the file and flipped through it. As he did, photos of the crime scene and the ballroom flashed by.

"May I see those?" I asked.

Officer Rodriguez didn't try to hide his condescending snort. "Ms. Williams, these photos are very graphic. You really don't want to see them," he said.

My gaze turned to the uniformed officer, and I sat a little taller. "Officer, I've been privy to police photos since I was ten years old. There's nothing in those I haven't seen before," I said sharply.

The two men looked curiously at me, and I sighed.

"My father was a police officer," I said, bracing myself for the next question.

Officer Rodriguez opened his mouth, but the detective held up his hand. He seemed to nod to himself, confirming a supposition he'd made, perhaps. His voice was soft and placating. "You're Brad Williams' daughter?"

"Yes," I replied, not totally surprised he knew. Over a thousand cops had attended Dad's funeral. The detective must have been there too—that would explain his extra concern about my welfare. Both Officer Rodriguez and Jason looked at me, but my eyes didn't budge from Detective Clark.

"Captain Brad Williams was a highway patrol officer in Northern California. He died protecting a woman and her child from an abusive husband five years ago," he said, saving me from having to explain.

Had it really been five years? My heart lurched, remembering that terrible day.

"We're sorry, Mrs. Williams," the officer had said. Mom had whispered "Brad" before she'd fainted, collapsing in my arms.

The detective's professional façade fell, and he smiled, revealing a kind, caring man behind the shield. I guessed he was a father, probably a good one.

"I doubt you remember, but I stood behind you at the funeral," Detective Clark said. "Your dad and I met several times at various conventions and seminars and became friends. We managed to play golf together at a couple of them, and shared many stories about our families. You're a couple of years older than my daughter. We'd hoped to get the two of you together one day," he added, smiling again. "Your father was a good man and a true hero."

"Thank you, Detective. If my father golfed with you, then you must've been important to him. He was very selective about the cops he'd take out on the links."

Dad's face appeared in my mind's eye. "Most cops can't slow down enough to enjoy the game," he used to say. I gulped, trying to get rid of the baseball-sized lump in my throat. Forcing the conversation back to the present, I held my hand out to the detective. "May I please look at the photos? They might jog my memory about last night."

Detective Clark took one more searching look at me and passed me the file. "This is strictly off the record, Ms. Williams," he said.

"Absolutely."

I was much more interested in clearing Jason of any suspicion than writing an article. I looked back at him before digging into the file. He'd recovered from the implied accusations, but I wasn't sure if he was up for viewing photos of a dead body.

"You want to see if room service is here yet?" I asked, giving him an out.

"No, I'm fine," he said bravely, then leaned down to my ear. "Thanks, though," he whispered, and I opened the file.

The first glossy paper showed the body of Vanessa Trammell splayed out on the grass. I recognized her green satin dress, but one of her matching green shoes had fallen off. It sat on the ground nearby. Piled next to her was a gold scarf—what she must have been wearing in the parking lot. Her head was turned to the side, her pale hair pushed back to reveal her purple throat. Hanging limply on her shoulder was one end of a black bow tie.

I examined the photo carefully, noting the blotchy water stains on her clothes before moving on. The next shot was a close up of Ms. Trammell's head. Her hair had been soaked, just like her dress, and was bunched into ringlets, some stuck to her forehead and ear. A few stringy locks clung to her neck, but the rest was fanned out on the grass. Her face looked undamaged, but her makeup was a streaky mess. As I inspected the numerous bruises around her neck, the questions multiplied in my mind.

"Detective, what was the approximate time of death?"

Officer Rodriguez cleared his throat loudly, and Detective Clark adjusted his tie before answering, still a little wary, I guessed. "The initial estimate is between midnight and three a.m."

"The sprinklers came on at three?" I asked and looked up at the detective. The fog was damp, but the body had been soaked.

Officer Rodriguez's mouth fell open.

"Yes. What else do you see?" Detective Clark asked with a proud smile.

"Well, looking at the bruising, it's obvious she wasn't strangled with the tie," I said, pointing to the set of parallel purple lines below her ear.

The detective stroked his chin. "You share your father's keen eye, I see."

I didn't reply. Instead, I flipped through the other photos, most of them different views of the body.

"No DNA evidence?" Jason asked.

Detective Clark shook his head. "Not so far. We won't know until the autopsy, but there are no obvious signs of sexual assault."

"The sprinklers washed away the blood," I murmured, my stomach churning. Only one faint stain remained near the hem of Vanessa Trammell's dress.

Jason's fingers curled into a tight fist next to me.

The next set of photos documented the ballroom. Racks of chairs separated the empty tables, and carts of dirty dishes lined the walls. My eyes were drawn to the frosting covering the plates. I flipped to another view showing the corner of the room where the cake had been.

"The cake cutting—that's when he took the tie," I said suddenly, turning to Jason. "You'd just put your tie in your jacket, and I set down my purse to help you with the button, then we went to watch them cut…" My voice trailed off. My purse had been left on the table while we watched Mitch and Ann. If Ron had searched the jacket, had he been through my purse too?

Detective Clark didn't miss a beat. "Is your purse here, Ms. Williams?" I nodded slowly. "Can you get it? You'll understand you need to touch it as little as possible. Rodriguez?"

"Fingerprint kit, right." Officer Rodriguez headed out the door.

I numbly walked to the bedroom. My tiny purse was next to my bag, and I picked up the strap with two fingers and carried it to the living room. I set it on the bar in front of Jason and Detective Clark.

"Have you handled anything in your purse since the cake cutting last night?" the detective asked.

"Only my car keys. They're in the outside pocket. I don't think I've even opened the main compartment since dinner," I said.

"So you don't know if anything's missing?"

"No. There isn't much in there." As I ticked off the contents in my head, I froze.

Jason looked at me, voicing my thoughts. "Your ID is inside, isn't it?" he whispered and wound his arms around me.

"My driver's license…*MY MOTHER!*" I screamed. My license listed Mom's address. Jason's arms tightened as terror washed through me.

"Where does your mother live, Ms. Williams?" The detective handed me his small notebook and a pen.

My pulse took off double-time at the thought of Mom being in danger. "San Jose," I said and quickly jotted down the address. It was only a six-hour drive from here. *Ron could already be there.* My hand flew toward my purse—and my cell phone. The detective caught me, causing the knots in my stomach to claw their way up my throat.

"Please, wait just a few minutes, Ms. Williams. Then you can have your purse back. I'll call the San Jose PD right now."

The shakes took over as I tried to get a handle on my fear. The thought of Ron anywhere near my mother…I couldn't lose her too. "I have to warn her," I cried, fighting back the helplessness that twisted in my gut.

Once again, Jason came to my rescue. "Use my phone, Melissa. Come on."

Before he led me to the bedroom he glanced at the detective. He nodded, his phone pressed against his ear.

We entered the room and Jason's face fell. His bedside table was empty. He scanned the room, muttering "Oh yeah" before releasing me and picking his pants up off the floor. He extracted his phone and handed it to me, giving me a quick kiss on the forehead. "I'm sure she's fine. Try not to worry," he said, rubbing my back slowly. The doorbell rang again, and Jason released me. "I'll give you some privacy, but I'll be right outside if you need me."

"Thank you, for everything," I said, grateful for his calm presence. He caught my hand, kissed it, and stepped out, not quite closing the door behind him.

It took me two tries to dial the number, my fingers were shaking so hard. One ring…two…three…I chewed my lip harder with each unanswered jingle. By the time the answering machine picked up, I could taste blood.

Hearing Mom's recorded voice, I panicked. "Mom, you need turn on the alarm—no, get out of the house and go next door to Kathy's…then call me. Please, I need to talk to you. There's a man who might be looking for me…he's dangerous. Just call me from Kathy's as soon as you get this message, Mom. I have to—"

Beeeep.

The machine cut me off and hung up. I covered my mouth, swallowing back the fear. *It was just the timer.* I knew Mom hated long messages, but what if she *couldn't* answer the phone?

I dialed frantically again, her cell this time. A writer for a West Coast travel magazine, Mom did most of her work from home, but her research took her all over. As I listened to more nerve-racking ringing, I tried to remember if she had any trips planned this week. She'd mentioned looking forward to seeing me, but I couldn't remember her saying anything about going anywhere.

The ringing stopped with a business-like "Bev Williams."

I nearly collapsed with relief. "Mom, it's me."

She definitely wasn't at the house; noisy conversation filled the silence after my frantic greeting.

"Melissa? Where are you?" she asked.

I remembered I wasn't calling from my phone, and for a split second I wondered what the area code for Ann Arbor, Michigan, was. As if I didn't have enough to think about.

"I'm still in L.A., heading up to Santa Lucia in a little while. I'm using my friend's phone," I explained.

"Your friend's phone? Why? How was the wedding?" she asked. She sounded distracted.

"Um, my battery died. The wedding was fine. Where *are* you?" Far from home, I hoped.

The noise got louder. Her office was never this busy, especially not on a Sunday. But she was safe.

"Oh, I meant to call you from the car. I'm at the airport. This morning I got a call from Jack; he's down with the flu and needs me to fill in at the Reno Rodeo, of all things. I'm about to jump on a plane. I'll be there for a week, so you'll have the house to yourself."

Thank goodness. "That's great, Mom. Stay away from the business end of the horses, okay?" The knot in my throat finally dissolved.

She laughed. "You're the expert. Hey, maybe you could come join me for a day or two. I'm supposed to have a big room, and I could really use your help getting the lowdown on the whole rodeo thing."

I took a deep breath and let it out slowly, hoping to calm my racing pulse. She was safe. There was no way Ron would know where she was.

My sense of humor even returned. "Only if I get credited, Mom. I thought there were rules about freelancers at the magazine."

"I'll have a talk with my editor and see what I can do. I'll call you tonight. You're coming home today, right?" She spoke quickly, and I heard a muffled "sorry" on her end. She must be about to board. The story of the murder would have to wait.

"Actually, Mom, I remembered a few things I have to do in Santa Lucia, so I'm going to stay down here a little while longer. I'll give you a call before I head home." The thought of hiding in my empty apartment, alone, sent a shiver down my spine.

There was one more thing I had to tell her. "Can you do me a favor, Mom? Please call me before you go back home, okay? Someone rifled through my purse, and I'm afraid they might have your address."

"Melissa, how many times have I told you to keep your purse with you? Was anything stolen?" my mother scolded, reducing me to a five-year-old.

I rolled my eyes in response. "No, I don't think so. I'll tell you all about it tonight."

A loud voice in the background called for group A to board the plane. "Have a safe trip, okay, Mom?" Once she was safely in Reno, I'd tell her what really happened.

"You too, honey. Be careful. I'll talk to you later. Love you," she said.

"Love you too, Mom." I looked down at the phone and pressed END. Behind the numbers on Jason's display was a photo of palm trees and sand—a memory of home, maybe? In the midst of all this chaos, it only reminded me how much I was going to miss him.

Adding insult to injury, the phone beeped and popped up a text:

AA 1624 will be departing at gate…

I closed the phone. There wasn't any reason to read on; I'd already gotten the message: my time with Jason was almost up.

Shutting out my sorrow, I walked back to the living room. Jason met me with a plate of pancakes covered in strawberries. "You have a message," I said.

"It can wait." Jason pocketed his phone without looking at it. "Is your mom all right?"

"Yes, she's fine." I caught Detective Clark's eye. "She's boarding a flight to Reno as we speak. She'll be gone for a week. The house is empty."

He nodded. "SJPD will be keeping close tabs on her house, in case anyone suspicious shows up. Hopefully we'll have a suspect in custody long before she gets home." He turned back to the bar where Officer Rodriguez had emptied my purse and was busy coating the contents with fine black powder.

I sat down on the couch next to Jason and cautiously forked a strawberry. My stomach had quieted after learning Mom was all right, but eating didn't seem very appealing.

"Didn't I choose well?" Jason asked. "Would you rather have eggs?" He lifted a silver dome covering another plate on the coffee table, revealing a fluffy pile of yellow.

"No, this is fine." I shoved the strawberry in my mouth, surprised when my stomach growled with gratitude. The rest of the pancakes disappeared quickly after that.

I poured myself a second cup of coffee and checked the officers bent over the bar, inspecting my credit card. "How's it going, Detective?"

"We have several clear prints. When you've finished your breakfast, we'll need to get your fingerprints for comparison. I'd also like you to inspect the contents to see if anything's missing," he said.

I grabbed a piece of bacon and nodded.

"I'll also need your fingerprints, Mr. McAlister," he added.

"That's fine," Jason said, finishing his breakfast. "Do you really think Melissa or her mother might be in danger?" he asked.

"Until we process the evidence, it's hard to say. But this case bears a striking resemblance to another recent homicide in L.A. County. The two may be related." The detective looked at me. "I'd appreciate you not mentioning that in your article, Ms. Williams."

The idea of writing about the murder had completely lost its appeal. "Don't worry, Detective, I'm a little too close to this story to report it." I wiped my hands on a napkin and walked over to the bar.

Officer Rodriguez snapped off his rubber gloves and smiled apologetically. "All finished. Sorry about the mess." He'd brushed away most of the black fingerprint powder, but a small, dark cloud still floated above my things. "You really don't keep much in your purse, do you?"

"This is my travel purse. Necessities only."

Rodriguez raised his eyebrows.

"Yes, my regular one is bigger." We shared a smile and then I found a paper towel under the bar to clean off my few belongings.

"Is everything there?" Detective Clark asked.

I surveyed the collection and squinted my eyes. Methodically, I reloaded my tiny purse. Money, credit cards, and license went in first; those were all in order. Makeup next…fine. Tissues, cell phone, keys. *What isn't here?*

"It feels like something's missing, but I can't figure out what it could be. Do you have a card, Detective, so I can contact you if it comes to me?"

He promptly fished two business cards out of his pocket and handed one to me and the other to Jason. "Call me at any time. My cell number is at the bottom. I think the only other thing we need is for you two to come down to the office and sit with the sketch artist. We're trying to get the wedding photographer's shots, but it'll take time to sort through them all."

"That's fine, Detective, whatever we can do to…" Jason stopped when I threw my hands up and furiously dove back into my purse. "What is it?" he asked.

I held up one finger. Finding my cell phone, I flipped it open and started madly punching buttons. I paused, checked the detective's card, then hit SEND.

"I have something even better," I said and proudly handed the phone to the detective. "Meet Ron."

"Why do you have *him* on your phone, Melissa?" Jason stared at me in shock.

"Beth took my picture before the wedding. I didn't know it, but Ron was standing right behind to me." Ron and his eighties fashion sense looked as comical as ever in the shot, but I stifled my snicker, remembering he'd probably ended a young woman's life with his bare hands. "I literally bumped into him after this was taken."

"Can you send me that photo, Ms. Williams?" Detective Clark asked.

I offered him a sly grin. "I just did."

Ten

We spent the next hour separated, each of us assigned a cop. While I repeated my story and Detective Clark filled out a statement form, Jason let Officer Rodriguez fingerprint him and search his jacket. By the time I'd read and signed my form, Jason had washed off his inky fingers, and we switched places.

Once my prints were completed, Detective Clark dismissed Officer Rodriguez and I cleaned up. When I returned the paperwork was gone, and the detective stood by the door reading over his notes. He'd just closed his notepad when the phone next to the couch rang.

"Yes?" Jason answered. "No, we haven't." He covered the receiver and looked at me. "What time is it?"

"Twelve thirty-eight," Detective Clark answered before I could find a clock.

Jason frowned and tilted the phone back up. "Yes, I know when check-out is, but…we *can* vacate the room…we're not *that* late!" he snapped. "I'd *love* to talk to the manager."

"What's wrong?" I mouthed.

With a huff he put the phone against his chest. "Checkout time was noon. They want to charge me for an extra night."

"Maybe I should have a word with them," Detective Clark offered, holding out his hand.

Jason passed him the receiver. "That'd be great, thanks."

The call didn't last long once the detective took over. After some terse words and a few not-so-veiled threats, he hung up. "The manager apologized for interrupting and agreed that checking out before two o'clock would be unreasonable."

"Did I hear you say the media could've gotten wind he was throwing key witnesses out of his hotel?" I asked.

"You *are* a reporter," Detective Clark said with a quick wink.

Jason guffawed. "Nice."

"I should be going. When we ID the prints, I'll call you, Ms. Williams."

I caught his hand, holding it between mine rather than shaking it. "Melissa, please. Thanks for everything, Detective."

"You're very welcome. Tell your mom Tim Clark says hello." Detective Clark—Tim—pointed at Jason. "Take care," he said with more emphasis than I would've expected.

Jason nodded, his face grave, and Detective Clark left without another word.

I looked at Jason. "What was that about?"

"Nothing," he said, but I wasn't convinced. He avoided my gaze, busying himself by stacking up our breakfast dishes.

Rather than argue I pushed the curtains open, revealing the view I'd imagined last night. The nocturnal fog had burned away, leaving a perfectly clear outline of the island rising above its watery confines. The sparkling azure ocean reminded me of Jason's brilliant eyes and the twinkle that accompanied his breathtaking smile. My mood turned a darker shade of blue as our final minutes ticked away.

I didn't hear Jason come up behind me, and I jumped when he spoke.

"Hey, come outside with me for a minute," he said and took my hand. The glass in front of me slid open, and he led me to a padded chaise on the balcony. He pulled me onto his lap, and we lay together, bathed in the bright sunshine.

"How are you?" he asked softly.

"I'm okay," I lied.

Jason didn't say anything, but his arms tightened around me.

Can he feel me coming apart? No more lies. "This wasn't exactly how I'd planned to spend the morning with you," I said. My breathing became erratic. "When do you…?" The rest of the question caught in my throat. In minutes he'd be gone.

Jason found one of my hands and began working his magic, rubbing my sweaty palm. "We need to talk about that. I'm not ready to let you go, and after this morning, I don't think you should be alone—especially if you're going to your mom's house."

His parental-sounding concern didn't elicit my inner teenager this time. Instead of rebellion, I was consumed with guilt. Over and over he'd had to save me, like I was a little child unable to take care of myself. That wasn't the only reason for the guilt, though. The truth was I *liked* being his damsel in distress. But I had to let him go, free from worry.

"I'm not going all the way north. I'll stay in Santa Lucia until Mom gets back. There wasn't anything in my purse with that address on it, so I'll be safe. You heard the detective—now that they know who to look for, Ron's days are numbered." I tried to hide my sorrow by playing with one of his belt loops. "When's your flight?"

"Not until Friday."

What? No, I can't have heard him right. "Friday? I thought you had to get back today." I fought back the dangerous hope that wound its way through me. If one day could lead to a week, what would a week lead to? *No, end it now. It'll only hurt more later.*

"I was thinking of checking out the Central Coast. Do you think you could recommend a good spot to stay?" He released my hand and traced my jaw instead, bringing to life the desire that had been forgotten in the stress of the morning.

He's leaving—no matter what. He has *to leave.* "But your flight! Beth said you were going home today."

"Since Mitch isn't around, and my summer classes don't start for another week, the plan was to return to Ann Arbor early. *That* plan has definitely lost its appeal," Jason said, twirling a lock of my hair around his finger.

No, I'm still dreaming. Just as I moved to pinch myself, he kissed my neck, proving I *was* awake…in more ways than one.

Nervous Melissa tried one last time. "But you can't change your reservation now—they'll charge you for it."

"Don't be ridiculous. It's already done." A smile danced in his tone.

"That's why it took you so long to wash up after the fingerprints." The hope spread like wildfire, and a completely unreasonable image of Jason meeting my mother flickered through my mind.

I jiggled as he laughed behind me. "Not much gets past you, does it?" He returned to caressing my neck with his lips. "I almost changed it yesterday," he murmured against my skin.

"Yesterday? Why?"

Jason laughed again at my confusion. "Why do you think? A certain lovely woman caught my eye at the wedding, and I thought maybe I'd see if she was available for dinner at a later date."

He thought about changing his flight after only seeing *me?* During the wedding, he'd been unable to keep his eyes off me—was that why? Apparently I wasn't quite as invisible as I thought.

"But you looked shocked when you heard Todd call my name after the ceremony."

"You *were* there!" he exclaimed. "I told you I wanted to meet you. I can't believe you snuck out before I caught you." He raised his head from my skin, whispering in my ear instead. "Your emails were very sexy, you know? Very…thought provoking."

"Right." My innuendo was anything but thoughtful. "Didn't Mitch tell you what I looked like?"

Jason played with my ponytail as if it was something he did every day. "No. Mitch wasn't particularly helpful. His take was that if I was seriously interested, I should move back to California." He shifted so his arms encircled me again. "He left me to figure out who you were on my own. It wasn't until the reception I found out such wit and intelligence resided in the irresistible woman I have in my arms."

His voice mixed with the sunshine pouring down on me, and I sighed contentedly.

Jason's hands stilled. "So you didn't answer my question. May I join you for a few days?"

Friday! I lay back, noting how my head fit perfectly on his shoulder as my fantasy took a new twist, showing me the immediate future this time. Jason in my car…checking out Poly…seeing my desk at the *Daily*. Then I remembered my vacant apartment, and the vision became comical.

"That would be great, but my apartment is just about empty. I don't even have a TV."

His fingers moved to my ear and circled it, following the ridges and valleys and sending chills through me in the midday heat. "That's all right. I think we can find some other ways to entertain ourselves."

I flopped over and pulled myself across his body in search of his lips. With a quiet moan I melted into him, our tongues engaging in an erotic game of cat and mouse. *Five more days!* My naughty side rejoiced, throwing even more fervor into the kiss.

I lifted my face from Jason's as his hands wandered down my chest. "We really should go. We have a long drive ahead of us," I said, catching his fingers over my heart. "Unless you *do* want to pay for another night…"

His lower lip popped out, tempting me anew, but I managed to resist kissing his pout away.

"I guess you're right," he sighed, wiggling his fingers against my sternum.

I slapped his shoulder playfully before pulling him up off the chaise.

It took longer to check out than to pack. After his previous faux pas, the manager fell over himself to take care of Jason's tie-less tuxedo until Mr. McAlister could pick it up. Jason politely cut off the man's groveling with an assurance that we had only good things to say about the hotel, should anyone ask. Refusing the bellboy's offer of help, we made a run for the door.

Without even a grunt, Jason hoisted his huge suitcase into my car. That, combined with his backpack and my computer bag, completely filled the tiny trunk. Giddy with excitement, I buckled up, and we hit the road.

I caught myself checking out Jason for the twentieth time since putting the car in drive. Lounging in the passenger seat next to me, he seemed unaware of how his presence skewed my view of the world. With him next to me, everything seemed brighter, clearer. Everything seemed right. Yup, I was in deep, deep trouble.

Poor me. I suppressed a giggle and peeked at Jason again. Twenty-one…

He adjusted the seat, sliding all the way back and reclining a bit to make more room for his long legs. After surveying the dash, he turned on the radio and was greeted with loud static.

"May I?" he asked.

"Sure, knock yourself out."

He fiddled with the buttons, tuning through various stations, looking for…I didn't know what. The man I'd been so intimate with was still largely a mystery. With four hours of driving ahead of us, I'd definitely remedy that situation.

"How's this?" Jason asked. I gave him a thumbs up as Sammy Hagar belted out *I Can't Drive 55*. "What kind of music do you usually listen to?" he asked, beating me to the punch.

I popped open a compartment in the console between us, displaying the few CDs I kept in the car. "Mostly rock, some pop, a little alternative…there's more on my MP3 player. Radio stations in Santa Lucia are few and far between, so I have to make do." He extracted a colorful jewel case and began inspecting the cover. I guess he approved, but I couldn't tell for sure.

"We're doing this completely backward, aren't we?" I said.

He looked up, scowling. "Backward?"

"Yes. Don't people usually sleep together *after* they know things about each other like, oh, what kind of music they enjoy…or what they're allergic to…or whether or not they get carsick?" I pursed my lips.

Jason's eyes sparkled, and he blurted, "*Carsick?!*" He put his hand over his mouth and puffed his cheeks dramatically. The fake puking sounds he made were overcome by raucous laughter when I snorted loudly trying to contain my own mirth. The uninhibited happiness in his laugh was as addicting as any narcotic, though I couldn't imagine any drug giving me such complete pleasure. I could fly on his brand of intoxication for a very long time. Already I was plotting how to get my next fix.

Catching his breath, his voice took a more serious tone. "You're right, though; we did kind of rush through the formalities. How about we rewind a bit and try a more traditional approach?"

Skeptical, I briefly took my eyes off the road to inspect his face. The humor had been replaced with a thoughtful stare.

"What'd you have in mind, exactly?"

"How about this: let's spend some time getting to know each other, pretending we just met. I could even take you out on a real date—maybe dinner and a movie? Start over again, the normal way," he said.

"Hmmm. Normal, huh? I'll have to think about that."

I took the ramp onto the freeway and considered his proposal. Baring my body to Jason had been a stretch, but baring my soul? That was another matter. I could already feel the connection between us strengthening, which would make breaking it that much harder. But we couldn't spend days together without getting to know each other; that'd be ridiculous. We'd have to talk and probably find something to do—besides repeating last night's activities—during the daylight hours, at least.

"After our date, there will be sex, of course," he said matter-of-factly, sliding his hand up my leg.

"How do you do that?" I asked. I grabbed his fingers and moved his hand to the arm rest. His touch was not conducive to my keeping the car in just one lane of the busy freeway.

"Do what?" He brought my hand to his lips and kissed it gently.

"Read my mind. Are my thoughts tattooed to my forehead or something?" The words came out louder than I'd intended, echoing back to me in the confined space.

Jason chuckled. "Thinking about sex again? We must be on the same wavelength."

I shook my head. "Never mind."

His shoulders slumped. "I'm sorry. You must think sex is all I think about." He turned away to stare at the urban sprawl flying past us.

"It's not?" I teased, but he didn't laugh. "Don't be sorry, I, uh, *was* thinking about…you know. Is it hot in here?" I flipped on the air conditioner, and he finally returned my sidelong glances. "It's just that you seem to pick the thoughts right out of my head pretty much whenever you want. I need to be more careful what I think about, I guess," I said. I squeezed his knee, and he ran a finger over my knuckles in response.

"I had no idea. We really *do* think alike," he said, seeming almost in awe.

The intensity in his words set butterflies loose in my stomach. Clearing my throat, I said, "So your idea is to get to know each other before we have another round of amazing sex. Does that cover it?" I wondered if he would classify what we did last night as "amazing" too.

Jason turned back to me, smiling. "Precisely. Are you interested?"

"Okay, but I think we need some ground rules. Is kissing allowed before this 'real' date?" *I sure hope so. His kisses are…mmmm…*

Jason sat back and pinched his bottom lip, lost in thought. How *I* wanted to pinch his lips—with mine.

"Well, I did kiss you when we were first introduced." He brushed his fingertip across the exact spot on my cheek.

"You sure did." I couldn't believe he remembered.

"You had that same beautiful surprise on your face. That settles it. Kissing is definitely allowed." He moved his warm hand to mine, which was still resting on his knee. "I'm not sure I could give that up anyway," he said. "Hugging and handholding are also acceptable."

"Acceptable? That's an understatement." I smirked. "But there's a line for touching, right?" I started to move our joined hands up his leg, trying to find out exactly where that line was. And to think I'd only met Jason twenty-four hours ago…

He tightened his grip as my fingers neared the top of his thigh. "Uh, yeah," he squeaked. He very deliberately moved my hand back to the steering wheel. "I'm thinking until our date things should stay PG-13." He took a deep breath and folded his hands in his lap. "Can Naughty Melissa handle that?"

I kept my eyes forward, trying not to dwell on the word *handle*. "Uh, I think so. I'll pretend Mom's in the room with us. So…when is this date? Not tonight, I assume. We'll be lucky to make it to Santa Lucia by dinner."

Jason nodded. "Okay, let's not make this too hard on ourselves. To-morrow night?"

I grinned at him. "You read my mind."

His teeth flashed as he returned my smile and settled back into his seat. With the rules agreed upon and time on our hands, I decided to start the get-to-know-you ball rolling.

"So, what kind of music do *you* like, Jason?"

He winked and rubbed his hands together, ready to play our game. "I like a little bit of everything—rock, classical, pop, but…" He paused and looked away shyly.

"Yes?" His self-consciousness made him even more attractive. Faint pink colored his sun-kissed cheek. I gripped the steering wheel a little tighter and forced my eyes back to the road.

"You'll get a laugh out of this—my favorites are movie themes. They're the first things I learned to play on the piano." He ran a hand through his hair, obviously uncomfortable with his confession.

"Let me guess…*Mission Impossible?*"

"Now who's reading minds?" he asked with a nervous laugh, but when I gave him an easy smile, he relaxed a bit. "I must've played that song a hundred times before Mitch burned the music. Of course, I had it memorized by then, so the torture continued."

"I'll have to change his ringtone the next time I get the chance," I said. How I wished I could see Mitch's face when his least-favorite song came blaring out of his cell phone. I wondered if I *would* get the chance. *If Jason were to move…*

I banished thoughts of the future before my imagination really ran away with me.

The miles rolled by as we took turns asking questions. Jason's stories about his childhood antics with Mitch were interspersed with short anecdotes from my past as a bookworm. Although we both grew up in California, Jason spent his spare time either playing piano or surfing, while I amused myself writing or skiing. We compared elementary schools, junior highs, and by the time we got to high school, Highway 101 brought us back to the coast in Ventura. Jason's witty stories had easily distracted me from the tedium of driving.

It was back to me to ask a question, and I finally broached the one subject the reporter in me was dying to discuss. "So, did you play any sports?"

"Yeah, I was a real jock in high school. None of that sissy stuff like football or baseball for me," Jason said.

I raised an eyebrow at him curiously.

"I lettered in tennis and golf." His laugh rang out again.

"Not quite good enough for either Tour, huh?"

"No, I decided science was much more to my liking. How about you? Badminton? Field hockey?"

I stuck my tongue out at him. "No, I played soccer for a season and a half in high school and nearly made all-state as a goalie, if you must know."

"What stopped you?"

"I dropped out mid-season my sophomore year." I glanced at Jason before I spoke again. "That's when my dad was killed," I said, trying to keep my voice steady.

Jason inhaled sharply. He put his hand on the back of my neck and rubbed it gently. "I'm sorry. Detective Clark thought very highly of your father."

"He was a good man. Somehow Dad arranged his work schedule so he made it to almost all my games. He really enjoyed watching me play, and I loved hearing him cheer me on."

I'd been at a game when I found out about Dad's death. I hadn't touched a soccer ball since.

"I'm sure he loved you very much," Jason said quietly.

I took a deep breath and smiled weakly. "And I loved him. I miss him every day."

Jason didn't speak again. I wondered if he didn't know what to say, or if he knew his presence was more comforting than any words.

The harsh ring of an old-fashioned bell telephone came from the cup holder. Jason picked up my cell phone and checked the display. "It's Linda."

Glad for the distraction, I threw him a warning glance. "She'll be on speaker."

With a flick of his fingers, he locked his lips and threw away an invisible key.

Linda didn't know I'd spent the night with Jason—at least I didn't think she knew. *So what if she does?*

With a guilty pang, I activated the speakerphone. "Hey, Linda, what's up?"

"MELISSA!" she screeched. "He did it! I'm ENGAGED!"

Jason and I both flinched when her high-pitched voice pierced our eardrums.

"Linda, not so loud! You're going to blow out my speaker," I said, trying not to scream myself. "So the bouquet worked its magic for you?"

"Of course it did! I wish you could see my ring, Melissa. It's huge! And gorgeous! And absolutely PERFECT!" she yelled.

"Calm down. Start from the beginning."

Jason rubbed his ear, trying to recover from Linda's screaming.

"Okay, okay. So let me think. You left before Mitch and Ann did, right?" She didn't wait for an answer and plowed on, her words gaining speed as she spoke. "We all went outside and did the birdseed thing. Ann'll be picking that stuff out of her hair for a week! Anyway, she and Mitch got in the limo and drove off. I started to go back inside with the rest of the crowd, but Chase wouldn't budge. When everyone else was gone, he raised his hand and *another* limo pulled up. It was for *us*, Melissa! Our own big, black limousine! I couldn't believe it!" She took a breath, giving me a chance to speak.

"I'm not surprised. Chase is quite the romantic. What happened next?"

"So we got in the car, and Chase knocked on the divider. Without a word, we drove away. I asked him where we were going, and he just smiled and put his hand in his jacket pocket. Guess what he handed me?"

I looked at Jason, who shrugged.

Not waiting for an answer, Linda hurried on. "*Disneyland tickets!* My favorite place, Melissa! He took me to Disneyland!"

Jason shook his head, and I chuckled. If Mickey had a spare room, Linda would move in with him, even if it meant polishing his ears.

"How sweet—" I started, but she didn't hear me.

"So it was almost midnight when we got there, and Chase says in his sexy voice" —which she then mimicked, causing Jason to throw a hand over his mouth— "'I know a great place to watch the fireworks.' He led me through the park with a blanket slung over his shoulder. We were still in our wedding get-ups too. Everybody stared at us. Finally, he stopped at the steamboat—you know the one?"

"Yes, I know, the long, boring ride we take when we're too tired to stand in line for one of the roller coasters," I said with a groan.

"It is *not* boring! I love it. Anyway, the ride was closed when we got there, so I was trying to get Chase to tell me what was going on when one of the park employees came over, shook hands with Chase, and let us on the boat—alone! We went up to the top level, and he laid the blanket out on the deck, cuddling up with me. The fireworks started right over our heads!

"Oh, Melissa, it was so romantic! It was like the show was just for us. When the finale started, the sky turned white there were so many shells going off. That's when Chase pointed up and said, 'Linda, this is what my heart feels like whenever I'm with you. Will you marry me?' Then he lifted my hand up toward the exploding fireworks and slipped on the ring!"

She was screaming again, and I quickly reached for the volume button.

"That's wonderful! Congratulations!" I shouted back to her.

"But that's not even the best part," she said. "When the fireworks ended, Chase got that I-want-you-now look in his eye and kissed me like you wouldn't believe. Every inch of my skin was on fire! When he tried to unzip my dress, it ripped and—"

"LINDA! *You're on speaker!*" I hollered and looked at Jason. No longer able to contain himself, he laughed out loud.

Linda finally stopped talking. Had she heard him?

"You're in your car, right?"

"Yes. How about I call you later, okay?"

Jason didn't even try to hide his laugh this time, and I slapped his shoulder.

"Hold on, Melissa. Are you alone?"

Busted. "No."

Silence…then Linda's angry voice. "Quit stalling. Who's with you? *Where* are you?" I knew she'd call me until she'd figured out why I was avoiding her, but I wasn't going to cave that easily.

I answered one of her questions. "I'm just pulling into Ventura."

Jason snorted.

"Ventura? You didn't go home last night?"

I didn't bother to answer, counting to twelve before she spoke.

"Melissa, you *didn't!* Mitch said you were joking around about sleeping with his brother…it *wasn't* a joke, was it?"

Thanks, Mitch. I sighed and changed lanes, avoiding Jason's arched eyebrow and smug grin.

"No, it was anything but a joke," Jason answered happily, and I groaned. "Best wishes to you and Chase, by the way," he added.

There was another long pause on the line. "Hello, *Jay-son,*" Linda sing-songed. "I thought *you* were heading back to school today."

"I changed my plans after the incident at the hotel. Melissa shouldn't be alone right now." He put his hand on my shoulder, suddenly serious.

"How nice," she said suspiciously. "Wait, what incident?"

"You're not going to believe this, Linda," I started, quickly detailing the murder and probable involvement of Ron.

"No way! You must be terrified! He touched your *things?*" The rising pitch of her voice got my own heart racing.

"The cops will get him—they probably already know who he is. Don't worry," I said. Seeing an exit, I pulled off the freeway. Maybe a cold drink could calm the knots bouncing around in my stomach. "Just out of curiosity, does Chase still have his bow tie?"

"Yes, I took it off him myself in the limo. Why?" she asked.

I explained how Jason's bow tie was stolen and left with the body. "Slimeball Ron got a really good look at Chase too," I said. "Just be careful, okay?" I couldn't see how Ron could find them at Disneyland, but better safe than sorry.

"Don't worry about us. I've got my own pepper spray, remember?" she laughed.

I *did* remember, and suddenly my hands began to tremble. I tightened my grip on the steering wheel.

"Listen, Linda, I've got to take a break from driving. I'll call you soon to get the full story of your night at Disneyland, okay? Catch you later."

I abruptly pulled into the parking lot of a hamburger joint and slammed the car into park with a jerk.

"Okay, Melissa. Be careful yourself. You too, Jason. I'll talk to you guys later."

It took me two tries to push END, Jason's worried stare making the task even harder.

He reached over and turned off the car, then unbuckled and faced me. "You're shaking all over, Melissa," he said, taking my hand in his. "What's wrong?"

"I know what Ron took out of my purse. My pepper spray. He *is* coming after me." Paranoid, I checked my mirrors, as if he could be right behind us.

Jason leaned over and put his arm around me. "He won't get near you, Melissa. I promise. He doesn't know where you are, and you said yourself there's no way he can find you. It'll be okay."

His voice was low and calm. Only a hint of fear lurked around the corners of his eyes. "Let's get something to eat, and then why don't you let me drive for a while? You can call Detective Clark and tell him what you remembered." He cradled my cheek in his hand and kissed me very softly. "It'll be fine, trust me."

I let my head fall onto his shoulder and closed my eyes, trying to muster my common sense.

Jason was right, of course. How *could* Ron find me? I took a deep breath.

"Thanks," I said, wishing there was a better way to tell him how grateful I was he'd stayed. Somehow I'd make it through this mess, with Jason's help. I tried not to think about what would happen when he left on Friday.

What would I do then?

Eleven

After a basket of fries and a large Diet Coke, I calmed down. Jason took the wheel, and I called Detective Clark—Tim, he reminded me—and told him about my missing pepper spray. He noted it and gave me a brief update on the progress of the investigation.

In the few hours since we'd left L.A., the police had confirmed unknown fingerprints on my driver's license and phone. The computer was currently trying to match them to a name. San Jose Police had put a remote surveillance unit in front of Mom's house in case Ron, or anyone else suspicious, showed up there. Tim assured us we were safe and promised to call if he found out any more information. All we could do now was wait.

After I relayed the information to Jason, he immediately changed the subject. "So what's next on the things-we-should-know-about-each-other list?"

The road took us inland again, away from the ocean and Santa Barbara's offshore oil rigs. "I know," I said and retrieved my stack of newspapers from the back seat. "How about 'what are you reading right now?'"

"I just started a Clancy novel. Spies and suspense are probably my favorite, but I've read a lot of different things over the years." He looked past me at the dead grass covering the rolling hills and frowned. "I'd forgotten how dry things are here. One thing I'll miss about Michigan is the green. It's much different than all this brown."

I giggled. "It's not brown, it's *golden*. The Golden State, remember?"

He rolled his eyes.

The rest of his statement took longer to register in my brain. "You're leaving Michigan?"

"Once I graduate in August, I'll be going on to medical school. U of M has one—a very good one—but I've applied to several around the country. I'm hoping to get into USC so I can come back to California. Brown or golden, I miss it here; and now I have even more reason to come home." He reached a hand out to me, and I felt the blood rise in my cheeks as I took it. "So what do *you* like to read, besides the news?"

I gave his hand a squeeze and then released it. "Murder mysteries mostly. Christie, Parker, Grafton, you know. I occasionally hit the sci-fi and fantasy sections, though, and I'll admit I've read all of Harry Potter."

I looked down at the papers in my lap. "The news is my favorite, though." The *Los Angeles Times* was still on the top of the stack, and the same article I'd read yesterday stared up at me. "I wonder if this is the murder Detective Clark thinks might be connected to Vanessa. Kerry Stanton was a USC student who was strangled in a similar way, with her sorority scarf conspicuously left behind."

"It could be, but USC isn't in the best neighborhood, you know. What sorority did she belong to?" Jason asked.

I scanned the article. "Theta Pi."

Jason's hand became motionless. "Ann's a Theta Pi," he said quietly.

"Maybe that's how Ron ended up at the hotel. I bet everyone at the sorority knew about the wedding," I said.

Did Ron learn about the wedding from Kerry? He'd said he was "a friend of a friend of the bride"—and he had an invitation. My stomach turned. Was that *her* invitation he'd been flashing around?

Jason shook his head as he looked out at the road. "I'm sure Detective Clark figured that out when he talked to Tricia. She's a Theta Pi too. I want to find out more about you, not do his job."

Keeping one eye ahead, he slid a different section out of the pile in my lap. The sports page landed on the top. "There's a much more important topic we need to discuss before this relationship can go any further," he said ominously.

My muscles tensed. *First he mentions Tee, and now this?*

"What's your favorite baseball team?"

I mirrored Jason's somber tone, hiding my relief. "The Giants, of course. You're *not* a Dodger fan, are you?" *Damn, he isn't perfect after all.*

His face fell. "I'm sorry, Melissa. I thought we had something special going." He couldn't maintain his false disappointment for long, though, and chuckled. "There had to be something we don't agree on."

"Oh, Jason, the *Dodgers? How could you?*" I wailed dramatically, throwing the back of my hand against my forehead, à la Scarlett O'Hara. Two seconds later we exploded with laughter. It felt good to laugh with him, so easy and natural.

After I caught my breath, Jason asked what I'd be doing over the summer and beyond.

I quickly ticked off my plans: summer with Mom, internship in the fall, graduation next spring. He listened intently, glancing at me often. I could tell he was curious, but something else lurked in his eyes. I had no luck reading *his* mind, however.

He caught me staring and changed the subject again, asking about my favorite movies. When we discovered our mutual love of *The Princess Bride*, we traded so many quotes we ended up reciting most of the script.

Before I knew it we pulled into Santa Lucia. I directed Jason to the closest market so we could restock my bare pantry. Luckily, I hadn't packed up the kitchen yet.

Walking through the grocery store with Jason was surreal. I'd pushed a metal shopping cart down these aisles a hundred times, listened to the same annoying music, shivered in front of the same freezers, and selected the same generic ingredients—always alone. Now he was here with me, and I was suddenly aware of how even this mundane task changed with his presence.

His eyes drank in everything, watching with marked interest while I chose a bottle of spaghetti sauce, as if it would give him some great insight into my being. We discussed the pros and cons of bagged salad as well as the economy of fresh parmesan versus canned. When I struggled to reach a jar of capers on the top shelf, Jason smiled and brushed his finger across my cheek before handing them to me.

He was constantly renewing that contact: a touch on my hand, a caress across my back, a whisper in my ear. The thing that scared me the most was how *right* it felt having him with me, and the déjà vu of my first vision of Jason returned. I could see us repeating this scene together for years to come.

It could happen! If he gets into USC *and you got an internship in L.A. then…*

Naughty Melissa ignored all ifs and coulds, distracted by the definition in Jason's deltoids instead.

Slowly I inhaled, trying to clear my thoughts. What might happen in the fall didn't matter. We'd already proven email didn't last long, and we had the whole summer between now and then. *Friday. It ends on Friday.*

After the market we switched seats again, and I drove the few remaining miles to my apartment. When I signaled at the driveway of my complex, Jason sat up with an astonished look on his face.

"This is your apartment?" he asked.

"Yes. What were you expecting?" My complex consisted of about twenty small, two-unit buildings spread over a hillside—not the most common arrangement. Someday they were destined to become condos, I was sure.

"I don't know, something more like those, I guess." He pointed to the long, brown, three-story apartment building next door. "But these are nice. You don't have to worry about anyone stomping around over your head while you sleep."

I could tell he was impressed.

"What's your place like in Ann Arbor?" I asked, pulling into the spot right in front of my unit.

"It's more like a high-rise dorm: eighteen stories with a couple hundred units. I live on the fourteenth floor. I have the place to myself all summer," he added, his expression unreadable.

I wasn't sure how to respond, so I popped the trunk and hopped out, grabbing the smaller bags. Jason's grin returned as he extracted his monster suitcase and waited for me to dig my house key out of my purse.

"Home, sweet home," I said and unlocked the door. Inside, the dark hallway contradicted my welcome. I flicked on the light, illuminating the stairs that rose to the left.

"I think we'll start the tour upstairs, if you don't mind," I said and walked up the steps. We passed an empty bedroom at the top.

Jason glanced in that direction as we passed. "You had roommates?"

"Just one, but she left right after finals." I tilted my head as we passed another darkened doorway. "The one and only bathroom," I said, pausing for a split second before continuing to the door at the end of the hallway. I pushed it open and flicked on the light. "Our accommodations."

My bedroom was completely empty but for an open suitcase, a digital alarm clock, and a lamp—all of which sat on the floor. The only decoration was the vanilla curtains covering the sliding glass door.

Jason set down his suitcase next to mine and peeked outside. The view wasn't that spectacular; the twelve-inch-deep "balcony" hung directly over the front door. All he could see was the laundry room in the center of the parking lot.

"Where's the bed?" he asked, mimicking my comment from last night and earning a poke in the ribs.

"I wish I could just lead you into another room and say 'Ta-da,' but I can't. All the furniture is in my mom's garage in San Jose, thanks to Dave. You know him, right? One of Mitch's groomsmen?"

Jason looked confused for a second, then nodded. "He's a good guy."

I couldn't help but smile. "Yes, he is. His folks live in the Bay Area too, and he managed to fit my stuff in his trailer. Everything got moved for a pizza and a case of beer a week ago." I opened the closet and grabbed a large gray roll. "Here's the bed."

"A sleeping bag? That'll be cozy," Jason said doubtfully.

I sidled up and slowly slid my arms around him. "It'll be fine. You'll see."

His frown disappeared. "I'll just have to trust you," he murmured, bending his head down to mine. It'd been hours since I'd kissed him, and when our lips met, all the electricity we'd been storing during our drive was released in one giant jolt. He held me tight, the mint he'd had earlier tickling my tongue.

When his hands wandered toward my waist, I pulled back and wagged my finger at him. "Hey now, I thought we had an agreement."

Puppy dog eyes greeted me. "We do," he said with a sigh.

I kissed him lightly and slipped out of his arms. "How about some dinner?" I took his hand and led him downstairs.

"It's going to be a very long night," he said.

Before unloading the groceries, I showed Jason the equally vacant downstairs. A couple of empty boxes, another lamp, a phone, and a boom box were all that occupied the family room. The half-full dish rack in the kitchen was the only evidence the place was inhabited.

"When you said your apartment was empty, I didn't quite understand what you meant. This is like camping, sort of," he said without enthusiasm, setting the groceries on the counter.

"I guess, except with clean bathrooms and a real kitchen. At least the electricity is still on." I reached into the lower cabinet, located one of the two pots I owned, and filled it with water. "So, do you cook?" Somehow I couldn't quite see Jason standing in front of the stove long enough to fix a meal.

"Just the basics. I spend a lot of time on campus, so I have a cafeteria meal card. All you can eat for one low price," he crooned. "And no dishes."

With the water heating, I took the skillet out of the dish drainer and put it on the stove. "I see. Well, hopefully my spaghetti will meet with your approval, though I'm not sure it'll taste like institutional cuisine." I stripped the plastic off the hamburger we'd bought and dropped it in the pan.

"I'm pretty sure I can handle—"

Jason was interrupted by the loud strum of a steel guitar coming from his pocket. It was…a country western tune?

"*That's* your ring tone?" I asked. He definitely wasn't a country music kind of guy.

"Only if it's Mitch," he said with a wink. "Excuse me for a moment." Jason stepped out of the kitchen, and I heard a muffled "Hey, bro" before he walked upstairs.

I wondered why Mitch would be calling…unless the police had contacted him too. What a way to start a honeymoon.

The meat sizzled in the pan, ready for some spices and herbs. I was enjoying the scent of basil and garlic when I heard my own phone begin to sing.

Journey announced the call from Mom. I fished the phone out of my purse and flipped it open, cocking it on my shoulder so I could drop the pasta into the boiling water. "Hi, Mom. How's Reno?"

"Hello, dear. It's fine." Her greeting was unusually terse. "Melissa, you need to tell me exactly what's going on down there. I just got off the phone with the police. Did you know they're watching the house?"

Uh-oh. "Yes, Mom, I did. I just didn't have a chance to call you." I sighed and quickly worked out my story in my head.

The murder was easy enough to explain; Jason wasn't. I'd never gone into detail about my love life with her, but I'd never lied, either. The line wasn't so clearly defined in this case, though. Too many of the specifics of my very short time with Jason were integral to the case, and if she was to understand the danger, I'd have to explain his sudden appearance.

I decided I'd withhold only one fact and hope she didn't dig too deeply.

She listened quietly as I told the story, saving her barrage of questions until I'd finished. Most pertained to the investigation, and I had little to add. Then she moved into more dangerous waters.

"So you spent the night with this Jason?" she asked, her disapproval loud and clear.

"Yes, Mom." First rule of parental interrogation: only answer the question that was asked.

"Have I met him? You've never mentioned him."

I glanced up at the ceiling. She hadn't met *any* of the guys I'd dated in college.

Next tactic: connect to a positive memory. "You've met his older brother, Mitch. Big cowboy, really funny…remember?"

The line was silent for a beat. "How long have you been dating Jason?"

I gritted my teeth. This was the question I'd been hoping to avoid. If she knew I'd jumped into the sack with a man hours after meeting him, she'd freak out. Honestly, I still couldn't believe I'd done it.

"I've known him for a while." *Not totally a lie.*

"And he's with you now? How long have you been sleeping together? Did you use—"

"MOM! Stop it. Do you want me to give you the play by play of *every* intimate encounter I've had?" I said angrily. "Jason isn't the person you need to worry about. He hasn't strangled anyone!"

Mom was silent for a moment. "I'm sorry, Melissa, but can you blame me for worrying? In less than an hour I found out you're being stalked by a killer, sleeping with a stranger, and hiding with him in an empty apartment. You have to admit that sounds…unsettling."

I took a breath and blew it—and my anger—out. "I know, Mom, but you really don't have to worry about Jason. He's a perfect gentleman who changed his plans just to make sure I'm safe. He cares about me too, you know." The spoon stopped moving in the pan while I considered the awesome weight of what he'd done for me.

"When this is over, can you introduce him to me, please?" she asked, breaking the spell.

I frowned. When this was over, he'd be gone. "We'll see," I said quietly.

"I won't embarrass you." Mom was nothing if not persistent. "Well, not too much."

Right. She was probably already bookmarking my buck-toothed baby pictures on her computer.

"Of course you'll embarrass me." But two could play that game. The floor above me creaked, verifying Jason was still upstairs. "I'm surprised you haven't asked if he's good in bed." I smirked, knowing she really *didn't* want those details.

"Melissa," she huffed, "your mind is in the gutter."

Winner! Or so I thought.

"Is he…good?" she squeaked.

I almost dropped the bottle of spaghetti sauce. "You have no idea, Mom."

She gasped quietly, and I laughed, ending this game of cat and mouse.

"Listen, if I hear anything else from the police, I'll call you, and you do the same, okay? Everything will be fine. I love you."

"Love you too, Melissa. Be careful, and I'll talk to you soon."

I gave the meat a quick stir before putting the phone back in my purse. Mom was worried, which was to be expected, but at least she knew what was going on. As I finished up the cooking, I couldn't help but wish Mom *could* meet Jason. I was sure he'd charm her too.

The soft thumping of footsteps reached my ears as I set out the plates. I looked up to see Jason's calm, thoughtful face dusted with a hint of five o'clock shadow.

"How are Mitch and Ann?" I asked, trying to hide my curiosity.

One side of his mouth rose in a fleeting half-smile. "They're fine, but tired. I'd left Mitch a message about what happened this morning, warning him the police would be calling. He wanted to find out what the story was," Jason said.

"Did he know about…us?" I surprised myself with my guilty tone.

"Not exactly, but I told him anyway. There's not a reason for our…activities to be a secret…is there?" Jason scowled, and I couldn't tell if it was at the word *secret* or the word *activities*.

I busied myself taking the garlic bread out of the oven. I'd been less than forthright with both Mom and Linda—why? Was I concerned about my reputation, or was it something else? I refused to be that shallow. "Good or bad, you have to live with your decisions," Dad had always said, and I had no regrets about my choices regarding Jason. It's not like my love life would make headlines anyway.

"I can't think of a reason, can you?" I asked. One thing I hadn't taken into account was whether our tryst would be a blemish on *his* reputation.

"No, though hiding you in the bedroom does have its advantages." He ran a finger along my arm, raising goose bumps. "Mitch wanted to ask you if I still snored, but I told him he probably got more sleep than we did." He smiled at me coyly.

"Jason, you didn't…" *No secrets indeed.*

"Yes, I did. Mitch says thanks for the gift, by the way. The lace didn't last very long, but Ann really enjoyed the chaps. Apparently cherry is her favorite flavor."

"TMI!" I cried, sticking my fingers in my ears.

His laugh lingered until I passed him a plate full of food. "This smells great," he said, taking a deep breath over the steaming spaghetti.

Jason flipped the empty boxes in the family room upside down and slid them together, creating a temporary table. We sat on the floor and ate in a comfortable silence. I chewed slowly, running the day's conversations through my mind. I realized *comfortable* applied to them as well. Nothing was strained or forced, and the only *un*comfortable moments were when I was reminded of the short duration of his stay. Somehow I had to stop dreading the future and enjoy the present. There'd be plenty of time to worry about the end later.

I looked up and found Jason staring at me across his empty plate. "What?" I said, and then took another bite of spaghetti.

"What were you thinking about?" he asked. "Your expression went from happy, to sad, to determined."

"You can read my mind; surely you know what I was thinking," I said between bites.

"Hmmm, I don't know. I'm guessing the sadness has something to do with our current situation, and I hope the happiness had to do with me, but I have no clue about the determination." He popped the last bite of bread into his mouth.

I swallowed and took a drink. "I decided I wasn't going to let worrying about" —*losing you*— "Ron ruin our time together," I said sheepishly. "But you were right otherwise. Pretty cheesy, huh?"

"*I* don't think so," he said with a wink. "Are you done?"

I nodded, and he picked up both plates. He went to the sink, and I followed, helping wash the dishes and clean up the leftovers. We could've been an old married couple, navigating the small kitchen like we'd lived there for years. *Yup, comfortable.*

By the time we finished cleaning my eyelids sagged, and the yawns were unstoppable. Jason wrapped himself around me, and I slumped against his chest.

"You look exhausted, Melissa. Why don't we call it a night?" he said.

"What time is it?"

"Nine thirty…but you really didn't get much sleep last night." His lips turned up in my favorite devious smile.

"Well…" I yawned again. "I should jump in the shower first." Jason looked at me with a twinkle in his eye. "Alone. PG-13, remember?" I scolded.

"Damn," he swore under his breath. "At least we'll have to figure out how to fit in your sleeping bag."

I laughed and started up the stairs.

Jason followed me, flicking off the lights behind us until we got to the bedroom.

Fighting another yawn, I picked up the sleeping bag and unrolled it so the top was near the wall. Jason unzipped it enough to turn down one corner, but I shook my head and pulled the zipper all the way around the edge. With a quick flip, the bag became a very, *very* thin queen-size mattress.

"This is just the bottom," I said sleepily. I opened the closet and pulled out a sheet and blanket. "These go on top," I said around another gaping yawn.

Jason took the linens out of my hands, set them on the open sleeping bag, then put his hands on my shoulders.

"I think I've got it. Why don't you hop in the shower before you fall asleep on your feet? I can handle it from here."

I turned my face up to his, and he kissed me sweetly.

"All right." I found my pillows in the closet, yanked my nightshirt—a gray, over-sized T-shirt with POLY in large, green letters—out of one of the pillow cases and trudged toward the bathroom.

The shower woke me up a little, but by the time I'd toweled my hair dry, the yawns had returned. Back in my bedroom, Jason had made up our "bed" and was lounging shirtless in his pajamas, reading a Clancy paperback. Even dead tired, my skin prickled at the sight of his bare, muscular chest. He looked up and patted the spot to his left.

"I didn't know which side you wanted. How's this?"

"Great." I flopped down next to him. The cool sheet felt refreshing after the hot shower, and I rolled onto my side, cuddling up on Jason's shoulder. He pulled the sheet over both of us, holding me close. The light winked out as my eyes closed, and Jason stroked my damp hair. Sleep was only moments away.

"Goodnight, my love," I thought I heard him whisper as my consciousness faded.

The sound of a car alarm woke me, but my eyes didn't open. My heart skipped a beat, and I realized it wasn't my car. The familiar sound of my neighbor's screeching siren ended with six short beeps and a slamming door.

Warm and content, I remembered I'd been dreaming about the most handsome man. I'd almost drifted back into his heavenly kiss when the alarm went off again. Frustrated, I gave up and opened my eyes. The fuzzy image around me came into focus slowly, erasing my morning fantasy for good.

I rolled over stiffly, looking for the vibrant blue eyes I'd seen in my subconscious yearnings, but I was alone. Every muscle tensed, and I sat up, looking for some tangible evidence Jason hadn't disappeared along with the dream. I barely managed to suppress my cry when I saw his suitcase next to the closet and heard the faint rush of the shower.

It's irrational to behave this way. Becoming completely immersed in Jason in just a day and a half wasn't normal. I'd lived my entire life without him…and yet I'd never felt alive until we met. *There is something seriously wrong with me.* I rubbed my face and wondered if Beth did phone consultations; I was in dire need of a psychologist.

Until I could seek therapy, I decided to spoil myself. I rolled onto Jason's pillow and inhaled deeply, letting his scent fill me.

Another sound joined the patter of water, one much more inviting than the car alarm. Jason's humming hypnotized me, drawing me to my feet and down the hall. In seconds, Naughty Melissa was wide awake and turning the doorknob.

Jason mixed in a few lyrics as I quietly closed the door behind me. The shower curtain breezed seductively but revealed nothing. *Damn it.* The steam smelled like soap, and I could picture the bubbly lather gravitating downward over the contours of his sculpted chest. I chewed my lip at the thought—it was so tempting to take one little peek, just to see if my imagination was remotely close to the real thing.

But we'd agreed, things were to stay PG-13 until tonight. Ogling Jason in the shower wouldn't help us reach that goal. I forced myself to pick up my toothbrush and face the sink, but couldn't help but notice the towel sitting next to me, quite out of his reach.

The tenor of the water changed, and I guessed Jason was rinsing off. I finished brushing my teeth and looked at the towel again. The two times I'd woken up last night, he'd kissed my forehead and encouraged me to go back to sleep, even though his lingering touch told me he had other ideas in mind.

I wasn't tired anymore. I picked up the towel and turned around.

Can't even wait a few hours? Who's treating him like an object now? My sense of propriety—what was left of it—stopped my hand before it touched the shower curtain.

No, I wouldn't give in to temptation, not when the anticipation of tonight was enticing on its own.

With a deep breath I unfolded the towel and hung it over the top of the shower curtain. The humming stopped abruptly.

"Melissa…thanks," he said, his voice uncertain. "How long have you been in here?" He turned the water off, and the towel slid into the shower.

I sighed. "Awhile. I'll see you downstairs." *Fully clothed.*

He may have thought last night was long, but tonight's date couldn't come soon enough for me.

Twelve

hen Jason came bounding down the stairs, he found me dressed and drinking a glass of milk. He carefully took the glass and set it on the counter before catching my face in his hands. "Good morning, beautiful," he whispered.

"Good morning, handsome," I breathed, catching the sweetness of his toothpaste. Just like the first time, Jason's kiss made the ground roll beneath me, and I swayed in his arms. He pressed me against the side of the fridge, preventing me from falling, and melded his long, lean body to mine. Every hard inch.

The kiss started playfully. Jason's biceps bunched in preparation to push himself off me, but after fantasizing about him in the shower, I wasn't about to let him go so quickly. I plunged my tongue between his minty lips, knowing the effect it would have.

Jason shuddered in my arms. His hands slid tantalizingly down the sides of my blouse before he managed to pull his mouth from mine. With eyes blazing in the bright morning light, he staggered back, hands in the air.

"Not until after dinner," he chided.

Mischievously I grinned at him, picking up the carton of milk. "As you wish," I said and bent over more than necessary to slide it into the fridge.

Jason slapped me on the ass. "You're quite naughty this morning, aren't you?"

I straightened up, rubbing the back of my shorts. "It's all your fault, just remember that."

He laughed, then picked up my glass and took a big drink before giving it back to me. Sexier than any model in a *Got Milk?* ad, he wiped away his white mustache with the back of his hand. Dressed in worn denim shorts and a deep blue polo shirt, he looked like he'd just walked off the set of a Ralph Lauren commercial. Part of me wished more of my friends were around so I could show him off.

"So what's on the agenda today?" Jason asked, leaning against the counter.

I finished the milk and rinsed the glass. "First would be breakfast. I was thinking we could head downtown, have a quick bite, and maybe walk around a bit before it gets busy. Then it's up to you. I'd be happy to show you the lovely Santa Lucia Polytechnic campus, or we could hit the beach, or go hiking, or something." The phone caught my eye. "And I need to call my landlord, but that should only take a sec. What sounds good?"

Jason buried his hand in his back pocket. "You said you owed two hundred?"

I grabbed his wrist, preventing him from extracting his wallet. "Don't you dare. I've already paid for the month—*he* would've owed *me* money for vacating early. It's no big deal, really."

"But—"

I held his hand fast. "No. Besides, I'd rather you worked it off."

"Promise?" His eyebrows did a little dance.

I let go of his wrist and pinched his ass. "Oh yeah. So, what's it going to be today?"

"I've only been to the campus once—years before Mitch knew a horse actually had four legs. I'd love to see where you spend your time." His teeth flashed in the sunshine.

"Okay. Then maybe I can add some variety to your wardrobe." I pressed a finger into the Michigan logo sewn into his shirt above his heart. He caught my hand and kissed my knuckles.

"My mom says I look good in this color. Don't you like it?" he asked with false disappointment. His eyes widened to demonstrate how his shirt accentuated their bottomless blue.

Trapped in his gaze, I answered hoarsely, "Yes, I like it." Jason laughed, and I finally tore my eyes away from him, fanning myself. "We'd better get going."

Breakfast was a quick stop for muffins and coffee, followed by a short walk through the tree-lined streets of downtown Santa Lucia, hand in hand. Summer was tourist season in my little college town, and the store windows were filled with T-shirts, knick-knacks, and souvenirs.

Catching the sightseeing vibe, I led Jason into one of the many shirt shops. It didn't take long to hunt down the rack of university-themed wear. After passing on the school colors of green and gold, I settled on a black golf shirt adorned with a small white Poly logo for Jason. At least he'd have one souvenir to remember me by, even if it didn't light up his baby blues.

One mission accomplished, we left the crowded sidewalks of downtown and drove to campus. Jason's head swiveled around, taking in the mishmash of architecture lining the main thoroughfare through the campus.

"The school adds and remodels whenever it finds the money," I explained. We passed a large, prison-like concrete structure on the right. "Those dorms were from the early seventies."

The road ended at a T-intersection. "Those are from the fifties, I think." I pointed at a set of long red-brick buildings.

"That's newer, though," he said, looking at the curving glass and steel of the Performing Arts Center.

"Yes. It opened in the nineties. My building isn't nearly so modern." I turned left and drove down the hill to the single staff parking place next to the aging Graphic Arts building. After tossing my parking pass in the window, Jason and I walked up the short set of stairs to my home on campus.

"The newspaper office isn't really that impressive. I hope your expectations aren't very high," I said, retrieving my keys.

With a quiet, "We'll see," Jason followed me into the dimly lit building.

"Here's the campus radio station," I said, pointing at a door covered in stickers and the graffiti-style letters KSLP. "And just down the hall…my office." I unlocked a door with a brass plaque announcing the home of the *Mission Daily.* I flipped on the lights, revealing the cubicle-filled bullpen. "It looks just like any other office, really."

"It's great. Which cube is yours?" he asked.

I led him down the second aisle of short, gray, fabric-covered walls to my "office."

"A window seat…nice," he said.

"Oh yeah, the view of the neighboring roof is spectacular." I collected the papers scattered across the desk—Craig had left quite a mess behind. "I share this cube with another reporter… Well, I used to. I should take some of this stuff down, I guess." I scowled at the walls, which were covered in research notes, Post-its, and old stories.

Jason smirked, seeing the stuffed horse labeled "Save a Horse, Ride a Cowboy" next to the phone.

"Mitch," I confirmed.

He turned his attention to the wall of paper. Closest to the doorway were clippings of the two front-page articles I'd written. The yellowing article about Mitch was pinned next to my more recent article about the first Poly football player invited to the Senior Bowl.

"Wow, this is impressive." He bent over so he could examine the scraps and printouts.

"It's what I do," I replied simply. "Have a seat." I offered him the single chair in the cube.

He sat slowly, his eyes darting from one scribbled note to another.

The office door opened, and a bushy mass of black hair headed our direction.

"Hi, Mark. What're you doing here?" I called. He threw a hand in the air when he saw me peeking, prairie dog-style, out of the cubicle.

"I thought that was your car, Mel. I'm just grabbing a few things before I take off for break. Are you hanging around here this summer?" Mark stepped into the cube across the aisle from mine with a smile on his face. A nice guy with an easygoing demeanor and friendly chocolate eyes, Mark made work enjoyable for everyone. The paper was lucky he'd agreed to stay on as editor-in-chief his senior year.

Out of the corner of my eye, I noticed Jason had stopped reading and was listening intently to our small talk. "I'm here for a few more days, then it's home for the summer. How about you?"

Mark disappeared behind the partition, rummaging through a drawer. "Same thing, basically. Hey, if you're not doing anything tonight, how about I treat you to Spike's for dinner?"

He'd barely spoken the words when Jason shot out of his chair like a rocket and snaked his arm possessively around my shoulders.

"Relax," I whispered. "The group goes out together all the time."

"What group?" he asked through his teeth.

"Sorry?" Mark replied.

Ignoring Jason, I raised my voice. "I said I wish I could. I didn't know anyone else was still in town."

Mark cleared his throat. "Actually, no one else is. I thought it would be nice to have dinner alone for a change."

I hoped he didn't hear Jason's *humph*.

He doesn't understand. Mark isn't interested in—

Just then, Mark's chair squeaked and he stood up. He continued speaking, slowly turning around to face me while sorting through his own pile of papers. "I've been meaning to ask you out for a while, Mel. With everyone gone, I thought tonight would…be…perfect…" His sentence trailed away to nothing when he saw Jason standing behind me.

Ask me out? Why? Stunned, I gawked at him. It wasn't until he glanced at me that I found my voice. "I…um…Mark, I'd like you to meet Jason McAlister."

Recovering my faculties, I turned to Jason. "Jason, this is the editor—editor-in-chief, actually—of the *Mission Daily*, Mark Caldwell."

Mark had gone back to staring at Jason. Neither man said anything, so I stumbled on. "Mark, Jason is Mitch McAlister's brother. You remember Mitch, right?"

Jason was the first to break out of the trance. "Nice to meet you, Mark. The newspaper has done well under your guidance. I've been happy to see more of Melissa's work on the front page since you became editor," he said smoothly. He rested his right arm casually on the low cubicle wall and made no attempt to shake Mark's hand.

What? My mouth dropped open. How'd he know that? Jason's icy stare erased my curiosity.

Mark returned the glare, his eyes narrowing. "Thank you, Jason. I assume you're here visiting?" he asked, his tone equally cool as his eyes slipped to the logo on Jason's shirt. I'd never seen such intense scrutiny.

Jason's expression didn't change. "Yes. And I'm afraid Melissa's already spoken for this evening," he said. His fingers started to massage my shoulder—softly but very visibly.

I hissed his name, but he ignored me.

Mark looked at Jason, then at me, and I smiled sheepishly. What could I say? It was just dinner.

Setting his jaw, Mark tried to stand a little taller. He had an inch or two on me but would need to stand on a box to match Jason. "So I see. Will you be staying long?"

"Until Melissa leaves for San Jose," Jason said, and I shuffled my feet. This battle for male dominance was unexpected and nerve-racking.

"Maybe we'll get together when you come back in the fall, Mel," Mark suggested, smiling widely at me.

I'd opened my mouth to explain my plans, but Jason cut me off.

"Doubtful, since *Melissa* will be on an internship then."

I slapped him in the stomach, but he didn't even flinch, winking at me instead.

My anxiousness gave way to irritation. Having two men fight over me wasn't the turn-on the movies made it out to be. And what exactly were they fighting over? Jason was leaving in a few days, and Mark…well, I had no explanation for his behavior.

Mark's eyes narrowed. "You're very well informed, Jason. You two must be close."

"Very," Jason said. He took his hand from my shoulder and tenderly traced my cheekbone, immediately raising my already-pink face to a blazing red.

I looked away, wishing I could crawl into a hole. If only Mark would forget this meeting while I was gone.

Before I could chastise Jason again, Mark stepped across the aisle, his fists clenched. I felt Jason tense as well.

"Don't," I said to both men.

Jason didn't move but stared down at Mark, refusing to even blink. Thank goodness the cubicle wall separated them.

The war of wills lasted a few more seconds before Mark flexed his jaw and snapped his head around to me. "Have a good summer, *Mel*," he said curtly. He eyed Jason one more time. "Jason," he said through his teeth.

"Mark," Jason replied, his expression cracking into a smirk.

"Thanks, Mark. You too," I said weakly before the door slammed.

Jason just stood there, a victorious sneer slathered across his face. For once, I didn't find him attractive.

"What the hell was that all about? I have to work with him, you know!" I shoved the chair back under the desk so hard the walls rattled three cubes away.

"Here you thought you were invisible to men," he chuckled. "That obviously isn't true, though while I'm here I wish it were." Completely unaware of my growing fury, he ran his fingers down my neck.

"What were you thinking? He's my friend—not a criminal. You didn't think I'd *accept* his offer, did you? Give me some credit." I slapped his hand away, disappointed to find the same streak of macho bravado in Jason that lurked in his older brother.

Jason tried unsuccessfully to wipe the grin off his face. "You've got quite a temper, don't you?" he said, reaching for me again.

"And you seem to think ruining my life is funny, don't you?" I fumed. Ducking under his arm, I turned on my heel and marched out of the office.

"Melissa, wait," Jason called, scrambling behind. "Are you saying you had no idea that guy was so into you?" Before I could answer he grabbed my arm, spinning me around just as his brother had, years ago.

Furious, I gave him the evil eye. "Do you know what happened to Mitch the *one* time *he* grabbed me like this?" I said.

Shocked, Jason dropped my arm and inched away.

"How would you like it if I treated your friend, your *boss*, that rudely the first time I met her? Is being a pig a McAlister family trait?" I roared. "And he's just that—a *friend*."

Understanding finally registered in Jason's brain, and his face fell. "I'm sorry, Melissa. I really am." He glanced back at my cube. "It was obvious he liked you, and you were so relaxed talking to him…" He turned back to me, shame filling his eyes. "I didn't think."

"No, you didn't. You're walking out of my life in four days and won't see Mark—or for that matter *me*—ever again. Don't make my life any harder than it has to be," I snapped. The thought of how empty my existence would be after Jason left suddenly crushed me.

Jason froze. "I never meant to make your life difficult, Melissa. That's the last thing I want to do." He took a deep breath as he struggled to hold my gaze with his distraught eyes. "Am I *ruining* your life?"

The razor-sharp edge of truth tried to slice me open. "No, of course not," I lied, looking down. *Not yet… Not until you leave.* I wanted to stay mad and yell at Jason more—and not just for acting like a possessive dolt. How dare he come into my life, steal my heart, and then leave? My hands clenched and flexed as I fought with my emotions. Then the bruise on my hand reminded me that punching something wasn't such a good idea.

When I looked up, I met Jason's drawn face, his eyes shining. "I'm sorry," he whispered again, taming my fury. I suspected the apology wasn't only for his run-in with Mark but for the pain he knew was coming. He took a careful step toward me, holding his arms open.

I clung to my last tinges of anger, letting him suffer for another second before melting into his embrace. How I wanted to tell him everything would be okay, but the words wouldn't come.

He held me tenderly, pressing his cheek against my hair. The sound of Jason's heart soothed the ache in my chest. "Is there anything I can do to repair the damage I've done?" he whispered.

You could stay and never leave.

I shook my head. "No, you were right. I won't see Mark for months. It probably won't matter then." I turned around, keeping one arm around Jason. "Let's get out of here."

Keys in hand, I closed the door behind us. I wished I could lock all my problems away this easily.

Once in the hall, Jason automatically turned back the way we came, but I pointed him in the opposite direction. I doubted Mark was still around, but why tempt fate?

"There's more to see this way," I said.

He frowned at my forced smile and took my hand, his shoulders slumped. His guilt rolled over me like the fog, thick and gloomy. I wrapped my arm around his waist, hoping to convey my forgiveness. He gave me a quick squeeze, but said nothing.

As we walked down the hall, I struggled to break through the silence that separated us. We passed a newspaper rack with a few old copies left in it. The large print of the headline caught my eye, reminding me of something odd Jason had said to Mark.

"What was all that talk about my being on the front page more? How'd you know that?"

Jason took another deep breath. "You might not want to know, now."

A finger of fear ran down my back. "Why?"

"It'll probably upset you more," he said as we descended the stairs.

I sighed. *What now?* "Just tell me."

"I knew about the changes at the paper because I've been reading your work for some time," Jason answered tentatively.

"You have?" *What interest could my stories have for him?*

"Yes. I've read everything you've written for the *Daily*," he admitted as we walked outside into the sunshine.

Dumbfounded, I uttered only one word. "Why?"

"You're going to think I'm crazy." He stopped in the shade and let go of me, leaning against the low wall that held back the hillside above.

He pressed his fingertips together, his hands forming a web in front of him. Staring at them for a long minute, he seemed to be gathering his thoughts. "I think I mentioned in one of my emails that Mitch talked about you?" he asked carefully.

I nodded, but he didn't look up. "Uh-huh," I said.

"At first he sent me a couple of the articles you'd written about him and commented about how refreshing it was to meet a reporter who really knew her stuff. As time went on, you came up in conversation more often. 'Melissa did the funniest thing' or 'You wouldn't believe what Melissa said.' I started to get jealous."

"Jealous? Of Mitch? But you didn't know me—"

"Not of Mitch—of *you*." He ran his fingers through his hair, leaving a few dark locks dangling across his forehead. "Before he met you, *I* was the one who made Mitch laugh, the one he'd get all his good jokes from. You stole my brother from me."

I started to speak, to apologize, but he put a surprisingly cool finger over my lips and shook his head.

"Don't say you're sorry. You had no idea. I was stupid to feel that way, I know. When Mom told me you were going to ask me for information about Mitch, I seriously considered blowing you off, but apparently your pull on me works over great distances. I read a couple more of your articles and realized I had a golden opportunity to find out more about you." He finally looked into my eyes, humor twinkling in the blue. "What if Mitch *was* planning on making you my sister?"

I stood on my toes so I could lightly kiss his lips. "Then this would be *really* awkward, wouldn't it?" In a fit of snorts and laughs, the cloud of gloom lifted for good.

"Too true. Your no-nonsense emails put that fear to rest quickly." A wry smile curled Jason's lips. "Through your notes, I saw how appealing you were—how smart and strong—and I created this picture of you in my mind." He looked over my shoulder, out toward the peaks leading to the ocean. "Perhaps *picture* isn't quite the right word; I didn't have an image of you—more of a voice, or a feeling…" He frowned, seeming at a loss for words.

"It must've been disappointing to find out it was me who'd sent the notes." I groaned. He probably had someone like Ann or Beth in mind. Someone tall, gorgeous, and perfect.

"No, just the opposite—my imaginary version didn't do you justice," he said quickly. He traced my pouting lips with his fingertip before returning to his original thought. "I really enjoyed those emails, Melissa, and I imagined what it'd be like to meet you. My jealousy turned to Mitch—he could see you and hear your voice whenever he wanted."

"But we lost touch," I said, curious about when he'd read the rest of my writing.

"When I stupidly let the emails stop, Mitch wouldn't share you anymore, and it pissed me off. I did almost email you at work, but Mitch was right—it wasn't fair for me to pursue you from so far away. So I settled on reading your stories instead.

"Your sharp wit comes through in everything you write, and the more I read, the more I felt like I was getting to know you. To me, the stories read like letters from home; many had something to do with Mitch anyway, so it wasn't too big of a stretch to pretend you were writing them to me. They weren't as much fun as the emails, but they still gave me a sense of you." He sighed and looked down at his feet. "Pretty sick, huh? Dreaming about a woman thousands of miles away who had no face?"

I rested my head on his chest, and his arms encircled me. *He'd been dreaming about me?* I couldn't believe what I was hearing. No wonder he could read my thoughts; he'd spent months practicing with my written words.

His breathing accelerated, waiting for me to say something, no doubt.

I pressed my face against his neck, embarrassed. "Then you saw my face, in the church, with my mouth hanging open like a fool. How many times did you ask me where I wanted to sit?"

"A couple," he confirmed with a chuckle. He cradled my cheek in his hand. "And you didn't look foolish. You stared at me with such complete wonder that I got a little lost myself. Remember, at that point I had no idea who you were, or if Melissa Williams had come to the wedding. I found myself with a beautiful, shy woman on my arm, and an intelligent, flirtatious one in my head, and I didn't want to choose. I wanted both of you. I'm really a very greedy person." I could hear the smile in his voice.

"Uh-huh. Speaking of greedy…" I lifted my face to his, and he eagerly met my lips. The memory of our first meeting came back in a flash, along with the accompanying vision. I had trouble believing it had only been two days since that pivotal moment; somehow it felt like Jason had always been part of me.

A wolf whistle from a passing student ended our kiss abruptly. "How about we grab a bite at the campus market and go visit Mitch's horse? We can take Buckeye a snack," I suggested.

"Sounds great." Jason automatically collected my hand, and we fell into step.

After a few feet, Jason stopped in his tracks. "Wait, did you say Mitch's horse is named Buckeye? That ass! Only my brother would name his horse after *them*."

It took a moment for me to comprehend what he was saying, but then I exploded with laughter. U of M's biggest rival was the Ohio State Buckeyes. Mitch and Jason might be close, but they were still brothers, complete with sibling rivalry.

We couldn't have asked for better weather to tour the campus. Summers in Santa Lucia were moderate, following a pattern of several warm days then a few foggy ones. Today the temperature was in the eighties, the heat tempered by a gentle breeze. We made a quick stop for sandwiches, sodas, and a bag of carrots. Lunch in hand, we hiked the sunny half mile to the equine unit.

I almost turned around when I saw the number of trucks and trailers parked at the top of the hill. The dirt lot was completely full, and a huge truck had backed in next to the stables. We heard a crash, and the truck lurched to the left. Somewhere in the distance a cheer went up.

"Is it usually this busy?" Jason asked.

"No. It must be moving day for something." Something big, judging by the way the truck shook.

I peeked in the stable, thankful to find only nervous horses staring back at me. "We'll just sneak in and out," I said, hoping we wouldn't run into anyone else for Jason to spar with.

Buckeye was waiting for us, stretching his long neck and sniffing for snacks.

"Hey there, big guy. You hungry?" I asked, letting Buckeye find the carrot I held under his wiggling nostrils. "Say hello to Jason."

The horse snorted on Jason's outstretched hand.

"Nice to meet you too," he said with a laugh. When he offered Buckeye a carrot, the horse's manners improved.

"So, did you ever let Melissa ride you?" Jason asked the horse.

I was about to answer for him when two guys wandered in the far end of the stable. "We should probably be going," I said. "Don't want to spoil Buckeye with too many treats."

Jason glanced over his shoulder. "Do you know them?" he asked softly.

"Sort of. They know me." I'd spoken to the cowboys a couple of times but had never been officially introduced. I wasn't sure they were on the rodeo team.

I looped my arm through Jason's, but he didn't take the hint to go.

Great, here we go again.

His blue eyes darkened. "Melissa, I made a mistake with Mark, and I'm deeply sorry. I won't embarrass you again. Please let me prove it."

Jason was asking for my trust. I hesitated, and his expression turned to anguish. I couldn't stand it.

"Okay."

Buckeye whinnied, begging for more carrots. With just a hint of a smile, Jason took the bag from me and busied himself with the horse.

"Hey, it's Lois Lane!" the first guy called. "Did you come by to welcome Diablo home?" His gaze dipped below my face, and I looked at Jason. He raised an eyebrow, but didn't move.

I watched the second guy's eyes sweep over me, and my heart skipped a beat. Did they always do that? How had I missed it?

"Is that what's going on?" I asked, thankful they now looked me in the eye. **Poly's Prize Bull on Loan**...I remembered the story now; Craig had asked me to look it over. Diablo had been making bovine girlfriends at UC Davis for the past month.

"Yup. It took us an hour to get the stubborn son of a bitch out of the truck. The smallest sound freaks him out," the other guy said. He nudged his friend when he saw Jason, and they kept walking.

To my amazement, Jason lifted a hand and offered a friendly "Hey."

The first guy slowed and pointed at Jason. "You look a lot like..."

His friend's eyes became saucers. "We'd better get back out there," he said and hurried his companion past. "Say hi to Mitch for us."

"Take it easy," I said, watching them go. I shrugged, then reached up and kissed Jason on the cheek. "And thank you."

"Any time." He leaned down to return the kiss but Buckeye nuzzled him in the side. Jason had to step back or fall down.

I laughed. "I guess you're not the only one who's jealous!"

We shared the rest of the carrots with Chase's horse before continuing our tour. Walking back toward the heart of campus, I thought about the last time I'd visited the stable with Mitch. I'd momentarily forgotten Jason wouldn't be the only one disappearing from my life. Mitch was already gone—would Buckeye disappear too? Adding Jason's impending departure to the list amplified the loss it in ways I couldn't explain. I found myself fighting for breath, unable to visualize any future, fantasy or otherwise.

Jason stopped suddenly and put his hands on my shoulders. "Are you okay?"

Get control of yourself, Melissa! I made my lungs expand with a cough. "Uh, yeah." I scrambled for some kind of rational explanation for my distress. "It's just that, sometimes…the horse dander gets to me, I think." I rushed through my lie. "Maybe I'm allergic. I'm okay now."

He cradled my face in his palm. "Are you sure? Your eyes were starting to bug out there for a sec."

Deliberately I sucked air in through my nose. "Yeah, I'm fine, see?" I could tell he didn't believe me, but I pretended not to notice and started walking again. "I wonder what'll happen to Buckeye now that Mitch will be living in the city."

Jason's critical gaze blanketed me as we made our way down the road, but he finally decided to play along. "Buckeye's moving down south too. Ann's parents have quite a spread in Rolling Hills, including a corral. They already have a stable for Buckeye and hands to take care of him. He'll live the good life, and Mitch will get to keep on riding."

"That's good. I know Mitch loves him." *Lucky horse.*

We reached the main campus and turned west, toward the library.

I pointed out various buildings and sights but continued to mull over my reaction. I knew Jason would disappear in just a few days—nothing had changed that fact. We'd made no commitments, and I expected to miss him just like I missed his brother. But what I'd felt was much more profound than mere sorrow. Why?

The answer eluded me, and my thoughts eventually turned to other subjects, namely dinner. Jason fiddled with his cell phone, subtly checking the time with increasing regularity. By mid-afternoon the anticipation of tonight's date had become a tangible prod, urging me to walk faster, to finish the mundane tour, and get Jason home. The car was a welcome sight when we made the final turn.

"So, we need to decide what we're going to do tonight—before the amazing sex, that is," I said, starting the car.

Jason shook his head with wily defiance. "No, *we* don't. I'm taking you out, remember? I get to choose tonight's pre-orgasmic activities."

I pressed my lips together, my heart doing a rhythmic double-take on the word *pre-orgasmic*.

He smirked. "Rest assured, reservations have already been made. We're starting with dinner at six. I'd recommend we head back to your place and change."

Without another word I put the car in gear and sped home.

We pulled up to the apartment and parked, but Jason caught my hand before I could get out. "Would you mind if I borrow your car while you get ready?"

"Why?"

A hint of pink touched his cheeks. "Well…among other things, I need to restock." He read my blank expression and with an exaggerated motion looked down at his lap and then back up. "For tonight."

I took the hint and dropped my gaze to his lap and his protruding fly. Oh, *restock*. Condoms.

"That's not necessary. I'm on the pill." It was my turn to blush—the last time I'd discussed birth control was with my mother in the ninth grade.

Jason cradled my face in his hands and kissed both cheeks. "That's good to know. But that's not the only thing I plan to get." His mouth captured mine, effectively erasing my questions—and my thoughts.

When he let me breathe, I just stared at him. What were we talking about?

"Your car?" he reminded me with a lopsided smile.

"Uh, sure. Just let me get the front door open."

Jason followed me closely to the door, and after I'd unlocked it I turned around to find myself in his arms. "Mmmm. You sure you don't want to join me in the shower?"

He stared at me the way a starving man looks at a juicy steak—ravenous. "Not until later."

"What should I wear?" My attention wandered as his finger chased a strand of my hair back behind my ear.

"Well, I'm planning on a jacket and tie, so something comparable? I thought I saw something black and sexy hanging in your closet." He lightly traced my nose with his finger as he spoke.

"You saw that?" I bit my lip and looked down. My black dress was something a former boyfriend had insisted I buy, but the relationship had ended before he'd ever seen it on me. It had never left the closet and was buried behind blouses and slacks I had yet to ferry home. I blushed, remembering the deep neckline of the dress. As I stared at the ground, Jason's finger lifted my chin.

"Maybe it's time to take the tags off, don't you think?" He gave me a quick kiss before hustling back to the car. "I'll be back before you know it," he called and slipped behind the wheel.

Stunned by his sudden departure, I yelled, "There's a GPS in the glove box!"

When he was out of sight, I dashed up the stairs. Naughty Melissa would be ready for whatever he'd planned. *Especially anything that leads to an orgasm!*

Thirteen

*I*t took me a few minutes to find the article about the murder. I knew a random slaying wasn't likely to be front-page news in Los Angeles, but the tiny story was hidden on page fourteen between a violent dock workers' strike and the current scandal in the mayor's office. **WOMAN FOUND DEAD AT POSH HOTEL**—the article read more like an advertisement for the resort than the account of a young woman's murder. I wondered if the hotel had any part in getting the story buried.

I shifted uncomfortably in my black pumps. Wearing a dress that revealed way too much and with no place to sit but the floor, I was left to read the paper standing at the kitchen counter. I didn't know exactly when Jason got back; he'd locked himself in my bedroom by the time I'd emerged from the bathroom.

He'd answered my knock with a muffled, "Wait for me downstairs, okay?" The door had remained closed.

I adjusted the straps on my halter-top dress, wishing more fabric would magically appear to cover the exposed center of my chest. The neckline—if I could call it that—extended all the way down to the bead-encrusted empire waist. My back and shoulders were also bare, adding to my discomfort. Even my hair, most of which was pinned back in a single large barrette, didn't conceal much. At least the skirt was full and long, falling to the middle of my calf. If I were a little girl I'd be twirling around the tiny kitchen.

Finally, I heard the bedroom door open and Jason's footsteps on the stairs. I pushed my hair over my shoulders and waited for him to find me.

He stopped at the bottom of the stairs. "Melissa?" he asked tentatively.

"In the kitchen." I clasped my hands in front of me, my arms pressed against my cold ribs.

He appeared in the doorway, one hand behind his back. "Wow," he purred at the sight of me. His free hand reached out, and I met it with my own.

"Wow yourself. You look amazing."

Jason had on a charcoal gray suit accented with a vibrant sapphire shirt and jewel-toned blue tie. Combined, they electrified his eyes. The matching pocket square was icing on the cake.

"There aren't words to describe how you look," he whispered. Gracefully he lifted my hand and invited me to spin.

My skirt flared as I circled, and when I rounded to face Jason, a huge bouquet of red and white carnations greeted me. "These pale in comparison to you, but they were the best I could do," he said.

I lifted the flowers from his hand, my smile growing. I held them close to my face, savoring the sweet scent. "They're lovely, thank you. Carnations are my favorite."

His lip curled suspiciously.

"Is there anything you *don't* know about me?" I asked.

"Plenty, but I hope to rectify that over time."

I set the flowers on the counter, and he pulled me close. His warm hands ran lightly over my shoulders and down my back as we kissed, setting my skin on fire. Our lips separated, and he brought his cheek to mine. "You're so beautiful, Melissa," he whispered, pulling my chest to his.

In his arms I felt beautiful…and protected…and wanted. His strong heartbeat, his enticing cologne, his fiery hands on my skin—forget dinner, I was ready to have Jason, here, now.

I squeezed him tighter, willing time to stop. Could he feel the desperation in my grasp?

He leaned in and kissed my neck, sending a shiver through me, then loosened his grip. "I think we should go. Do you have a wrap?"

I laughed. "A *wrap*? No. A jacket? Yes. I'll be right back." After a quick trip to my closet and a careful walk down the stairs, I was ready to go, my black coat draped over my arm.

Jason had found my lone vase and was arranging the carnations when I reappeared.

"I'm ready," I announced. "Where are we eating?"

He handed me my purse and escorted me out the front door. "Have you ever been to the Olde Port Inn?" He walked to the passenger side of my car and opened the door.

"I've heard of it, but I've never eaten there. It's supposed to be really nice." I gathered my skirt in the car, and he closed the door. He glided around to the driver's seat, and soon we were headed toward the freeway.

"Do you know where you're going?" I asked.

"Yeah, I'm pretty sure I do. If I get lost, I promise I'll ask for directions," he said, raising his right hand.

We spoke very little during the twenty-minute drive down the coast. I spent most of the time watching Jason, noting the now-familiar curl of hair above his collar and the tiny freckle below his ear that wiggled when he grinned. Every once in a while he caught me staring and would wink or stroke my arm in response. His expression intrigued me; his guarded smile was a sharp contrast to his intense gaze. *Read my mind*, his eyes pleaded, sending my nerves into high gear. I tore mine away, afraid I might hear what he couldn't say.

Friday. This all has to end on Friday. He knew that…didn't he?

The Olde Port Inn sat at the end of the pier in a tiny seaside town just south of Santa Lucia. The restaurant resembled an old, weathered sea shanty, not a fine dining establishment. Jason drove slowly onto the wooden jetty and parked in one of the few spots next to the restaurant.

He opened my door with a flourish, and I gladly took his offered hand, welcoming his support as I extracted myself—and my dress—from the car. After straightening my twisted skirt, I started for the entrance. I didn't get far.

"Hold on a sec," he said and pulled me close. He held his cell phone at arm's length and softly kissed the spot just behind my ear.

I gasped.

"Smile," Jason whispered.

The phone made a clicking sound—taking a picture, I realized too late. "Our first date," he said playfully, displaying his handiwork. Ignoring my dopey grin, I stared at his elegant face. "I can send you a copy," he offered.

I wanted a copy, more than anything. That one photo could be the only evidence I'd have of Jason's existence a few days from now. But how wise would it be to fawn over a picture, knowing I'd never see him again?

"Maybe later," I said, my smile fading. Avoiding his eyes, I looked toward the restaurant. The aroma of smoky mesquite and buttery garlic were a tantalizing complement to the salty air. "I'm hungry, and it smells wonderful."

"Melissa," Jason said, his lips curving down. He cupped my cheek in his hand. His eyes questioned me, though I was sure he already knew what I was thinking.

"It's nothing," I said, covering his hand with mine. This wasn't how I wanted to start our evening. I struggled to recover the sensation of his lips on my skin, to recreate the image stored in his phone.

Jason's expression didn't ease, so I tried a pout instead. He set his jaw stubbornly, though the corners of his mouth twitched upward.

Not one to back down from a challenge, I decided to let Naughty Melissa off her leash. I nuzzled his hand, sliding his palm over my lips, tracing the lines and grooves with my tongue. He inhaled sharply, his mouth falling open.

"Shall we go?" I asked sweetly.

Jason shook his head, waking from his lust-induced trance. "You really are dangerous, you know?"

I just laughed and banished all thoughts about the future from my mind—with the exception of those pertaining to our sensual plans for later. Jason walked to the door with his arm around me, protecting me from the light breeze coming off the water.

The hostess greeted us and led us through the restaurant's clean, light interior. My heels clunked against the wide-planked hardwood floor, the sound echoing off the walls of the sparsely populated dining room. All conversation stopped when we walked by.

"They're looking at you," Jason whispered in my ear.

Pulling my coat tighter around me, I was glad when the hostess seated us on the empty patio. Sheltered from the wind by high Plexiglas walls and warmed by a propane heater, I took off my jacket. The Pacific sparkled with a thousand tiny suns reflecting off the wind-driven ripples. Above the sea, a few wispy clouds crossed the sky, waiting to color the coming sunset.

"Magnificent," Jason said softly.

I turned to find him gazing not at the scenery, but at me. I smiled back and slipped my hand into his. Our fingers danced, lightly touching and circling until the waiter interrupted us, asking if we'd seen the wine list.

Before I could open the leather-bound folder, Jason said, "We'd like the Corbett Canyon Riesling, please."

He'd selected one of my favorite wines. I raised an eyebrow at him.

"Yes?" he asked innocently.

"You read my mind." It wasn't too hard to guess his co-conspirator, but I was surprised Mitch had any idea what wine I liked. Pizza and beer were more his speed.

The waiter left, and we opened our menus.

I was more interested in Jason than food, so rather than read I watched him peruse the pages. He inspected the list line by line, squinting at some entries while licking his lips at others. His hair captured the sunlight, a few of the brown strands reflecting the golden rays when he tilted his head to read the next page.

"What looks good to you?" he asked without looking up.

"You do, of course," I replied without hesitation.

With a slow, seductive smile, he glanced at me through his lashes. "On the *menu*," he said. "You're going to need your energy for later, you know." Jason found my hand again and stroked it lightly.

Naughty Melissa immediately took the dare implied in his words. I stood and slowly leaned over the table, bringing my face just inches from his. He didn't fail to notice the view down the front of my dress as gravity tried to liberate my breasts from the thin black fabric. "Bring it on, lover," I whispered.

Jason's blue eyes locked on mine. He exhaled, blowing his hot breath down my chest. The shock on his face was consumed by burning desire, and my skin tingled at the sight of such wanton lust. Before he could act on his yearning, I heard the doors open behind me, and I sat back down just as the waiter returned with our wine. I grabbed my menu and held it in front of me as I subtly readjusted myself and verified that I was indeed still *in* the dress.

"Are you ready?" the waiter asked, and Jason looked at me with one eyebrow cocked.

"Definitely," I said, not taking my eyes off of Jason. With a cough, he quickly spread his napkin across his lap and looked up at the impatient waiter.

Every movement I made, every word I uttered, affected Jason in some way—and this realization brought with it an unfamiliar confidence. Smiling, I casually made my selection. While Jason placed his order I tested my new-found power. When his eyes flitted to me, I licked my lips, causing him to stumble over his words.

Pinching my lips together, I barely contained the giddy laughter threatening to bubble out. I wondered how much more of this he could take before throwing me over his shoulder and whisking me away.

The waiter repeated our orders and asked if we needed anything else. Jason refused to look at me as he requested a large glass of ice water. When the brimming goblet arrived, I couldn't contain my giggles any longer.

Jason watched my near hysterics, his exasperation vanishing in his own fit of laughter. Only when the hostess seated another couple at the next table were we able to get a handle on our hilarity. Our hands came together again as we caught our breath.

"I knew you were sexy, but *good Lord*," Jason said, after a long drink. "I don't suppose you could save some of that for later? I'd like to survive dinner."

I shrugged, promising nothing.

After another sip of water, he loosened his tie. He fingered the button at his throat, just as he had at the reception. Was that really only two days ago?

"Would you like some help with that?" I asked slyly.

His eyes locked on me, and he immediately cinched his tie back up. "No, thank you," he said firmly and promptly polished off the rest of his water.

He cleared his throat and folded his hands together in front of him, denying my touch. "So you mentioned you had a summer job lined up in San Jose?" he asked lightly.

I tried not to laugh again, recognizing his attempt to turn the conversation toward something resembling small talk. "Yes, but it's nothing special. For the last couple of years I've worked at the local library, helping out with the summer reading program. It's really just something to do—the pay sucks. If I'm lucky I'll sell an article or two to the neighborhood paper."

Jason leaned forward. "You don't need the money for school?"

I sat up a little straighter, startled by his question. "No. My parents planned for me to go to college since the day I was born, and they started saving then. My dad also left me some money specifically for school. He was adamant that I complete my education."

Jason's expression brightened. "I have a tough time believing your father had many harsh words for you."

I laughed. "No, he didn't. I'd needle him once in a while so he'd tell me about *his* college days. He had the best stories." In my mind I heard Dad's contagious laughter, which wasn't so different from Jason's. "I think the two of you would have gotten along very well."

"If he didn't shoot me first," Jason chuckled.

My hand slid across the table to him, and he gave it a squeeze. I was having a tough time not touching him.

"True. You have corrupted his daughter quite thoroughly."

"So what does your mom think of me?" Jason's forehead creased slightly.

Does my mother's opinion mean that much to him? I squirmed a little, afraid to admit what I had, and hadn't, told her. "She doesn't know *what* to make of you. I haven't gone into great detail about…you know…us."

"Hmmm," was his enigmatic reply.

The waiter returned with our dinner, thankfully ending that train of thought. My stomach growled at the grilled shrimp and scallops on my plate, but Jason's bacon-wrapped filet mignon looked awfully appetizing too.

"Yours looks good," we said in unison.

"How about we share?" Jason sliced his meat down the middle and slid half to the side. "It doesn't really feel like we've only known each other only a couple of days, does it?" he asked.

Not nervous or self-conscious—well, except for the dress—I felt…at peace. "No, it doesn't. You're very easy to be with," I said.

We exchanged samples, mmm-ing and ahh-ing when we tasted the food.

"So what classes are you taking this summer?" I asked after a sip of wine.

"It's a very easy session for me, actually. Only General Ed classes are taught in the summer, so I have English Lit and Philosophy, and that's it. I'll see if one of the local bands needs a pianist this summer. If not, I might give lessons for a few weeks."

He took another bite, and I tried to picture him teaching a ten-year-old how to play scales. I was surprised at how easily I could imagine it.

"Sounds like you aren't hurting for cash, either," I observed.

He chuckled. "No. I was lucky enough to win a scholarship that covers most of my expenses. My parents had big plans for me too, and they also saved up. Life's been good for both me and Mitch," he said.

We continued to chat about summer until the waiter cleared our plates. We ordered coffees in lieu of dessert, and I wondered what he had planned next. The PG-13 restriction on our date was about to expire.

Jason took a deep breath, glanced at me, then watched his finger circle the top of his wine glass. "Sounds like your summer is pretty flexible, Melissa," he started.

"I suppose," I said carefully. His seemingly offhand comment was reminiscent of the roundabout way he'd trolled for information in his emails.

He interlaced his fingers, distracted by his own movements.

Is he nervous? I braced myself for what he might say next.

"Have you ever thought about doing any traveling?" he asked.

I looked at him blankly. "Traveling?"

His eyes creased at my confusion. "I thought you might like to check out the Midwest, specifically a certain town in Michigan," he said.

Caught completely off guard, I stared at him. "I…uh…I don't have *that* much extra money, Jason. Airline tickets aren't cheap." My mind raced. I'd been given a reprieve until Friday, but now—what was he suggesting? "My mom…I…" I couldn't untangle my conflicting emotions enough to form a coherent sentence.

Jason leaned toward me and touched my arm. "It's just a thought, Melissa. That's all."

My mouth opened, but nothing came out. Michigan? Even my imagination failed me this time.

Jason shook his head. "I'm sorry I brought it up—forget I said anything." He brought my hand to his lips. "Did I chase Naughty Melissa away?" He brushed his mouth across my wrist, his tongue lightly stroking my throbbing pulse.

Future be damned! Naughty Melissa couldn't care less; she wasn't about to disappear. The distance separating me from Jason was quickly becoming unbearable.

"No, she's definitely here." As proof, I fished a single ice cube out of his water glass and dragged it down the exposed center of my chest.

Jason's face turned red as he watched my fingers descend. Waving his hand at the waiter, he croaked, "Check, please."

Minutes later we were driving down the narrow access road toward the freeway.

"What's next? A steamy movie?" Could he have found a theater showing *Body Heat* somewhere nearby? Or *9½ Weeks* perhaps?

"Nope, no movie. Something quite different," he said. The rhythmic clicking of the turn signal should have warned me, but I didn't look up in time to see the sign announcing where we'd turned. We stopped in front of a group of mission-style buildings nestled against a hill. "Wait here for just a sec, okay?" he said. Before I could reply, he'd popped the trunk and hopped out.

I'd reached for the door handle when the trunk closed with a loud *thump*. When Jason opened my door, a bulging sack was hanging from one hand.

"Where are we?" I asked.

"You really don't know?"

I shook my head.

"Let's find out," he said mysteriously and offered me his arm. He avoided the largest building, leading me into a smaller one tucked into the trees to the right.

The surprises continued when we entered what seemed to be a hotel gift shop. Jason led me through racks of wind chimes, lotions, and swimsuits to a desk in the back. I looked for some indication of where we were, finally finding a clue when we made it to the cashier. "Reservation for McAlister," Jason announced, and I read the sign on the counter: *Welcome to Sycamore Springs.*

My breath caught. A secluded resort hotel, Sycamore Springs boasted natural mineral springs that fed a set of hot tubs hidden on the hillside. I'd never been here before, but the place was a favorite make-out spot for many of the athletes I'd interviewed over the years.

Jason finished with the clerk and smiled broadly. "Shall we?" Consulting the map provided by the cashier, we followed a dimly lit trail up the hill. Every once in a while a faint light would mark a turn-off for one of the hot tubs, but all I could see was black. Occasionally we'd hear a giggle somewhere in the darkness. The path forked and we followed the sign marked Rendezvous. It led us to redwood deck, a wooden bench, and an empty hot tub.

A single light illuminated the controls for the water. Jason kissed my cheek, then set the bag down and knelt by the dials. Soon the water swirled and bubbled to life, filling the tub at my feet. With the flick of a switch, a faint glow emanated from the bottom. I shivered, not from the cold, but from the nervous excitement racing over my skin like sparks dancing on steel.

Jason pulled me close. "What do you think? Look like fun?" he whispered seductively.

I looked around, but I couldn't see or hear another soul. "Fun? I suppose that's one word for it. I'm assuming there are no swimsuits in the bag." My hands ran up his jacket to his tie, and I began to finger the knot gently.

"No. Just towels and flip-flops. I didn't think you'd want to walk back down the hill in heels." He ran his fingers through my hair as he spoke, finding my barrette and unfastening it. After depositing it in his left jacket pocket, he pulled my face to his. "Swimsuits would just get in the way." He traced my lips with the tip of his tongue.

My mouth opened to receive his, but he didn't come closer; rather he backed away. I looked at him and pouted, but he slipped his jacket off, folded it, and set it on the bench. "It's much warmer in the water," he said, giving me a sly smile before he turned and removed his shoes and socks.

I slipped my shoes off and sat on the nearest bench to watch Jason undress. He didn't look at me as he removed his tie, his long fingers making quick work of the offending knot. His shirt was the next to go; he was down to his slacks when he realized I was still dressed. "Aren't you going to join me?"

"Oh yes, I plan to, but I didn't know dinner came with a show," I said with a snicker.

"Are you looking for a show?" he teased, giving his hips a swivel as he unzipped his pants. I laughed, but as he slowly slid his pants down, I fell silent. There were no briefs tonight. There was nothing but skin, muscles, and beneath a tuft of dark curly hair…*him.*

With a smile, Jason stepped out of his slacks and hung them over the back of the bench. My heart stopped when he moved toward me, completely naked, and leaned down.

"Show's over," he whispered, running a finger down the center of my dress and earning a standing ovation from my nipples. But then he turned away, leaving my hands hanging in mid-air as I reached for him. With a chuckle, he pulled a red bottle out of the bag and turned to the hot tub.

Sitting on the edge, he emptied the bottle into the water. The smell of sulfur was replaced with that of roses and strawberries. Jason glanced over his shoulder at me and grinned. "Better?"

"Yeeeaah…"

My answer caught in my throat when Jason's broad shoulders flexed. Every muscle in his back tightened for an endless second while he balanced on his hands. In one smooth motion, he elongated his body and disappeared under the bubbles.

My mouth dropped open when he rose from the foam to face me. The water swirled around his navel, his perfectly defined arms shimmering as he pushed his dripping hair back. His hands ran down his face before falling back into the water. Glittery droplets cascaded over every hard ridge and taut valley of his body.

I envied the beads of liquid licking at Jason's skin. My jacket fell behind me; I was shivering, but definitely *not* cold.

"Melissa?" he said softly, holding his hand out to me.

I swallowed and blinked, but didn't move. *Surely this is another dream.*

Jason moved to the edge closest to me, resting his head casually on his arms. "Or do I get a show, too?"

"I don't have nearly as much clothing to tease you with," I said. I stood, keenly aware that parts of me were as wet as he was.

"I was hoping you'd say that," he said, his voice husky. The sound sent Naughty Melissa into orbit.

My eyes never leaving him, I lifted the back of my skirt. I swayed my hips back and forth, slipping my underwear down my bare legs. I bent over to retrieve my black panties and Jason sighed, peering down my dress again.

"See something you like?" I chuckled.

"*Like* is not the word I would use."

A flurry of tingles coalesced in my chest, raising hard peaks beneath the black fabric. I tried not to dwell on the implication woven into his words as I straightened up. Jason shifted in the hot tub while I took my time with the zipper on the back of the dress. The sight of his naked body stretched out in the water below me was quite distracting.

"Melissa, it's been two long days, and one incredibly long night." He ran his hand through his hair again.

"Trust me, I'm well aware how *long* it's been," I said, releasing the hooks holding the halter top behind my neck. The dress floated to the deck, leaving me standing above him *au naturel.*

He exhaled loudly and licked his lips. After I laid the dress across the bench, his hand rose to me again.

I reached for his outstretched fingers and stepped into the water. I almost ruined the moment by jumping right back out.

"It's really hot," I gasped.

"I'm sorry," he said, and stroked my legs under the surface. "Does this help?"

I nodded, slowly becoming acclimated to the water.

"Maybe I should give you something else to concentrate on." His hands slid up out of the water and rested on my hips. Standing on the step, I towered over Jason, but he used that fact to his advantage. Starting just below my ribs, his lips nipped and nuzzled as they wandered higher, sending spikes of pleasure through me.

"If we increase your body temperature, it won't be such a shock," he mouthed against my skin, occasionally tasting it with the tip of his tongue. My fingers wove into his hair as he kissed his way up the center of my chest.

The heat of the water, the steam, and his body seeped into me from all sides, taking away the sting. He dipped his hands in the water again, reheating them before wrapping one around each of my breasts. With his sizzling thumbs, he circled and flicked my engorged nipples. The water could've been a thousand degrees, and I wouldn't have cared.

"Jason," I moaned, hoping the rumble of the Jacuzzi would mask my exclamation.

He hummed in response, his lips still against my chest. My cheek brushed against the top of his damp hair, filling my lungs with another blast of sweet berries and strong sulfur. His mouth found the hard center of one breast, tonguing and sucking it.

I gripped his shoulder as he blew a cool breath across my freshly kissed nipple, eliciting another squeak. "You're torturing me," I croaked.

A low, sexy laugh was his reply. "Now you know what I was going through at dinner," he said, leaning away from me.

"I didn't mean I didn't like it," I complained, refusing to let him go.

He just smirked. One of his hands disappeared, and I started to sink into the water. When his hot, wet fingers slid up between my legs, the surprise stood me back up instantly. Fire and water combined when he touched me, stroked me. I threw my head back and rocked against the rhythm of his very long, very talented fingers.

"Do you think you're hot enough now?" he teased, slipping a warm finger into me.

My reply came out with a grunt, "Hot? Uh…on fire." I lowered myself down to him, throwing my knees wide. We kissed again, but he caught me in the water and set me down on the edge of the submerged ledge. His hand continued its torturous exploration, and I panted in pleasure when his touch found that perfect, sensitive spot. I moved my lips to his ear and explored it with my tongue. "I want you, Jason," I whispered.

"Mmmm, do you?" A tremor rocked through me when I tried to answer, and he chuckled. "I'm not quite done teasing you, Melissa," he whispered in a low, silky voice. He sucked my earlobe and let it gently slide between his teeth.

"I'm so close, Jason…*please*…"

But he didn't move. Instead, he began a different dance with his hand, kneading my flesh gently between his thumb and finger.

I pinched my eyes shut and threw my head back, silently screaming for release. "Jason…" I warned, quickly reaching the point of no return. As the wave of orgasm crashed over me, I moaned, and he sighed.

Jason's voice was barely audible over the rushing water. "You're so intense when you come, Melissa. I had to see it…the first time."

My eyes popped open, and I inhaled, seeing the wanton look in his eyes. His fingers had stopped moving when I peaked, but hadn't left me. A smile bloomed on his face, and his fingers slid inside me, starting a new rhythm.

At first the sensations were almost too much to bear, sending violent spasms through me. After the third quake, he moved to my ear. "Do you want me to stop?"

The next climax was already building, and I shook my head, unable to speak. Slowly the overwhelming sensitivity became an even deeper longing, and my hand wound its way under the water.

"You're coming with me, this time," I growled, wrapping my fingers around him. Slowly I traced his every contour, letting my hand rise and fall along his hard length.

"Oh yes," he breathed. His lips crashed into mine, and he kissed me hard, forcing his tongue into my mouth. His fingers emerged and returned to their erotic stroking, pushing me close to the brink again. But fingers wouldn't be enough for me this time.

Gasping for air, I couldn't speak. My body was screaming—no, begging—for more than just Jason's touch. *Enough foreplay! I want more! Please…please, Jason…*

Hands and fingers disappeared, and with a single satisfying surge, we became one. His eyes burned through me, and I returned the stare with desperate longing. We'd done careful, I wanted ferocious. I crushed myself against him, driving him even deeper.

Jason grabbed the lip of the hot tub, still locked in my gaze, and started to rock. The blue of his eyes enveloped me; I saw nothing that wasn't him. I reached down and found the edge of the step and braced myself as he plunged into me again and again. Deeper and deeper… I couldn't get enough.

"The way you feel, Melissa…so right…"

Every sensation was heightened. I felt every bubble wiggle past my skin, heard every sigh and moan that left Jason's throat. I tasted the remnants of his coffee-tinged kiss on my lips, smelled the bitter sulfur slowly overpowering the fruity bath oils. His teeth sparkled in the dim light, clenched together with concentrated determination. Most of all, I could feel every millimeter of him as the friction between us increased to overwhelming levels. Water sloshed out of the tub onto the deck, an appropriate herald of the coming ecstasy.

I fought to stave off my second orgasm until the last possible moment, alternately panting and holding my breath, aching for the glorious end. *Now, Jason, NOW!* I thought, and my resistance crumbled. Jason's cry of sheer elation answered my unspoken words, and I felt his first pulse as I contracted around him. We climaxed together, flying to a level of euphoria I didn't know existed. I was barely aware of his movements when he pulled me across the tub, holding me tightly on top of him.

As the rapture faded into exhausted contentment, I watched my lover. Jason's eyes were closed, and with a melodic sigh, a very relaxed grin filled his face. I kissed him gently, running my fingers through his hair. "How did I end up here, with you?" I wondered out loud.

His eyes opened halfway. "I could ask you the same thing, lover," he whispered. "I wish I had another way to say it, but you are simply incredible."

I brushed my lips against his, sharing a breath with him. "Well, you're perfect," I said and laid my head on his shoulder, letting the water tickle my chin.

We held each other for a long time, staring up into the trees. The branches blocked out the night sky, forming a canopy of blackness above us. The water continued to swirl and bubble, relaxing our tired bodies while we sat, silent, each lost in our own thoughts.

My mind drifted back to the beginning, to the first moment I saw Jason and my imaginary life with him. Although I knew I shouldn't, I pretended it could all be true, that I could be with him always. I could hear the words on his lips—"I love you, Melissa"—said with such deep affection that my heart fluttered out of control. My reply would be a simple, plain "I love you too."

But that's perfect! When even Naughty Melissa approved, I knew my attraction to Jason was much more than physical. I truly loved the peaceful stranger in my arms, whether he shared the sentiment or not.

My thoughts were interrupted by a bell ringing at the bottom of the hill. I counted twelve chimes, then Jason took a deep breath, kissed me softly, and slowly slid away. Our watery bliss had come to an end. Without a word, he climbed out of the hot tub and wound one of the huge beach towels around his waist. Always the gentleman, he held the other one open, wrapping it—and himself—around me when I emerged from the tub.

"Thank you. This was wonderful," I said with as much sincerity as I could muster. I stood on my toes and gave him a chaste kiss.

He didn't say anything at first, watching his fingers fall through my hair. The crease between his eyes told me he was debating what to say. After three passes, he spoke.

"You're very welcome," he said. My heart wrung itself inside out, trying to read his expression. The devotion in his eyes was tinted with something dark. Sadness perhaps?

I was about to apologize—for what I wasn't sure—when he leaned in and kissed my neck. When he looked up again, the sorrow was gone.

"Time to go to bed," he said, a genuine smile returning to his face.

We slipped on a minimal amount of clothing and walked back down the hill. I was thankful for the flip-flops; Jason was right. I probably would've slid down the hill on my ass if I'd been wearing heels. 'Course, I didn't complain when he kept his arm securely around me.

Jason remained quiet on the drive home, but kept his hand in mine. Now and then he'd steal a glance at me or squeeze my fingers, but these contacts were different—not thrilling or electric, but thoughtful and loving. I stroked the back of his hand with my thumb, hoping he felt the same emotion from me. We both sighed, and I smiled, convinced he did. I wished this spectacular night would never end.

By the time we snuggled together in my makeshift bed, it was past one a.m. Rolling over on the less-than-fluffy sleeping bag, I had to laugh.

"What's so funny?" Jason asked, his eyes twinkling.

"Just look at us…we had a romantic dinner and erotic sex, yet here we are, decked out in our old T-shirts, trying to get comfortable on the floor. Kind of anti-climactic," I giggled.

Jason stretched across me and turned off the light. "Anti-*climactic?*" he whispered. "Are you trying to tell me something?" He slipped his leg over mine and dipped his head to suckle his way down my neck.

Sleep would have to wait awhile longer.

Fourteen

*T*he transition from sleeping to waking was slow and easy for a change. Before my eyes opened, I savored the warmth of my surroundings. The birds chirped happily outside. Somewhere in the distance a leaf blower hummed. The sheets rustled beside me, assuring me I wasn't alone.

Jason brushed the hair out of my face with one finger. "Good morning, beautiful," he said.

Slowly I opened my eyes and was greeted by a phenomenal view of my own personal Prince Charming. "Good morning, handsome."

"Do you always wake up with such a lovely smile on your face?" he asked. His finger moved to my lips, tracing the grin I couldn't contain.

"I doubt it," I said with a laugh. "My alarm clock isn't nearly this pleasant." I shifted slightly, feeling a twinge in my neck as I did. "Did you sleep well?"

"Yes, but I woke up a while ago. I've been watching you dream. It was quite entertaining."

"Entertaining? How?" I asked. I tried to nonchalantly wipe my chin. Had I been drooling in my sleep?

"You displayed quite a rainbow of expressions this morning. Do you remember any of your dreams?"

I closed my eyes, searching for some flicker of memory, but found none. "Nope. I'm sure it was all good," I said and rolled onto my back. I must've slept in one position the whole night; everything was stiff and tight. The pain in my neck became more pronounced and threatened to migrate into my head. I was contemplating finding the aspirin when Journey started playing next to me. It was Mom.

When I picked up my cell phone, I groaned. It was only eight o'clock—too early for her to be calling. Something was wrong.

"Hi, Mom. What's up?"

"Oh, thank God, you're all right," she said. "I was so worried. Where are you?"

"I'm still in Santa Lucia, remember? What's going on?"

"Thank goodness. The alarm at the house just went off. The police are on their way, but I had to make sure you were okay."

I covered my face with my free hand, trying to contain the fear rising from the pit of my stomach. Jason touched my shoulder.

"I'm fine. Everything here is quiet, so don't worry. I should hang up so you can talk to the police when they call. After you hear from them, call me back, okay?" I tried to keep my voice steady. I hadn't thought about Ron in a day and a half, but he'd obviously been busy.

"Okay. Hopefully I'll talk to you in a few minutes. I love you," she said.

"I love you too, Mom." I closed the phone—and my eyes—and lay there. The headache I'd been dreading made its full-blown debut with invisible daggers penetrating my temples.

"What's wrong?" Jason whispered.

"The alarm went off at my mom's house a few minutes ago. It has to be Ron." My own voice made my head throb. I cocked my elbow over my face, blocking out the equally irritating light.

Jason sighed. "The house was empty, right?"

I nodded, but then grimaced.

"You don't look so good," he said.

"I think I'm getting a migraine."

I felt a warm hand stroke my arm. "I've got ibuprofen in my kit. Would you like some?" His voice was so soothing, *it* was almost enough to stop the pain. Almost.

"Thanks. That'd be great."

Jason must've left, but I didn't hear him. I was aware only of the ominously silent phone in my hand and the timpani pounding inside my skull. I couldn't help but imagine what the police might find. At first I pictured the inside of Mom's house—my home—a complete disaster. Shattered glass, upended furniture, emptied cabinets—the manifestation of violent rage. Superimposed on the destruction was Ron's face, filled with evil satisfaction, laughing maniacally. I gritted my teeth, and the pain in my head intensified.

That's not the only possibility. Another image filled my mind, a more pleasant sight: Ron in handcuffs being thrown into the back of a blue-and-white San Jose Police cruiser. He cowered in the back seat, weak and impotent. Maliciously, I hoped he'd suffer the same sexual violence in prison as he'd inflicted on his victims.

My grisly musings were interrupted by the enticing hum of the coffee grinder. The ache eased a bit with the promise of caffeine. Jason's continued thoughtfulness struck me, filling me with something deeper than gratitude. I tried to embrace the feeling, but one word doused it. *Friday.*

"Here you go," Jason said.

I moaned when I took my arm off my face and forced myself to sit up. He handed me two brown pills and a big glass of water. "Thanks," I said, tossing both pills in my mouth. The cool water quenched a thirst I didn't realize I had, and I finished the whole glass without thinking. When I handed it back to Jason, my phone came to life.

"Mom," I said with the phone halfway to my ear.

"Hi, Melissa," was her subdued reply. "The police didn't find much at the house. They saw some scratches on the front door, but it didn't appear to have been opened. The deadbolt is still intact, and none of the windows are damaged."

"Which sensor went off?"

"The front door. The sound of the alarm must've scared off whoever was messing around." She didn't sound particularly pleased.

"What else, Mom…is there something you're not telling me?" I asked.

"They reviewed the tapes from the surveillance van and saw a light-colored sedan stop in front of the house right before the alarm went off. What did you say that guy's car looked like?"

I caught Jason's eye. "The cops said he drives a tan Saturn. Crap."

"Damn it," he whispered and sat down next to me, putting his hand on my back.

"The police are canvassing the area, but I doubt they'll find him," Mom continued. "It's rush hour. You know what that's like." She sighed, her frustration mirroring mine.

"You're staying in Reno, right?"

"Until Sunday night. I'll call you before I leave, and we'll figure out what to do then. You stay in Santa Lucia and keep your doors locked," Mom commanded.

Any other time I would've questioned her authority—we're both adults—but in this case her worry was more than justified.

"Okay, Mom, I will." I twisted my head around, trying to loosen my cramping neck. While I was relieved the house was okay, Ron was much too close for comfort. "How's the rodeo?" I asked, changing the subject.

Jason slowly rubbed my back while I conversed with Mom about steers and lariats. I promised to call her tomorrow before hanging up.

"They didn't catch him," Jason stated, rather than asked. The angry glare in his eyes didn't help—the last thing I wanted was for him to confront Ron again.

"No. They only caught a picture of his car. Apparently, he tried to break in through the front door, but the alarm scared him off."

Something wasn't right, though. Why would he try to break in at eight in the morning?

"At least the police know where he is," Jason said. "It shouldn't be much longer before they catch him." His fingers moved up to my neck, working a particularly stubborn knot.

"That feels good." I took a deep breath and let it out slowly, trying to clear the image of Ron from my mind.

"Take off your shirt and lie down," Jason said.

I gave him a sideways glance, in too much pain to turn my head, let alone have sex.

He rolled his eyes. "I'm not going to molest you, promise. Lie on your stomach."

Still wary, I slipped the T-shirt over my head before lying down and curling my arms up at my sides. His knee touched my elbow. "Comfortable?" he asked.

"I guess. A little chilly, maybe."

"Not for long." I heard him rubbing his hands together, and my skin tingled in anticipation. I jumped when he touched the base of my spine; his hands were blazing hot, but felt wonderful. His thumbs pressed into my tight muscles, his fingers wrapping around my sides as they slid up to my shoulder blades. "Try not to think, just relax," he said hypnotically.

"Okay," I said, exhaling slowly. He methodically kneaded my back, working each tense muscle. Amazingly, his touch didn't ignite the passionate desire I usually felt; rather it drew the pain and stress out of me like a magnet. His hands moved firmly over my skin in rhythmic patterns. First he made circles with his fingers, then waves with his knuckles, then lines up and down my neck with his thumbs. Within minutes, I became a lifeless puddle of goo.

"How do you feel now?" he asked, lightening his touch.

"Ung," I grunted. "Like a jellyfish. I'm yours," I sighed. The ache in my head was a distant memory.

He chuckled softly. "That's exactly what I wanted to hear."

The peace of the moment was broken when my phone rang again, the harsh bell signifying one of my friends calling me. "Noooo," I moaned, and Jason increased his pressure again before lifting his hands from me.

"Don't you dare move." He found the phone and answered it. "Hello, Linda."

I remained perfectly still, listening to Jason deflect her curious probes with short "yes, Linda" and "no, Linda" responses until she must've gotten to the purpose of her call.

"Just a second, I'll ask her," he said. "Melissa, would you like to go to the beach with Linda and Chase today?"

"Uh-huh," was all I could manage.

"I think that was a yes. Hmmm? Okay, hang on." I heard him shift, but per his instructions, I didn't move. "Linda wants to tell you something. Here."

The phone touched my cheek.

"Melissa, can you hear me?" Linda said loudly.

"Yeah."

"Wear that bikini we got you last month. If you show up in that one-piece you wear to do laps, I'm going to cut it in half. Got it?"

"'Kay." *Whatever*. At this particular moment she could've told me to come buck naked and I would've said yes.

The phone disappeared.

"What time…? Great. See you then." He snapped the phone shut, and I heard him rubbing his hands again. I welcomed their return with a sigh.

"You seem to be pretty agreeable now," he said, feathering his fingers across my shoulders.

"Uh-huh." Anyone who could make me feel this good could have whatever they wanted.

"So you'll give me whatever I want?" he asked slyly. I was too lazy to even roll my eyes at my mind-reading masseuse.

"Uh."

He took my vague response as a yes. "Good," he said. His fingers walked down my spine with tiny baby steps, covering every millimeter from my hair to my hips and erasing coherent thought. When he got to the base of my spine, he fanned his hands out and slid them back up slowly. He stopped, and I felt his warm breath in my ear.

"I want *you*. *Forever*," he whispered, then started massaging my scalp with his fingertips.

"Okay," I sighed, ignoring the garbled warnings running through my gelatinous brain.

"Deal." Jason laughed again, then slowly removed his hands from my hair and covered me with the sheet. "I'm going to take a quick shower. You stay here and try not to melt into the floor."

"'Kay," I replied.

I don't know how long I lay there, but when the shower went on, I finally collected enough energy to move. It was like the day had started all over again, cleansed of Ron's disruption. Not bothering with my t-shirt, I slipped into the bathroom and started my routine at the sink. We shared my lone bathroom like we'd been living together a year, not a couple of days. Jason hopped out of the shower, and I stepped in, wasting barely a drop of water. He was just finishing at the sink when I turned off the water, and he passed me a towel.

The familiarity continued in the kitchen, where we enjoyed cereal and bananas for breakfast. I was impressed when Jason poured my coffee and added a teaspoonful of hot chocolate mix to it. With a knowing smile, he closed the canister of cocoa before handing me the cup. Mitch must've been very thorough when he clued Jason in on my likes. I'd have to thank him someday.

We chatted easily about nothing, eventually coming around to the weirdest things we'd eaten for breakfast. Since Jason ate at the dining hall every day, he rarely had anything that wasn't considered breakfast food. I, on the other hand, ate anything that was in the fridge. When he raised a skeptical eyebrow, I quickly grabbed a fork and the container of cold spaghetti.

Before I could take a bite he emptied my hands.

"No, I believe you. Please don't eat that—the garlic will ruin the banana I just ate." He then ended the discussion by sealing his lips to mine, reminding me how much I loved bananas.

We'd barely finished our breakfast when Linda knocked on the door. She took one look at me and smiled.

"You actually wore it!" she screeched.

Doubling as a windbreaker and cover-up, my beige long-sleeved shirt was unbuttoned and tied at the bottom, revealing my navy blue bikini top.

"I said I would, didn't I?"

Seeing Jason, Linda lost interest in me and looped her arm through his. She escorted him out to the car while I locked the door. When she dragged Jason into the back seat of Chase's Suburban with her, I yelled "Hey!" but she just stuck her tongue out at me and buckled up. Sulking, I hopped in the front seat next to Chase.

"So you made quite the romantic proposal, I hear." I said, trying to ignore the chatter behind me.

Chase grinned and backed out of the parking space. "I guess. She liked it."

I waited for Linda to chime in with more gushing about their engagement, but she continued to grill Jason. When she asked about the details of our time at the hot springs, I'd had enough.

"Rumor has it a ring was involved, but I haven't seen it yet," I said loudly, glaring at her.

Linda stopped talking immediately, her whole face turning red. "There definitely *is* a ring," she said and dangled her hand over the front seat. "I'm sorry, Mel. Here."

"Wow, this is gorgeous," I said, inspecting the large solitaire. I tilted the ring back and forth, sending tiny rainbows spinning through the car.

"Isn't it? I told Chase it was perfect, but he's taking me with him to shop for a wedding set in the jewelry district in L.A. next weekend." She glowed at her boyfriend—no, fiancé.

"Wow, even more diamonds coming. I hope you have a lucrative summer job, Chase," I said.

He laughed, shaking his head. "No, unfortunately not. Thank God for credit cards. I'm going to have to design the next Eiffel Tower to pay off the bill, though." An architecture major, Chase wanted his name on the next "world's tallest building."

"Good luck with that," I said with a grin.

Jason had been listening quietly, and when the conversation lulled, he leaned forward and put his hand on my shoulder. I automatically touched it with my fingers, wishing he was closer.

"I noticed the boards on top of the car, Chase. Are there any decent surf spots around here?" he asked.

"It's not too spectacular, but there's a ground swell in right now. I brought my extra thruster and spring suit in case you'd like to catch a few sets," Chase said.

I looked at him dumbly, not understanding anything he said, but Jason replied with an enthusiastic "Wicked!" The guys launched into a detailed conversation about Central Coast surfing, but I stopped paying attention to the words and just listened to the lilt of Jason's voice. Linda didn't speak either, and I could guess she was busy trying to figure out how Jason and I fit together. Her curiosity was insatiable.

It didn't take long to drive to Pismo Beach, and we lucked into a good parking spot near the stairs leading down to the sand. Linda and Chase practically lived at the beach during the summer and had everything we'd need for a full day of sun, surf, and relaxation. The guys took the umbrella and cooler, and we followed with the chairs and towels. By the time the surfboards made it down, Linda and I were lying in the bright sun in our bikinis, oblivious to the world.

"Now, *this* is a Kodak moment," Jason said.

I opened my eyes to find the guys standing in front of us, clicking off photos on their cell phones. I threw one hand over my face and gave Jason the finger with the other. He laughed and took another picture. He'd changed into a black, short-sleeved wetsuit. It only enhanced his muscular body.

Changing tactics, I smiled sweetly. "Come here. I'll give you something to remember," I said.

I heard a choking sound next to me.

Jason leaned down and gave me a quick kiss. "Later, Naughty Melissa," he whispered in my ear. "Things are a little too revealing in this." He ran his hand across his neoprene-covered chest.

My hand followed his. "I noticed. It's quite sexy, you know." I tried to pull him down for another not-so-quick kiss, but he resisted with a groan.

"You…ah." He wiggled out of my grip and stood, holding his hands together in front of him. He was right, the wetsuit was quite revealing, and very elastic, as demonstrated by the way it was expanding below his waist. "Good thing the water's cold. Chase, we'd better get out of here," Jason said, picking up his surfboard.

I tried not to look, but couldn't help but see that Chase's wetsuit was also form-fitting, and that Linda had a similar effect on him. She glanced at me, and we laughed as the guys headed for the waves, carrying their boards waist high.

They swam out past the kids playing in the shallow water, and I soon lost sight of them. Just as I closed my eyes again, Linda spoke.

"So, you and Jason seem pretty serious after—what, three days?" she said.

Here we go. "Define serious."

"He can't take his eyes off you. Did you know that? The entire ride over he was looking at you, even when he was talking to Chase." I peeked at Linda, only to see her peering intently at me.

"Can you pass me a water?" I pointed at the cooler next to her.

"And look at you. I've never seen *you* like this," she continued.

"Like what? I'm just relaxed, that's all." *At least I* was.

"Exactly. You swore I'd never see you in that bikini, that you were too embarrassed to wear it in public. Yet here you are, showing more skin than I've ever seen, perfectly at ease. I'd say Jason's had quite an effect on you, Melissa." Linda cracked open her water bottle and took a long drink. "How long have you known him, really?"

I sighed. My feelings were still all churned up. How could I explain...without sounding completely insane?

I stalled, picking up my chair and moving it under the shade of the umbrella before opening my water. Maybe I was going about this wrong. If I gave her *some* of the story, there was a slim possibility she'd let the rest go.

The beach was pretty crowded, and I waited for the mother next to us to finish yelling at her disobedient son before answering.

"It's complicated. I met Jason online at the beginning of the school year, and we had some fun via email for a few weeks. We didn't share pictures, I never spoke to him, and when we lost contact, I didn't give him another thought. When I saw him at the wedding, I didn't even know who he was."

If I *had* recognized him, would we have ended up here?

She dragged her chair next to mine. "But you figured it out."

"Yes, and I thought for sure he wouldn't want to have anything to do with me."

Linda's brow wrinkled. "Why?"

"Look at him, Linda." I waved toward the ocean. "He belongs with a debutante, or a supermodel. Plus, I wasn't exactly alluring in my email notes. I said some pretty raunchy things." My gaze shifted to the seagulls circling over the pier.

"You really need to give yourself a little more credit. Why you think you're not pretty, I'll never understand. If you saw how the guys on the team look at you whenever you walk away from them…" She picked up her sunscreen and squirted a thin ribbon on her arm. "That's why Mitch wouldn't let any of them ask you out," she said casually.

Mitch wouldn't let *them? Some reporter I am!* Perhaps that explained the strange behavior in the stable yesterday—Mitch must have intimidated the guys before he left. They probably saw Jason as an informant. But the larger question remained. "Why would he do that?" I asked.

"To keep them from fighting over you, that's why. You remember the brawl last summer, don't you?" She looked at me.

"What brawl?"

"After Santa Margarita."

I shook my head, and she lowered her sunglasses. "You really didn't know?"

"No. What happened?" Santa Margarita…I'd driven down to watch the rodeo in July, more as a fan than a journalist, and had spent most of my time in the stands. The guys had acted kind of weird that day, but I'd heard something about a filly and assumed they were bickering about some new girl they'd seen at the event—not me.

Linda nudged me, breaking me out of my stupor. "Remember Mike's black eye? Dave gave it to him after getting punched in the jaw. They both had big plans for you. Chase and Mitch had a heck of a time breaking up the fight."

Plans? For me? "No one ever said anything to me—before or after that. I really had no idea," I said. The breeze came up and blew my hair across my face. I caught it and tucked it behind my ear.

Linda chuckled. "Like I said, you need to give yourself more credit. What I really don't understand is why you never asked any of *them* out. Any of those guys would be a great catch." She turned back toward the ocean and let some of her water splash across her neck.

"I hate to burst your bubble, but I did ask one out. He turned me down," I said, enjoying the gape I got in return.

She recovered quickly and shook her head, brushing off my statement as impossible. "You got turned down? I don't believe it. Who'd you ask out?"

"Mitch," I said, realizing too late I should've kept my mouth shut.

"*He* turned you down?" Her eyes threatened to pop out of their sockets. "When was this?"

"Oh, I don't know…a couple years ago maybe? At Wednesday coffee."

Every Wednesday morning during rodeo season, the team met at Starbucks for morning coffee and to shoot the bull, so to speak. As an unofficial member, I was invited. Some days the guys filled the shop, other times only a couple showed up. Only once had Mitch and I been the only two there—our one and only "date."

Somehow we'd gotten onto the topic of my love life, and why I didn't have a boyfriend. "Why don't you ask more guys out?" Mitch had asked.

"Like I need more rejection in my life," I'd snapped back.

"Mel, you shouldn't quit before you try. Lots of guys would jump at the chance to go out with you."

"Right." I took a sip of coffee while he huffed. There was only one guy I'd ever thought about asking out, and he was sitting in front of me. "Fine. How about you, then? There's a new Bond movie out. We could catch the nine o'clock."

The words were hardly out of my mouth before I regretted saying them. He froze, and I tried to play off my request as a joke. "Or maybe we could catch the matinee on Saturday, if it's past your bedtime."

The shock on his face dissolved into an apologetic frown, and I knew what was coming.

"It's not that I don't want to," he started, sliding his coffee cup between us, "But…"

Did you really think he'd say yes? I stared at the table, wounded, embarrassed, and sure I'd just ruined our friendship. "I understand. I'm sorry I—"

That's when Mitch had put a rough finger under my chin and forced me to look at him. "No, Melissa, don't be sorry. It's just that you're more like my little sister. I couldn't. But you'll find the right guy eventually." He'd then slid his boot out from under the table and wiggled it. "And he won't be wearing shit kickers, either."

"Besides," I said, running my finger in the sand and avoiding Linda's stare, "he'd already seen the movie. It wasn't a big deal." I wasn't about to let Linda—or Mitch, for that matter—know exactly how much his rejection had hurt.

"He said he thought of you as his little sister?" Linda asked.

"Yup."

"Maybe you will be, someday," she quipped, earning a swat on the leg. "So back to Jason—how do you feel about him exactly?"

The water bottle in my hands was now covered in condensation, and I collected the droplets with my finger. "I don't know. Physically, he's…fantastic. And I wish I could describe how I feel when I'm with him…it's not like anything I've ever experienced with a man before. I don't have to pretend to be something I'm not. He seems to accept everything about me, no matter how bizarre. It's very…refreshing."

A huge grin stretched across Linda's face. "There's a name for that feeling, you know."

The smile I discovered on my own lips vanished and became a scowl. "Names don't mean anything. He leaves Friday, and I won't ever see him again." The crushing emptiness returned, and I struggled for a breath.

"Hmph. You can try to deny it, Melissa, but it's written all over your face. You're in love." She held her hand up, refusing to hear any more argument from me. "And the way Jason looks at you, I'm pretty sure he feels the same way. Aren't you even going to *try* to hang on to that?" she scolded.

"In love? After three days?" I snorted. *Is it that obvious?*

"Why not? It didn't take much longer than that for me and Chase. 'Course we didn't jump into the sack hours after we first met," she teased.

"Your loss," I said, gloating.

She giggled. "I still have trouble believing you did that. Just another piece of evidence that points to Jason being someone very special. You'd better not let him walk out of your life."

Reality slapped me across the face yet again. "I don't have a choice. His life is halfway across the country, and mine is here. All we have is today."

"I'm guessing Jason won't let you go that easily," she said in her annoying know-it-all tone.

I tried to brush her comment away with a sweep of my hand, but one phrase wouldn't leave me. *You're in love.* I knew she was right, but it didn't matter. Friday was only three days away.

I decided it was time to change the subject. "So, Linda, now that you've got the ring, when's the wedding?" I asked.

She sighed and admired her new piece of jewelry. "Not soon enough. That's for sure. It'll be next summer, after we both graduate."

"Have you decided where you're going to get married?" Linda's mom lived in Fremont, not far from my mom, but her dad lived in Texas.

"Actually, we were thinking about Hawaii. Just a small ceremony with close friends and family on the beach at sunset," she said, almost like she was asking my permission.

"That sounds beautiful, Linda."

"Would you come if we did that?" She looked at me with pleading eyes.

"Of course." By then I'd have the money from my internship to cover the cost. I wondered if she'd invite Jason. *Don't be ridiculous.*

Linda bounced in her seat. "That's great, Melissa. It wouldn't be any fun getting married if my maid of honor couldn't be there."

"Me? You want me to be your maid of honor? What about Beth or—"

She cut me off with a wave. "No, I want you. You've always been there for me, like a…*sister*," she giggled. "Will you? Please?" A preschooler couldn't beg any more effectively.

"Wow, Linda. I'm just so surprised. Thank you! I'd be happy to do it." I gave her hand a squeeze. "What is it I have to do exactly?" I asked timidly.

"Don't worry. It'll be easy. I'm so happy you'll be there!" Her eyes lit up. "Then you can catch my bouquet, and we can start planning *your* wedding," she chirped.

Before I could argue, Jason and Chase emerged from the crowd at the water's edge, grinning from ear to ear.

"That was great," Jason said. Breathing heavily, he stood his board up in the sand and unzipped his wetsuit.

"Catch any big ones?" I asked. He peeled the neoprene down to his waist, exposing his fantastic chest. At the sight of his wet, bare pecs I stopped listening, instead wondering what he did to stay in shape. My eyes wandered over his rippled six-pack…*hundreds of crunches?* The fantasy improved as my gaze rested on his broad shoulders and well-defined deltoids. *Oh, he could be a swimmer.* I imagined Jason in a tight, tiny Speedo, racing toward me, muscles bunching and straining, water dripping…

"Well, Melissa?" Jason asked, leaning down so all I could see were his eyes. Tiny laugh lines creased their corners, and I knew I'd been caught.

"What? Here," I said, flustered. I tossed him a towel, and he snorted.

"Thanks, but Chase asked if you wanted a hot dog. We're going up to the car to change and get some lunch." He slowly dragged the towel across his chest, his lips curving into an uneven smile that told me he knew precisely why I hadn't heard the question.

Blushing, I shrugged. I might be guilty, but he *was* magnificent. "Sure. Hurry back."

He bent down and kissed me with cold, salty lips before picking up his board and following Chase.

"Yup, you two are in love," Linda teased when the guys were out of earshot.

I sighed. I knew there was no point in arguing with her anymore. Loving Jason didn't change anything; I knew that too.

The guys weren't gone long. When they returned, they were wearing long, baggy swimming trunks and sunglasses. In their hands were boxes of hot dogs and French fries. Jason's shirt dangled from his back pocket, so I happily continued my ogling as we ate.

The afternoon progressed slowly, and I enjoyed every minute of it. The weather stayed warm, but occasionally a cool wind blew in from the ocean—a reminder the fog was never too far way. For most of the afternoon we continued our lazy lounging in the sun, enjoying the freedom summer brought. Linda and Chase accepted Jason without question; it was as if he'd been a part of the group all along. Linda still looked at me curiously every once in a while, giving me a knowing smile when I caught her. I rolled my eyes or stuck my tongue out in response, repeating what had become an annoying tune in my head. *Friday. It all ends Friday.*

Our fun ended just before sunset when Jason received a call from Detective Clark. He listened intently, saying very little, and thanked the detective before hanging up. While he was on the phone, I brought Linda and Chase up to speed on the Ron situation and what had happened this morning.

"He was at your mom's house?" Chase asked, stunned.

I nodded. The fear this morning's call had triggered tried to make a comeback, but a reassuring hug from Linda helped keep it bottled. "That's probably the police telling us they've caught him," she said.

"That'd be great." My hopes were short lived once I saw Jason's ashen face.

He closed his phone slowly. "The police have identified the prints on your driver's license. They belong to Ronald Hancock, an auto mechanic from San Fernando. They confirmed it was his car spotted in front of your mom's house this morning, Melissa, but it was last seen headed north, toward San Francisco."

"What else?" I asked. Nothing Jason had said explained his pale features.

"They've connected him to another murder—a month ago, not far from where he works. A teenager."

Jason looked at me and swallowed, like he was about to be sick. "He did the same disgusting things to her as he did to his other victims…including the wedding hostess."

And I'm next. Sand and sea became one nauseating hue as my vision blurred.

"Animal," Chase snarled. "I wish we'd known. We would've beat the living shit out of him."

I didn't realize I was trembling until Jason put his arm around me. "They've put out a statewide APB, and Detective Clark is confident they'll catch that scumbag soon. Try not to worry. You and your mom are both safe."

The four of us looked at each other. No one seemed to know what to say.

The beach around us emptied as the sun sank in the sky; families headed home, and only a few fishermen walked along the waterline.

Eventually Chase rose. "Why don't we pack up and watch the sunset from the pier?" he suggested.

We collected our things, threw our clothes back on, and walked onto the pier arm in arm. Directly ahead of us the setting sun turned the cloudless sky blood red. As it dipped below the horizon, Jason pulled me close and kissed me.

"Too bad we can't just stop time right now," I whispered when his lips left mine.

He smiled back. "But you're mine forever, remember? There's a lot of time for sunsets in eternity."

Jason pulled me close again, and his kiss filled me with the love I'd been trying to fight. I wanted to share his optimism, but one hated word canceled out my hopes for the future.

Friday.

Fifteen

"So, what do you think?" I asked, staring impatiently across the table.

Jason took an inordinate amount of time chewing the bite of burger, paused, looked up at the ceiling, then chewed some more. Annoyed, I picked up my own burger and took another bite. Finally, he swallowed.

"Well, after much consideration, I have to agree with you," he said. "This very well could be the best hamburger I've ever had." He gave me a thumbs up.

I rolled my eyes. "Told you," I grumbled through my mouthful.

He started laughing, and I barely got my food down before I joined him.

Chase and Linda had invited us to share a movie with them, but we'd declined. After they'd dropped us off at my apartment, we'd opted for a late dinner instead. I'd shared Jason enough for the day, and though I loved Linda, I'd reached my limit with her suggestive prodding. I wanted Jason all to myself, to take him somewhere away from everything and everyone. And I knew just the place.

"I especially love the décor," he said, pointing up. Thirty or so toothpicks were stuck in the acoustic ceiling tiles, their colorful cellophane tails creating a shiny rainbow in the fluorescent light.

I took a long drink of my malt before speaking. "Oh, come on. There must be lots of places like this in Michigan. I'll bet the ceiling in every diner in Ann Arbor has those." Every college hangout had a similar look—it just happened the Burger Factory had great food as well.

Jason shrugged. "I wouldn't know. I spend nearly all my time on campus. It's a very sheltered life."

"It's time you got out more." I plucked a couple of straws from the dispenser and passed him one. Then I grabbed the toothpick that'd come in my hamburger.

"Melissa!" He dropped the straw and scooted into the corner of the booth.

"Come on. Live a little." I put the toothpick in the straw and blew as hard as I could. The tiny dart stuck in the ceiling directly over Jason. The lady in the next booth groaned and shook her head.

"You're such a wild woman," he said, stuffing the last of his burger in his mouth.

"You know it." I fished some cash out of my wallet and dropped it on the table. "Finished?" I asked.

Jason didn't answer. He picked up the straw and his toothpick and looked at me with one eyebrow raised.

"Give it all you've got," I coached with a grin.

Jason looked around quickly, took a deep breath and blew through the straw. The toothpick flew straight up, but instead of hitting one of the soft, white tiles, it hit one of the steel supports and, with a *tink,* ricocheted across the aisle. It landed, point down, in a stack of pancakes on the table across from us, as if placed there by the chef. The two people in the booth were locked together in a torrid kiss and didn't notice.

I bit back my giggles and waved Jason toward the exit. "I think we're done," I choked and pushed him out the door.

We dashed out, holding our sides. Jason beat me to the car and opened the driver's door with a bow.

"Why thank you kindly, sir," I said in a very bad Southern accent.

"Mah pleasure," he replied in an equally poor drawl, then got in the passenger side. "So what's next, cow tipping?"

The clock on the dash read twelve minutes past ten. "Nope, too early for that. The cows aren't really asleep until after eleven. Have you *been* cow tipping?" I asked, surprised he knew the term.

"No, Mitch told me about it a long time ago. He seemed to think it was fun."

"It's not, really. But there are other reasons to go to the back forty at night."

I rolled down my sleeves and started to button up my shirt, earning a frown from Jason. We'd donned pants before heading to dinner, but he'd insisted I keep my bikini top on, and be as exposed as possible.

"It's getting cold," I said, leaving a few of the top buttons open for his benefit.

"I bet I can warm you up," he said, slipping his fingers behind my neck and pulling my lips to his.

"I'm counting on that," I said breathlessly when he released me. "But not here."

Ignoring his curious expression, I started the car and drove to the back entrance to campus. The road wound through the school's outlying fields, used for farming and grazing. The only building we passed was the campus dairy before turning toward the stables.

I parked between two horse trailers and hopped out, grabbing my monster Maglite from under the seat. Jason caught my hand, and I pulled him close, snaking my arm around his waist.

"Where are you taking me?" he asked. He hugged my shoulders, following the circle of light at our feet.

Saying nothing, I pulled out my keys and unlocked the stable door.

"You have a key? We're not going for a night ride, are we?"

"Ha! No." Mitch had tried to teach me to ride once, with disastrous results, including a sprained wrist. "Mitch gave me his spare, just in case he lost his."

We walked down to Buckeye's stall. The big horse lumbered over and stuck his head out, sniffing loudly.

"Sorry, Buckeye, no carrots today." I gave him a few pats before unlocking Mitch's tack box. Jason occupied Buckeye while I dug out a couple of old blankets. "See you later, big guy," I said, giving the horse one more rub.

I led Jason around the side of the building, away from the car. The road continued past the stables, next to a large grassy pasture.

He squeezed my hand. "Are we there yet?" he teased.

"Just about."

We stopped by the fence at the edge of the pasture, and I draped the blankets over the top. Clicking off the flashlight, I stuck it in my back pocket and took both his hands in mine. In the pitch black of the moonless night I could barely see his face. "Close your eyes and listen," I said.

I did the same, concentrating on the low whistle of a distant train and the occasional rustling of a nearby animal. Everything else was quiet, even the insects. A breath of air mixed the sweet smell of freshly cut hay with the saltiness of the ocean lingering in Jason's hair. After I counted to a hundred, I looked up at Jason.

"Open your eyes," I whispered. "Can you see better now?" My eyes had adjusted to the dark, and I could easily see the surprise on Jason's face.

He dropped my hand, reaching for my cheek instead. "Yes," he breathed. His smile caught what little light there was, and his eyes reflected it back to me. He leaned toward me, but I put a finger on his lips, stopping him.

"Look up," I said.

Jason's eyes widened as he turned them skyward. "Amazing," he whispered. I'd guessed, having grown up in L.A., he was used to a barren sky where all but the very brightest stars were obscured by city lights. In Santa Lucia, the lights were less numerous, and here on the outskirts they were nonexistent. Countless stars filled the sky, making finding something as conspicuous as the Big Dipper a challenge.

While Jason stared up at the heavens, I wrapped my arms around him, resting my head on his chest. "We can take the blankets out in the field and lie in the grass. If you stare at the sky long enough, you might see a satellite fly by."

"Maybe in a minute. I'm quite comfortable right here," he said, tightening his arms around me. The rhythm of his heart filled my ears, and I sighed, content. The last few days had been so wonderful, and I wished, more than ever, they didn't have to end.

Three more days. I pinched my eyes shut, reminding myself I wasn't supposed to be thinking about the end. But was it really his departure I feared, or something else? I hadn't admitted my true feelings to Jason—I'd barely admitted them to myself. Was that what I was afraid of? Not being left alone, but being rejected…again?

No, it had to be losing him. Jason had all but told me he felt the same way. He'd been open and frank with his feelings from the beginning. I was the one hiding. Here under the stars, enveloped in his arms, I decided no matter what happened on Friday, it wasn't fair to keep my feelings to myself any longer.

"Jason," I whispered.

He lightly stroked my hair. "Yes?"

I lifted my face from his chest and looked into his eyes. They seemed to glow in the dark—becoming navy blue beacons, both patient and encouraging. He cupped my cheek, his thumb lightly caressing my face as I struggled to compose some kind of preamble.

Instead, I blurted out, "I love you, Jason."

His thumb stopped, and with it my heart. *Oh crap! I read him wrong.* The hesitations and pregnant pauses I'd assumed were silent I love yous—were they really unspoken regrets? *I'm such an idiot!*

His hand moved again—not away, but into my hair. He tilted my head up and kissed me with a new intensity, a blistering confirmation. Breathing heavily, he lifted his lips from mine and leaned back, his eyes reflecting the fiery passion burning through my veins.

"How I've wanted to hear you say that," he whispered, his voice pouring over me like molten steel. "I love you too."

My heart exploded in my chest. Joy and hope and love combined into something indescribable, filling my entire being. I felt more awake—no, alive—than I ever had before. I rose on my tiptoes, dying to show him exactly what he'd awakened in me.

As he bent down to kiss me again, the silence was broken by a different sound.

"How sweet," said a low, mocking voice.

In an instant, the atmosphere changed. It was as if the ground had suddenly turned to ice, sapping all the warmth and love away and replacing it with frigid fear. Jason froze for a split second then whirled around, shielding me from the intruder.

We both knew who had spoken.

Ron stood in the middle of the road, about eight feet away. He didn't have a light, but one arm was extended toward us. I couldn't tell what he had at first; it wasn't a weapon I recognized. He gave it a shake, and I heard the familiar clinking of a steel ball inside a metal canister.

My pepper spray.

You have a weapon too. Dad's voice rang clearly through my head. The long metal flashlight poked me in the back.

"You're quite a difficult woman to find, Melissa Jean Williams," Ron sneered. His coarse voice matched his bedraggled appearance. His shirt was hanging out of his ripped jeans, and even in the dark I could tell he hadn't shaved recently. "It was a long drive to San Jose. But it was worth it in the end. My little distraction this morning gave me the time I needed to look you up."

"How did you find me?" I asked over Jason's shoulder. I slid the flashlight out of my back pocket slowly, hoping Ron couldn't see it.

In his other hand he waved a white rectangle. "Having your mail forwarded is quite a convenience, isn't it? The post office was nice enough to leave your old address visible on your report card. *Very* convenient," he said. "By the way, your grade in Spanish slipped to a B."

He threw the envelope toward us and reached into his pocket. "Of course, I had to wait for you to come home this evening. You two made quite a couple at dinner." With a sharp *snap* he produced another weapon, a switchblade. "But I enjoyed the chase, Melissa. It makes the end that much sweeter."

Ron crept closer, and Jason pushed me back, intent on keeping his body between me and the knife. "You won't get near her," Jason snarled. He continued to nudge me behind him, and I readied the light.

With a smug snort, Ron bared his teeth in a feral smile. "Maybe not…at first." His finger twitched over the pepper spray. "But I owe *you* a little something, don't I?" He raised the canister to eye level.

I flicked on the flashlight, aiming its powerful beam directly at Ron's face. The spray flew wildly off line, and Jason sprang forward, fists flying.

"Jason, NO!" I screamed. The knife in Ron's hand glinted in the beam of light, slashing toward him.

"Run, Melissa!" Jason yelled and smashed his fist into Ron's face. The force sent them both tumbling to the ground. Ignoring his plea, I stood and watched, trying to figure out a way to help him.

Ron recovered quickly. When he tried to block Jason's next punch, the pepper spray flew out of his hand, bouncing across the asphalt toward me. I kept the light focused on them, watching in horror as they wrestled on the ground, their hands locked together. Jason struggled to get control of the knife while Ron kept him from landing any more punches. I picked up the spray, but it would just as likely disable Jason as Ron, so I pocketed it. Heavy in my hand, the fourteen-inch metal flashlight was my best weapon, and I watched for an opportunity to club Ron with it.

They continued to scuffle, and I gasped when spatters of red stained Jason's white T-shirt. Ron still had the knife, but Jason seemed to be getting the upper hand, slowly overpowering his weaker foe. They rolled to the opposite side of the road, near the edge of a deep drainage ditch. Just as I thought Jason was about to pin Ron, he let out a terrifying scream. I echoed the cry when I saw the knife buried in his thigh.

Ron quickly turned the tables, pinning Jason. With blood dripping from his nose, he grabbed the hilt of the knife, bringing another scream to Jason's lips. He savagely pulled it out and brought it plunging down again.

Jason's face twisted in agony, but he caught Ron's hand, stopping the knife inches from his chest. "Go, Melissa! NOW!" he yelled. The pain in his voice cut me deeper than any blade, and my grip on the flashlight tightened.

Ron cackled hysterically. "Once you're gone, who's going to protect her?"

He yanked the knife high out of Jason's reach, laughing as he prepared to stab him again.

Screaming "*NO!*" I swung the flashlight and its four heavy batteries as hard as I could. The metal hit Ron with a loud *crunch*, snapping his head to the side. His arm dropped harmlessly to his side, and with one push from Jason, he fell into the ravine. He tumbled down the six-foot drop, hit the bottom, and was silent.

"Oh my God, are you okay?" My voice trembling, I dropped to my knees, fumbling to point the flashlight in the right direction.

"It's only a small…small cut. I'll…I'll be fine," Jason stammered. I turned the shaky light on his leg and was horrified to see the entire side of his jeans soaked in blood. A long, deep gash exposed the muscles and tendons in his thigh.

Swallowing back my shock, I steeled myself. "No, it's not. We have to get you out of here." I handed him the flashlight, ripped off my shirt, and tied it around his leg, trying to pull the cut closed and stop the bleeding. Jason cried out, and I winced, sharing his pain.

"I'm so sorry," I said.

He shook off my apology. "Don't be. You're doing exactly the right thing," he said through clenched teeth.

A faint moan came from Ron at the bottom of the ditch. He was coming around.

"Come on. Let's go," I said, reaching for Jason's hand.

I helped him to his feet, trying to steady him as we made our way back to the car. Ron thrashed around in the dead bushes in the ravine, coming closer. We'd barely passed the stable when I stopped.

"*Shit!*"

"What?" Jason looked up and echoed my curse.

Sitting directly behind my car was a dirty two-door Saturn. Ron had blocked me in.

"Melissa, go. I have my cell phone; I'll hide and call for help. Just *go!*" he commanded.

"Jason McAlister, if you think I'm going to leave you here alone, bleeding, and unable to walk, then you really *are* crazy."

I guided him back to the stable instead. Ron was struggling up the embankment, swearing every time his feet skidded on the graveled slope.

Once inside the building, I opened Buckeye's stall and pulled Jason inside. His eyes drooped as he half-sat, half-fell in the corner of the hay-strewn floor.

I put my hands on his cheeks, praying he didn't pass out. "Listen to me. Just stay here and be quiet. I'm going to lead him away."

My mind was already two steps ahead, remembering the nearby corral and its angry occupant. If I could get Ron to follow me, I'd make sure he had more than enough to keep him busy.

"Melissa, no. Just go, before he gets here. I can't let you get hurt," Jason protested weakly.

"Trust me. I know what I'm doing." *I hope.* "When I get him far enough away, call 911. Tell them you're in stable number two of the equine unit at the end of Via Carta. Got it?" The adrenaline pumping through my bloodstream made the words come out fast, and I had to work to keep my voice down.

Jason tried to hand me the phone. "Maybe you should…" but I closed his hand around it, hearing Ron's yelling coming closer.

"We don't have much time. Say it—stable number two at the end of Via Carta!"

He sighed. "Stable two, Via Carta," he repeated, then clenched his teeth as he tried to reposition his leg.

I leaned down and kissed him hard, trying to impress how much I loved him into a single, frantic act. "It'll be okay," I whispered, telling myself as much as Jason. Then I let him go.

Buckeye huffed when I caught his halter and pulled him toward the door. "No matter what you hear, Jason, you have to be quiet, or this won't work. Promise?" I pleaded. Of course my half-baked plan might not work in any case, but at least Jason should be able to get the police out here.

He nodded slowly. "I promise. Please be careful. I love you."

The desperation in his voice brought tears to my eyes. "I love you too. I'll be back soon." I clipped Buckeye's halter to the short rope next to the stall door, not only preventing the horse from stepping on Jason, but effectively shielding him from view.

Outside, Ron pounded on the door to the stable. "You can't hide for long, Melissa. I'll find him…then I'll find you!"

The horses around me shuffled nervously when he forced the door open. I ran to the other end of the cavernous building, purposely tipping over a pile of shovels before running out the back.

"I'm growing weary of this, Melissa," he hissed.

He's too close to Jason! I had to get Ron out of the stable so Jason could call for help. I stopped halfway between the building and the corral and yelled at the top of my lungs. "Jason, get up. We have to go. GET UP!"

I was about to turn back and yell again when Ron crashed through the pile of shovels. That was my cue to run to the corral fifty yards away.

I threw my leg over the top of the metal rails and waited. My plan was working—so far. When the back door of the stable flew open, I jumped into the corral. Where was its occupant?

"Damn it, bitch, you're going to pay when I find you," Ron screeched, stepping out into the open. I waved the flashlight wildly, not-so-subtly guiding him toward me. I carefully made my way to the center of the iron-enclosed circle. To my left was a wooden wall—a safety barrier. Only one animal required such a thing, and with almost debilitating relief, I heard his heavy breathing under a piece of dented siding that served as a makeshift roof. I swung the light around just long enough to find him—all eighteen hundred pounds of the aptly named Diablo. His glassy eyes and short, downturned horns definitely gave him a devilish aura. The bull didn't move, but without the light I doubted he could see me. Noise triggered this animal's rage, and I planned to provide him plenty.

Swinging the light around, I caught Ron climbing the fence. I slowly withdrew the pepper spray from my pocket and slid my finger over the plunger, praying it wasn't empty. The breeze sliced across my bare shoulders like icy fingernails. I should be terrified, trapped between a vicious murderer and a living, breathing battering ram, but it didn't occur to me that the animal in the corner could just as easily come after me until Ron spoke.

"I like the new look, Melissa." He raked his eyes across my bikini top and licked his lips. "What happened to your boyfriend? I'm sure he'll be sorry he missed out on this." He jumped to the ground and stalked toward me. "I guess I'll move you to the top of my list, but I *will* find him, I promise you that."

"I don't think so," I said, taking a step back. Ron looked around, but didn't slow. Diablo's pitch black coat was just another huge shadow in the darkness, invisible.

"Of all the places to hide, you brought me *here?* After such a long wait, it's a shame to finish you surrounded by this shit." Ron kicked a pile of manure toward me. "But this doesn't have to be the end. Maybe I'll take you home with me, keep you for a while. Show you what you've been missing, wasting your time with Prince Valiant." His voice became shriller, the closer he got.

Just a few more feet.

"How many women have you hunted down, Ron?" I asked, trying to keep him talking.

"I like the way you say my name, Melissa," he said, his voice lowering an octave. "A few. They all wanted me, in the end. None were as—" he inhaled, as if smelling flowers "—intoxicating as you. Your little game of hide-and-seek proves how much you want me. To go to such trouble to turn me on… You'll beg me to take you with your last breath," he promised. He slowed, still too far away for the pepper spray to reach him.

Again I heard Dad's voice. *Keep him talking.*

"What about Vanessa? Did she want you too?" I asked.

Ron took another step toward me. *Just a little farther…*

His laugh sent imaginary spiders running up and down my arms. "Vanessa? Of course she did, but she was nothing. A way to let off some steam after your rude friends interrupted our little chat. Don't worry. I've been saving up for you, Melissa," he said.

I shuddered and another jolt of adrenaline hit my system. I fingered the button on the flashlight.

Ron's knife flashed in the rising moon's light as he spun and flipped it. "Usually I prefer a more hands-on approach with my women, feeling the last beats of their heart with my fingers around their throat," he sneered. "But I'll make an exception for you. I'll enjoy seeing your blood mixed with his."

He waved the darkened blade in a figure eight in front of his sadistic grin. "Will you scream for me, Melissa? Yes, you'll scream…you'll scream for more," he taunted.

Diablo kicked at the dirt in the corner. "Bull," I snapped and raised my arm.

"Feisty to the end," he said with a high-pitched laugh. "Say it louder, baby. Scream for me!"

"BULL!" I yelled and pointed both my flashlight and the pepper spray at him.

His twisted grin disintegrated into a blood-curdling, girlish shriek when the spray hit his face. The knife fell to the ground, but I continued to cover him with the caustic liquid—his head, his hands, his shirt—emptying the can. Arms thrashing, Ron doubled over, madly scratching at his burning eyes.

With a loud snort, Diablo took off. Ron's tortured screams couldn't mask the earth-shattering hoof beats speeding in his direction.

I backed away, my heart pounding as fast and as loud as Diablo's hooves. He passed me with only feet to spare, and I yelped in the wake of his massive charge. The bull's attention didn't waver from Ron, even when his howling degraded into mindless curses and sobs.

Then, with a loud *thud*, the murderer's cries abruptly ceased. Diablo's head reared up, throwing Ron through the air like a broken puppet, his arms and legs flailing out of control. He crashed into the steel fence on the opposite side of the corral with resounding *clang,* falling into a motionless heap in the dirt and dung.

Diablo came to an abrupt halt and spun around, his breath visible as twin clouds of dust swirling above the ground.

I threw the flashlight aside, hoping to distract the beast, and dug my toes into the soft earth, running as fast as I could to the barrier. With a grunt, the bull charged again, thundering toward me. Seconds after I threw myself behind the thick wood, Diablo crashed into it, shaking the ground. I threw my hands out and shut my eyes, waiting for the beams to collapse around me. With what I expected to be my last breath I whispered, "I love you, Jason."

Nothing happened.

I opened my eyes, amazed to see wood, not angels, towering straight and tall above me. The wall had held, and I patted it lovingly. I slumped against the timbers, breathing as hard as the huge bull panting a few feet away. For a moment the world shimmered and turned black, but I leaned forward onto my knees and forced my head down. Slowly the lightheadedness retreated, and my mind filled with one thing.

Jason.

I stood carefully, testing my balance before climbing the fence behind the barricade. Diablo stomped around his corral, huffing and snorting, but ignored me. Ron didn't move; his legs pretzeled out in opposite directions, obviously broken.

"I'll *never* want you, asshole," I snarled, breaking into a run. Bursting through the stable door I yelled Jason's name over the strengthening wail of sirens. Only a nervous Buckeye stood in the way.

Seeing the door at the back of the stall, I remembered the small pen on the other side. After unclipping Buckeye and shooing him through, I fell to my knees.

Jason didn't move when I shook his shoulder.

Blood soaked the shirt tied around his leg. "Jason, please, wake up," I begged, touching his face, his hands, his hair. His breathing was so shallow, I had to hold my own breath to hear it. "It's over. We're safe. It's okay, you can open your eyes now." I coaxed. *No, no, no, I can't lose him like this!*

I had to do something. Frantically I tried to tighten the makeshift bandage, tried to slow the leak that was stealing his life away, drop by drop. Suddenly Jason moaned in pain.

"I'm so sorry, sweetheart. Stay with me, okay?" I implored. His eyes fluttered open, and relief washed through me.

"Melissa?" he mumbled. The sirens stopped, replaced by flickers of blue and red visible above the stall door.

I squeezed his hand, pressing it against my heart. "Yes, Jason, I'm here. Stay awake. Stay with me. The ambulance is coming."

"Don't cry, beautiful," he said, the ghost of a smile flitting across his lips. His eyes didn't stay open long.

Tears I hadn't felt dripped onto his cheeks as I bent down and kissed him. His icy lips only fed the panic growing in me. "Jason, I love you."

"I love…"

He didn't finish, and his head lolled to the side.

"Jason!" I shook his limp hand. "Don't leave me, *please!*" I sobbed. *Please, God, please don't take him too.*

God's answer was the crackle of a police radio.

"In here!" I shrieked. "We need help!"

Sixteen

*T*he campus police reached us first, answering my shouts with assurances that medical help was on the way, followed by questions about our attacker. I waved them toward the back of the stable, refusing to look away from Jason's chalky face. An agonizing two minutes later, the ambulance arrived. Jason regained consciousness momentarily when the stretcher was wheeled in, and he whispered my name.

Someone pulled me away, saying something about letting the EMTs work. Then questions flew at me like bullets.

"How old is he? Is he allergic to anything? Is he taking any medication?"

With a helpless shrug, I watched them locate Jason's wallet, which held more answers than I could give them.

"Where are you hurt?" a woman asked. She blocked my view of Jason, forcing me to look up. I was mildly surprised to see her face under a fire-fighter's helmet.

"What?"

She took my bloodied hand and wiped it with something cold and wet. "Where are you hurt, honey?"

"I'm not. It's…the blood's not mine," I stammered, fighting another wave of tears.

"They're taking good care of him. You don't need to worry," she said, thoroughly cleaning my fingers.

"Is he going to…" I stopped, afraid to finish the question.

She wrapped a piece of shiny plastic around me. "Keep this on, it'll help you warm up." She pressed her fingers against my wrist. "Would you like to ride with him to the hospital?"

"Yes."

She bent over the closest EMT. I heard the words "shock" and "exposure" before the tech nodded and glanced at me.

"He's going to be okay, miss," he said over his shoulder. "We're just about ready to go."

A few clicks later, Jason was strapped to the stretcher and being rolled out of the stable. My escort, the firefighter, kept an arm around me until I was lifted into the ambulance, then she slammed the door behind me. I lifted a hand at the dark window in belated thanks.

The trip to the hospital passed in a blur. I sat in the corner of the ambulance, staring at Jason. He drifted in and out of consciousness, mumbling incoherently. The EMTs continued to assure me he'd be okay and even let me hold Jason's hand. His skin was so cold…

At the hospital, doctors and nurses surrounded Jason's gurney, barking out numbers and shouting orders as they whisked him through a set of unmarked double doors. An arm stopped me from following, and before I knew it, I was on my own gurney in a curtained-off exam area. Above my protests, the nurse took my vitals. Tersely, I answered her questions, my eyes glued to the doors.

Finally, she stopped asking and gave me a T-shirt and a warmed cotton blanket to replace my Mylar one. She left me in the lobby with a curt, "Wait here. The doctor will be out shortly."

Numbly I sat in one of the cold, hard plastic chairs. My mind shut down; after three days of trying to keep reality and fantasy separate—and failing—this latest event had sent me over the edge. Only one image filled my thoughts: the sight of Jason on the stretcher, bruised and battered, deathly still, and frighteningly pale.

I leaned over to put my head in my hands and was surprised to find they weren't empty. Somehow, during all the confusion, I'd picked up Jason's phone; not even the insistent nurse had been able to pry it from my hand. I flipped it over, carefully scratched off the dried spots of blood, then opened it.

The background picture on his display had changed. The shot of sunny L.A. I'd seen before had been replaced by two happy people about to enjoy a dinner at the pier. In the picture, Jason's grin was for the camera, but his eyes were on me. My pink cheeks and goofy expression reminded me of his warm touch and his sultry voice when he'd coerced me to smile.

Please let him be okay.

I scrolled through his phonebook, preparing myself for the call I had to make. Though it was nearly midnight, I found his parents' number and dialed. Thankfully, the conversation was short. I repeated to Mr. McAlister what the EMTs had told me: "A transfusion may be necessary, stitches and possibly surgery, but he should recover." Mr. McAlister asked for the name of the hospital and directions. I hoped the news would be better by the time they arrived.

"We'll see you soon, Melissa. Thank you for being there for Jason," he said before hanging up. I pushed END and looked through the contacts one more time. This call would be even more difficult.

I pushed SEND again, wondering what the time difference was between Tahiti and California. Did cell phones even work there? Maybe I should wait…but then the ringing stopped.

"Hey, bro, how'd the date go? Did she like the flowers?" Mitch answered, with a laugh.

I choked on a rush of grief.

"Jason?" he asked, his tone now subdued.

With a deep breath, I forced the words out. "Mitch, it's Melissa. There's been an accident. Jason's been hurt." I pinched my eyes shut.

He didn't respond. I pulled the blanket tighter, waiting.

"How is he?"

"He…he was stabbed in the leg. The EMT said he would be okay, but he lost a lot of blood. They're still working on him."

Mitch exhaled slowly. "What about you? Are *you* okay, Melissa?" His concern reached through the phone and yanked my heart up to my throat.

"I'm fine," I said, willing the tremble out of my voice.

"What happened?"

I closed my eyes, cringing as I recalled it all. Ron's sneering face. Jason's scream. The smell of blood. "We were attacked. It's a long story."

I felt a hand on my shoulder and looked up to see a man in scrubs standing over me.

"Hang on, the doctor is here." I held the phone out, hoping Mitch could hear the conversation.

"You're Jason McAlister's friend?"

"Yes."

The doctor smiled. "He's going to be fine. We've stabilized him, and he's not in any pain."

The invisible load I was carrying lightened a little. "And his leg?"

His smile shrunk a bit. "We're prepping him for surgery to repair the damage. Considering his age and physical condition, I don't expect there to be any complications. Barring any nerve damage, the procedure shouldn't take too long. With rest and physical therapy, he should be as good as new in no time."

He glanced to the side, acknowledging someone. "I'll have the nurse show you to the OR waiting area after you've finished your call," he said.

"Thank you so much," I said weakly.

He smiled and turned to address the man three seats over.

"Mitch, did you hear that?" I asked, bringing the phone back to my ear.

"Yeah. I'm not surprised, Jason's too stubborn to let some prick take him out," he said. "I need to call my folks. They'll want to know what's happened."

"I talked to them already—they're on their way." I tossed off the blanket and paced around the waiting area, anxious to be closer to Jason.

"Thanks, Mel. We'll make arrangements to head back too." He paused. "Was it the guy at the wedding?"

"Yes."

"I'll kill that son of a bitch with my bare hands," he snarled.

My voice turned cold. "Too late."

I'd overheard the EMTs talking in the ambulance. Diablo had thrown Ron so hard he'd broken more than the killer's legs; he'd snapped the bastard's neck. Ron hadn't been brought to the ER, but to the morgue.

"Good." Mitch said solemnly. "We'll see you in a day or so. I'll let you go—I'm sure Jason needs you."

"Thanks, Mitch. See you soon."

The nurse was waiting for me at the counter and led me through a maze of corridors to a small room with a few hard chairs and a table with a half-finished puzzle on it.

I spent most of the two hours Jason was in surgery alone. At some point a police officer joined me, but I had no idea what he'd asked or how I answered. He'd left by the time the nurse reported the operation was successful.

I couldn't stop thinking about Jason. Three days ago he'd been no more than words on a computer screen, and now here we were, ready to sacrifice our lives for each other. Why didn't I feel more grateful he was alive and well?

Because in three more days he'll be gone, and you'll be alone again. That's why.

Was I really that shallow?

Anguish and anger—at myself—battled it out. Neither side had declared victory by the time I was allowed to see Jason in the recovery room. The nurse told me he would probably sleep until morning and pointed at yet another plastic chair next to his bed. I gently took his hand in mine, careful to avoid the bruises and scratches covering his knuckles and arms. He didn't react when I touched him, which disturbed me deeply. I wanted to scream and shake him to get a response—some kind of confirmation he was truly alive.

Even though monitors all around me beeped and blinked, verifying Jason's vital signs, I put my hand on his chest to feel the rhythm of his heart and lungs for myself. Some relief did breeze through me, but his slack face broke my heart. His expression was one of profound sadness, not peaceful sleep. I kissed him lightly on the cheek, careful to avoid his blossoming black eye.

"Get better, Jason," I whispered.

He stirred briefly a couple of times but didn't wake completely. Eventually some of the noisy apparatus was removed, and he was transferred to a semi-private room on the second floor. The other bed was vacant, and though it tempted me, I remained at Jason's side, our fingers intertwined.

Mr. and Mrs. McAlister arrived just before sunrise. After reviewing Jason's chart and checking his pulse herself, his mom—Dr. McAlister, I remembered—stationed herself at his other hand.

"He's going to be fine," she said, more to Jason than to me or her husband.

Around seven, Jason's eyes cracked open.

"Melissa," he rasped.

The sound of his voice restarted my heart.

"Jason, I'm here. We're safe. You're in the hospital," I said. "It's over."

He pulled his hand away from his mother and rubbed his eyes. "You're okay? He didn't hurt you, did he?" Jason croaked, squeezing my fingers.

"I'm just fine," I said, my lip quivering. After all he'd suffered, his first thoughts were for me. "Your parents are here." I motioned toward them.

He slowly turned his head and saw his mother. She was fighting back tears.

"How are you, sweetheart?" she asked, staring deeply into his eyes.

I loosened my grip on Jason's hand and inched back toward my seat. He probably wanted some time with his parents. I couldn't leave, but I could give them a little space.

"I'm fine, Mom—just groggy. It's the meds." He searched for the controls on the bed and raised his head so he could see around the room. I slipped my hand out of his, but he grabbed it and pulled me back to the side of his bed. "Please don't go, Melissa," he said, his voice small and vulnerable.

I didn't argue.

His parents didn't comment, but his mom nodded her approval at me.

Jason's clarity returned slowly. He perked up a little when breakfast arrived, nibbling on the toast and fruit offered by the nurse, but he rejected what she claimed was oatmeal. By the time the attending physician came in at nine, Jason was able to discuss his injury with the interest expected of a pre-med student. Now fully awake, he didn't protest when I hesitantly let go of his hand.

The doctor predicted Jason would be released the following morning if there continued to be no indication of infection or swelling. I sat by the window during the exchange, watching Jason analyze his own condition. Finally the doctor finished, and Jason smiled at me.

His mom took the doctor aside for a few more questions, and Mr. McAlister filled her spot next to Jason's bed.

"When you're released tomorrow, we'll drive you home," his father said.

I inhaled sharply. Tomorrow was Thursday.

"We brought the minivan, so you'll have lots of room to spread out," he continued, unaware of my rising panic.

No! Friday—I have until Friday!

Questions finished, Mrs. McAlister joined her husband. "A good night's sleep in a real bed wouldn't hurt, either," she added, poking at the plastic-covered mattress.

I turned away, my jaw tight. Her unintended insult sliced through me, another reason for Jason to leave. Excusing myself, I hurried to the bathroom, my chest heaving.

"Melissa," Jason called, but I didn't stop. I barely got the door closed before I broke down.

I sank to the floor and buried my face in a towel. Sobbing violently, I couldn't stop the enormity of the situation from burying me. I'd nearly lost Jason last night, and now I was losing him tomorrow. *Tomorrow!* I'd focused so hard on Friday that this simple change crushed me.

It was completely logical for him to go home with his parents, and I knew it was in his best interest…but piled on top of everything we'd been through, it was too much. I wanted to scream—but gagged myself with the towel instead.

When I heard the faint knock on the door, I jumped up. Had they heard me? How long had I been in here?

"Just a sec," I choked. I turned on the faucet and doused my face. Both the surprise of the knock and chill of the water helped re-bottle my emotions, but my eyes remained puffy and bloodshot.

"I'm just tired," I mouthed to the mirror, preparing to face Jason again. I had to pull myself together to make it through these last hours.

With one last deep breath I opened the door. Mrs. McAlister met me, worry creasing her forehead. "Are you all right, Melissa?"

I swallowed quickly, unable to dislodge the lump in my throat. "Yes, I'm fine. Just tired, thanks. Sorry for taking so long." Jason's dad had replaced me in the chair. He followed Jason's eyes when they rose to me.

Mrs. McAlister touched my arm. "Why don't we take a little walk? I could use a cup of tea. How about you?" she asked.

"I'm fine, really," I said. Jason's gaze flashed to his mother and then back to me. *Uh-oh.*

"A Coke sounds good too. Melissa, do you think you could scrounge one up?" he asked. "Please?" His eyes said *trust me*, and I sighed, defeated.

"Okay. I'll be back soon," I promised.

His eyes bore into me and my heart lurched. "I'm counting on that," he said.

I followed his mother out of the room, directing her toward the elevator. "The nurse said the cafeteria is downstairs."

Once inside the descending car she took my hand. "I just wanted to thank you for taking care of Jason. We spoke to the police when we arrived, and they explained how you risked your life for him. Thank you so much."

Her gratitude made the lump in my throat grow larger. I looked at the ring on her finger as I spoke. "You're welcome. He protected me first, Mrs. McAlister."

"Please, call me Lynn," she said. The doors opened, and a different beige hallway appeared in front of us, along with a sign pointing toward the cafeteria. Lynn invited me to lead. "You really should think about going home and getting some rest, dear. I can imagine how tired you are, with everything that's happened. We'll keep an eye on Jason while you nap." She wasn't condescending or demanding; she actually sounded like my mom. But with so little time left, there was no way I was leaving.

"No, I'm okay," I said. We entered the sparsely populated cafeteria, and I went directly to the drink station. I picked up the largest cup I could find and filled it with coffee. In lieu of my normal hot chocolate addition, I added three packets of sugar. I needed the extra kick to fight off my growing exhaustion. Lynn met me next to the cooler, waiting while I picked out two Cokes.

We were halfway to the cashier when I remembered I had no money. Everything was in my car—back at the stable. I looked apologetically at Lynn. "I just realized I don't have my purse. May I—"

She put her hand on mine and nodded. "I was going to insist, in any case," she said. Lynn had much more than tea on her tray; she'd filled it with pre-made sandwiches, pudding cups, and chips. I waited by the exit while she completed the transaction.

With everything paid for, Lynn pointed at the tables. "Can we sit here for just a bit? I think Frank would like a couple minutes with Jason alone."

Checking the wall clock, I sat. *Five minutes.*

I stirred my coffee in time with the second hand, inadvertently sloshing some out. *Four minutes, thirty seconds.*

Lynn sipped her tea and stared across the room. "Jason cares quite a lot about you, Melissa. He's very worried about you," she said.

Apparently Frank wasn't the only one who wanted a private conversation.

"Why? I wasn't hurt," I said.

"True, but he can see how exhausted you are. And your reaction earlier..." She paused, and I cringed. "He's concerned about leaving you alone." Her voice became hushed. "It's obvious the two of you have become very close in just a few days."

I took a drink of the steaming black liquid in front of me. It scalded my throat on the way down, briefly taking the lump with it.

"Yeah, I guess we have." Thankfully Naughty Melissa remained silent.

"Between phone, email, and texting, it should be easy for the two of you to stay in touch this summer," Lynn probed.

If only. I didn't want to have this conversation—not now, and especially not with her. I answered with a vague *hmmm* and set my stirrer aside.

She didn't respond immediately, and I checked the clock again.

"Did you know Jason's hoping to come back to California in the fall?" she asked.

I looked up at her. Her eyes, identical to Jason's, stared back at me.

"He'll only be gone a couple months." Her soft features relaxed into a warm smile.

Again, I was reminded of my mother. Maybe it was because I had no energy left to argue, or because I was barely awake, but I nodded in agreement. I could see where Jason got his talent for persuasion.

We sat for another minute but didn't speak any further. When Lynn went to refill her cup, I stood in the hall outside the cafeteria. This time she took the hint, and we headed for the elevator.

Frank met us at the door to Jason's room, showing yet another police officer out.

"I'll contact Detective Clark. He'll be able to fill in a lot of the details," the cop was saying.

Tim… Jason must've mentioned him. I probably should've said something, but I slipped past without a word, eager to reclaim my spot at Jason's side.

I opened the door quietly in case he might be asleep, but was greeted by his tired smile. "Here you go," I said, handing him a Coke.

He stroked my fingers as he took the bottle but didn't say anything. The silent communication with his mother continued with another long look in her direction.

Rather than speculate on what they were plotting next, I sat down, grateful to reclaim my chair.

Frank started to close the door, but Lynn caught his arm, giving him a meaningful glance.

"Um, well," he started, and she tipped her head toward the door. "Your mother and I are going to stretch our legs and reserve a hotel room, okay? We'll be back later."

"Thanks, Dad. See you then," Jason said and yawned.

Lynn blew him a kiss before pushing her husband out the door.

Jason exhaled loudly. It took all his energy to open the Coke, and he only managed a couple swallows before handing me bottle back to me.

"You need to rest," I said.

His blue eyes disappeared under heavy lids. "So do you. You don't have to stay, Melissa. I'll probably sleep all day." His eyelids only rose halfway as he struggled to smile.

"Shhh, quit worrying about me. Just rest and get better." I stroked his hair and his eyes closed for good. I leaned over and kissed him gently. "I love you, Jason. I'll be here when you wake up."

"I love you too," he mumbled, then fell asleep.

Jason slept most of the afternoon and into the evening. I caught a few winks too, sitting in the chair next to him. Our hands stayed interlocked the whole time, and whenever the nurse came in or Jason made a noise, I woke. The sandwiches came in handy; I ended up eating two of them over the course of the day. When his parents returned around five with hamburgers, Jason woke up looking much stronger, though his black eye had worsened.

His mother kissed his forehead. "I'm sorry we bothered you, dear. We can go so you can get back to sleep." She gave me an appraising look.

Jason gave my hand a squeeze before releasing it and stretching his arms over his head. "No, I'm awake now." He winced as he shifted in the bed, but quickly smiled to hide the pain.

"We brought an early dinner, just in case the two of you wanted something besides hospital food," Mr. McAlister said, waving a familiar red-and-white bag.

"Great, I'm starved," Jason said. His parents went to work laying out the spread on the bedside table. Jason's eyes tightened again when he shifted, trying to find a more comfortable position.

"You should call the nurse. You're due for more medication," I whispered.

"It's not that bad, really. I don't like the fog that stuff puts me in." He reached up and touched my cheek. "You really need to get out of here and get some sleep, Melissa. You look dead on your feet."

I fiddled with the edge of the sheet. "Where would I go? There's nothing in my apartment, remember? My car isn't even here."

Jason frowned but couldn't argue further because Frank pushed the table over and handed us hamburgers. While we ate, Lynn told us about the hotel where they were staying and about their drive down, laughing at how much traffic there was on the L.A. freeways at one in the morning.

The doctor came in an hour later on his evening rounds. He told Jason everything looked great and he'd be back in the morning to sign the discharge papers. My heart fell when Lynn offered to make her son's favorite meal when they got home. I didn't even know what his favorite food was.

Jason stole worried glances at me throughout the evening. With only hours left, I stubbornly planted myself in the chair beside his bed, intending to stay there until he was wheeled out to his parents' minivan. My eyes kept betraying me, though, becoming heavier with every blink.

I hadn't realized I'd dozed off until loud shushing jerked my head back up.

"Sorry, Mel," Mitch said, hugging his mom.

Mitch? When did he get here? "No problem," I said, clearing my throat. I scooted my chair over, releasing Jason's hand after a quick squeeze.

Mitch took my spot. "Nice shiner, bro." He linked hands with Jason and leaned in for a careful hug. Ann was right behind him and gave Jason a little wave. She didn't linger, choosing to sit on the empty bed next to me.

"How're you doing?" she asked, her eyes wandering from my unruly mane down to my manure-stained shoes.

"I'm all right," I said, finger-combing my hair. "How was Tahiti?" Ann's tan had darkened considerably in the few days since the wedding.

"It was great. Nothing to do but eat, sleep, and—" she turned her head away from her parents-in-law "—Mitch."

My snort became a full-fledged laugh when the corner of Lynn's mouth curled up.

Ann continued, unaware her mother-in-law had heard her. "Thanks for the gift, by the way." In a surprisingly friendly gesture, she touched my arm. "You contributed the chaps, didn't you?"

Lynn covered her mouth and coughed.

"Yeah, I did," I admitted. "I'm sorry you didn't have more time to use them." Ann pushed a stray lock of hair over my shoulder. "Don't worry about it. You and I both know Mitch needed to be here. Thanks for calling him."

I think I smiled at her, but I wasn't sure if this new, caring Ann was real or if I'd fallen asleep again.

The sound of my name woke me up in any case.

"Melissa, you look like hell," Mitch scolded. He stood over me, his hands on his hips, glaring.

"Asshole," Jason muttered.

"Thanks, Mitch. Your manners are as gracious as usual," I said. I was about to comment on his raccoon tan lines when he yanked me to my feet.

"Come on, let's go get your car. You need to breathe some fresh air."

"No, I'm fine. I'll stay," I insisted, unable to free myself. What I really wanted was to crawl into bed with Jason, but that was out of the question.

"Melissa, please," Jason said. "Just go with Mitch for a little while. The nurse is bringing my meds, and I'll be asleep again in less than an hour. You need a nap—and a shower and change of clothes wouldn't hurt." He cocked an eyebrow at my baggy *Property of Sierra Vista Hospital* T-shirt and blood-spattered jeans.

"But there isn't much more time," I said, my voice barely a whisper.

Jason shot his brother a scathing look, and Mitch let go of me. He took both of my hands in his. "I know, and this didn't come out at all the way we'd planned. But I need you to be awake tomorrow, all right?"

He pulled me close so the others couldn't hear. "I want to be able to give Naughty Melissa a proper goodbye." His eyes twinkled under his dark lashes, but the word *goodbye* sucked away my sense of humor. "Please. I promise I won't go anywhere. You do have my clothes, after all."

I opened my mouth to argue, but Ann nudged me. "He needs your strength, Melissa. Take a little time to recharge for *him.*"

She was right, but I couldn't help feeling like everyone was ganging up on me. I took a wavering breath, knowing if I didn't give in, Mitch would physically remove me from the premises. I also knew I was too tired to fight back.

"Fine. I'll take a short nap, but I'll be back in a couple of hours, okay?"

Jason smiled and pulled me to him, kissing me softly. "Thank you. I'll see you soon, my love," he whispered.

I kissed him once more on the forehead and let go. Jason's parents said good night, but I assured them I'd be back soon. I tried not to think about how I'd be repeating this scene tomorrow. There'd be no such promises then.

Ann and Mitch led me out of the building and into the parking lot, catching me when I tripped off the curb. The evening sun was hidden behind a thick blanket of cold fog. I hugged myself, realizing it'd been nearly a day since I'd been outside. The fresh air did feel good, but as I took one last look at the hospital my lungs suddenly felt like they were filled with water. Time was almost up.

Mitch pointed at a bright red car in one of the visitors' spots. "Here's our ride. Nice, huh?" he grumbled. The tiny car would've easily fit in the bed of his pickup truck.

"Just your style, Mitch," I said.

My large friend carefully squeezed himself into the subcompact, hitting his head twice in the process. Ann giggled, unable to keep a straight face.

I slid into the back seat, crinkling my nose at the new-car smell that still permeated the fabric. We drove through the hospital parking lot, and my eyes drooped again. I dug my fingernails into my knees hoping pain would keep me awake.

Mitch glanced at me in the rearview mirror. "So, Mel, I heard you had a dance with the devil. Is that true?" he asked.

I inhaled, confused by his statement. *The devil…oh, Diablo.* The memory had become blurry in the intervening hours. "I guess you could say that. Is he all right?" I owed my life to my four-legged accomplice.

Mitch laughed. "I'm sure he's fine. There's not much a 200-pound man can do to a bull that size, not without a sword and a cape." When he turned south on Santa Rosa Street, I sat up, confused.

"Mitch, my car is back at the—" I started.

"Settle down, Mel. Ann and I will go get it after I drop you off at your apartment. You're in no condition to drive. Don't worry, we won't take it joy riding."

I slumped back in my seat. Everything was out of my control.

No one spoke after that, making the ten-minute ride feel more like ten hours. When Mitch pulled up in front of my apartment, I climbed—no, fell—out of the car.

His strong hands grabbed me before I hit the concrete. "Let's get you in bed," he said gently.

We walked to the door, and I didn't even try to put the key in the lock. I handed it to Ann instead. She unlocked the door, and I noticed a large white object at my feet—an envelope of some kind. Bracing myself against the side of the building, I bent down and picked it up. I couldn't focus on the label, so I gave it to Mitch.

"What's this?" I asked, teetering in the doorway. *This is worse than tequila.*

He read the faint writing, then ushered me inside. "It's for Jason, actually. I'll take care of it."

"Oh." I should've been curious about the delivery, but it took all my concentration to climb the stairs. When I resorted to my hands and knees, Mitch hoisted me up in his forklift arms and carried me to the top. He hauled me into my room and set me on the sleeping bag. I crawled to my pillow, searching blindly for the T-shirt I normally slept in.

"Mitch, I'll meet you downstairs," Ann said, untying my shoes.

She's still here?

"Get some sleep, Mel," Mitch commanded and shut the door, leaving us alone.

"You don't hafta do this, Ann. I can taycare of myself," I slurred, tugging weakly at my clothes.

"No, I don't think you can," she said. With a few swift movements she undressed me and threw my pajama shirt over my head.

When she was done, I forced myself to stay awake long enough to set my alarm for ten o'clock, making sure it was on the p.m. setting. I turned the volume all the way up and then fell back on my pillow. A two-hour nap would be plenty.

"Thanks, Ann. I owe you," I mumbled.

"Sleep well," she whispered as I lost consciousness.

Seventeen

*Z*ZZZZZZ…

Somewhere in the blackness, something buzzed in my ear. Ghostly images of bloody knives and charging monsters faded away as the sound grew louder. I resisted waking for another moment…then took a deep breath and stretched. The feeling of dread wouldn't quite leave me. *I bet Jason can erase the nightmare.*

I rolled over and opened my eyes.

A figure knelt next to the suitcase in the corner, slowly unzipping one of the pockets.

"Jason? I had the most horrible—"

His head turned and I gasped. *Mitch.*

It wasn't a nightmare.

"Sorry, I didn't mean to wake you." Mitch jumped up and raced to the door. The light shining through the curtain cleared my head with burning truth. Jason was leaving…*today!* With a terrible shudder, I realized I'd slept all night.

"Hold it right there, McAlister," I barked. I swallowed, trying to dislodge the frog in my throat. Over my shoulder sat my alarm clock, completely black. Unplugged, it'd been rendered useless. I'd lost so much time…

"What have you done, Mitch?" I cried, my voice cracking. I crawled to my suitcase and whipped out the first clean clothes I touched.

He slapped a hand over his eyes when I peeled off my shirt without any show of modesty.

"You needed more than two hours' sleep—you were a zombie. Don't worry, Jason's fine," he said to the wall.

"Damn you, Mitch! I'll have more than enough time to sleep after he's *gone*," I shouted. "What time is it?"

"Almost nine," he whispered, and opened the door.

"Nine!" I cried. *Nine o'clock!* I'd slept for nearly thirteen hours…and Jason would be discharged from the hospital any minute now. Mitch had stolen my time with him. Desperation exploded into fury.

"You *bastard!*" I picked up the lifeless clock and hurled it at him. "GET OUT!" I screamed.

He easily blocked the flying appliance and ducked out the door. "I'm sorry," he said, slamming it behind him.

I flung my hair out of my face, catching the unpalatable smell of dirt, sweat, and cattle. Clad only in underwear, I dashed into the bathroom, slammed *that* door, dumped my clothes on the floor, and jumped into the ice-cold shower. Standing under the frigid water, all I could think about was the time I'd wasted sleeping. I could've been with Jason—touching him, watching him…for the last time. Instead, I'd been comatose, useless.

After five minutes of scouring and shampooing and another two of drying, dressing, and brushing, I yanked the bathroom door open. Hollering, "WHERE THE HELL ARE MY KEYS?" I tore down the stairs and into the kitchen.

"You don't need to rush, Mel. Jason isn't going to be discharged for a while." Mitch dumped a scoop of chocolate into the travel mug on the counter. "He only woke up about a half-hour ago. The doctor has to check him one more time, and he has to get fitted with crutches."

"Give me my damn keys, Mitch," I warned. He might be my best friend, but if he didn't give me my car keys… My hands balled into fists.

"Have something to eat before you go," he said hesitantly. "There's one other thing…"

My jaw flexed. "What?" I said through my teeth. What else had he done?

"Your mother's on her way here," he said.

My mother? Everything came to a grinding halt. I'd totally forgotten about her. She'd been expecting me to call yesterday while I'd been at the hospital. My eyes drifted to the floor in shame. She must've been terrified, not being able to contact me.

"Did you talk to her?" I asked, my anger subsiding. "Is she mad?"

Mitch put an arm around me, pressing my damp hair against my back. "She called your cell last night after I picked up your car. She was kinda upset. I guess she'd been calling all day. I told her what happened and that you were safe." He handed me a piece of paper with numbers scribbled on it. "She's flying in this afternoon. I think she plans to ride home with you."

I took the paper, read it, then carefully folded it and put it in my back pocket. Her flight was scheduled to arrive at two; Jason would be long gone by then. So would Mitch.

"Thanks." I squeezed him, knowing this, too, was a last. *God, I'm going to miss you!* After today, there wouldn't be *any* more McAlisters in my life. But the longing, the ache to have Jason in my arms overshadowed everything else.

"May I please have my keys now, Mitch?" I begged quietly.

He frowned. "Will you at least have one donut? Jason'll kill me if you pass out in his hospital room because of low blood sugar." He pointed at a pink box on the counter next to my mug. The rich aroma of coffee filled my nostrils, and my stomach gurgled in anticipation.

"Fine," I snapped. I snatched a donut out of the box and shoved it in my mouth. Mitch watched me as I downed my breakfast in three bites, then chugged what was in the mug, incinerating my mouth.

"There. Happy now?" I held out my hand.

He took it in his and placed his other hand—and the keys—in it before locking his ebony eyes on me. "Melissa, I know how hard this is for you, having to let him go. My heart tore in two every time I had to leave Ann to come back to school. If you need to talk, I'm here."

But you knew you would see her again. It's not the same. My insides disappeared, leaving me cold and empty.

Mitch released my hand and wrapped himself around me in a bear hug. "It'll be okay. He loves you, you know?"

I nodded against his chest. "I know. I just wish it was enough."

Mitch laughed as he let me go. "Oh, it's more than enough. Jason isn't going to give up on you. He's way too stubborn for that." He pulled on the end of my ponytail, his dark eyes dancing. "Here, don't forget your purse."

"Thanks for taking care of me, Mitch."

"Hey, what're friends for? I'll grab Jason's stuff and meet you at the hospital." He gave me a playful shove. "Go! He's waiting for you."

I managed a small smile and then rushed out the door.

"Don't get a ticket," he added as I headed to the car.

I only blew through two stop signs on my way to the hospital, and that was due to inattention, not speed. Mitch's words wound themselves around my heart like a vice. "Jason isn't going to give up on you…"

A thrill shot through me at the thought, but I beat it back. I knew Mitch meant well, but reason superseded hope. Maybe if Jason were staying in Southern California, or if we hadn't already had an aborted online relationship, I would've found more comfort in his words. I'd known all along this would only be a whirlwind affair; now I had to deal with the consequences.

When the hospital came into view, my sorrow threatened to overflow, bringing my donut with it. I inhaled slowly through my nose. The only thing that kept my anxiety in check was that Jason was so close. He was here, with his warm hands and endless blue eyes. I'd pay later for this one last indulgence, but I was going to get all I could out of these remaining moments.

The hospital lobby bustled with patients and visitors this Thursday morning. I picked my way through the people, sunglasses firmly in place. Like a shield, my glasses hid not only my tired eyes but my competing emotions. It wasn't until I knocked on Jason's door that I slipped them off.

"Come in," he replied.

I crept in, not sure if he still had the room to himself. I was greeted by a crowd of smiling faces. Jason's parents sat comfortably on the empty bed near the window, while Ann touched up the dark circles under her eyes, seated in the lone chair. Jason beamed at me from his bed, sitting nearly upright in his new black polo shirt—the one I'd given him. He looked nearly normal except for the black eye and the thick white bandage peeking out from under his baggy tan shorts.

He held his arms out to me. "Good morning, beautiful," he purred.

My face flamed as I walked over and melted into his embrace. The rails of the bed had been lowered, and he pulled me close and kissed me tenderly, at first. Unfazed by the fact by the fact his family surrounded us, he deepened the kiss, sending chills all the way to my toes.

Thoroughly embarrassed, I hid my face next to his ear after the exchange and listened to his parents discuss the weather.

"Good morning, handsome," I whispered. The warmth of his cheek and his fresh scent made me forget the hospital. "You smell good this morning."

Jason wove his fingers into my hair and gently held my face back so he could look into my eyes. "I got a sponge bath this morning. All clean." He smirked.

"On the outside," Ann murmured.

I couldn't help but smile. "I'm sorry I missed it."

"Me too," he said with a sly grin.

Another knock on the door interrupted us. Without waiting to be invited, a beefy blond man wearing blue scrubs came in carrying a pair of crutches.

Reluctantly, I slipped out of Jason's arms.

His parents stood too.

"Melissa, we're going to get another cup of coffee. Can we bring you something?" Lynn asked. "Ann, how about you?"

"No, thank you," I said. I took Lynn's seat on the bed while the therapist worked with Jason.

Ann shook her head. "Nothing for me. Thanks, Lynn." With a sigh, she snapped her compact closed. "You look better," she observed. "You must've slept well."

"Yes, I did…though I didn't mean to be gone so long." I hesitated, wondering if she'd been the one to tamper with my clock, but my anger had run its course. Better to end on a good note, I decided. "Thanks again for helping me. You didn't have a good night?"

"Not really." She paused to watch Jason balance on the crutches. He sat back down and the therapist adjusted the supports. "Your floor is very hard."

"You slept on my *floor?*"

The therapist helped Jason into the hall. "We'll be right back," he said over his shoulder.

Ann gave her lips a coat of gloss. "Mitch didn't want to leave you alone, so we snagged some blankets and pillows from his folks and slept in the other bedroom. It was awful." She twisted her head to the side and her neck cracked. "No offense."

"None taken." Ann's helpfulness through this ordeal continued to stun me. "I don't know what to say… Thank you."

She just shrugged and loaded her makeup into her purse.

The door opened and Jason hobbled back in. The therapist appeared behind him, wearing a satisfied smile. He waited while Jason signed the forms on his clipboard, then wished us well and left.

Setting the crutches aside, Jason sat on the edge of the bed and stared at me. His brilliant eyes had lost their luster; the bright blue was now clouded in gray gloom.

This was it. The end.

Jason glanced at Ann. "Could you excuse us for a few minutes, please, Ann?"

"Sure, no problem. I'll go down and wait for Mitch in the lobby," she said, rising gracefully.

Despair slowly suffocated me as the door swung closed.

"Come here," Jason said.

I didn't make it into his arms before the first tears fell. All the emotions I'd been holding in for days came pouring out—I couldn't keep them locked up any longer.

Jason didn't say anything. He just held me, stroking my cheek or rubbing my back every time the sobs swelled.

My voice cracked when I spoke. "I don't…want you…to go."

He took my face in his hands and brushed his lips against my cheeks, kissing away my tears. "I wish I didn't have to," he breathed.

Sniffling, I kissed him and tasted the salty remnants of my crying. The fire in his kiss overwhelmed the agony for one glorious moment, but in the back of my mind I knew I was fooling myself. There would be pain, and the longer I waited, the worse it would be.

With a sniffle, I backed away.

"Is there anything else you need before you leave?" I asked. I tried not to look in his eyes, but I couldn't help but notice glistening trails of tears on his cheeks.

He wiped his face and took an unsteady breath. "Actually there is. See that?" He pointed at the rolling table that had been pushed into the corner. A vaguely familiar FedEx envelope lay on top of it. "That's for you."

Reluctantly I slipped my fingers out of his so I could retrieve the mystery package. It was already open.

"Look inside."

I sat on the bed next to him and followed his instructions, extracting a business-sized envelope. "What's this?"

"Another opportunity for us." He took my hand in his. "You've given me such a gift, sharing your life with me, and I'd like the chance to…well…return the favor."

The donut churned in my stomach as I opened the smaller envelope. The blue and orange airplane on the corner told me nearly everything I needed to know, but I looked inside anyway. The computer cards I found weren't like any airline tickets I'd ever seen; covered with so much fine print, they were impossible to decipher.

"These don't have any dates on them," I said.

"They're not tickets, Melissa. They're vouchers. And before you ask, they didn't cost me a cent. I gave up my seat on an overbooked flight a couple months ago and received these as compensation. I'd already purchased my tickets for this summer, so I don't have a use for them."

"So you want me to…*what* exactly?" I asked, once I found my voice.

"I'm officially inviting you to come visit me. I'll be in Ann Arbor until late August. You can come for a day, a week, or more—as long as you want." He stared at me earnestly.

Ann Arbor…*Michigan?* I looked at Jason. His face was calm, but he nervously stroked my palm, waiting for me to say something.

"Visit? As long as I want?" I repeated.

"Yes. My roommate is long gone, and I have tons of space. You can even have your own room." Jason squeezed my hand. "I told you, I'm not disappearing from your life."

Slowly his words began to register. What he was describing wasn't a visit—it was a living arrangement. Though he veiled it well, Jason was asking me to come live with him—*all summer.*

My mouth fell open, and his eyes widened in response. But what could I say? I had to be fantasizing again. This couldn't be happening. There's no way this was real.

Me, fly to Michigan… The thought of boarding a jet, suitcase in hand, reminded me why I couldn't even consider it. Mom. She was expecting me to come home. This would be the last summer I'd have with her before moving out for good. She'd talked about girls' nights out and wine tastings and mud baths for weeks. The piece of paper announcing her impending arrival suddenly became a lead weight in my pocket. *No, I can't go.*

But what if you did? I could wake up next to him every morning, explore a new place through his eyes, experience his life even more fully than he'd seen mine. I loved him…

No, I can't go. What would I do in Michigan while Jason was at school—sit in his apartment? No job, no friends, nothing. *Nothing but Jason.*

"Please, Melissa, tell me what you're thinking," he pleaded.

Don't you know?

Strain showed in tiny lines above his perfect eyebrows. He deserved an answer. Why wouldn't the words come out?

Jason tried again, his smooth, persuasive voice flowing over me like warm water. "You said yourself there wasn't much in California for you this summer. I have a couple of friends in the journalism department at U of M who could hook you up—maybe you could publish something there. I'm sure the Ann Arbor library has a summer reading program too."

It was clear he'd put a lot of thought into this plan. I hated to admit it, but I was starting to feel cornered. *What more could you want?* My thoughts reeled as I stared at the printed cards.

"It's a very generous gift, Jason. Thank you. I honestly don't know what to say." Only one thing was clear: I couldn't possibly make this decision right now.

"Melissa—" He started to argue, but then changed his mind. When he spoke, his tone matched his defiant squint. "You know I intend to keep seeing you. If this doesn't work, I'll find another way." He set his jaw stubbornly.

"It's just, well, there's my mother…and my stuff," I added lamely.

His face fell with my words, and his eyes moved away from mine. This tiny separation hit my heart like an arrow—the first shot heralding the coming onslaught.

"I understand, I really do. Your mom's probably dying to see you, especially after this." He flexed his fingers and inspected the bandage on the back of his hand covering the spot where his IV had been.

I touched his face with my fingers, softly tracing his features, nearly giving in and agreeing to go. But what if we got tired of each other? It'd only been *five days*, after all…five magical, unbelievable, terrifying days. Of course I wanted more of the magic, but what happened when my "visit" ended? We'd end up in the same place we were right now: Jason going his way and me going mine.

The arguments continued to build, adding headache to heartache. *But how can I deny him?*

I caught the tear that leaked out of the corner of his eye. "I just need some time to think about this. It's a huge surprise, Jason. Can you understand when I say this just adds to the surreal nature of our…relationship?"

He seemed to relax a bit, and a tiny smile flickered across his face. "Yes, I really do understand. But you know, surreal or not, I love you."

"Yes, and I love you too," I said with a resigned sigh.

The sparkle hadn't returned to his eyes. Knowing I caused him such sadness broke my heart. But I *did* need time to think, to sort out how I'd become completely engulfed in this man in slightly more than a hundred hours. It couldn't be healthy…but I wasn't sure anything could possibly feel more right.

"You're not going to come," he whispered, finally picking up on the thoughts screaming through my head.

"I'm not saying no. I'm just surprised," I repeated. "We've been together constantly since we met, and I'm having trouble remembering what I was like before. You've changed me so drastically—I'm still trying to figure out who I've become." The next words burned my throat. "As much as I hate to say it, I need time…alone."

He gazed out the window, unblinking. "How long?" he asked.

I hadn't thought of that. How long *would* it take? If I chose not to go…no, when I gave up the fantasy that I *could* go…I'd have to tell him. I couldn't lead him on, couldn't give him false hope from two thousand miles away. He deserved better.

"Can I have a couple of days? I'll call you on Saturday," I said. Two days…then a phone call. I could do that, couldn't I?

"Saturday night at seven my time, okay? That's four your time," he said sternly, taking the envelope from my hands. Grabbing a pen off the bedside table, he wrote his phone number across the front, followed by the agreed time.

Pulling me close, he snuck his hand behind me and slid the envelope into my back pocket. "Promise…" he whispered against my lips.

The feathery touch of his mouth on mine tempted me again. I could just visit…*and prolong this agony*. "Four o'clock my time on Saturday, I promise," I breathed before he kissed me, sealing the pact.

Gentleness became desperation as I pressed myself to him, shaking from the flood of emotion. The sparks of lust ignited when he sought out my tongue with his, but anguish chilled my back where his hand rested. Hope blazed when he fisted my hair, holding me fiercely; grief pricked my fingers when I brushed a scratch on his neck. Blanketing everything was love, warm and soft, insulating us from the future—no matter what it held—for this one last timeless kiss.

Reality broke the spell with a harsh rap on the door. Without a word we separated as the discharge nurse and Jason's parents filed into the room.

"I should go," I said, fighting back tears. I'd already done my crying, and if I started again I'd never leave.

Jason started to protest, but I shook my head slightly, willing him to understand.

Biting his lip, he nodded reluctantly.

I thanked Lynn and Frank and turned to the door. Jason caught my hand.

"If I don't hear from you by seven thirty, I *will* track you down," he said, his red-rimmed eyes brimming.

I carefully kissed his bruised knuckles. "Don't worry, I'll be on time. Have a safe trip."

"You too," he said and let go. His blue eyes followed me to the door, and I paused, memorizing his face.

The door closed silently behind me as I made my exit. The word I hated most had gone unspoken, but it hung over me like a shroud.

Goodbye.

Eighteen

*T*he chirping of my phone broke me from the trance.

The first thing I noticed was my hands, tightly gripping the steering wheel. White knuckles and pins-and-needles tingling told me my fingers had long since gone to sleep. Painfully I stretched them and looked through the windshield at my apartment. When did I get home?

The phone's electronic cry for attention repeated. The three beeps meant I'd received a text message. When I saw Mom's name at the top, I inhaled with a hiss.

> *I'm boarding the plane.*
> *See you soon. Love, Mom*

I checked the time. Twelve twenty? That'd explain the sweat dripping down my face. I'd been sitting in my car for almost two hours—just sitting. At least that's what I guessed I'd been doing.

My mind blank, I tried to recover my most recent memory. Something poked my back. Scratching the itch, I found a long envelope in my pocket. The vouchers. *Those* I remembered. My eyes still hurt from the crying I'd done this morning.

Rather than relive Jason's farewell, I started from my present situation and tried to work backward. The drive home was a blank. Getting in the car? Nothing. Leaving the hospital? Nothing. The lobby? Finally I found a speck of memory.

I'd run into Mitch and Ann in the lobby on my way out of the hospital. Mitch had hugged me, I was pretty sure.

"Hey, Mel. How're you doing?" he'd asked.

"Um, I'm not really sure," I'd said. The memory became slightly clearer.

"Things will work out. You know that, right?"

I'd ignored him. "Thanks again for everything," I think I'd responded.

"Say hi to your mom for me," was the last thing he'd said.

Ann had hugged me too, but she hadn't said anything.

I was pretty sure I thanked her, and then I must've gotten in my car and driven home. Everything after her hug was a blank, though.

I shook my head at the missing memories and got out of the car. It'd been a long time since I had a lapse like this—at least four years. What had the therapist said…that they're caused by emotional shock? *No, not again.*

Since my phone had woken me from my stupor, I set it to go off again at one thirty. Leaving Mom waiting at the airport would be a bad thing, especially if I'd had another episode. She wouldn't be happy to learn they'd come back; it'd taken a year to get rid of them after Dad died.

I was about to shove the phone in my pocket when I noticed the voicemail icon on the screen next to the words "Eleven missed calls." Could I bear to hear my mother's worried messages?

I could just delete them—she'll never know.

Guilt won out, and I lifted the phone to my ear. "You have four new messages," the computerized voice said. At least Mom didn't leave a message every time she'd called.

"Hi, honey. I'd kind of hoped to hear from you by now. Call me when you get the chance. Love you."

The voice time-stamped the message Wednesday at eleven thirty a.m. I pressed delete.

The next message was unexpectedly happy. "Hey, Mel! Chase decided he didn't want to wait to go ring shopping, so we're heading back down south. I'll call you this weekend and let you know how it went."

Linda's message ended with a giggle. At least she wasn't waiting by the phone.

Mom's next message was at two minutes past three. "Melissa, where are you? I tried calling your apartment, the house, even the number you used before, and I got no answer. I'm getting worried. Please call me." She spoke fast, her voice higher than usual.

I deleted this message too, wishing I'd thought to call her. The next message would be even worse, but I was surprised to hear a man's voice this time.

"Hello, Ms. Williams, it's Detective Clark. I just spoke with the Santa Lucia police. I'm sorry you and Mr. McAlister had to face Mr. Hancock.

I'll see what I can do to persuade the authorities here to close the case as quickly as possible. Considering what happened, I expect the investigation into Mr. Hancock's death will be very short. It's clearly a case of self-defense. Call me any time if you have questions or would just like to talk. Please give my wishes for a speedy recovery to Mr. McAlister."

His voice was comforting, but it only made me miss my father, and Jason, even more. I waited for Mom's next message to start, but heard "End of new messages" instead.

She must've given up leaving voicemails and just kept calling. I could imagine how worried she'd been…and then to find out what happened from Mitch?

As much as I'd like to think I was worried about Jason yesterday, really all I'd thought about was myself. I closed the phone and slipped it in my pocket. There was no point in calling now, she was on a plane. *I hope she'll forgive me.*

I dragged my guilty ass into the apartment and set the envelope on the kitchen counter, face down. I fingered the flap for a moment, imagining what Jason was doing. He should be nearly halfway home by now, riding in the back seat of his parents' minivan. Was he asleep? In pain? Thinking about me?

He's gone! It doesn't matter. Forcing my thoughts back to my mother, I surveyed what I had left to do. I could at least be packed when she arrived. The carnations Jason gave me were still flourishing, filling the kitchen with their scent. As I debated the wisdom of taking them home with me, I noticed a new envelope, with my name on the front, propped against the vase. My hand trembled as I picked it up. I recognized the handwriting instantly. Inside were two crisp one hundred dollar bills and a note.

> My love,
> I promised I'd take care of the inconvenience caused by your extended stay in L.A. I believe this covers the cost of not turning your key in on time.
> Hoping to see you soon,
> Jason

His generosity—and stubbornness—were endless. I traced the words, written in his swooping hand, with my finger. *He writes entirely too neatly to be a doctor.* I leaned down to smell the flowers, trying to ignore the memories the word *doctor* conjured.

For the next hour I forced myself to focus on one task: packing up my few dishes. This was part of my old life, the time before Jason, so it shouldn't be too hard. I was wrong.

Something that should've been simple turned into an excruciating test of willpower. The glass we'd shared for milk, the pan I'd used to cook us dinner, the cabinet filled with food he'd never eat—reminders of Jason were everywhere.

We only ate one real meal here. There's no reason to be so sentimental. But the emptiness seeped deeper into my soul with each dish I packed.

My phone alarm finally went off, giving me a reprieve from the past.

Located a few miles south of my apartment, the Santa Lucia Regional Airport boasted two airlines and four gates. While sitting in the car, I watched Mom's tiny passenger jet land and then walked across the street to the terminal, easily beating her there. I saw her walk in through the glass doors beyond the security checkpoint, her short, brown waves ruffling in the breeze.

"Melissa, thank God!" she called, hugging me tightly. "I was so worried about you!" Faint crow's feet framed her gray eyes when she smiled.

Many people had commented that we looked alike, but I'd never been able to see it. I did recognize the mixture of love and relief in her expression, though.

"I'm so sorry, Mom. I should've called earlier. I wasn't paying attention to the time," I said, lifting her computer bag off her shoulder.

She refused to let me pull her carry-on. "Mitch explained why you couldn't call. You look tired. How's your friend? Jason, isn't it?"

Her dark eyes told me she hadn't gotten much sleep either. Her automatic forgiveness added to my guilt, and her well-meaning question made me cringe. Jason was so much more than a friend. *Was* being the key word.

"He's going to be okay. His parents are driving him home right now. He flies back to Michigan tomorrow." The invisible knife in my chest dug a little deeper.

"Michigan? I thought Mitch's family lived in California."

Crap. Mom didn't know the whole story. "They do. But Jason goes to school out of state." I popped the trunk, then threw myself behind the wheel while she stowed her suitcase.

The radio was blaring when she got in the car. "When are you going to see him again?" she asked, after turning down the music.

I squeezed the steering wheel so tightly it made a cracking noise. "I don't know."

Out of the corner of my eye I saw Mom frown. She didn't say anything else until I turned into my apartment complex.

"Is he coming back to California?" she finally asked.

"Maybe in August," I said, flexing my jaw.

"You won't see him before then?"

Did Jason talk to her too?

"That depends," I replied, pulling the car into my parking spot. I jumped out and had the front door unlocked before she'd unbuckled.

Mom caught up with me in the kitchen. "Depends on what?"

With a heavy sigh, I handed her the vouchers. "On this."

She looked at the envelope, then back at me. I returned to my packing, leaving her wondering. Without thinking, I threw the last few pieces of plasticware in the box and sealed it shut.

Discussing Jason's…proposal…wasn't high on my to-do list, but apparently Mom had other ideas.

"These are airline vouchers—a lot of them. Where did you get them?" She counted the cards in the envelope. I hadn't bothered to understand exactly how many there were or how they worked.

"Jason gave them to me. He wants me to come to Ann Arbor and visit him." I stalked past her to retrieve the other empty box from the family room.

"How long does he want you to stay?" she called, leaning around the corner to watch me.

"You don't want to know," I muttered. Mom put her hand up and caught me on the way back into the kitchen. I couldn't look at her. "He said it's up to me, but he'd like me to come for the whole summer."

Her hand dropped. "I see."

I hazarded a glance at her. She searched my expression, but she wouldn't find answers I didn't have.

I couldn't look at her anymore, seeing the disappointment in her face. "I'm going to pack the bedroom. Can you finish up the last things in here?"

She nodded, and I dashed up the stairs.

Most of my clothes were already packed, and I quickly threw the sheets into my pop-up hamper. Rolling up the sleeping bag was a new form of torture after what had transpired on it, but I did, and pushed it into the top of the hamper. The last piece of clothing to pack was the black dress, and I carefully folded it and zipped the suitcase shut. Sniffling, I hauled my bags down to the car.

The only things left in the bedroom were my pillows, the lamp, and my defunct alarm clock. When I returned for these last items, I couldn't stop myself from picking up Jason's pillow and burying my face in it. His scent still lingered on the pillowcase, and my injured heart started its assault. *You could be in Ann Arbor tomorrow.*

"Do you need any help?" Mom asked, spooking me. "Sorry, Melissa, I didn't mean to startle you. I finished in the kitchen and put the boxes in the car. Looks like you're done here." She spoke quietly, and I wondered how long she'd been standing in the doorway. She picked up the alarm clock lying in the middle of the floor without another word.

I passed her the other pillow and unplugged my lamp. We tossed the last few things in the car, and I made one more pass through the apartment, grabbing the forgotten lamp in the family room. The only thing left was the flowers. Mom picked them up and carefully stowed them in the back seat. I locked my apartment for the last time, and got in the car.

After dropping off my key, we headed north. Mom drove, leaving me free to sit, motionless, trying not to think about how Jason had looked in the driver's seat. *Is there anything that doesn't remind me of him?* If only I could remember what had made me happy before I met him…but I drew a blank. Had he changed me that much?

Time lapsed for me again, and it seemed like only seconds had passed before we pulled into a gas station in Soledad.

"I'm getting you something to eat," Mom said.

I turned to her, confused. "What?"

"Your stomach has been growling for the last hour. Didn't you feel it? When did you last eat?"

I had to really think about her question—had to force myself to remember what happened before that last conversation, last touch, last kiss.

"Um, I had a donut for breakfast?" I shrank in my seat, expecting her to start chewing me out.

Mom didn't yell or even complain but sighed loudly and shook her head. I thought I heard her mutter something like "it's happening again," but I wasn't sure.

Mom made me eat a hot dog and chips she bought before she'd start the car. The food went down, but since I hadn't felt my hunger earlier, I didn't feel any satisfaction now. When I finished the last bite, she tossed a granola bar at me.

"You need to eat more. One donut is not enough to keep you going for a full day," she said.

"I know. I just forgot about lunch." She didn't need to know I'd spent two hours in my car, catatonic.

I managed to stay alert for the remainder of the drive. Mom talked about her trip to Reno and actually smiled when I asked her a question or made a comment. Our conversation ceased when we turned onto our street. I guessed she was remembering the same thing I was. Ron had been here just a few days ago, looking for me.

"I still can't believe he stole our mail. I should've stopped it while I was gone." Her voice wavered, and I put my hand on her shoulder.

"It's not your fault, Mom. Try not to think about it." I'd regret forgetting to call her for a long time. No matter how much I cared for Jason, my negligence was inexcusable.

"How did you do it? Fight him, I mean," she asked.

"Didn't Mitch tell you?"

"He just said you were attacked and that you saved his brother's life. He mentioned something about a bull, but it didn't make a lot of sense."

I told her exactly what happened while we unloaded the car—omitting the details of the conversation I'd had with Jason prior to Ron's appearance. She listened closely, trying to hide the fear in her eyes when I described how I let Ron chase me through the stable. By the time I finished the story, we were sitting on the bed in my room.

"I can't believe how calm you were, hon. You're so brave, just like your father," she said.

I glanced at the picture next to my bed. My father and a twelve-year-old me smiled up from inside the black frame. He looked indestructible in his dress uniform and brand new captain's bars.

"He's always watching over us, you know," I said, remembering his helpful whispers.

"I know." Mom patted my knee. "I should let you get some rest. Why don't you go to bed early tonight?"

In answer to her question, I yawned. "Okay. Thanks, Mom. I've missed you."

She hugged me before she got up. "I've missed you too. It's good to have you home." The door closed quietly behind her.

It *was* good to be home, but I still felt empty inside. I looked at my nightstand again but not at the photo. Sitting next to it were the vouchers. Would it hurt too much to go for a weekend?

The thought of seeing Jason again energized me, and for the first time since we'd parted I took a real breath. Reality was quick to set in, though, and I recalled how painful it'd been to leave him this morning. Could I go through that again?

The sadness threatened to reclaim me, so I slipped off my shoes and grabbed the closest pillow. If I was going to cry, I'd rather do it under the covers so I wouldn't upset Mom.

I fished around the bulging pillowcase for my pajamas. The T-shirt I found wasn't Poly's gray and green, but dark blue. My hands shook as I held it up, though I knew exactly what I'd find on the front. Once I saw the bright yellow lettering, I collapsed on the pillow, pulling the shirt close. *Why is he punishing me?*

"I have plans for that shirt," Jason whispered in my memory, and the tears came freely. I wanted to be with him so badly the center of my bones ached. I remembered all the things I loved about him: the sound of his voice, his laugh, how his forehead crinkled when he read my mind, the way his touch made me tingle. And then there were his eyes. I'd seen my whole life in his brilliant azure eyes. What was left to see now?

As I cried myself to sleep, I wished more than anything that I could still see them.

When I woke up, Mom was sitting on the bed next to me, frowning. "Good morning. When I said go to bed early, I'd kind of hoped you'd at least change first."

Stiffly I rolled onto my back. "I guess I was more tired than I thought."

Mom touched Jason's shirt, still clutched in my fingers. "I don't think that's it. I think it's time you tell me what's going on between you and Jason. The way you're acting is like..." She stopped and looked away.

"Like what?" *What have I done now?*

Mom took a deep breath. "You're acting just like you did after Dad died, Melissa, and it's scaring me. I talked to you for an hour in the car yesterday, and you didn't so much as blink. This morning, I find you in a ball wrapped around this." She lifted the corner of Jason's shirt. "And I'm pretty sure it's not yours. Why don't you just call him? He gave you tickets; plan a trip to go see him, for goodness sake." She tried to mask the worry in her eyes with an exaggerated sigh.

"It's not that simple, Mom. I can't go back to him—I'd just be leading him on. There isn't any future for us. What if he goes to medical school in New York? What if I get a job in Seattle? It's just easier to let him go."

I realized I was still clutching Jason's T-shirt and quickly shoved it under my pillow. "I'll get over him," I lied.

"Hmmm," she said, watching me. "It sounds like you two have been together awhile. Why haven't I heard more about Jason?"

I closed my eyes. "We met online a while back…but…I only met him in person on Saturday."

Silence. The seconds ticked by, and still I heard nothing. Finally Mom took a slow, deep breath, and I knew the fuse had been lit. I braced for the explosive lecture on online predators and date rape that had to be coming.

"So it was love at first sight, then," she said almost thoughtfully.

My eyes popped open. The anger and disappointment I'd been expecting to see weren't there. She actually looked calm and almost happy. Why wasn't she telling me how irresponsible I was, how childish?

"Mom, do *you* believe in love at first sight?"

She took my hand and started tracing my fingers with her thumb. "Honestly, I don't know. I've never experienced it. Your father, however, swore he knew we were going to be married the first time he looked into my eyes."

She looked at Dad's photo, the special smile she saved only for him growing on her lips.

"Brad had just moved in across the street from me and came over to ask where the school bus stopped. When I pointed at the corner, he got the funniest expression on his face. I was only sixteen at the time and didn't think anything of it. He was two years older than I was, after all. The next time I saw him he surprised the heck out of me and asked me out. The day I graduated high school he proposed."

She turned back to me with one of those things-were-better-then looks on her face. "Of course *we* didn't have sex until we were married."

I rolled my eyes. "Well, I'm just a tad bit older than you were, aren't I?"

Wed at nineteen, I'd always considered my mother a child bride, much to her chagrin. Her story piqued my curiosity, though.

"What did you do when you were in high school and Dad went to college?"

"In those days"—she squeezed my hand playfully—"we actually *talked* on the phone. Brad called me every evening, *and* he sent me a weekly letter. I have boxes of them in the attic. He'd come home every other weekend and pamper me with flowers and picnics. The time apart wasn't so bad because we knew someday we'd be together forever."

"You were lucky he was so close," I said. Jason was a world away.

Mom smiled, but then a shadow crossed her face. She fingered her wedding ring, and I knew she was thinking about Dad's death. I tried to distract her.

"So what would you do, if you were in my place?"

Her morose expression evaporated, and she tapped her chin with her finger. "I'd probably go see him—over the Fourth, maybe—and see where things stood after that. I bet you could take a week off without any problem."

A week. A week would double the time I'd spent with Jason. But it didn't solve my problem; I'd still have to repeat the heartbreaking separation I'd just experienced. How much more would it hurt to leave a second time? A short visit seemed like a Band-Aid on a gunshot wound. We'd made the break—why reopen the injury?

Mom wasn't finished. "Your father would have done something completely different," she said with a grin. "And I have a feeling you're more like him in this case."

We talked some more about Dad and Jason. I was surprised how good it felt to open up to her. The pain became manageable enough that I got up and changed. Maybe the next two days wouldn't be so bad, and I'd be able to make my decision without so many more tears.

I spent the day on mundane tasks like laundry and email, all the while thinking about Jason. I folded my clothes while weighing the pros and cons of what Mom and I had discussed. Objectivity regarding Jason didn't come easily, and my emotions swayed from excitement to despair to anticipation to grief in a matter of minutes as I visualized the possibilities.

Mitch's words also resonated in my mind as I worked. "Jason isn't going to give up on you." I worried about what Jason would do if I *didn't* take his offer, if I told him it—us—was over. He'd fought to keep me with him that first night. Would he do it again? Would he come and find me? I was pretty sure he would, as unbelievable as that was. My heart took off again at the thought, and my emotional roller coaster climbed toward another peak.

He seemed so sure of his feelings—he had from the very beginning, I realized. Was I unsure of mine, or was I just afraid to accept them? No, I knew I loved Jason; I'd risked my life for him. It was something else. *But what?*

At dinner Mom questioned me again.

"You've been quiet all day. Have you made any headway?" she asked over her Kung Pao shrimp.

"Maybe. I've thought a lot about what you said, but I still can't shake the feeling I'd only be in for worse heartbreak the next time I left." I picked up a shrimp and examined it before popping it into my mouth.

Mom stared at me. "That's what's been bothering you? The fact you'll have to say goodbye again?"

Again? I hadn't even been able to say it the first time. I flinched at the memory of Jason's distraught face when I'd walked away.

"But goodbye isn't forever," Mom said, as if it were obvious.

"What? You're not making sense." I chased a grain of rice around my plate. *Of course it's forever. Jason and I have separate lives. A weekend visit won't change that. Goodbye is always the end.*

"Goodbye is always the end? What?"

My teeth came together with a *clack*. Had I said that out loud?

Mom put down her chopsticks. "Well, that explains a lot." She paused, inspecting my face as she tried to articulate her discovery. "Do you remember the last thing you said to Dad?"

I gaped at her. "Mom, you know I don't think about that day."

In all my grieving, the one thing I'd never been able to remember was the last time I'd seen my father. I felt like if I allowed myself to dwell on that moment—my last seconds of happiness with him—all my memories of him would disappear. He'd truly be gone, and I wouldn't feel his presence any longer.

Mom ignored me, her eyes bright. "The last words you said were, 'Love you, Dad. Good—'" Before she could finish, I clamped my hands over my ears.

"No! Don't say it." All the pain I'd felt over leaving Jason exploded tenfold. I refused to think the last, despicable word. *No, Dad. Don't go!*

My hands moved to my face. It was too late. She'd said it. Dad was gone. Really gone.

"After all this time…I had no idea. That's why you never tell me goodbye," Mom said, as much to herself as to me. "It's always 'Love you' or 'Talk to you later.' For you goodbye *does* mean forever, doesn't it?"

My grief spilled out in a shower of tears. "Yes," I choked out between sobs.

Mom rushed to my side and threw her arms around me. "A word won't hurt me, Melissa. Nor will it hurt Jason. What you said to Dad didn't have anything to do with what happened, you know that."

"Of course I know that. But *knowing* the truth and *feeling* the truth are two different things."

My admission didn't do much to comfort me. In all the years since Dad died, I'd never been able to say goodbye to anyone—not Mom, not Mitch, no one. No wonder I was so worried about having to say it to Jason.

Slowly, the discovery sunk in, and my sobs subsided.

Mom kissed the top of my head. "Jason has stirred some very deep feelings in you. Maybe understanding them will help you to decide what to do."

She released me and returned to her seat, finishing her dinner in silence.

I poked at my rice but my appetite had disappeared. If saying goodbye was what kept me from fully embracing Jason's love, how did things change now that I knew it? I closed my eyes to think and was filled with sudden, overwhelming hope.

I'll never leave you, Melissa. Dad's voice was still with me, still strong. *You know what to do. Listen to your heart.*

Nineteen

I paced in a tight circle, waiting for the time on my cell phone to change. We'd agreed I would call Jason at seven o'clock, only three minutes from now. It'd been two days since I'd seen his face, felt his touch, or heard his voice, and with clammy palms and trembling lips I waited impatiently, like an addict craving her next fix. The excessive humidity didn't help; my forehead was covered with sweaty droplets.

I swiped at the drips with the back of my hand, frustrated. What had he said? "How's it supposed to feel when you finally find the one who makes you whole?" I still didn't have an answer—the completeness he instilled in me was indescribable. He was the one, I could see that now.

Our indefinable connection lay at the heart of my conversation with Mom last night. I now understood why I'd been convinced I'd never see Jason again. My experience losing Dad colored every relationship I had. Whenever someone I cared about left me, I'd subconsciously equated it with the day Dad said goodbye for the last time. A loving farewell had come to mean death. And it wasn't just Jason—I'd felt the same fear after the wedding when Mitch had said goodbye, even though he hadn't actually said the word. I was still afraid to say goodbye to anyone, but Mom had helped me identify the root of my fear.

"It'll always be with you," she'd said, recounting the sleepless nights she'd spent worrying about Dad when he was on patrol. "But love is stronger than fear. If you look into your heart, you'll see you already know that. Was it fear that made you stand between Jason and that killer? Or love?"

Both, actually. "But what about Dad?" I whispered. "Fear won, in the end."

Mom's face turned to stone, and her hazel eyes iced over. "No, Melissa, fear did *not* win. We lost him to mindless evil, not to fear," she said, her voice steely. "If fear had won, do you think I'd let you out of this house? I said goodbye to him that day just like you did, remember?

"I loved him, I trusted him, and even though I can't hold him anymore, I still feel him. He's in my soul, Melissa, and always will be. Fear will never take him away from me." She didn't cry, didn't even tear up as she spoke. "It'll only steal Jason from you if you let it."

Hearing that, I'd made my decision.

Six fifty-eight. As tempted as I was to call Jason early, I didn't. Instead I changed direction and circled clockwise. If we'd made it through last night, we could make it two more minutes.

Sleep had been a fleeting thing for me, crowded out by other doubts and worries. What if, once Jason had time to think about what had happened over the last few days, he regretted his actions? What if he'd decided a week with me was enough? What if…what if…what if…

What if I showed up at his door wearing nothing but a trench coat and high heels?

After much tossing and turning, the what-ifs had eventually subsided, and I'd managed to get a few hours of rest. Daylight did little to calm me, erasing the apprehension and replacing it with anxiousness. I'd tried to keep myself busy today: reading, watching videos—heck, I even tried my hand at the crossword puzzle—but my mind kept coming back to this moment. All day long, I'd tried to visualize this conversation, wishing I could see his face as I spoke, wondering what his reaction would be. He'd be happy with my decision, wouldn't he?

I checked the time again. One more minute to go.

Below the time, another word caught my eye. *Saturday*. Unbelievably, it was one week ago that I first laid eyes on Jason McAlister. Here I was, just seven days later, unable to think without his face appearing in my mind, unable to breathe without tasting his scent. The memory of the moment our eyes first met was so strong, I shuddered recalling it. How much longer could this feeling last?

A lifetime.

Finally my phone beeped. I dropped it, trying frantically to silence the alarm. Dialing the number was equally difficult with shaky hands, and I cursed myself for having that last can of Coke. My pulse raced, but I forced myself to dial slowly and accurately. I rehearsed my story one last time while I listened to his phone ring. How I wished I could see his eyes as I explained myself.

"Melissa," Jason said. Relief poured out of the phone.

He didn't think I'd call. A small smile crept across my lips.

"Hi, Jason. How are you?" Could he hear my nervousness? Another bead of sweat slid down my back.

He didn't answer immediately, sending my pulse skyrocketing.

"I'm surviving."

"How's your leg?" I swallowed, trying to control my trembling.

Jason sighed. I hoped he knew I needed to work up to the difficult part of the conversation. "Good. This morning I called the clinic and set up an appointment to get the stitches out later this week. Hopefully I'll be off the crutches soon." I could hear the edge in his voice—he wasn't going to wait much longer. "How are *you* doing?"

"I've been better, actually." The words wobbled over my tongue as my heart tried to pound its way out of my ribs.

"I know what you mean," he said.

The silence that followed nearly undid me, and I took off down the hall. He shifted the phone, and I imagined him sitting in his apartment, running frustrated fingers through his hair.

"How was your—" I started, but Jason interrupted me.

"Have you thought any more about my offer?"

My heart skipped a beat.

"I'm not the only one who's no-nonsense, am I?" I said with a laugh verging on hysterics. I touched the white circle on the wall in front of me as he spoke.

"I guess that's a trait I picked up from you," he said wistfully. I heard a soft ringing in the background, but Jason ignored it. "Have you?" he pressed. "Melissa, will you come to see me *sometime* this summer?"

I knew the stress in his voice well; it'd been my constant companion for the past two days.

"What was that sound?" I asked, avoiding his question.

"Nothing—just the doorbell." The ringing started again, louder and longer this time. "Just ignore it. Nothing is more important than you." He paused, and I strained to hear his next words. "Please don't toy with me, Melissa. The last few days have been hell. Being alone hasn't helped *me* at all. I can't tell you how many times I picked up the phone to call you. Tell me now. I need to know if I'll ever see you again," he begged.

The doorbell continued to ring, and I thought I heard him swear under his breath.

"Answer the door, Jason," I said.

"NO!" he shouted. I jumped involuntarily, the sound of his shout ringing loudly in my ears. "Not until you tell me. I can't take this anymore. I have to know. Please, you're *killing* me!"

The shock of his anger rendered me speechless.

"I'm sorry, Melissa, that was uncalled for," he said with another sigh. "I just miss you so much. Please forgive me?"

My heart ached, hearing the pain, the defeat so clear in his voice. Before I could answer him, a couple of guys stepped out of the elevator, laughing loudly. Giving me the onceover, they squeezed past.

"Hey, if Jason's not around, come on down to my room," the taller one said, giving me a wink. I turned away, my lips pursed. The phone had gone silent.

His friend pushed him farther down the narrow hallway. "Cut it out, Chris. If Jason catches you checking her out, he'll kick your ass again—even on crutches."

The two disappeared behind a slammed door at the end of the corridor.

It was another long second before Jason found his voice. "Melissa, where are you?"

"Just answer the door, *please*," I whispered.

With a crash the call ended, and the door in front of me burst open. Jason towered over me, balanced on one crutch. He was more beautiful than I remembered, dressed in a very familiar gray-and-green Poly T-shirt and faded cutoffs. The white bandage covering his stab wound peeked out below the tattered denim. His eyes were blue blowtorches glowing above dark, sleepless circles and yellowing bruises. He *had* been pulling his hair; one side stuck straight out like a poorly styled Mohawk. But the most handsome look of utter surprise covered his face.

I slowly lowered the phone from my ear, awed by the sight of him. Cool air rolled out of the apartment, but my shiver had more to do with the way Jason's eyes devoured me than the change in temperature.

I smiled carefully. "I forgive you. I was wondering where my nightshirt—"

He swooped down and captured me, stealing my words when his lips crashed into mine. The crutch fell behind him with a thud.

My memories were shamed as I reveled in the intensity of his kiss. His touch surged through me, accompanied by a swell of warmth that had nothing to do with the humid Michigan air. Slowly I tilted my head as his lips parted, inviting mine to follow.

Almost timidly, our tongues met, reintroducing themselves with small, gentle movements. The tender touch didn't last long—I couldn't resist his alluring taste. He eagerly explored my mouth, kissing me with the fervor of years of separation, not just days.

I swayed dizzily in his arms, gasping around his lips. He turned me toward the doorframe for support, pressing himself against me. My body answered his call, the fiery need centering itself where his hips met mine.

When our lips separated, Jason cupped my chin with one hand and stared into my eyes. Tears rolled down his face, and as his thumb brushed my cheek, I discovered my eyes were damp too. "You came," he barely whispered.

I smiled up at him innocently and wiped his cheek with the back of my fingers. "You always make me come," I said.

He chuckled, his laugh warm and inviting. "Welcome to Michigan, Naughty Melissa."

His hands couldn't stay still, caressing my face, my shoulders, my hair. "I can't believe you're here," he repeated over and over between kisses.

"*How* are you here?" he finally asked.

"I decided you were right. There has to be a way to make this work. I'm yours for as long as you'll have me."

"How did you find me?" he asked, his grin stretching so wide it had to hurt.

"You're not the only one who can pump Mitch for information, you know," I said, smiling. I'd called him after deciding, with Mom's blessing, to follow my heart and come to Michigan as soon as possible. Mitch had heartily endorsed my plan and was more than happy to give me directions to Jason's apartment.

Impossibly, Jason's eyes shone even brighter. "He does come in handy, doesn't he?"

"Definitely."

Jason put his arm around my shoulder and pulled me into his apartment. I picked up his crutch, lying in the middle of his kitchen, and he led me past the immaculately clean sink and stove. The only dish visible was a dirty mug sitting next to the stained coffeemaker.

He hobbled into the living room and eased himself down on the black couch. Pizza boxes and soda cans littered the floor next to his upended coffee table. I righted it and replaced the items, leaving a space for Jason to prop up his injured leg.

"Sorry about that. I was in a hurry," he said. He hastily picked up the remote and wrinkled newspaper cluttering the couch, then patted the seat next to him, inviting me to sit down. "What do you think?"

I sat, letting my eyes wander around the room. The couch and coffee table dominated the space, facing a set of brick-and-board shelves that held a small TV, a few books, and a stereo. Above the window the air conditioner hummed quietly. Through an open door to the right of the kitchen I saw a synthesizer tucked next to a dresser—his bedroom, I assumed. Two doors on the left were closed, probably the bathroom and the unoccupied bedroom.

"Pretty clean for a bachelor," I admitted. "Not a dirty sock in sight. It's great." I cuddled up next to him, lightly touching his face and the dark marks of exhaustion around his eyes. "You look so tired," I said.

He smiled weakly. "I haven't been sleeping so well."

"I heard." Another tidbit Mitch had passed on was that Jason had woken up more than once in L.A. yelling my name. "I'm sorry I made you wait so long. It wasn't easy for me either."

His arm tightened around me, and he kissed the top of my head.

"Don't be. The fact you're here now is all that matters."

Jason's other hand rested on mine, his knuckles still black from the fight. I never realized that punching someone hurt the aggressor as much as the victim. A fresh scratch on his hand reminded me of something else Mitch had said.

I must've frowned, because Jason suddenly tensed.

"What's wrong?" he asked.

"Your hand…" Maybe now wasn't the time for this. "Never mind."

Jason ran a warm finger across my jaw, turning my face toward his. "Tell me," he said.

"Well, Mitch said you gave him a fat lip, and I was wondering why."

Mitch had brushed it off as tough love between brothers. Jason didn't say anything.

"Did it have something to do with me?"

"He said something less than flattering about you. Can we just leave it at that?" I stared at him with one eyebrow raised. Mitch cracked plenty of jokes, but he wasn't one to insult someone behind their back.

Jason returned my stare but eventually gave up and rubbed his eyes. "He asked what else we'd done in Santa Lucia, and I mentioned we'd gone to the beach. He couldn't believe you wore a bikini, by the way." He took a deep breath and rubbed his new scratch. "Then he asked me what I thought of your tattoo."

"You hit him because he mentioned my tattoo?" Something was missing. My body art was hardly worth fighting over.

Jason's head snapped around. "It's true?"

"Yes," I said slowly. "Mitch was with me when I got it. Was that why you hit him?"

"Not exactly. He said all his friends had seen it. I told him he was full of shit, and he laughed and said, 'It's just above her left—' and *that's* when I decked him." Jason's eyes hardened with the words, but I giggled.

"Ankle," I finished between laughs.

"What?"

"My tattoo. It's above my left ankle," I repeated, enjoying the flush on Jason's cheeks. "I don't know how you missed it."

I suddenly felt warm, remembering the way he'd ogled me from head to toe the first time we'd made love. He did the same now, and I fought the urge to fan myself.

"While I love every inch of your body, it isn't your feet I'm most interested in." His eyes locked with mine.

The intensity of his stare set my skin on fire. "You owe Mitch an apology," I said, my voice hoarse.

Smirking, Jason raked his fingers through his hair, smoothing it down a little. "I guess you're right. He's still a prick, though."

I pulled his face down and kissed him deeply. When I leaned back I caught him eyeing my feet, balanced on the edge of the coffee table.

"You want to see it?"

He nodded, and I rolled down my sock to reveal a small blue heart.

"It's the exact color of Dad's uniform tie. I used to tease him about it."

Jason sat up, tilting his head so he could get a better view. "What does 5947 mean?" He touched the black numbers in the center of the heart.

"It's my dad's badge number. I put it on my ankle because that's my kicking foot."

I shivered when his fingers wandered higher up my leg.

"It's beautiful, just like the rest of you."

I slid my foot back down and snuggled under his arm, resting my hand on his chest. This summer was going to be better than I could've imagined.

Jason raised my fingers to his face, lightly rubbing them against his lips, lost in thought. As I watched, his brow creased. When his eyes closed, I knew something was wrong.

"What's bothering you?"

He took a deep breath and gazed down at me. "How long did you say you were staying?" The fear in his voice hit me like a brick, and I sat up.

"I thought you wanted me to stay…" My voice trailed off as I realized I must have misunderstood. "I can change my ticket. I don't want to impose." I rolled to the side so I could fish my cell phone out of my pocket.

Jason pulled me close so fast my head spun. "When *exactly* is your return flight?" he said, the edge returning to his voice.

"August nineteenth. I'm sorry, I thought you meant…I mean, I thought you said…" *as long as I wanted.* My throat closed, and my ears grew hot. *What a mistake.*

"That's *precisely* what I meant. This isn't a dream, is it?" He caressed my jaw with one finger. "You're really staying until I leave?" The hope and wonder in his eyes took my breath away.

This is *a dream, no matter what he thinks.* "Yes, if it's okay with you," I whispered, kicking myself for doubting him.

"Oh, Melissa, it's so much better than okay." His mouth found mine again, his kiss so deep that time stopped. Panting, he lifted his head and stared, silently loving me. Just like the first time we met, my eyesight faded, and I got another glimpse of a future with him.

The vision was simple this time. The same loving eyes looked down on me, surrounded by gray hair and soft wrinkles. This was where I was meant to be, I knew that now.

"What are you seeing?" he asked, running his fingers through my hair, looping it over my ear.

"The same thing I saw the first time."

He smiled, just like he had in my imagination.

I traced the collar of *my* shirt on *his* marvelous body. "In those first seconds when I looked in your eyes in the church, I saw a wonderful future with you. I felt your kiss, your touch. I saw our marriage, our children, everything. I saw my entire life, with you."

His smile faded a little.

I felt the blush rising in my cheeks. "I know, it's completely crazy. I had no idea who you were, but somehow I envisioned myself with you, forever."

"And I thought the lightning bolt I felt was eerie," he said. The smile returned, wider than before. "So, how do I look with gray hair?" he said, reading my thoughts again.

"Just as handsome as you do now," I said and touched the spot where I'd seen the laugh lines just moments ago. "I love you."

Jason squeezed me even tighter, and his lips brushed my ear, sending a wonderful tremor through me. "I love you too," he breathed. He took my hand in his and held it against his chest, over his heart. "Welcome home."

"I like that." We sat, comfortably resting our heads together, and I realized those two words signaled both an end and a beginning in my life. I'd finally resolved my grief, after all these years, and with that acceptance found a new beginning in a love that could possibly last the rest of my days. In Jason's love, I'd finally found my home.

Enough with the mushy. Naughty Melissa was growing restless.

"I've got one question though," I said with a smirk.

"I bet I know."

"Where's the bed?" we said together.

ACKNOWLEDGMENTS

Whirlwind wouldn't be what it is without the help of many incredibly smart people. Thanks must first go to Elizabeth Harper: This journey started with you, and most fittingly has come full circle back to you. Thank you for your faith, support, and hard work on my behalf.

Thank you to Meredith Stratton, Linda Rusiecki, Lorraine Gabbert, and Kindra Cherry for the many hours you put into critiquing the various incarnations of *Whirlwind*. To Amy, Cindy, Kathy, Killian, Linda, Meagan, and Rie, and my NoDisclaimers critique group: Thanks for your time, honesty, and sense of humor.

There's much more to a book than a manuscript, and many thanks go to Sherry Wilson, Rosana Rivera, Sarah Huchel, and Raquel Cochran for your expertise in bringing those extra pieces to fruition.

Thank you to my editor and new friend, Jessica Royer Ocken, for your great insights and long hours, and to all of Team Whirlwind at Omnific Publishing.

This book would not be complete without a huge thank you to my family. You are my biggest fans, having endured take-out dinners, piles of laundry, and an endless train of Jason-this and Melissa-that without a single complaint. My kids, my husband, our parents…I couldn't have done this without you. I love you all.

And finally, thank you, dear reader, for letting yourself get caught up in *Whirlwind*.

ABOUT THE AUTHOR

Originally from Arizona, Robin DeJarnett has lived most of her life in Northern California. A former engineer, computer administrator, and saleswoman, she draws on her experiences, as well as her love of travel and sports, to make her stories as realistic as possible.

When not writing, Robin is a cook, chauffeur, housekeeper, maid, life coach, travel consultant, psychologist, roadie, financial advisor, and EMT—for her loving children and husband, at least.

Robin loves to hear from her readers. You can contact her through her website: robindejarnett.com